W9-BWQ-626

03/2018

S M

"*Smoke Eaters* is a thrilling, exciting, funny and strangely heart-warming book, and Grigsby's experience as a firefighter shines through on every page, lending grit and realism to this rollicking ride of a tale in which firefighters become dragon-slayers. It's exactly as bonkers – and as brilliant – as you'd expect and I look forward to more from this author."
    Anna Stephens, author of Godblind

"Sean Grigsby has conceived what promises to be a brilliant and harrowing series. Dragons have returned, bringing fire, revenant spirits and ash in their wake. Cole Brannigan, a grizzled no nonsense fire-fighter, is there to stand in their way. Profane and exhilarating, filled with unforgettable characters and scorching action, *Smoke Eaters* is an amazing mix of adventure, fantasy, and science-fiction. Grigsby is an electrifying new voice."
    John Hornor Jacobs, award-winning author of Southern Gods *and* The Incorruptibles

"I've been waiting for a book like this for years. Original, exciting, *Smoke Eaters* is a red-hot page-turner."
    Adam Christopher, author of Made to Kill

"I love dragon stories in which the dragons are real monsters, laying waste to everything around them; and I love novels with protagonists who aren't callow young adults learning that they're chosen ones. *Smoke Eaters* has terrific dragons, and a hero with some miles and e..wicked sense

    Alex

PALM BEACH COUNTY
LIBRARY SYSTEM
3650 Summit Boulevard
West Palm Beach, FL 33406-4198

and strangely.

xperience on him, plus great writing and a
of humor. I flew through it."
Stoker, author of The Hum and the Shiver

SEAN GRIGSBY

Smoke Eaters

ANGRY
ROBOT

ANGRY ROBOT
An imprint of Watkins Media Ltd

20 Fletcher Gate,
Nottingham,
NG1 2FZ
UK

angryrobotbooks.com
twitter.com/angryrobotbooks
Rain of fire

An Angry Robot paperback original 2018

Copyright © Sean Grigsby 2018

Cover by Lee Gibbons
Set in Meridien by Argh! Nottingham

Distributed in the United States by Penguin Random House, Inc., New York.

All rights reserved. Sean Grigsby asserts the moral right to be identified as the author of this work. A catalogue record for this book is available from the British Library.

This novel is entirely a work of fiction. Names, characters, places, and incidents are the products of the author's imagination or are used fictitiously. Any resemblance to actual events, locales, organizations or persons, living or dead, is entirely coincidental.

Sales of this book without a front cover may be unauthorized. If this book is coverless, it may have been reported to the publisher as "unsold and destroyed" and neither the author nor the publisher may have received payment for it.

Angry Robot and the Angry Robot icon are registered trademarks of Watkins Media Ltd.

ISBN 978 0 85766 773 1
Ebook ISBN 978 0 85766 774 8

Printed in the United States of America

9 8 7 6 5 4 3 2 1

For Owen and Scarlett,
Daddy will always keep
the dragons away.

CHAPTER 1

You never forget the smell of burning flesh, no matter how long you live. I'd been fighting fire for almost three decades, and had successfully dodged that particular bullet up until seven years ago, when the dragons came.

"Came back" would be more accurate. But these scalies are nothing like the old stories.

They're worse.

So, there I stood on the outskirts of the city, taking a piss with my duty shirt stretched over my nose to block out the scorched-hotdog smell cordoned zones were known for – careful to avoid the ashes flying up from my stream – and keeping the front of my turnout bottoms dry.

The year was 2121 and they still hadn't put toilets in fire engines.

"Captain Brannigan," Giuseppe, my engineer, shouted behind me, followed by one of her two-fingered whistles.

I was nearing sixty and had never been able to whistle like that. When I looked over my shoulder, my shirt threatened to fall off my face, so I lowered my head to keep it secured.

Giuseppe pointed from behind Fire Engine 30's steering wheel, calling my attention to the wasteland behind me.

Growing up in Minnesota, we used to get the best snows. I mean, the frigid stuff covered everything when you stepped out of your front door every winter morning. The landscape before me, as I shook myself dry, looked the same, but it sure as hell wasn't snow. Ashes covered the ground as far as I could see, except for the crumbling shells that used to be houses or businesses, and the distant salvation of Parthenon City. Miserable clouds blotted out any patch of sun, so the sky looked as bleak as the ground.

But Giuseppe pointed to something else.

A wraith floated over the desolation, with its black mouth agape and tattered flesh where legs should have been. I couldn't tell if it had been a man or woman; patches of ethereal hair floated from its head, and its flesh sagged everywhere. This wraith was silent – since it hadn't seen us. It hovered a couple hundred feet away, at the bottom of the embankment where I'd been pissing.

The wraith's white eyes, white clawed hands, and gray-speckled white skin blended against the sea of ash like camouflage, but I would have smelled it coming if I hadn't had my nose covered, even above the regular quarantine zone funk. They all stank like barbecued babies.

A documentary I watched on the Feed theorized that because wraiths had died so terribly at the hands of a dragon, the burnt stench stuck to their souls, bringing misery to living people like me who had to breathe it in. I once caught wind of a wraith from a mile away. No shit.

If the smell alone wasn't bad enough, the dead bastards attracted dragons like flies to rot. It's why one fatality caused by the scalies was a death sentence to an entire neighborhood. I could imagine the dragons having a fire orgy among the ashes of their destruction after that.

Me and my crew were OK, though. There was nothing around left to burn. The dragons usually returned underground after a while, when the food ran out, and they'd laid their eggs – if the smoke eaters didn't get to them first. Still, I should have known better than to stop in the middle of a quarantined zone. But when you get as old as me, your bladder tends to call the shots.

Wraiths usually stayed among dragon ash heaps. But this one was floating right by the road.

"Hey, old man, you done peeing?" DeShawn hopped from the engine, chewing bubblegum.

I pulled my shirt down and winced against the wraith's funk. God damn, I was upwind of the thing, too. By then it had seen us and stretched its mouth wide, wielding its electric teeth and shrieking in that frog-getting-electrocuted roar that dissuaded anybody from ever getting close to one.

Twirling my finger in the air, I told DeShawn to get back in the pump as I circled around to hop into my seat beside Giuseppe.

"Mind if we hang around for a second?" Giuseppe asked. "I've never seen a wraith disappear. Might get lucky."

"Yeah, come on, Cap," DeShawn said. He rubbed a hand over his bald head. "We can always outrun it if it gets too close."

"Or hose it away with the deck gun," Giuseppe said.

"That'd be stupid," DeShawn said. "Didn't you see its teeth? That thing's got electricity running all through it."

Giuseppe shook her head. "It's a ghost, dub. We wait around; it'll get sucked up to Heaven."

"Or Hell," DeShawn said.

We lived in a country full of ash and theories but short on answers. Rumor had it the Canadians were far ahead of us in dragon research, but those weirdoes weren't sharing.

No one had seen a wraith vanish, to my knowledge. After a horde of dragons decimate an area, the wraiths might stay around for a few weeks, but then they just disappear – poof – and then the city moves in to rebuild the neighborhood, jacking up prices while they're at it, touting dragonproof foundations and a less-impoverished neighborhood. One might call this morbid gentrification the circle of life, but whoever did would be a dickhead who'd never seen what a dragon can do.

"Let's not hang around," I told Giuseppe. "We have to get back to the station. Chief wants us to–"

Our radio blasted out the emergency tones, only slightly more comforting than the wraith's shrieks.

"Structure fire response," the dispatcher said. "3509 Brentmoore Way. Multiple calls saying visible flames are coming from the roof."

I tensed. Held my breath. Not today.

"No indication of dragon involvement."

With a smile on my face, I released my breath. My crew did, too, filling the cab with a whoosh of relief. I remember when a confirmed structure fire wasn't such a relaxed affair. The fire department's standard operating procedure on dragon calls was to stay the hell back and wait for the smoke eaters to arrive and kill the scaly. What that amounted to, usually, was watching a house burn down, and if God was just that day, the smokies would slay the dragon without any civilian casualties and inevitable wraiths.

I'd seen a few dragon fires. It was either on the Feed or through binoculars at a good distance. Shittiest feeling in the world, being unable to do anything while people's lives went up in flames. But what could we do? My dragon knowledge was limited, but I knew bullets and bombs didn't make a scratch against their scaly hide.

Water streams and axes would only piss them off.

At the end of the week, I'd be retiring.

I'd let the fire department know as much a few months before. No one could believe Cole Brannigan would put up his helmet and settle down. It wasn't the money. The dragons had tapped the city's budget and shat all over our pension fund. I guess I was just ready to sleep in until my wife, Sherry, woke me up for breakfast. I was ready to spend my days having great sex and teaching myself how to oil paint. Thirty years on the job is a long time.

In the back of Engine 30, Theresa, who'd been sleeping before the call came in, jolted awake and leaned forward, ogling me with bloodshot eyes. "What was the call?"

"Structure fire," I said. "Gear up."

Theresa didn't move. "Dragon?"

"No, I would have told you. Let's go."

Theresa placed a hand on my shoulder. "You're the best, Cap."

I put my hand on hers and nodded my thanks.

Beside her, DeShawn stared at our hands as he got his turnout coat on, almost like he was pouting. Not wanting to leave out one of my crew, I held out my fist for him to bump. With a weak smile, he punched his knuckles against mine.

Sometimes being a fire captain is like fathering a bunch of jealous four year-olds.

I waited to turn on our engine sirens until we were well away from the wraith. Really, I didn't understand the purpose of using sirens and lights out in the wastes. It wasn't like there was traffic to get around. But that's the thing about the fire service: hundreds of years of tradition unimpeded by progress.

When we were about a mile away, we could see dark

smoke reaching to the sky. The fun had barely started. Over the radio, Truck 1 announced they were en route, so I told Giuseppe not to let up on the gas. I'd be damned if another company beat me to what would probably be the last fire of my career.

On our arrival, flames gnashed from the eaves of a single-story house. No cars in the driveway. The smoke churned out more dark brown than the black I'd assumed – a good sign. But it was picking up velocity – a bad sign.

Fire has a way of drawing the human eye, but I'd learned a long time ago that smoke is what tells you what the fire is doing, and more importantly, what it's about to do.

This one was about to go nuts if we didn't stop it quick.

Giuseppe pulled a few feet past the house, how I'd trained her, allowing room for the ladder truck, but also letting me see more of the trouble we were about to get into. Truck 1 parked behind us as I jumped out and gave dispatch a report of what I saw. From rundown front porches, neighbors gawked as a few of the younger, braver residents inched closer for a better look.

"I need all of you to get back," I yelled. "Anybody in the house?"

They jolted with droopy mouths and shrugged their shoulders before retreating to their homes.

"The ground shook," an older lady shouted from her porch chair.

The neighbors argued against it, said the older woman had imagined it.

"I watch the Feed," she said. "I know the signs to watch for."

None of the houses showed any indication of quake damage, but I told DeShawn to be on the lookout for signs of weakness. Quakes usually meant a dragon was in the area, but you could never tell if it was a scaly or just baby shocks from fragile crust.

Any other time I would have told my crew to surround and drown the house from the outside, but with the potential for someone being trapped inside, we had to make entry.

Giuseppe connected a supply line from a nearby hydrant to our pump. DeShawn and Theresa stretched a hose line to the front door and put on their air masks as two of Truck 1's crew forced open the entrance and began setting up a ventilation fan while Giuseppe charged the hose line.

Things were running smoothly.

Truck 1's captain ambled over to me, his big gut swinging from side to side under his open turnout coat. "Hell of a way to start the day."

He was in the rookie class a few years after me, and a total asshole, but he knew his way around the fireground. I was about to tell him to place the ladder over the roof when a huge moving truck barreled past Engine 30 and blocked the street.

"What the hell?" I took a quick glance at the fire, seeing that DeShawn, Theresa, and the two guys from Truck 1 had gone inside and were already spraying water. I stomped toward the moving truck, ready to tear somebody a new orifice.

A scrawny guy in an oxford button-down jumped from the driver's seat, studying a clipboard as he jogged to the back of the truck.

"Dispatch," I said into my radio, "can you have police respond to block traffic?"

She acknowledged my request.

"Hey, man." I waved a hand in front of the guy's clipboard.

He looked up as if I was asking if he'd like fries with that.

"We've got a fire going on here."

"I know," he said, stepping over to a lever. "Watch out."

I looked up as the truck's back door rose open, and a heavy metal track flew toward me. Nearly getting creamed, I jumped out of the way before the track extended down to the street. Two huge carts rolled out, filled with metal men standing at attention, featureless glass heads and water cannons on each arm.

Fire droids.

I made sure the guy saw me point down the street. "Get the fuck off my fire scene."

"But…" The guy swallowed, blinking like a bug had flown into his eyes. "Mayor Rogola ordered us to test out the fire droids on the soonest incident. That's why I'm here."

"The mayor can eat a dick. This is a life-and-death situation for real people to handle. I'm done talking about this. Police are on their way." I turned, ready to hustle back and get a status report from my crew.

But the fire had grown larger, hotter than when we'd first arrived. The curious neighbors ran away, no longer able to handle the heat. It didn't make sense. My crew was one of the best at interior attack. The fire should've been smoldering by now.

"30-C to 30-A, what's going on in there?" I waited for Theresa to answer me. After a minute of silence, I tried again.

My question was answered by the ground rumbling and a roar from inside the house. Something alive and hungry.

Oh, damn.

I didn't think about what I did next, I just did it. Standard operating procedures be damned. Opening the captain's bin, I removed my air pack and a pickhead axe.

"Cole." Truck 1's captain grabbed my arm as I turned to the house. "You can't go in there."

I shoved him away. "You're in command. Call in the smoke eaters."

"But there's a dragon."

In under a minute, I packed up and entered the house. I crawled as fast as I could with a hand tracing the pressurized hose, but even that low, the smoke blocked all sight past my fingertips. When I hit a corner, I straightened and called out for anyone who could hear. Nothing. Puffs of smoke flew at my face and sparked orange and blue when they touched my mask. In thirty years of fighting fire, I'd never seen anything like that. I was like a giant stumbling through an active storm cloud. Dragon fire wasn't what I was used to combating, and a shudder across my back told me I was in way over my head.

Get 'em. Get out. Get 'em. Get out, I kept telling myself.

I found the hose nozzle, but no sign of anyone near. The heat bore down on me even more, and falling back on my training I raised the hose to the ceiling and sprayed a quick shot of water.

A flashover happens when everything inside a fire reaches its ignition point at the same time and the house becomes an inferno. This happens when the ceiling temperature reaches between 932 and 1,112 degrees Fahrenheit. If my quick spray of water came back – and I could hear it hit the floor – it meant that temps were still below flashover. If the water became steam, I'd have to get my ass out of there before becoming barbecue.

Flashing images of Sherry's face, half-covered with her red, graying hair came to mind. The pleasant image morphed into her standing over my grave, and then the surrounding cemetery crumbling into ash as my wife mutated into a flesh-rotted wraith.

I shook it away. My mind loved to jump to the worst-case scenario at the worst time.

My spray of water dripped onto the floor in front of me. No flashover, yet. Grabbing the nozzle, I crawled farther into the house.

I called again for Theresa and the others, keeping still to detect something. Anything.

"Cap!"

It was too hard to tell if that's what they said, but it was a sound, and it was human, coming from deeper in the house and off the safety of the fire hose. Taking a slow breath from my mask and checking my air level, I crawled for the voice in the dark.

Normally, I would have expected furniture or other household items to traverse, but there were only piles of ash to crunch through with my gloves and knees. I was about to call out again, when I spotted a red glow to my left. A PASS device blinked nearby as well.

The ashes scattered under my scrambling until I came to DeShawn hanging from the lip of a pit in the middle of the floor. Red fire raged below DeShawn's dangling boots. I got on my stomach and slid toward him, reaching out for his air pack's shoulder straps.

In the pit below, an enormous dragon – about the size of a bus – lay on its belly, crunching on a charred corpse and tearing away the turnouts with its claws. It was as red as its fire, jagged scales over every inch of its fat body. It didn't have ears, but a shitload of evil-looking horns. No wings. That's one thing different about real dragons compared to the ones from fairy tales. Real dragons don't fly.

I couldn't tell who the dead firefighter was. Pain and anger bubbled up to my throat, but I had to swallow it. This was no time for revenge. I grabbed DeShawn and helped him out of the hole.

The dragon rolled over as it bit off the firefighter's head and swallowed, snorting gleefully and puffing flames from its snout. This bastard had crawled from beneath the ground, through the concrete foundation, and stamped out a comfy spot to munch on one of my brothers or sisters. The headless body rolled over in the dragon's grasp, and the flames illuminated the name on the back of the turnout coat. It was Theresa.

My axe grew heavier in my hands. I wanted this scaly dead.

"Follow the hose and get out," I told DeShawn. I had to shout for him to hear me, pointing back the way I'd come.

He nodded and crawled away. I still had to find the Truck 1 firefighters, even though I was sure they were dead, swallowed. Only a self-serving asshole would leave people behind, but I'd be lying if I told you the thought of escaping didn't play through my mind like a bad song on repeat.

My HUD said I was at half a bottle of air, and my nerves weren't helping me conserve breath. When DeShawn disappeared from view, the floor shook. A roar followed. My ribcage rattled. The dragon towered over me, clawing at the walls and having to hunch with its back against the ceiling. Still, it was small as far as dragons went. Smoke rolled from its nostrils into its yellow, glowing eyes. From behind its countless teeth, red fire flickered in the back of its throat.

I put the nozzle on a straight stream and shot into the dragon's mouth. Not only did that not extinguish the flames, I think the growling and puffs of smoke from its nostrils meant I'd done nothing but annoy the bastard.

I had to get the hell out of there.

Crawling as fast as I could, I heaved huge gulps of air,

following the hoseline. Jaws clamped onto my air pack, and my hands and knees left the floor as the dragon lifted me into the air. It shook me to and fro like my dog, Kenji, treats trespassing backyard squirrels. I bounced from one wall to the other, each hit bringing a new flash of pain.

When I first got on the job, I had a captain who once told me, "If you're going to eat a shit sandwich, you might as well swallow it in one bite."

Well, I was in the middle of a supersized quarter pounder of shit, and the only way I saw out of my predicament was to do what they'd trained us to never do, under any circumstances. I loosened my air pack's harness straps and slipped my arms from them. When I unbuckled the waist straps, I fell until the air hose yanked my head up, ripping the helmet from my head and the mask from my face.

I braced myself for the superheated air inside the house to enter my lungs and burn my throat. Dying from that and smoke inhalation would have been better than letting some ugly ass scaly get me. Maybe I wouldn't become a wraith going out that way.

But I didn't succumb. Uncomfortable as the heat was, it wasn't hurting me.

The hell?

I was so surprised I was able to breathe, I almost neglected the dragon dropping my air pack from its teeth and opening its mouth, the sound of a high-octane crescendo rising in its throat.

My axe lay in front of me, so I threw it at the ugly bastard. I'd only done it to distract the scaly, but, as if God owed me a favor, the axe twirled through the air and landed in the back of the dragon's throat. It rose, smashing holes in walls and breaking through the roof, shooting its fiery breath into the afternoon sky. The dragon was throwing an all-out temper tantrum, and I was caught in the middle of it.

I crawled for the fire hose, but the dragon swung its tail into the corner, dropping smashed bits of wood and sheetrock to block my escape route.

Shit.

"Hey," someone shouted from above.

Through the hole in the ceiling, Truck 1's captain stood at the tip of their ladder fifty feet up, lowering a harness at the end of a rope.

I was going to kiss that man.

The dragon coughed up the axe as I secured the harness around my middle. Yanking twice on the rope, I yelled for the other captain to take me up. That's when the house began crying.

A structure, like any other entity, makes certain sounds when it's dying, ones I've developed a knack for identifying. This house was coming down. The dragon clawed against the collapsing walls, too focused on me to realize it was being pinned down by the collapse.

Truck 1's captain could only pull the rope so fast, considering he was an out-of-shape, middle-aged man pulling another guy on the end (me) who wasn't Jack Spratt either.

Kicking off one crumbling wall, I dodged another that would have flattened me. Below, most of the dragon's body lay under the rubble, but its long, ugly head was out in the open and snapping toward my wrinkled ass.

I was done for, seeing, almost in slow motion, the trajectory of the scaly's coal-black teeth. They'd pierce my legs, rip me from the harness with a back-breaking snap, and then the bastard would drag me underground to enjoy its meal.

But something flew into the side of the dragon's throat, stabbing it with a blade of white flame. It was a someone – a smoke eater. They'd jumped nearly fifty feet with the aid of the thrusters in their power suit, and plugged the scaly with an enormous laser sword on their right arm.

Smoke eaters always got the coolest toys.

I was just above the roof, and Truck 1's driver rotated the ladder to get me and his captain out of the battle, when the dragon roared louder than ever, a huge sound wave rippling from its jaws. The pulse racked the ladder truck, along with me dangling from it, and killed the truck's power. The ladder stopped moving, and I was stuck above an angry dragon trying to shake a smoke eater from its neck.

The smoky looked at me. They wore a slick green fire helmet, and what looked like tactical wraparound sunglasses covered their eyes. I knew it was a woman by her lips, but I guess it could have been a man with particularly nice kissers. She shouted something I couldn't decipher.

Another smoke eater flew in from above, the heat from his thrusters wapping against my head. He landed on the dragon's bottom lip and, with a hand holding on to the top of its snout, shot a thick stream of foam into the dragon's throat. Before the scaly could chomp him, he hovered down to the ground and blasted the dragon with laserfire from his other arm.

Damned dragon never had a chance.

The smoke eater hanging on to the scaly's neck removed her sword and flew onto its head. With a quick steadying of her weight, the smoky plunged her sword into the scaly's skull. As the big bastard flopped to the ground, the woman jetted to the front yard like the Angel of Death.

Truck 1's captain lowered me to the ground. I removed my harness and took the next moment to throw up the big breakfast DeShawn had cooked that morning.

"You the one who was inside?" The foam-shooting smoke eater jogged over to me.

I wiped my mouth, head beginning to ache. "Yeah. I went in after my crew."

"You lost your mask. You could breathe in there." The way he said it was a mix of inquiry and confusion. Hell, it seemed he knew more than I did about that shit. He hit a button at the side of his head and the tactical goggles split and retracted into his helmet.

He was a black guy, and had red irises. I knew they weren't contacts, because that kind of crap wasn't tolerated in our line of work, but some people had a strange allergy to the dragon ash that turned their eyes weird colors. Others just developed a bad case of silicosis. It's why you saw a bunch of people walking around wearing surgical masks.

"Yeah," I said. "I guess the hole in the ceiling vented the smoke pretty well."

What did this guy want from me? I just wanted to retrieve my crew and mourn like every other red-blooded American.

"Then you're going to have to come with us." The voice behind me was feminine and stern.

I turned as she retracted her goggles.

"They only sent two of you clowns?" I said. "And a little too late."

She looked almost like Sherry when she was younger. Except her eyes were closer together and her nose was bigger. Her helmet prevented me from seeing what her hair looked like, but by the way she gave me the evil eye, I would have bet my life's savings she was a redhead.

A policeman ran over. "Holy cow! Did you see that?"

"Officer," the Angel of Death said, as Foam Shooter closed in on me.

"Huh?" The cop started at the smoke eater's voice.

"Hand me your cuffs," Angel said.

I'm too old and tired for this shit. I would start swinging fists if I needed to.

It wouldn't take a genius to figure out what she wanted to do with those cuffs. What's that saying? Out of the fire, into the frying pan?

I spit. "You guys are on some drugs if you think you can kidnap people in broad daylight. Firemen especially. Clean up your own dragon mess. I'm calling my chief and going home."

A black apparatus with flashing purple and green lights drove up and parked behind Truck 1. More smoke eaters.

Foam put his hand on my chest.

The cop fidgeted the handcuffs from his belt, all smiles. "Sure thing. You're the boss."

I turned to run, but Angel caught me in the back of my legs. My knees hadn't been on the ground more than a few seconds when she clicked the cuffs onto my wrists.

"You assholes have no right," I shouted. "I was doing my job and trying to help my crew. If you fuckers had showed up sooner–"

Angel pointed to Foam, who pulled a black bag from his turnout pocket.

I continued to yell and curse until he put the bag over my head. It tightened around my face where I couldn't breathe, so I had to shut up.

"Calm down," Angel said.

I couldn't see anything. But my silence caused the bag to loosen a bit, allowing me to breathe. I heaved, ready for the air to be taken away again.

"The bag you're wearing," Angel said, "tightens if you talk, cutting off your air. If you didn't already figure that out."

I nodded.

"I normally don't like to do things the hard way, but you aren't making this easy. So this is what's going to happen. We're calling in the cleanup crew to quarantine this area. We'll try to retrieve any of your firefighters' bodies. But, whether you like it or not, you're coming with us."

CHAPTER 2

I could deal with the quiet of the man-sized terrarium they'd put me in; it was a nice change from the dragon fire I'd managed to crawl out of, even though Theresa's headless corpse kept popping into my mind. I could deal with the occasional green-shirted smoke eater who walked by without paying me any attention. I didn't want to talk to those assholes unless they were going to let me go home. I could deal with the stink of my sweat-soaked duty shirt and my ash-covered turnout bottoms. I could even deal with the hard-on-the-ass chair I sat in, which highlighted my lack of anatomical cushioning.

But damned if these smoke eaters didn't give me lukewarm coffee in a chipped, Parthenon City Fire Department mug. Terrorists are treated better.

I didn't see what kind of vehicle they used to bring me here, but it had sounded and moved like any other fire apparatus. I also had no clue how long the trip had taken. Time has a way of escaping you when you have a kill-happy, near-sentient bag over your head.

Outside my glass prison, movement drew my eyes to the left, where a black man in a crisp, flame-orange uniform shirt walked up and looked in on me. A golden badge shone on his chest. Pinned on the collars, where a fire officer's bugles would normally be, were some other decorations I couldn't make out.

This guy was high up on the smoky ladder for sure.

He smiled and waved at me. Then, lowering his head, he pushed something on a panel next to him. Sirens buzzed inside the glass room. Thirty years of slowly losing my hearing with each emergency run did nothing to block out the sharp robo-bird-like squawking. I covered my ears.

From vents in the room's floor, black smoke rolled out, engulfing my feet and ankles.

The hell with this.

I threw the mug of insulting coffee at the glass wall in front of me. The porcelain shattered, leaving brown liquid dripping down the unscathed glass, where, on the other side, the man in orange stared at me, scrunching his lips as if I was the one behaving poorly.

So I threw the chair, which had even better luck surviving the impenetrable wall. Before the smoke closed around my head, I flipped off the man in orange and stole a big gulp of air. Then the smoke blocked everything from view. It wasn't hot like in a fire, but I sure as shit didn't want to breathe it in.

Over the years, smoke had become more dangerous due to all the different chemicals they used to make couches and holostereos. Not that the old, wood-only fires were safe to breathe in – it's where the original term "smoke eater" came from to describe firefighters – but modern times created the type of smoke where one puff could kill you. A nasty combo of hydrogen cyanide and carbon monoxide that would displace your oxygen or send you into cardiac arrest.

I closed my eyes, holding air in my cheeks, drawing it into my lungs, and then inflating my cheeks again. I was fooling myself if I thought I could keep doing that forever.

I don't want to die!

If the chair or coffee mug couldn't break the glass, I'd have been stupid to think slamming my fists against it would do anything more. But since my fire training wasn't offering me anything useful...

...I went shamma-lamma-ding-dong stupid.

The first glass wall I found got a flurry of punches until my knuckles ached.

I couldn't hold my breath any longer. The point of no return was miles behind my anatomical rearview mirror, and I was so damned tired. I'd gone past fight or flight and sailed directly into "fuck it."

After emptying my lungs and a three-count, I opened my eyes and breathed in the smoke. Might as well get it over with, huh? If these smoke eaters wanted to punish me for fooling around with their dragon, I wouldn't let them have another second to torture me. I just wished I could have seen Sherry one more time.

The black smoke rolled over my lips, tasting like coffee grounds and the ashy bottom of a nuclear reactor – or what I'd imagine it would taste like. I held the smoke in my lungs like a toke of marijuana, waiting for a fatal coughing attack, waiting for the toxins to kill me. But they didn't. I exhaled the smoke from my nostrils, smelling the charred essence. After another moment, I breathed in again with no lightheadedness or signs of asphyxiation.

What the hell is going on?

Air whooshed into the room as the man in orange entered with a slight limp and a clang with every other step. Behind him, what I'd thought to be solid glass resealed, and the black clouds swirled around us both. The vents in the floor hummed like a vacuum cleaner, sucking away the smoke as quickly as they'd spewed it out.

"What the hell is wrong with you people," I shouted. "I don't have much for a lawyer, but I swear we're going to sue the shit out of you!"

The man in orange bent over and picked up the chair I'd thrown. "Relax, Captain Brannigan."

The smoke hadn't bothered this guy either. No one knew all the secret shit the smoke eaters were into when they weren't slaying dragons, but messing with old firemen for the hell of it was apparently part of that protocol. With the room clear, I saw that this man's collar pins were crossed lances, like the knights used back in medieval days.

"Who are you?"

He sat in the chair and held out his hand, smiling. "I'm Chief Donahue."

"Never heard of you." I shook his hand, mainly out of habit and respect for the rank. The fire service has a way of doing that to you.

"I'm chief of the Smoke Eater Division."

"I guessed so. With the orange shirt and the collar pins, and the way you almost killed me!" I walked over to the wall and leaned against it. "Listen, Chief, I'm not trying to be disrespectful. But it's been a real bad day, no thanks to you guys, and I'm sure my chief will want me to file a report and do some debriefing, and I really just want to go home. You've had your fun scaring me with the smoke. So if you don't mind–"

"That smoke wasn't for my enjoyment. And it was as much for your understanding as it was for mine." He unwrapped a thick piece of colorless gum and began chewing.

I stifled a laugh. "Well, I'm sorry to tell you I didn't get anything out of this dog and pony show. I've seen fog machines before."

"That wasn't fake fog. That smoke was real. Dragon

smoke, actually. As was what you breathed in the house fire today." Donahue nodded his head, smacking on his gum. He hadn't blinked once.

At that moment, I knew he was telling the truth. But that just confused me even more.

He directed a hand to the other chair in the room. "Have a seat, Cap."

I took my time getting there, watching the chief the whole way. When I got to the chair, I plopped down.

Donahue leaned forward. "I want to apologize for the way my smokies handled things this afternoon. I bet you can understand how your adrenaline goes from zero to a hundred at a structure fire. It's compounded when you're fighting a dragon."

"She put a bag over my head that suffocated me if I wasn't compliant."

Donahue held his hands out like a sympathetic guidance counselor. "I know. I know. We've had issues with citizens interfering with dragon scenes in the past. Idiots who want to get a selfie with a dragon and put it on the Feed. The mute bag is supposed to be a last resort. And my smoke eaters are instructed to bring in anyone who can breathe smoke."

"I'd get sued for that kind of thing. And then I come here to be experimented on? Because my old ass can handle a little smoke?"

Donahue cocked his head, thinned his eyes. "You kidding me? That wasn't a little smoke. And this room isn't an experiment. Like I said, it was to show you that what happened today wasn't a fluke or a result of your firefighting experience. Don't you know what it takes to be a smoke eater?"

"More balls than brains."

Laughing, Donahue shook his head. "My guess is we never caught wind of your ability because you were already well on in your career and age when the dragons emerged."

"My ability? I've got a bum knee and a weak bladder. What do you mean?"

Donahue stared at me, as serious as a heart attack. "Captain Brannigan, you can breathe smoke, withstand intense heat. You're a smoke eater."

I think I'd known since that dragon ripped my air mask off, but I'd been denying it. How could anyone believe something like that was possible? Up until that point, when Donahue smiled at my visible realization, I'd been calling bullshit.

Looking back over the years, I could pinpoint certain instances where I'd showed signs of a smoke eater, besides the recent house fire: eight years old, out camping and my mom telling me not to sit so close to the bonfire as I danced my fingers over the flames; hanging out in a smoke-filled garage with my uncle, Teddy, who burned through American Spirits as if his lungs depended on it. I just thought everyone was like that.

Even in my whole career as a firefighter, smoke and heat had never bugged me like I'd seen it affect others on the job. I thought I was either lucky or they were pansy-asses.

All of this ran through my mind as I glared at Donahue. "Well, too bad for both of us, huh?" I stood and walked toward where I'd seen Donahue enter. "Now, if you pricks can take me back to my fire station…"

Donahue turned the chair around to sit in it backwards. "There aren't many of us smoke eaters around. Not that we know of. We're the only ones who can effectively fight these dragons. Especially within a structure. And the scalies love to hole up in buildings. Our little group here has to cover the entire state. We need you."

"No, what you guys need is an attitude adjustment

and more tact. I don't know if you read up on me or not – though, the cloak-and-dagger thing you have going on says you did – but I'm retiring at the end of the week. In fact, I was going to cash in on the vacation days I had left, but now I think I'll just use them to get on with my life." I punched the glass wall in front of me. "How the hell do you open this door?"

The chief drummed his fingers against the top of the chair, biting his lip and breathing a little heavier. He was trying to contain his frustration, not let it show. When I became an officer, I read a book on body language, thinking it would make me a better leader. It was pretty obvious Donahue was pissed. And that made two of us.

"Smoke eaters are born, not made," Donahue said. "This room we're in, it's where all smokies discover themselves, it's where we test those who think they've got what it takes. Children whose parents saw them move a hand over a flame unscathed, or born to a mother who chain-smoked throughout the pregnancy. We indulge these fruitless tests because it keeps city hall's checks coming and keeps them off our backs. But real deal smoke eaters aren't carnival attractions. I believe nature or genetics has given us the means to fight the scalies, but we need every ounce of help we can get, every smoke eater we can find. I don't know why you got into the fire service, but I don't think you would have climbed the ranks if you didn't care about people. It's why you went into that house to rescue your crew. It's why your hoseman is still alive."

"But it wasn't enough." I turned to Donahue. "Was it?"

"Then make it mean something. Put off your retirement. Transfer over to the Smoke Eater Division and use your gift for the greater good. We can definitely use your fire experience. And you'll get a big raise to go along with it. I'd say another twenty thousand more a year."

Holy balls.

The man wasn't going to let it go. I had to tell him what I told vacuum salesman and Jehovah's Witnesses who wouldn't get off my porch. "Let me think about it."

"That sounds fair enough." Donahue stood and removed a card from his pocket. "This is my direct line."

I took the card and got a whiff of the strange gum in Donahue's mouth. "What the hell is that you're chewing on?"

"Oh." He laughed and spit it into his hand. "Nicotine gum. Trying to quit cigarettes. I thought about switching to a bubble vape, but people look so ridiculous blowing those glowing blobs from their mouths."

"Cigarettes, huh? Abusing your gift?" I made bunny ears with my fingers for the last word.

"Wife's making me. For the grandkids. You have any children?"

"Wasn't in the cards."

Donahue limped closer, with the sound of a metallic crab.

"If you don't mind me asking, what happened to your leg?" I asked. "I can hear it clank against the floor."

Donahue smiled as if I'd complimented his uniform, and knocked knuckles against his right leg. "Titanium alloy. Lost it to a dragon. If you transfer over here, maybe I'll tell you the story."

"That might be worth it."

It was almost like looking in a mirror with Donahue. Obviously we looked nothing alike, but we were cut from the same cloth. Old hands still squeezing the Devil's throat. Brotherhood is a word that gets tossed around the fire service a lot, but it's always nice when you can feel it.

Donahue stepped closer to the glass and pushed something in his pants pocket. Angel and Foam, the two smoke eaters from before, rounded the corner. Angel had her favorite little torture bag in hand. My guess about her being a redhead had been wrong. She was of Indian heritage and had hair darker than dragon smoke.

I froze in my tracks and Donahue turned back when he saw I wasn't walking beside him out into the hall.

"I hate to do this to you," he said. "But we're going to have to put the mute bag on you again. At least until you're sworn in. We like to keep our activities out of public knowledge – not many of them are happy with us, thanks to Mayor Rogola – and fire captain or not, in our eyes you're a citizen."

"Couldn't imagine why anyone wouldn't like you guys." I groaned. "What is this place?"

Lowering my head to Angel, I gave her my best "fuck you" glare. She grinned as she put the bag in place.

I was once again in the dark.

"We're the only line of defense against the dragons, Captain Brannigan." Donahue patted my shoulder. "And you're one of us. Sink or swim."

CHAPTER 3

I should have been home twelve hours before. Fire families get used to loaning you out for twenty-four hours at a time, but anything more than that is hell for everybody.

If I could have sat in my pickup a while longer, I think I might have come up with a good plan on what to say to Sherry. You might say telling the truth was the only thing I had to do. What else did I have to think about? I had a bad day and fell into a terrible situation. Why wouldn't she be OK with that?

But sometimes the truth has to be sold, and not long after your honeymoon phase, you learn that being married means being a good salesperson. Those who can't wheel and deal end up losing half their shit and sleeping on a friend's futon.

The lights were off inside my house, but that didn't mean no one was home or awake. I stared at the second floor window for a minute, where a bad storm had once sent sixty-mile-per-hour hailstones through the glass. Apparently, dragons scorching the earth didn't stop natural meteorological events from occurring. The only difference now was that when it rained, we had to slog through wet ash as much as mud.

I'd taped cardboard on the other side of the upstairs

window, but hadn't gotten around to putting in a new pane. That had been six months ago, and my plan was to use the first week of my retirement to finally get it fixed, along with other household projects I never had any time for.

I couldn't decide what Sherry was going to be more pissed about. Being gone all day or considering a new career. No, I was pretty sure it would be the dragon incident.

Readjusting my overnight bag on my shoulder, I climbed the front steps to the door. I'd barely gotten my head inside when a baseball slammed into the door frame just centimeters from my ear.

"Shit!" I jumped back.

"Watch your language in this house."

The light turned on in the kitchen, and Sherry stomped away, humming a lilting song stuffed with frustration, the kind of noise combination only wives are capable of. I sighed. Sherry always asked me to leave my firefighter attitude at the station. I couldn't help that foul language was as much a job-related tool as a spanner wrench.

News about dragon emergences travels fast, especially between firefighters. And their spouses. Want to share something with the entire world? Tell one firefighter. I swear we have a gossip network that goes viral quicker than anything on the Feed.

I should have called to let Sherry know I was OK, but with the smoke eaters kidnapping me, and spending the next several hours giving my battalion chief a verbal report of what had happened at the fire, and then being sent between different chiefs within the administration and then to a psych evaluator, I'd been too busy and had only snagged a half hour of sleep every time they dragged me to a new office and a new chair to sit in.

I'd also tried like hell to tell my chief about the smoke

eaters nabbing me, but he didn't want to hear about it.

"None of my business," he'd said, waving it away and closing his eyes, like I was blowing bees in his face.

I touched a few fingers to the dent Sherry's baseball left in the door frame, taking account of the other two dings above it. In our whole marriage, Sherry had only been pissed enough to get out her old Rawlings ball – signed by Waterman Schultz, some major leaguer I'd never heard of – and show me she still had an abundance of power in her throwing arm. People still talk about her no hitter at the 2092 high school state championship. She could have gone off to play college ball, and who knows after that? But instead she married me a year later.

I dropped my bag at the door and followed my wife into the kitchen. Sherry sat at the table with her arms crossed. When she got upset her eyes would glow green and the pale areas around them would redden. She tapped her lips with a couple fingers, inviting me to kiss her. I did.

Hunching over, she scratched a red-painted nail into the tabletop.

"I've had one weird day," I said. "I would have called, but I've been through the wringer."

"I thought you were dead." She lifted her eyes to me, sparkling green. "I had to hear about it from Scott Pierson's husband. And you know how he blows things out of proportion."

"What did he tell you?"

She swallowed. "That you went into a house with a dragon. An actual dragon. That you lost your air mask and almost died."

It sounded like Scott Pierson's husband had gotten the facts fairly correct for once.

"Yeah..." I sat down across from her, rubbing my chin and trying to find a good way to tell her about what happened.

"You didn't really do that, right? He was just making it up. Right?"

"I had no choice."

Sherry jumped from her chair. "Are you crazy? One week from retirement. One week! What were you even doing at a dragon fire?"

"We didn't know it was a dragon. The quake must not have been big enough to detect. And I wasn't going to let my crew burn."

"Now you probably have that silicosis stuff or some black lung disease you'll die from in a year."

I loved my wife with a fury hotter than a scaly's insides, but she was really starting to tire me out. She'd brought up the whole "breathing smoke" thing, and it was as good a time as any to tell her.

"That's another thing." I cleared my throat. "The smoke eaters took me today."

"What? What did you do?"

"Nothing. It's... it's more about what I can do than what I did. This is going to sound nuts."

With a soft kick, Sherry toppled the chair she'd been sitting in. "We're already in crazy town, so you might as well tell me."

OK, then.

"I can breathe dragon smoke. And the smoke eaters want me to join up with them."

Her demeanor didn't change a bit, but the rhythm of her chest looked to be calming. "You told them 'no'. Right?"

"I was heading that way. But in the end, I told them I'd think about it."

She trudged past me, heading for the front door.

"Where are you going?" I turned to watch her.

"To retrieve my baseball."

As if reading her mind, Kenji, our robotic dog, bounded in with the baseball in his metal teeth. He leapt onto my knees with his front paws and lifted his head with pride. The digital screen that acted as his eyes showed closed eyelids surrounded by dancing hearts and exclamation points.

I took the ball from Kenji's jaws and grinned at Sherry, who leaned against the wall, arms crossed.

"Jjoh-eun achim, babo gat-eun namja!" Kenji said, panting happily with his rubber tongue dangling.

The dog spoke nothing but Korean, and he used that same phrase every time he saw me. I tried looking up the translation after we'd gotten him, and after some rough research on the Feed, I was pretty sure it meant, "Good morning, dumb man." I didn't take too much offense to it. For one, it was rarely morning when he said it, so I knew he was confused. For another, I'd called him dumb first, so he probably took it as a term of endearment.

I'd spray-painted gray spots on his blue steel, attempting to make him look like a robotic Dalmatian – which I always thought he resembled – but it only gave him the appearance of a mechanical mutt. I never claimed to be an artist.

Just before the dragons emerged, and not long after the quakes of 2114, all of the dogs hightailed it somewhere they wouldn't get chomped or burned, like they could sense something in the world had changed. I could just see someone's Pomeranian finishing their last bowl of kibble and barking, "Thanks for the food and companionship, but you're all fucked," as it galloped into the sunset.

I'd heard urban legends that massive packs of dogs took up residence in the Nevada desert, sneaking into open bedroom windows and dragging children off in the middle of the night.

Man's best friend my ass.

Cats stayed around, and I'm convinced it was only to witness humanity's demise and put in a bid to take over as the dominant species once the dragons had finished burning everything down.

Sherry and I had never owned a pet. After the dragons emerged, some enterprising businesspeople saw an opportunity to fill the gap left by the dog exodus with artificial intelligence – I use that last word very loosely – and Sherry just had to have one. Two Christmases ago, the Feed had a sale on robo-dogs, so I folded. My wife came up with the name Kenji, said it fit his personality. I pointed out that he was made by a Korean company and that Kenji was a Japanese name, but it didn't sway her a bit. So, Kenji it was. He preferred me over Sherry, much to her chagrin.

"I have other things I can throw," Sherry said, giving me her death glare.

"Why don't we talk about this instead of bludgeoning each other and getting reported for domestic abuse?"

Kenji turned to Sherry and barked. "Eongdeong-i kkaji mueos-ibnikka?"

I taught him that one. Translated: What's up your ass?

I laughed and petted Kenji's gray-blue head. Wonderful invention. You didn't have to feed it or walk it, and it took your side in marital spats.

"I don't know what he just said, but if you think you're going to go fight dragons, you and the dog can find another place to stay." Sherry was never one to argue with finesse. If it was a fencing duel, Sherry would pull out a submachine gun.

I normally would just roll my eyes and ignore it, knowing she didn't mean whatever hurtful thing she said. Not today.

I stood, and Kenji perked up his ears. "The day I let

you tell me what I can and can't do is the day I'll start crapping fire. All I said was that I'd think about it. These smoke eaters seem like consummate jerks, but they have top-of-the-line equipment, way better pay, and maybe I was meant to do it. The smoke eaters think I was literally born to do this. That scaly killed Theresa, burned her up and bit her head off – someone I trained from day one. And it also killed two other brothers. Did Scott Pierson's husband tell you that? DeShawn almost died today, too.

"I want to make sure that never happens again."

She didn't say anything. For a few minutes, she just stared at me, eyes blazing green and swelling with tears hanging at the corners. It lasted an eternity, but I kept my eyes on her.

She walked over to the kitchen counter and brought back a holopamphlet.

"What's this?" I stared at the thin metal in her outstretched hand.

"It was going to be a surprise," Sherry said. "I thought it would be a good time to have what we never could. What you never had time for with the department."

I took the holopamphlet from her hand and opened it. Moving pictures of smiling kids floated at me. One in particular caught my attention: a red-haired little girl with the bluest eyes. My gut twisted and sank. I could have cried. The pamphlet was from an adoption agency.

"Oh, Sherry," I said. "I didn't know."

"I love you," Sherry said. Then, with a spin of her heels, she stalked away to our bedroom and shut the door.

"I love you, too," I said softly.

For my wife, my retirement wasn't just about me being home more often or having the time to fix the damn upstairs window. Sherry was looking forward to finally starting a family, something that nature had denied us, something the fire service and time had put a wall between. I'd always wanted to be a dad. And now that I finally could...

What an ass I'd been.

I patted Kenji again before raiding the fridge for some edible comfort. Then I dug out the bottle of bourbon I hadn't touched in a year. It was far beyond the drinkable date, but I didn't care. If super-heated, toxic smoke couldn't kill me, it'd be a wonder if past-due booze could bump me off.

I stayed up surfing the Feed on my holoreader. Instantly, I was inundated with words and images floating in the air in front of my face.

People were resharing posts from Mayor Rogola about how the firefighters and the smoke eaters, and even the police were doing such a horrible job. I didn't follow that idiot, but I still ended up seeing the bullshit he spouted on a continual basis. Someone should have taken away his holoreader. He would have still been a cowardly ingrate, but at least he wouldn't have infected the public with his propaganda.

Firefighters got paid too much. Firefighters caused more damage than help. Firefighters sat on their asses unless they were dicking around at the grocery store, all while tax dollars filled their pockets.

Well, Rogola and his supporters had never been under a flipped hover car, trying like hell to dig a five year-old out of the wreckage while his mother lay dead beside him. That kid's cries would never fill their heads and wake them up in the middle of the night for the next thirty years.

They'd never had to fight a dragon.

I flipped to the news, seeing if their drones had captured the house fire or me dangling from the ladder truck like a worm on a hook. Instead, they were doing a piece on Canada: The Mysterious White North.

Such a play on words.

"Shortly after E-Day, Canada severed ties and communication with the United States," said a reporter with too much eye makeup. "Why? At a time when sharing resources and intelligence is most crucial, our northern neighbors have elected to deal with the dragons on their own. And, despite limited information, from all accounts they are succeeding. We took to the streets of Parthenon City to see what you think is going on up north."

The screen switched to a stubble-faced, ball-cap-wearing man in his forties, a microphone shoved in his face. "I tell you this much, if those dragon worshipers have something we need to kill these dragons, we should just storm the border and take it."

A black woman in a tank top said, "I bet it's all that snow. The dragons don't like it."

The reporter's voice cut in, saying, "Mayor Rogola recently released this video, explaining his take on the situation."

Rogola's ugly mug floated from my holoreader. "We need to put America and Parthenon City first. Whether Canada has something or not, it doesn't matter. We need to take care of things ourselves. I am the only one who knows how to move forward. Droids are the best–"

I turned off my holoreader, couldn't listen to another damn word. The quiet of my house, the wood settling with the occasional creak, the sound of Kenji humming next to me, was way more comforting. I cracked open the bourbon and reminisced about all the memories Sherry and I had made in that house. How many more there could be. Maybe a red-haired little girl running through the halls.

That was the last night I stayed in that house. And it was on the couch.

CHAPTER 4

Sherry had already left for work when I woke up the next morning. I brewed an entire pot of coffee with the intention of drinking every last drop by myself. While the coffee dripped (all our advances in society and we still had to wait), I grabbed my holoreader and Donahue's business card.

As the old advice suggests, I'd slept on it, and decided that I didn't want my marriage to end over some job opportunity. Boiled down, that's what it was.

I'd done my time. Society owed me for thirty years of carrying morbidly obese people out of houses full of hoarded junk, for waking up at three in the morning because someone's knee ached, for seeing death more and more increasingly over time. I was done, and that's what I'd tell the smoke eaters.

My finger hovered over the first digit in Donahue's number when the holoreader rang.

The caller ID said "unknown."

I hit the button to answer the call with audio only. It was quickly overridden. I hate when people do that.

"Brannigan." It was the floating, holographic head of my battalion chief, Tom Elwood, looking to be in as shitty a mood as ever – wide nostrils and ruffled, white mustache. "You must have really screwed the pooch yesterday. You need to get downtown. Right now."

I wasn't going to lie down and take that. "I'm off the clock. You called on a restricted number?"

"You wouldn't have answered otherwise."

He had me there. "Well, I already told you everything yesterday."

"You're not coming to see me, you cocky son of a bitch. The mayor wants you in his office, like yesterday."

"What for?"

"I don't know. But you shut up and listen and do what he says. If this makes me look bad, I will ruin your retirement in every way I can."

Parthenon City, Ohio, hadn't been attacked by dragons since the first scaly emergence, what everyone began calling E-Day. I guess D-Day was taken. Sherry and I were visiting family in rural Minnesota, a coincidence that still plagues my mind. Sherry was thankful I hadn't been on duty, but I wished I could have been with my brother and sister firefighters that day. Maybe some of them would still be alive.

In any case, the city put a ton of money into making downtown "dragonproof," which drove real estate sky high. I don't think they did anything different besides slap a few safety stickers on stuff. Those who couldn't afford big-city living had to make do in the suburbs scattered across the ashen wastes, or in the more rundown parts of Parthenon, where some joked that a dragon would be an improvement.

I've always been a firm believer in cause and effect. Things don't just happen without reason. The scalies didn't just decide to quit hiding underground and pop out to say hello. Thing is, the dragon emergence was only the most recent calamity that struck our planet. What do they say about things happening in threes? First it was the earthquakes. They weren't huge, but they happened all over the globe. I can still feel phantom quakes when I walk down the street sometimes.

Our part of the country was fortunate not to be close to a fault line. We lost most of the west coast to the Pacific, and I heard Japan had split in half.

Then the dragons hit us.

It was chaos. The world governments went to pot, only some of them maintaining the illusion of control. Most Americans huddled toward the major cities, and normally that would seem like a bad idea, but I guess they figured there was safety in numbers.

Each US city became its own little nation in a way, abiding by its own laws and way of life, even though nothing was ever made official. Besides, calling it the United City States of America was more than a mouthful, and it would be too much work to change the flag and all that government stationery.

Farm highrises were built to grow crops and raise livestock indoors. Soon, the ashen land between the cities was abandoned and left to time and dust and rednecks. Sometimes I would imagine scavengers and marauders flying in aircars over the wastes like some bad apocalyptic movie. But it hadn't really been an apocalypse. People were still living and surviving, being kind to one another. It was just a change in scenery, and eventually the earthquakes became rarer.

Any time there's a tragedy, people look for someone to blame. Well, our glorious leader, Mayor Rogola, decided that the fire department would be the first place to direct everyone's extended fingers. He said we had been ill-prepared to face these attacks.

You know, because ancient monsters crawling out of the ground to scorch a Wal-Mart is something we'd been training for.

The city took our pension to help fund the effort to rebuild and fortify the city. The smoke eaters were placed under the umbrella of the fire department – presumably for budget reasons – even though they had complete autonomy. After the active dragons were hunted down – only about fifty in our state – all that was left to do was wait for a dragon to rear its ugly head. The smoke eaters had some classified tech to monitor seismic activity. And we firefighters just had to be good little boys and girls, transporting people to the hospital and putting water on the occasional conflagration.

All this lowered my opinion of city hall and Mayor Rogola to even less than it had been before the scaly crisis. And now I was at the hub of my hatred, sitting in a leather chair that smelled brand new, listening to the Muzak version of a tune I was ninety-nine percent sure was a heavy metal song, and watching the receptionist exhale multicolored bubbles after taking hits from her bubble vape.

It amazed me how human beings would continue to invent strange things to put in their mouths for no purpose.

After the second pass through a six month-old gossip holo-magazine, I stood up. "I'm leaving."

The receptionist had been in the middle of blowing a ridiculously large, green bubble that burst when I'd spoken. "Let me check with him again," she said with a huff.

This was a power play on the part of the mayor. He'd had my chief rush me here, only to keep me waiting. Any other person would have been fidgeting and wondering why they were there to begin with. Not I, said the cat. I'd run out of fucks to give.

"He'll see you now," the receptionist said.

Imagine that.

The receptionist pointed toward the large door behind her desk as she sucked up a blue bubble from her nicotine vape.

I went in without knocking. A skinny man with glasses and a bowtie jumped at my entrance, shaking as if I was a dragon. I didn't know who the guy was. He stood at the front of the mayor's desk holding a holoreader, carrying the weak obedience of an assistant.

Mayor Rogola sat at his desk, greasy black hair split down the middle, hunched over and leaning on crossed arms. My body language book would have said he wasn't happy to see me. His frown made him look just like the shī, Chinese guardian lion statues, at either side of his desk.

"So you're Captain Brannigan," Rogola said.

I nodded to him. "And you are?"

Rogola turned to the skinny assistant, who dropped his jaw and shivered even more. Then, going from a stern ronin to a happy monk, the mayor laughed in a slow, gravely bark. "He's funny, Jenkins."

Jenkins didn't look so sure, relaxing his quaking, but keeping his eyes wide.

I once saw a video on the Feed of a dragon that had emerged in the middle of an emu farm. Jenkins looked just like one of those birds spazzing out before getting torched and eaten.

"Have a seat," the mayor said.

I shrugged and took the one farthest from Jenkins.

"Funny, yes, that's you." Rogola ran his tongue behind his upper lip. "That must be what you were going for yesterday. When you spoke to the man with the fire droids. Right?"

So that's what this is about.

I smiled. "It was such a chaotic scene, I don't remember what I said."

Rogola pointed to Jenkins, but kept his eyes on me.

The assistant poked his holoreader. "Captain Brannigan stated, 'The mayor can eat a dick.'"

Mayor Rogola raised an eyebrow as Jenkins turned red and blinked his eyes at hummingbird speed.

"Am I in trouble?" I was ready for another shit sandwich to swallow.

Rogola sniffed. "You're here because you interfered with city property. I wanted those droids tested in a real fire situation."

"Those droids don't belong on a fire scene, much less one with a dragon."

"Don't you think, Captain Brannigan, that if you'd told your crew to back out of that house and let the droids do their job, your coworkers would still be alive?"

This asshole had gone below the belt.

"We call each other brothers and sisters," I said. "So the loss hits me more than if it was just a 'coworker.' And my point is that it's not the droids' job in the first place. You already took our pension away. Now you want to take our careers?"

Rogola turned to Jenkins. "Give us a moment alone."

With a nod, Jenkins left the room.

"That's what guys like you don't understand," I continued. "A robot can't make the tough decisions in the heat of the moment. Have you even been out of your office in the last few years? Do you do anything but fill the Feed with your bullshit? Or are you too much of a coward to do the right thing?"

All of the mayor's appearances on TV had been from his office or via hologram. Rumor was the dragons had turned him into an agoraphobic. He never left. I didn't mind making cracks that went below the belt either.

"See these?" Rogola pointed to the sh⬛ statues.

"I know what they are."

"They're a family heirloom."

"I thought Rogola was Italian or something."

The mayor groaned. "My mother's parents were from China. They believed these guard lions warded off evil spirits."

"Is that what you think the dragons are?"

"I know what the wraiths are." He soured his face as if he'd bitten into a lemon.

The rumors just might have been true.

"Sometimes it's best to hang up your helmet and let others do the guarding," Rogola said. "Do you see what I mean?"

"What do you want from me?" I yawned. "I've got a long day of doing nothing ahead of me."

"I wanted you fired," Rogola said.

I thinned my eyes. "For the droid thing?"

"I don't like bumps in my road. You represent everything holding this city back. You hold on to tradition like a life preserver and you can't see that your time is done. But it looks like the smoke eaters want you. So, I can't interfere."

"Well, they do love to help the elderly. But I was retiring anyway. Firing me would have just simplified things."

"Yes," the mayor nodded. "But that other captain who was there at the fire. He was hoping for a few more years of pay."

Truck 1's captain, the guy who'd saved my life. Rogola, the prick, wouldn't dare lay him off.

"You had him fired?"

"I can't make Donahue do anything, but your current fire chief works directly for me, and does what I tell him. If you want to blame anyone, blame yourself."

I stood up, ready to flip the desk. "You asshole! He did nothing wrong."

Rogola laughed. "Let me give you some free advice, Brannigan. Don't become a smoke eater. Their short time is over just like any other firefighter. The people of this state are tired of losing their homes because of such slow response. Technology and society are moving forward. Your kind is old news. We can save money and lives by using droids instead of grumpy old men like you."

"Let me give you something for free." I held up both of my middle fingers and backed toward the door.

Rogola grinned from his seat and waved goodbye.

Back in my truck, I pulled out my holoreader and Donahue's card.

"Chief D," he answered.

"I'm in. But only on one condition."

"Hello to you, too, Brannigan. Go on. I'm listening."

"At the fire department, get Truck 1's captain his job back. You do that, and I'll slay any damn dragon you want."

Donahue laughed on the other end. "Is that all?"

CHAPTER 5

Donahue said he'd send some smoke eaters to retrieve me, and that I wouldn't need my truck. So I left it at city hall.

There was someone I needed to see, so I asked them to pick me up at my DeShawn's house. I gave Donahue the address and he told me to be ready by three o'clock.

I tried calling Sherry, but she didn't answer.

Taking the hover bus was always something I avoided. It smelled, and the other people onboard would constantly hack into their facemasks or argue about what a wraith was made of. Or there'd be some guy blowing a bubble vape – there was one in every crowd. That day's two o'clock bus to the south side of town was sparse though, and it gave me plenty of time to think.

Maybe some coughing, bubble-blowing companionship wouldn't have been half bad.

After a while of looking out the window at the ash blowing in like a blizzard, I changed my gaze to the advertisements posted along the bus's ceiling.

Dirt won't settle when you leave it to a man of metal!
Stop by the Droid Factory today to talk
about payment plans.
Everyone can afford some help around the house.
Droids make life easier!

What the fuck was this? The 1960s?

Rogola had secured a deal for the Droid Factory to be the sole provider of municipal droids. That was just fine for the company, since most of Parthenon City's citizens couldn't afford a droid, or were too creeped out by the bastards to allow one in their home. Of course, there was the offhand socialite who owned a droid butler.

I could just feel the singularity on the horizon, when that socialite would wake up to find a metal hand squeezing the pearls around her neck.

Rogola liked to spout about how he wanted the best for the city, yadda yadda yadda. It was all about money, and that meant it was ultimately about power. Sniveling bastard couldn't leave his office, so he'd probably get some kind of hero hard-on by replacing all of us with his robots.

DeShawn was single and lived in a duplex in a part of the city where the ash only blew in every other week. When I pulled up, an older black woman wearing a face mask was hugging him in the doorway, patting his back and refusing to let go. I recognized her as Mama P – I never found out what the P stood for.

When I walked up to the edge of the driveway, Mama P turned to give me the evil eye.

DeShawn smiled, embarrassed, and raised his hand in greeting. "What's up, dub?"

"I'm telling you," Mama P said to DeShawn, "I can stay here for awhile. So you can get better."

DeShawn shook his head. "Go on home, Mama. I'll be fine."

She sighed and turned away. When we crossed paths in the middle of the walkway, Mama P grabbed my arm. "What's the matter with you?"

"Mama," DeShawn called from the door.

Mama P shook her head. "You should have known

there was a dragon in there. My boy almost died because of you."

She bent over in a coughing fit, holding a hand up that told me to stay back.

My heart, guts, and every other organ sank to the ground. If it had been the mayor or my battalion chief, hell, maybe even Sherry, I would have smarted off and walked away, knowing I was justified. But not with DeShawn's mother. I guess on some level, I knew she was right.

"Captain saved my life, Mama," DeShawn said. "Don't blame him."

"I'm sorry," was all I was able to say to Mama P.

She stared up at me with watery eyes and pocked, aged skin. She pulled down her mask, and when she pursed her lips it looked like she was gearing up for an extended ass-chewing. Instead, she let go of my arm, walked off to her tiny, spherical smartcar, and told the vehicle, "Home."

It zoomed away.

"Don't mind her, Cap." DeShawn said.

I waved my hand, like brushing away dirt. "Nothing to mind, dub. She has a right to be upset."

DeShawn had a good heart, and I didn't want to put him between his captain and his mother. Whenever there was the typical station drama at our firehouse – arguments about someone's cheeseburger getting eaten or a lazy shift not pulling their weight – it would upset DeShawn to the point he would shut down and stay quiet for a few days, no matter what I said to cheer him up. He liked everybody and only wanted the same in return.

"I wanted to come by and check on you," I said.

He smiled. "Thanks. There was something I wanted to tell you anyway."

"Yeah, me, too."

"Come on in." He held the door for me.

Inside, he'd turned on every light and had set up dozens of extra lamps that hadn't been there the last time I'd visited. I don't think I could have cast a shadow if I tried.

"Sorry about all the lights," DeShawn said. A box of folded firefighter-related t-shirts sat on the couch, and he was quick to hoist it into his arms. "Go ahead and have a seat. Can I get you a drink or something?"

"No, I'm OK."

"I've got beer."

That gave me second thoughts. "Well, shit, I'll take a beer."

After throwing the shirts into his bedroom and heading to the fridge, he came back with a cold one in each hand.

We both took long swigs from our bottles. I was damn thirsty, for alcohol especially. The past-due liquor from the night before had tasted like vinegar, so I'd thrown it out.

I also had a lot on my mind, things I was trying to sort before I said them. DeShawn was in the same boat.

But, being the elder, and his officer, I broke the tension first, "I'm–"

"Cap, I…"

"You go first," I said.

"I'm quitting the department."

I sat there for a second, scratching at the beer label. "You always told me this was your dream job, since you were a kid. And you've never quit anything in your life, not since I've known you."

"There's things you need to know."

"Like what?"

He sighed. "Theresa and I were close. We were

hanging out off the job."

"Yeah, it's hit me hard, too. I keep thinking I'm going to hear her high-pitched squealing coming from around the corner at any minute. Those awesome cinnamon rolls she'd bake."

"No, Cap." DeShawn shook his head, rubbing his face slowly. "We were sleeping together. Like, intimately. When her husband was at work."

Double damn.

"Um." I had no idea what to say. I thought I had problems.

"And then the dragon burned her. Ate her. Almost killed me, too. It was like our number came up, you know. Like our sins had brought that scaly from underground to judge us."

I finished my beer, desperately wanting another one, but too ashamed to ask for it. "That's nuts, dub."

"No," he said. "The Bible says Satan is a dragon. And it all makes sense. I feel horrible about Theresa. But Mama P says I've been given a second chance and shouldn't waste it. I'm going into the ministry."

If any beer had still been in my mouth, I would have spit it out. "Like a preacher?"

DeShawn nodded.

"What the hell happened in that house?" I asked. "We should have known there was a dragon way before they gave us the call."

He took a huge breath as he closed his eyes and tensed, like he was getting ready for an amputation. "Everything was normal. Smoke was hazy and growing, so we figured it must have been confined to the attic. We were looking for the attic entrance while the truckies made a search for occupants. Then we came around the corner and…"

"And what?"

DeShawn shook his head, stifling a laugh. "I thought I had gotten a whiff of smoke or something, seeing things. Hallucinating, maybe. But then Theresa pointed it out too. The TV was shooting white flames toward the ceiling, like a flamethrower. It covered the whole wall."

"That's weird."

Dragons were always the cause of the fires they were involved with. They never showed up after one had already started.

"Then the floor crumbled from under us," Deshawn said. "Theresa fell in, and the dragon came out. Fire everywhere. Man, that roar… I hung on to the edge, and I didn't want to move 'cause I thought I'd drop in too and get burned. Truck 1's crew came into the living room then. That's when the dragon killed them. The smoke got so thick. The heat. I just kept hanging on, hoping it wouldn't see me. That's when you crawled in and got me out."

"You tell all of this to the chief?"

DeShawn stared at me. "All except the white flames and the television."

"You tell him you're quitting?"

"Not yet."

I tapped my fingers against the side of the beer bottle. "Sounds like there's nothing I can say to dissuade you."

"You can't."

I sighed. "Well, you were a damn fine firefighter. The brotherhood is losing a good one."

"Two," DeShawn said, smiling. "With you retiring."

"Yeah." I cleared my throat. "I'm actually going to stay on for a while longer."

Pity crossed his face, might as well have been a blinking neon sign. He hadn't been a preacher for even a day and already had a knack for the holier-than-thou routine. "What for?"

"Smoke eaters."

His face went from pity to fear before he looked at the blazing lamps around us. "You're a braver man than me."

"No, I'm just crazy. Or stupid."

"I didn't sleep at all last night. Had to turn on all the lights, asked my mom to bring some lamps over. I can't be in the dark. Not even a little. I see things crawling around."

"Like what?"

"Theresa," he said. "Headless and burned up, as clear as you sitting here beside me. I just know her wraith is going to come and finish what the dragon couldn't."

I watched him rock back and forth. "Are you sure you're OK?"

He smiled. "I get my psych eval tomorrow, if you're worried. But, yeah. I'll be all right."

I wanted to say something to change DeShawn's mind, or at least convince him that God wasn't going to send a dragon or Theresa's ghost to kill him for some infidelity. But before I could open my mouth, an air horn blasted from the street outside.

"What's that?" DeShawn jumped and turned toward the noise.

"I'm guessing my ride."

DeShawn followed me outside where a big, black fire apparatus waited. It looked almost like an aerial ladder truck, but instead of a ladder, a huge laser cannon sat on top. The black paint glistened in the sun, and instead of the standard red and white lights, the truck had been outfitted with green and purple strobes and beacons. On the side of the truck, the words "Sink or Swim" had been painted in green.

The lady smoke eater from the day before hopped out of the captain's seat while the black man with red eyes circled from the driver's side. They'd substituted their power suits and helmets for the green smoke eater dress shirt and navy blue duty pants.

"Well if it isn't the Wonder Twins," I said. "Are you trying to start World War Four with that thing?"

Angel smirked. "That's why we don't typically go joyriding through residential areas. Makes people nervous. But Chief D told us to come…" she looked at DeShawn's duplex and the surrounding, meager neighborhood "…here to pick you up. So let's get going."

"Is that a laser cannon?" DeShawn asked, his eyes glued to the monstrosity in front of his place. He looked like a five year-old boy visiting the firehouse for the first time.

Foam's eyes flickered red in the sun. "It is."

I waved a hand to my former firefighter. "This is DeShawn Peyton. He… was on my crew for a long time."

"James Renfro." The guy I'd been calling Foam shook DeShawn's hand.

Angel stuck her hand out. "Captain Naveena Jendal."

I snorted.

Naveena raised her eyebrow. "What's funny?"

"Nothing," I said. "I just had different names for you guys in my head."

"Hm," she said. "You can enlighten us on the ride. Let's go."

I glanced at DeShawn, who was still ogling the cannon truck, and then turned back to Naveena. "Can I talk to you for a sec?"

Naveena huffed but followed me off to the side. "What?"

"DeShawn, over there, is thinking of quitting the fire service."

"Condolences to the Brotherhood."

I smirked at a fellow smartass.

"Can you take a couple minutes to show him around the truck?" I asked. "Maybe it'll remind him how much he loves the job."

"We don't give tours or do fire safety day at schools. That's what your former career was about. Smoke eaters don't do that kind of stuff. We're too busy killing dragons."

"Well, I don't get the Secret Squirrel stuff, the public sure doesn't like it, but he's a firefighter, not some Joe Blow off the street."

Naveena cracked an indignant smile. "That's something you're going to have to get used to, Brannigan. We're not the same as firefighters. Not even close."

"Potato, pa-ta-tow," I said. "You owe me for sticking that suffocation bag over my head. I need to look over this truck myself, and the quicker you hurry this up, the quicker we can be on the road."

She turned with a groan and stomped back to DeShawn. "Let me show you around the truck. Looks like you've already pointed out the cannon."

"How long does it take to recharge?" DeShawn asked.

Renfro bobbed his head, thinking. "About two minutes. That's why we try to be as accurate as possible. But we try to slay the scalies while they're still in the house, if we can. The cannon is a last resort."

Naveena went around the truck, opening every bin door, before coming back with hands on her hips. "Let's hurry this up."

A few of the bins contained the same kind of equipment we carried on our fire engines and ladder trucks: jugs of water and cups, forcible entry tools, pike poles. But most of it was a completely different world, right out of science fiction.

"This is my power suit," Renfro said, pointing to it inside the bin. "We step into the boots and slide into the arms. The suit does the rest, sealing in the front. Our thrusters allow us to jump up to fifty feet every thirty seconds or so."

The suit was a monster, made of metal but not the clunky armor of the knights of old, or even what some classic videogames had envisioned as a symbiotic human and robot war machine. By the way I'd seen the smoke eaters maneuver, it couldn't have weighed terribly much.

Renfro got into his suit to show us how it closed around him. There was an emblem on the chest – two crossed lances over a dragon skull.

"Renfro's suit has a foam gun and a plasma repeater," Naveena offered no further explanation of the weapons. "Mine has a laser sword."

"What about those?" DeShawn nodded to the, by comparison, ancient-looking tools in the large rear bin.

"Those are backup," said Naveena.

Renfro took out a large, black iron lance. "Some dragons can send out an electromagnetic wave when they roar, as you guys saw the other day. If it hits our equipment, poof! Then we have to go old school."

I pointed at Renfro. "That roar didn't hurt your suits, though."

"Because dragon EMP doesn't spread in a circle," Naveena said. "It's focused like a beam."

"Cool." DeShawn rubbed a hand over a harpoon gun, smiling.

Maybe there was still hope for him. God could have him long after his fire career was in the books, when he died in his sleep at ninety-nine or one hundred.

"All right," Naveena said. "Enough of the gun show. Let's go. Brannigan, you can close the bin doors."

It had been a long time since I'd been treated like a rookie, but I nodded agreement and stepped over to DeShawn. "You're a good man, DeShawn. No matter what you think you've done."

I held out my hand.

DeShawn shook it, but didn't look up at me. "Thanks, Cap."

I watched him go back inside his duplex, where the lamplight poured out to shame the sun. When DeShawn closed his door, the cannon truck's air horn blasted behind me.

I flinched. "Shit!"

"Hurry it up," Naveena called through her window. "You're late for training."

CHAPTER 6

"Have you guys ever heard of white flames shooting out of a TV?" I asked Naveena and Renfro as we rode through a desolate landscape.

"Nope," Naveena said, keeping her eyes on the barren road.

I'd never been that far out of the city on Highway 42 since the dragon emergence. Most people didn't travel anymore. It was too dangerous with the potential for random dragons popping up. And the roads were terribly neglected, so what was the point?

The holoreader manufacturers went into high gear a few Christmases ago, promoting expanded, full body holographics so you could visit with family for the holidays without leaving your local ash heap. The American road trip was just another thing the scalies killed.

Most of the city's surrounding towns had been burned to ash, not counting a few caravans of nomadic rednecks and RV fanatics. We were driving through the largest of the quarantine zones and Parthenon City showed no desire to rebuild that far out. The idea was that a ring of ashen waste surrounding the city would cut down on dragon incidents.

It was bullshit. There hadn't been a drop in scalies. I'd have even said they were on the rise.

"Why do you ask?" Renfro had been more approachable than Naveena on our long drive to wherever we were headed.

"Just something DeShawn said."

Ahead, through the ash like a ship through fog, appeared a huge building, similar to a smaller Pentagon – when it was still intact and operational. More of the compound became visible as we crested a rise in the road. In an adjacent field, a small cabin stood a hundred feet in the air on metal stilts. Below, a running track circled a vacant, concrete square.

My already sore muscles and bum knee ached with weariness.

"What is this place?" I asked.

Naveena turned around in her seat. "You've been here before."

"Ohio's Smoke Eater Headquarters," said Renfro, once again the only one I could rely on for understandable information.

I nodded. "Yeah, I should have guessed."

Renfro parked the truck just outside the front steps – two separate stairways that curved up toward large, glass doors.

"No guards?" I asked. "With all the secrecy you guys are so fond of, that seems a little lazy."

"No one's stupid enough to go this far away from the city." Naveena let down her pitch-black hair, and when she turned to me, a thick curl of it fell to the side of her eye, ending just beside her lips. "And everyone here is the guards. We can take on any scaly or trespasser with the same amount of ease."

I cleared my throat and looked away, pretending to study something outside the window. A woman with a down-do always did something to me. Call it an Achilles' heel.

I hoped Sherry would call me back soon.

"Well, go on in, rookie." Renfro smiled.

"You guys aren't coming with me?"

Naveena sputtered her lips. "We have to get back to more important duties. I had my fill of you ten miles back."

"Thanks for the ride, Renfro." I winked at Naveena before I shut the door.

She thinned her eyes and turned away. "Sink or swim."

I was halfway up the steps, knee aching like a sonofabitch, when my bladder decided it wanted to empty the beer I'd had at DeShawn's house. I'd needed to piss the whole ride over, but now I'd crossed the point of no return.

It took slow, steady steps, but I managed to get through the building's front doors, my head swiveling for the nearest bathroom. Instead, I found a smiling, orange-shirt-wearing Chief Donahue.

"Brannigan!" He stuck out his hand. "Good to see you. Welcome to the Smoke Eater Division."

I shook his hand quickly. "Yeah, great. Where's a bathroom?"

"The bathroom? It's…" he cocked his eyebrow then looked around "…right down that hall. First on your right."

I was dancing the Pachanga at this point. "First on the right. Got it."

To hell with my bum knee; I ran. A green-shirted smoke eater holding a mop jumped at my charging through the door, but I paid him no mind as I hustled to the urinal. After too many minutes of wonderful relief, I cleaned up, told the smoke eater he missed a spot, and met Donahue back in the foyer.

This time I was able to take in my surroundings

without a bladder threatening to rupture. The ceiling was high, and two upper floors were visible behind Donahue, between a pair of green, marble columns. Statues were displayed at each side of the nearby stairs. The one on the left depicted a warrior woman piercing a dragon's throat. An open mouth full of teeth and claws on the stone woman's chest suggested the dragon didn't like it too much. The one on the right showed a shirtless, muscled man riding a winged scaly like a jet ski.

"Not very accurate." I pointed to the flying dragon. "Dragons can't fly."

Donahue laughed. "What do you want from us, Brannigan. These weren't commissioned. Probably from some theme park originally." He looked me over, like a new statue he was considering. "You good to go? Or are you going to have to take a potty break every hour."

"Getting old sucks."

"Only if you let it. Follow me. I'll get you up to speed."

I jogged after him.

He led me down another hall where the overhead lights were spaced enough to allow patches of darkness between the lit areas. We were clomping along so fast that my knee was about to pop as the transfer from light to shadow almost mimicked a strobe light. Donahue's false right leg pounded the floor like a blacksmith at the anvil.

"Where are we going?" I asked.

"Training," Donahue said.

"Seriously?" I huffed as I continued to follow. "Today? How'd you even schedule me in?"

Donahue stopped at a door where a man's voice boomed from the other side. "That's the thing. We had to drop you in the middle of a class already mid-session."

"What?"

Donahue shrugged. "Sink or swim, Brannigan."

"What does that even mean? We fight dragons, right? Not giant squid."

Donahue had pulled out his holoreader, tapping a few buttons. "There are all kinds of dragons, and they can pop up anywhere. Even Lake Erie. But 'sink or swim' is our motto. It means we jump in and learn as we go. We don't have the luxury of waiting until we're ready. Not that we're reckless. There are too few smokies for that." He held out the holoreader to me, green-glowing words hovering in the air above the device. "Scroll down and sign at the bottom."

"What the hell is that?" I stepped back as if the words would bite me.

"A contract. Basic stuff. All smoke eaters have to sign it."

"Yeah, well, I don't sign anything I don't read first."

Donahue shoved the holoreader into my hand. "Brannigan, I've got a tar scaly cleanup in Dayton to get to, and a report of a Fin Fang serpent in an abandoned factory in Columbus. I don't have time for you to read a simple contract."

I thinned my eyes, but Donahue just stared back at me, impatient.

"You guys aren't Satanists or anything?" I asked. "I'm not signing over my soul or riding lawn mower?"

Donahue smiled. "It just says we can't fire you. The only way out is in a box."

I scrolled through the holographic paragraphs, watching them dance as they appeared and disappeared within the boundaries of the reader. Nothing crazy jumped out at me – blood orgies, mandatory union participation – so I signed the empty space at the bottom.

"Great," Donahue said, returning the holoreader to his side. "Sergeant Puck will get your uniforms to you. And a holoreader."

"Sergeant who?"

"You can use the reader to catch up on the material in your dorm room at night, to make sure you're in line with the rest of the rookie smoke eaters."

"Dorm? I'm not sleeping here. Wait just a damn—"

"Come on."

He opened the door before I could retort.

Standing in front of a holographic board covered in pictures of different types of scalies and illegible scribbling, was a woman dressed in the green smoke eater uniform. A black remote dangled in her hand, and her mouth was still open from her last statement. She had a head bigger than a fire hydrant, with a forehead and cheeks sunburned just as red. Her hair was pulled back with a green scrunchie, but several strands had come loose.

That booming voice I'd heard was definitely not a man.

"Sergeant Puck," Chief Donahue said. "Sorry to interrupt. This is Cole Brannigan, our newest smoke eater recruit. Formerly a captain with the Parthenon City Fire Department."

There were only three rookies sitting at long, white tables – two men and a woman, all about half my age. One of the men flinched and blinked rapidly as if he'd been napping. Nostalgia hit me like a hover train. I remembered my own firefighter rookie class and the mind-numbing classroom hours. There'd been a hell of a lot more recruits, though.

"More fresh meat for the scalies, huh?" Sergeant Puck said, in a bone-shaking baritone. "Thanks, Chief." She lifted her chin to me and then pointed toward the other rookies. "There's an empty seat next to Williams over there."

The only available chair was next to the female smoke

eater, a thick, black woman who sat with a finger against her lips and eyes still on the floating dragon pictures.

One of the male recruits, the freckle-faced one, grinned as I passed, as if my presence was equal to a dirty joke on a bathroom wall. The other rookie looked like a Samoan guy I was friends with back in high school. My friend had been a teddy bear most of the time, but you never wanted to piss him off.

Intricate tattoos poked out from the neck of the Samoan rookie's shirt, and he had tied his dark hair back with a rubber band. His top-heavy frame would have made him a great addition to a truck company in the regular fire service – made for breaking shit.

You know why truckies cut holes in roofs? So they can look down at the engine company and see the real firefighters working. It's a playful old joke. Us engine guys had to get our digs in somewhere. Long ago, Hollywood had only made firefighter movies and TV shows about truck companies. It made sense; people were more interested in firefighters carrying babies and climbing ladders. Watching water sprayed on flames wasn't that interesting on the screen.

But all of us smoke eaters in that classroom were the same.

Donahue was gone by the time I took my seat and looked up to the front of the room. Everyone was staring at me. The only sound was the buzz of holographic pictures floating around Puck's head and the freckle-faced guy snorting softly.

The sergeant cleared her throat. "Brannigan, right? I'm going to tell you what I told these three from the first day, and they could benefit from a refresher."

I waited for her to continue. Freckle Face sighed.

"This is on-the-job training," Puck said. "If we get a call to back up a dragon fight, we all go, ready or not. We can't hole you newbies away while the few smokies we have kill themselves needlessly. Got that?"

"Yes, ma'am," I said.

She nodded, seeming to be satisfied, and brought up a diagram of a dragon, kind of a scaly anatomical chart. The drawing showed the dragon's muscles and organs, the way the bones curved at different points in the spine.

"We're going to take a minute, for Brannigan's benefit, to briefly cover basic dragon anatomy."

Freckle Face groaned under his breath, but Puck must not have heard him.

"Brannigan," Puck said, "do you know how dragons breathe fire?"

"Some kind of organ?" I shrugged. "I don't remember. I've watched a few nature shows, but I mainly read about ancient dragons," I said. "Quetzalcoatl and that sort of thing."

Puck wrinkled her nose. "Quetza-what?"

"Quetzalcoatl. Aztec god that was a winged serpent. They'd sacrifice–"

"Shut up, Brannigan. I don't care." Puck rubbed her temples before zooming the hologram to an organ in the middle of the illustrated dragon's body. "The supra ignis gland here, which connects to the epiglottis. Our propellerheads are still studying how fire–"

Williams, beside me, raised her hand.

Puck groaned. "What, Williams?"

"What about those hard things on the sides of its body?"

"Side plates," I said. "They help the scalies move underground."

I did remember that part.

Puck actually looked impressed. "Very good, Brannigan. But don't speak unless you raise your hand."

The big guy with the tattoos stirred awake and raised

his arm. "It'd be a good place for wings."

"Well," Puck said, "despite what some of our propellerheads have theorized, dragons don't fly. Come on Kekoa, even ten year-olds know that."

"I never heard of a sergeant in the fire service," I said.

"I just knew you were going to be a problem." Puck gave a frustrated laugh and rubbed her oily face. "Smoke Eater Division is different from the fire department. I earned my title, and whether you realize it yet or not, I outrank you. You are no longer a captain. You are a piece of shit rookie, and for getting off topic and wasting my time, you're going to give me fifty pushups."

I hadn't heard that kind of talk since my first year as a firefighter. In a way, it brought back good memories. But she couldn't have been serious.

The other rookies stared at me, waiting. Freckle Face laughed.

Puck snapped her head toward him. "Shut up, Thomlin, or you'll be right beside him. Hurry up, Brannigan. Time is our greatest resource, and you need to pay up."

She and Donahue were real clock Nazis. I knew full well how response time to an incident was critical, how every second counted. But this was ridiculous.

I didn't want to let the other rookies think the "old man" couldn't do a measly fifty pushups. And hammering them out would be a nice "fuck you" to Sergeant Puck. I got into position on the floor and began the exercise. I'd quickly done three when Puck stopped me.

"Hold it right there, Brannigan. Stay in that position."

I was at the top of the pushup, arms fully extended, basically in a plank, already starting to tremble from the exertion.

"We do pushups differently around here," Puck said in a sing-song voice. "We do everything different. You're a smoke eater now. We're going to have to sweat the firefighter out of you."

Not in a million years, I told myself.

"When I tell you," Puck said, "you'll go down. When I say 'up', then you push up. Not before. Ready?"

Not really.

"Down."

I went down. For a second, the pain eased and I was in a better position, but then the soreness kicked in again, and I began shaking from the effort to stay off the ground.

Damn it, say "Up!"

After an eternity, Puck finally shouted, "Up!"

It went on like that for several more minutes. I wasn't even counting after the twelfth pushup. The room was silent, besides my blood pounding in my ears. Sweat poured down my face, and I swore I was about to black out. It had been a hell of a long time since I'd worked out that hard. The fire department required us to do an hour of physical training every shift, but that usually constituted a few bicep curls and walking a couple laps around the firehouse.

When Puck said, "Up!" followed by "Forty-eight," my energy renewed.

Puck made the last two drag on longer than the others, but I was too close to give up. After the last pushup, I hobbled back into my seat and glared at Puck, letting the sweat pitter-patter onto the table in front of me.

"Now we can get back to the lesson," Puck said, turning back to the holographic board. "We only have thirty minutes left in the day, thanks to Brannigan. Let's move on to the different known types of dragons and their weaknesses."

This caught my attention, despite mainly focusing on catching my breath. Sergeant Puck began talking about different broods and how every year different types of dragons would appear, meaner and more dangerous than the last.

Wyrm dragons worked their way into high-rises and set different floors on fire.

Williams, the recruit to my left, handed me a slip of paper. Those pushups suck. That's why we call her Sergeant Puke, the note said.

I lifted my sweat-soaked face to her. She smiled quickly, a pencil to her lips, and then turned back to the sergeant, who expanded a drawing of a long, snake-like dragon. With her free hand, Puck dragged a picture of a towering inferno – the Chrysler Building in New York. I'd heard about the incident, seen it on the Feed. It had to be the worst dragon-related disaster to hit the country since the beginning. The picture showed the building just before the top half fell to the street below. A scattering of glass and fire circled the point of breakage like a ring.

"This is what a wyrm can do," Puck said. "So far, the best way we know to kill 'em is to–"

The holographic pictures disappeared, and in their place flashing red covered the screen. Speakers in the ceiling blurted out a grating alarm. The other three recruits covered their ears.

Amateurs.

"Shit," Puck muttered.

She grabbed each side of the red-flashing screen and shrunk it into her palms. Reading something on the screen, she put her back to us. When she turned around, her face was grim, and she stared right at me.

What did I do now?

"Prepare to suit up," Puck shouted.

The other recruits jumped from their seats and stood at attention. I did the same, with less enthusiasm, although my heart raced like it was my first structure fire.

"Some smokies need our help just outside of Buzzard's Roost," Puck said. "Looks like you'll get to see some poppers firsthand. Sink or swim."

CHAPTER 7

"What the hell is a popper?" I jogged behind Williams on the way to the apparatus bay.

"Poppers," she said, breathing as heavily as me. "Plural."

The other two rookies had jogged ahead of us and were already in their power suits and climbing into a black rig with "Slayer 3" painted on the side in green. It carried no laser cannon or anything else that I could see. I guessed it was solely for transporting manpower.

The bay looked like a multi-airplane hangar and even had an old jumbo jet collecting dust at the far end. Multiple oil-stained spaces lay empty at each side of Slayer 3. The bay door split open with a hum.

Puck pulled up in a hover cart that heaved to and fro when she jumped from it. "Brannigan. Williams. Hurry up and get your power suits on."

I looked down at my sweat-soaked "Firefighters Find 'Em Hot and Leave 'Em Wet!" T-shirt and old pair of jeans. Williams ran toward the driver's side of the truck.

I followed behind. "I don't have a clue what I'm supposed to do."

"Put this on." Williams lifted a bin door.

A shiny, green power suit waited inside with a helmet hanging above.

"I'm trying to tell you," I said. "I've never put one on!"

Williams huffed. "Watch me."

She hefted the power suit from her bin and set it on the ground. It stayed upright like one of the fire droids I'd seen the day before. With her back to it, Williams slipped into the power suit like a onesie. It instantly enveloped her, finishing with a loud click. The tips of her boots and the elbows glowed orange.

"That's it." She secured her helmet, which, to my disappointment, worked like every other one since the dawn of protective headwear.

The helmet looked much like a traditional firefighter's helmet with a rear bill – originally meant to shed water – except it also had two metal pieces that would extend over the wearer's ears, reminding me of a Roman centurion helmet.

I took out my power suit.

It wasn't as heavy as I'd expected. I stepped backwards into the suit, slipping my arms and feet into the right holes, and then it felt like a robot was grappling me from behind. The suit's inner lining, including the gloves and boots, cinched around my body, and when I heard that same click, I moved my arms and legs to get a feel for the suit. The metal was only a tiny bit more cumbersome than my own body. One size definitely fit all.

Smoke eaters always get the coolest gear.

Williams nodded. "OK. Afu can show you how to power jump. He's better than me. Now let's go!"

I grabbed my helmet and followed her into the rig. The other rookies glared at us as we took our seats. Williams pointed to my helmet and then her head. I took the hint and put it on.

"Brannigan." Sergeant Puck's voice barked into my ears from speakers inside my helmet, even though she was seated at the wheel. "Since you can't seem to move your old ass fast enough, you owe me fifty more pushups when we get back. If you survive."

Freckle-faced Thomlin laughed.

Firefighters avoided talk about not coming home. It was bad juju. Apparently, there was a thing or two I could teach Puck about tact.

"Williams," Puck said. "You'll be right there with him. Fifty for you, too."

My fellow recruit dropped her head, looking more terrified about the pushups than the dragons we were headed for in Buzzard's Roost. The truck rumbled into the sunlight and we rolled onto Highway 71 faster than you could say "Dead silent in Slayer 3."

"How old are you?" asked the bulky recruit I guessed was Afu. He stared at me, waiting on an answer.

I smiled – it shows confidence, according to my body language book. "Just a little over the same number of pushups I keep racking up."

Afu laughed and stuck his hand out. "Afu Kekoa."

"Cole Brannigan."

"Yeah, I know," Afu said.

I offered my hand to the freckled guy named Thomlin, but he kept his arms crossed and looked at my hand like it was a dead scaly. So I made a circle with my extended hand and shook a "jerkoff" gesture.

Afu snorted and Thomlin glared at him. The big recruit cleared his throat and dropped his smile.

"How do the jet packs work?" I asked Afu.

Thomlin rolled his eyes.

"Oh, you have something to add, Gingerbread?" I leaned forward, arms on my knees.

"It's not a jet pack," Thomlin said.

"Not really," Afu added. "All you have to do is jump, and the suit will launch you a little farther. But if you want an extended jump, just hit the button on the side of your left index finger."

I looked down at my armored hand. Sure enough, there was a large black button where Afu said it would be.

"I'll show you how to deploy your sword when we get out of the truck," Afu said.

Thomlin groaned. "We won't have time."

"What's your problem?" I asked.

Thomlin sneered and shook his head, not like he was saying "no," but that he was appalled I kept talking to him. "I just don't know why you're here."

"I'm going in blind here, but I'm a smoke eater, same as you."

"You're also older than dirt, and too full of yourself."

"Thomlin!" Puck shouted through our helmets.

The feedback stabbed at my eardrums.

"Quit being an ageist dick and tell Brannigan what poppers are. We're almost there."

Thomlin waved a hand in front of him, as if he was casting the information like seeds. "Poppers are dragons."

"I gathered as much," I said.

"They pop out of the ground," he added. "That's where they get their name."

Shit, this guy was going to be as useless as tits on a dragon.

"All scalies come out of the ground, dub." I said.

Thomlin wrinkled his nose, twisting his freckles into weird shapes. "Dub?"

Old habits die hard. "Never mind. It's what we called each other. In the fire department."

"This isn't the fire department." Thomlin spit the words.

"You ever play Whack-a-Mole?" Afu asked.

I nodded.

"This won't be too different. At least, from the video Sergeant Puck showed us."

I blinked a few times, piecing together what he was saying. "You mean you've never fought these types of dragons before?"

"This is the first call we've gotten to join in on," Williams said.

Oh, boy.

Thomlin had already drifted from the conversation, looking out the window.

"Hey!" I snapped my metal fingers at him, and it sounded like blades crossing. "We're a team. If you hold back information just because I was walking into dangerous situations while you were still a load in your mom's uterus, we all could get killed. Drop the asshole routine and get in the game."

"You're not in charge," Thomlin said.

"Shut up, all of you," Sergeant Puck said. "We're here."

I'd been too busy yammering with Thomlin to get a look at where we were. It was different riding in the back seat, without a good view of the approaching incident, with no power to dictate a plan of action. Craning my head, I looked through the windshield.

The woods were ablaze, mostly on the ground, but it was picking up speed. Dark smoke churned in the wind, coursing through the treetops.

Great. Brush fires sucked to begin with. I couldn't imagine how much more of a bitch this was going to be, also dealing with peek-a-boo dragons.

I took the lead and opened the door. Williams jumped down behind me while the other rookies got out on the other side.

"Command mode activated," a feminine voice said in my headset.

"To communicate with the rest of us now," Williams said, "you have to say the word 'cast' first."

Williams's last word sounded through my helmet.

"And to stop it," she said, "just say 'end cast.'"

Walking toward the gathered rookies in front of the truck, Sergeant Puck secured her helmet. "Cast. Command to Slayer Three."

"Go ahead." The voice through my helmet sounded exhausted and terrified.

"We're on scene in the southwest corner," Puck said. "What are your orders?"

There was static and then what sounded like screaming. The wind shifted and the smell of burning wood and ash intensified. I could taste it, tingling on my tongue.

"They're fucking everywhere!" the incident commander shouted.

I was still green on how smoke eaters operated, but anytime I'd cursed over the radio at a fire, the shit had annihilated the fan.

"Slayer 3," the IC said. "They're headed right for you!"

All of us gathered closer to Puck. I swiveled my head to each side, searching for movement in the dirt.

"Your sword." Afu tapped me on the shoulder. "To deploy it, you–"

"Hey!" A shirtless man ran through the woods, headed our way. Ash covered his long, blond hair and beard. He waved a skinny, tattooed arm at us as he lurched his way over logs and rocks. "My RV is on fire back there and–"

The ground swelled underneath the man, tripping him, but he kept his balance as he fumbled forward. Just ahead of his path, the dirt disappeared like a sinkhole, and fire blasted out, scorching the poor bastard. As the burning man screamed, flailing fiery arms and falling forward, a large yellow snout snapped out of the hole and dragged him under.

"Holy shit," I said.

"Put your eyes on!" Puck shouted.

The other rookies hit the side of their helmets, which brought out the tinted goggles I'd seen Naveena and Renfro wearing the day before. Williams touched the button on my helmet before I had to ask.

When the goggles connected, the forest in front of me changed. I saw the fire deep in the woods, blazing in brilliant purple. Below, however, there were at least six or seven red dragon-shaped blobs swimming through the dirt underneath. They all registered a few hundred degrees hotter than the wildfire.

"Spread out," Puck said.

The other rookies obeyed. I was too busy looking at the thermal goggles and trying not to shit myself. Dropping my head, I looked at the ground below my boots. An enormous, red shape sped toward me.

Adrenaline is a hell of a drug, and it makes you do crazy things. I jumped. Straight up. It was like a catapult had launched me toward the sky, effortless. But I was too scared to appreciate the exhilaration of my first jump.

I retracted my therma goggles – that infrared stuff was annoying – and hit my suit's jump extender. The ground, now twenty feet below, exploded in chunks of dirt before a popper dragon emerged, gnashing its fat jaws and countless teeth from side to side, searching for me.

I laughed. "Fuck you!"

The dragon leapt out of the hole and raised its head toward me. Looking like a cross between a frog and a crocodile, the popper was yellow-scaled and the size of a Buick. A large, shovel-shaped horn protruded from the top of its snout, and its neon orange eyes flickered in the sun.

Something I'd like to have learned earlier in class was

that poppers have exceptional hearing. And damn good aim. With a wet, forceful choking sound, it shot a ball of fire at me as my power suit eased toward the ground and the awaiting popper.

I scrambled in the air like a fish out of water, trying to shift my position, but physics wouldn't allow it. The popper's fireball hit my leg and sent me flying into the nearest tree trunk, ten feet from the ground. I hit a couple branches and oofed when I finally hit the dirt.

My muscles were sore, but I was able to get to my feet. I think I might have also peed in the suit a little.

Quick steps pounded the ground as the popper stampeded at me, grunting like a sumo running a marathon. I tried to jump again, but the suit was still charging from the last one. I threw my arms forward, hoping the laser sword would extend by sheer will. Nothing happened, and the popper was about to tackle me.

I didn't know what else to do, so I readied myself and grabbed the popper's horn right before it would have impaled me. I dug in with my heels as the dragon pushed me back, snapping its slobbery teeth. The power suit gave me some extra strength. There was no way in hell I would have otherwise been able to stop a charging scaly.

I shoved back against the popper and held it from charging forward any farther, then punched it in the eye as many times as I could before I started to lose my grip on it.

The popper roared and gnashed more violently, until it suddenly stopped and made that nasty choking sound again.

I flinched and let go, rolling out of the way as it blasted another ball of flame from its gullet. I smelled hot metal as I crawled away from the popper. Bastard nearly flame-scalped me.

The ground behind me bloated, and I grabbed the closest thing I could get my hands on – one of the popper's three-toed hind claws. I pulled with everything I had and put the scaly between me and the churning dirt, where another popper burst forth. The new arrival snapped its jaws as expected, but its teeth found the yellow ass of its sister scaly.

The bitten dragon roared and snapped toward its attacker, but the second popper didn't realize it was munching on one of its own until after a huge chunk of dragon meat had been ripped away and the victim lay on the ground whimpering in its death throes.

The new popper jumped out of the hole and nudged its dead sibling with the tip of its shovel horn. I readied for another fight while searching my periphery for any other smoke eater.

"Cast," I shouted, remembering the voice command. "Mayday, mayday, mayday. I need help!"

Turning to me, the dragon growled and damn it if it didn't sound angry. Its orange eyes burned like coals before it charged, just like the last one. Seeing no reason to change my previous strategy, I dug in and prepared to grab another scaly by the horn.

But this one turned its head to the side as it came at me, swallowing my hand and forearm as it shoved me onto my back. It bit down onto the armor, shaking its head so fast, my vision blurred. I didn't feel much pain besides the terrible pressure on my power suit, but I was pretty sure the armor would give way at any second.

I tried to pull my arm from its jaws, but that just made it bite down harder, grunting as thick gobs of spit dripped onto my face like gasoline-smelling honey. I gagged, but had to keep my mouth closed so the spit wouldn't drip in.

Punching the bastard's eyes with my free fist, I again yanked my arm back. The popper loosened its grip enough for my arm to slide a little, and when it did, the sides of my suited arm extended like vertical car doors, and a thick, white laser sword lengthened, right through the back of the popper's head.

The dragon screeched once before it dropped dead – right on top of me.

Scaly spit covered my face, and my arm was still lodged in its teeth as my laser sword continued cooking its flesh, and on top of all of that, the crushing weight allowed me only a tiny bit of air each breath. But, thanks to the power suit, it was something.

"Will… one of you… guys… come help me," I managed to squeak out.

Afu's voice crackled into my helmet. "On my way. Where you at?"

"I'm the… asshole… under the… popper."

"I see you," Afu said. "Oh, man." My fellow rookie appeared behind the popper's dangling head and grabbed it by the horn. "End cast. You push, I'll pull."

It took more time and energy than I cared to expend, but we got the scaly off me with a wet flop of its body to the ground.

Afu nodded to my right arm. "Guess you figured out how to use the laser sword without me."

"The popper did that," I said. "I have no idea how to shut it off."

I waved the wide sword to and fro. It thrummed and shimmered with each slash.

Afu said, "Just hit that button behind the sword."

It would be that damn simple, wouldn't it? I pressed the button he indicated, and the sword dissolved back into the suit before the two "wings" sealed back onto my arm.

"What about the foam gun, or the laser?" I stood, bending over, hands on my knees as I gulped air.

"That's your partner's weapons. You're supposed to stay together and work in tandem."

"And my partner is?"

Afu wrinkled his lips. "Thomlin. He's been pairing with Sergeant. Maybe he just followed her again this time, you know, out of habit."

"I'm sure that's what it is. Where is everybody else?"

"I told Williams to go with Puck and Thomlin when you called for help. They'd be farther into the woods by now. They found another cluster of poppers."

I hit the button for my thermal goggles and looked at the ground around us.

No red blobs. Groovy.

But the forest fire still raged, growing hotter and faster. I hadn't heard anything about fire crews arriving or even being on the way, which wasn't a surprise. On dragon calls, firefighters stayed back until the smoke eaters had done their thing. But I'd have at least expected them to radio that they were waiting to be called in. Buzzard's Roost was close to several homes – a wild land urban interface, we used to call it. They didn't have the benefit of an ash barrier like some of the other neighborhoods.

"What about that shirtless guy?"

"Nothing we can do for him," Afu said.

"All right," I said. "No reason to stay here yapping, then. Let's go join the others."

Afu nodded and we jogged deeper into the roasting woods. When we came to a steep climb, I considered just power-jumping to the top, but didn't want to be in a situation where I needed it and would have no juice for my suit. So we trudged up the rise. My legs and muscles burned, and I seriously wondered why I hadn't just retired or let the mayor fire me. This shit was exhausting. But we made it to the top...

…and found three fire droids digging a trench in the forest floor.

"Who called in these clowns?" I stopped in my tracks as Afu came up behind.

He wiped sweat from his eyes and watched the fire droids working on the fire break – a technique to contain forest fires. "I have no idea what they're doing here."

The droids' eyes glowed blue, and their hulking bodies were bent over as they used huge, metal rakes at the end of their arms to dig a thick line through the woods. They moved in sync, digging and stepping backwards, repeating the same process, like a mobile factory line.

"Forget them," I said. "We need to find Puck and the rest."

We moved forward, and the droids rose from their work. In unison, they stomped over to meet us, creating a three-droid-wide blockade.

"We're sorry," they said as one, their blue eyes shaking to the movement of their robotic, used-car-salesman voices. "There's a fire, and we can't let you through."

"We're smoke eaters, you metal idiots," Afu said.

I couldn't give a damn about having a conversation with a bunch of rust buckets, so I moved to walk around them. They shifted to block me, clanging their metal arms and legs against their bodies as they did.

"We're sorry," they said again. "There's a fire, and we can't let you through."

"Our crew is trapped back there!" Afu yelled. "They're going to die."

"You can either move," I said, glaring at the middle fire droid's fake eyes, "or I'll make a path."

The fire droids raised their pointy rakes. "We're sorry. There's a fire–"

I pushed the button for my laser sword and cut two of their rakes off. With the backswing, I severed the middle one's head, and then shoved my white laser blade into the next one's torso until I'd shoved it onto its back. The droids continued their incessant pre-scripted bullshit, dropping the octave until their voices warbled into nothing when the circuits died.

To my left, I could have almost sworn the remaining fire droid had moved to swing at Afu. But the big man had followed my lead and sliced the robot into two dead hunks of metal.

"Did that thing try to attack you?" I asked.

Afu smiled, raising his sword. "I didn't give it a chance."

"That's not what I meant. They're not supposed to be able to do that."

There was no such thing as artificial intelligence. Even Kenji's actions were programmed into him. He couldn't start giving his opinion or dictating Walt Whitman – unless we paid for those upgrades. If these fire droids had the capacity to attack people, it was because someone had included that option in their metal heads.

Afu slapped my armor with the back of his gloved fingers. "Come on."

"Would you two quit gabbing and come do some work like the rest of us?" Puck's grating voice came in. "Brannigan, turn off your radio, for God's sake."

I rolled my eyes. "End cast."

We found Puck and the other two in a clearing in the middle of the woods. A wall of fire lay behind them, speeding closer, and three poppers were running around them like a herd of ostriches avoiding capture.

"Oh shit." Afu launched himself into the air.

I did the same, leaping with him toward the other smoke eaters.

From the higher vantage, I got a good view of the surrounding fire and my team below. It wasn't looking good. We were uphill and leeward to the fire. In layman's terms: we were fucked. Fire travels uphill at incredible speeds, and with the aid of wind, it was even worse.

Thomlin and Williams shot their lasers at the poppers and missed terribly. The dragons were too damn fast. Puck swiped at one with her laser sword and caught it in the leg, sending it tumbling over the dirt. Seeing the one dragon fall, the other poppers quit their marathon and moved in to attack.

I dropped in and landed near a popper, sinking my laser into its head. Afu landed in front of the other and kicked it in the face. If I'd tried that, I would have been on my back with my head in a popper's jaws. But Afu's kick sent the popper flipping onto its side. Williams ran up and blasted it with her lasers.

"Now that's team work," Afu said, giving Williams a high five.

I had no one to celebrate with when I turned around. Instead, I saw two big-ass, flaming trees falling to block our only escape.

"Uh oh." I turned back to the others.

Their faces reflected my sentiment.

The wind shifted, and that's when things got interesting. Strengthening from the fresh blast of air, the fire flew up the trees, creating a circular inferno around us, burning everything wherever we looked, and we were next.

"Let's jump over those trees," Thomlin said.

I stomped over to him. "You mean the ones on fire? You'll be incinerated if you try. Plus, Afu and I are still charging our thrusters."

"Better some than all," Thomlin shouted.

Afu said, "Let's jump into those popper holes."

"You want to ring the dinner bell, too?" Puck grabbed him by the back of his neck. "Dig in!" She looked at me.

"I'm rusty on this. Do you know much about wildfires, Brannigan?"

"A little."

I looked around at the flames approaching like a fiery mouth. I'd never been in a situation like this. I was used to fighting house fires, cars, maybe a dumpster. A two-day course on wildfires was just a boring necessity too long ago to remember.

Balling my right fist, I looked down to my sword arm.

"How much heat can we take?" I asked. "If the flames get within a few feet, would we be able to stand it?"

"Better than a normal person." Puck jerked her head toward where a branch snapped in the fire. "But we'll still burn if it touches us."

"Bunch together," I yelled.

They were quick to do what I said, even Douchebag Thomlin, who cringed at being so close to the other rookies. I extended my laser sword and pierced it into the ground. The dirt smoked and churned as if I was making mud pie.

Bent over, I dragged the sword around the other smoke eaters, much like the droids had been doing earlier with the fire break, making the diameter as big as I could with such limited time.

When I'd connected the lines to finish the circle, I pointed to Williams and Thomlin. "Fill it with foam."

Williams punched a button on her arm and shot the thick goop into the moat I'd made. Thomlin bent over and did the same. When they'd finished, I jumped into the circle with everyone else, just shy of getting my ass burned by the oncoming inferno.

"This was a stupid idea!" Thomlin hollered as if a centipede had crawled up his rear end. He leaned into Puck for protection.

"You want out?" The sergeant looked like she'd shove

him out of the circle.

The firestorm blew in, eating every twig and leaf it touched, giving off heat worse than anything I'd felt before. But it was mainly uncomfortable, barely painful and only slightly stinging to the eyes.

The fire passed us by as quickly as it'd come. The flames never crossed the foam circle we'd made, and the radiant heat didn't sear our lungs thanks to our gift. None of us wanted to leave the circle until we were certain we wouldn't get cooked, as if the fire was going to backtrack and nab us outside our ring of protection.

I was like a wizard.

An engine roared above as a water bomber aircraft doused the surrounding fire with gallons of water. There'd be at least one other bomber hitting the flames from the opposite end. They couldn't have showed up a little sooner?

"All right, it's done," Puck said after a while, being the first to step away. She probably wanted Thomlin's claws off of her. "Brannigan, Thomlin. Go see if you can find any info on that RV guy the scalies nabbed. We have to inform his next of kin. I'll call in the quarantine crew."

I nodded, even though the thought of working with Thomlin made my stomach churn.

Puck pointed to Afu and Williams. "We'll meet up with command. They'll want us to look for dragon eggs."

Scalies liked to take a break from their rampaging to knock boots. I guess the ashes are romantic.

Thomlin groaned and led the way back to where we'd parked Slayer 3. Hopefully the fire hadn't shifted too bad and scorched our only way back to headquarters.

"You know your way around here?" I asked Thomlin.

"It's called a basic sense of direction." He stopped and turned back to me. "But yeah. My dad used to take me out here sometimes as a kid. Taught me the laws of nature."

"Worms on hooks, how to undo a bra with one hand, that sort of thing?"

Thomlin grinned and I quickly missed his creepy frown. "More like he'd tie me to a tree in nothing but my underwear and leave me overnight. He said that's how Native Americans toughened up their children. I still never lived up to his expectations, though."

"Holy fuck," I said. "I'm sorry, man. And I'd say that I don't think Native Americans actually did that, but something tells me you already know your dad is a lying piece of shit."

"Was," Thomlin said.

"Oh."

"Yeah, and you remind me of him."

With that, he turned and trudged forward. I followed, but at a safe distance. We were literally walking through Thomlin's childhood abuse, and I was not going to stand in for Daddy when Thomlin decided to go berserk. When we came to the empty popper holes, I brought out my therma goggles.

All clear.

Except when I retracted my goggles, white flames sparked from one of the holes, the one the shirtless RV man had been dragged into by one of the poppers.

"Hey," I called ahead to Thomlin, who was focused on getting to the dead man's RV and ignoring me at all costs. "What's with this white fire?"

He turned back, looking to where I pointed. When he saw the pale flames, his face sagged. "Oh, great."

A white claw crept from the hole, followed by a wailing, ashen face. Its electric blue eyes were set deep within darkened sockets, and tattered flesh hung where legs should have been as it floated out of the pit.

It was a damn wraith.

"Sweet Jesus!" I ran ahead of Thomlin. My knee ached, had the whole time, but the adrenaline flowing through my system had numbed it for a while.

"What's the matter?" Thomlin called, as I neared the burned shell of an RV. "You never seen a wraith being born before?"

CHAPTER 8

Chief Donahue entered the bay as I was crawling out of my power suit.

"Brannigan, follow me." His normal, almost goofy, disposition had flown the coop, and the Donahue that turned away and marched toward the hall was a pissed off tower of ass-whooping. He yelled, "You too, Sergeant Puck."

Puck glared at me, pulling her hair back into the scrunchie. She shook her head as she brushed past my shoulder.

Well, jumpin' dildoes. My first day as a smoke eater wasn't even over and I was already on the shit list. Seeing no way out, I followed Puck and Donahue, jogging on achy knees to catch up, even climbing several flights of stairs, for God's sake. Donahue's metal leg gave him the speed of a cheetah.

Chief D didn't say anything as I fell in behind him and Puck. Around the corner, several smoke eaters, wearing the green duty shirts and pants I still lacked, walked toward us. The smokies were in relatively good moods, laughing and in the middle of a game of Grab Ass – until they saw Donahue storming by. The smokies stopped in their tracks, widened their eyes, and straightened their backs as if someone had planted TNT in their underwear.

After we passed, a stampede of retreating boots against tile filled the hallway behind us.

The chief stopped in a brightly lit hall, where a window on the right looked down into a big, white room where sparks from a laser splashed shadows up across Donahue's face.

He paced back and forth a few times before launching toward me with a pointed finger. "Mayor Rogola called me today, right before you did. Told me it would be a bad idea taking you on. Said you weren't only old and far gone, but that you were a loose cannon, someone who does whatever he wants, a freelancer. I stuck up for you, Brannigan, mainly because I think Rogola is a pompous windbag. I told him we can't afford to turn away any smoke eater, and that I'd make sure you were squared away."

"I didn't think you answered to the mayor," I said.

"I don't. I was just being diplomatic. He has a knack for stirring up the public and most people already see us as a necessary nuisance. And when one of my smokies destroys city property, expensive property, then I have to answer to that smug sonofabitch, and I'd rather castrate myself with a scaly tooth."

I cringed at the thought. "Are you talking about the fire droids?"

"What else? Those things record video, you know. He's got you slicing and dicing those droids without cause out at Buzzard's Roost. It's all over the Feed. 'You can either move, or I'll make a path.' That's what you said, right? Makes us all look like mercenaries. Rogola's going to have a field day with this. If we don't get shut down, he'll have the support to–"

"Those droids wouldn't let us pass," I said. "And why were they there at all?"

Donahue's eyes looked like they'd pop out. "That's

not the point, Brannigan!"

"Chief," Puck spoke up. "Can I say something?"

Donahue nodded.

Oh, great. More pushups for me.

"I agree that Brannigan is older than Lincoln's balls, and he has a lot to learn. But it's his first day, and he performed better than a lot of the smokies we have out in the field."

I turned to her, trying hard not to smile. Or stare in confusion.

Puck continued. "His dumb ass also forgot to shut off his radio, so I heard everything that happened between him and those droids. After he killed two poppers by himself–"

Donahue raised his eyebrows.

"Yeah, two – him and Afu got stopped by those robots while they were trying to find me and the rest of the crew. The droids wouldn't let them by, so they did what they had to do. If it weren't for Brannigan and what he did out there, we'd all be crispy critters and you'd be out at least three smoke eaters."

"Kekoa cut up a droid, too?" the chief asked.

Both Puck and I nodded.

"Guess they didn't show that on the Feed. Rogola's got a grudge against me. It's cute."

Donahue looked at the floor and rubbed his face with thick, dark-skinned hands. "Let me talk to Brannigan alone. Thanks, Sergeant."

Puck gave me a small nod, but I was still too in awe of her to reciprocate it. When she'd left, Donahue went to the window overlooking a laboratory and leaned on the sill.

I remembered that I'd left my holoreader in my pocket during the fire and dug it out quickly, as if I could have prevented the inevitable. The thing was fried, destroyed beyond all recognition by the heat in the forest. Sherry was going to kill me.

"Motherfucker!"

Donahue stared at me as if in pain, like I'd done something else to ruin his day.

I held up the blackened brick that used to be my phone. "My holoreader got burned up in the fire. I haven't talked to my wife since last night. I think I might be in the doghouse before long."

"I'm partly to blame for that I guess." Donahue sighed. "I figured, the sooner I got you out here in the work, you'd be more enthusiastic. I didn't even think about your family. Maybe I can help you get out of the doghouse somehow."

"Do you guys have a spousal memory remover I can borrow?"

Donahue laughed. "What did you think of your first day?"

"You mean I'm not in trouble and my first day also isn't my last?"

"You really ought to read your contract tonight, Brannigan."

I paused, thinking of all the terrible legal traps contained in that holo document. And I'd been dumb enough to sign it.

I shrugged. "Then my first day was pretty awesome."

Donahue smiled.

"I mean, I think it's stupid that you threw me into it without any knowledge or even a damn uniform–"

"Remember our motto?"

I blew air across my lips, shaking my head. "Yeah, that's not how we did things in the fire department."

"I knew you could handle it. And besides, does somebody become better through reading books or through experience?"

"I think it's a combination, but I guess if I had to pick one, it'd be—"

"Experience," Donahue said with me. "Sink or swim, Brannigan. Plus, Sergeant Puck is one of our best. As hard as she is on you rookies, she'd give her life if she had to."

"You know, I really thought I was through with this kind of work. But, it's weird. It feels like I was always meant to do it. I couldn't walk away if I wanted to."

"The smoke eater's curse." Donahue pressed his head to the glass.

I walked over to join him at the window. "You could say that about firefighters, too. I mean... Holy shit! Is that...?"

In the room on the other side of the window, and about ten feet below, a huge, red dragon lay on a giant metal slab. A yellow-shirted woman operated robotic arms with lasers that cut into the scaly's body and peeled back the skin. The woman at the controls wore clear goggles, but was otherwise unprotected from the dragon. The scaly's teeth were as long as the woman's legs, and reptilian eyes lay open so the dead bastard looked right at me.

"The dragon from your house fire," Donahue said. "The monster that set you on the path of a smoke eater."

"You make it sound too poetic." I squinted my eyes to see better through the glass. "What is she doing to it?"

The lasers cut into the scaly's neck, sending a tiny plume of dark smoke into the air.

"The yellow shirts are our scientists." Donahue nodded to the woman below. "Propellerheads."

I raised an eyebrow. "Puck kept using that word in class. Thought she was just insulting somebody."

"It's not an official title," Donahue said. "Just a nickname that stuck. They've come up with all kinds of neat tools. Most the public doesn't know about. And their research tells us all kinds of things, like the best way to kill the scalies."

"A laser sword to the jugular seems to work all right."

Donahue clicked his tongue and shook his head. "Some are tougher than you think. Not everything we have works against every dragon. That electromagnetic pulse from yesterday is just one surprise a scaly can throw at us. Sometimes we have to improvise. Adapt and overcome, is what you firefighters say, yeah? That dragon down there, we're calling a Fafnir."

"Gesundheit," I said. "Who makes all this stuff up?"

"The propellerheads, mostly. Naveena and Renfro told them what the Fafnir did with that EMP blast. It's not the first dragon to do so, but definitely the first to do it with so much power. Yolanda down there is inspecting the dragon's throat to get us some answers."

Yolanda was a light-skinned black woman with a fantastic afro. She wore her yellow uniform shirt as if she was born for it, and the protective goggles she wore brought it all together.

"So you guys don't know everything about dragons." I hummed with interest.

Crossing his arms, Donahue turned to me. "Seven years of dragons isn't long enough to learn much beyond the basics. I think we've done all right with the short time we've had, but we're still getting through our growing pains. We have a national network of smokies in other states we share information with. I'm working on making it international."

"Yeah, maybe you can find out what the hell Canada has been doing."

Donahue smiled like he knew something, but ignored me. "We've never seen a dragon like the Fafnir before. Who's to say there aren't a ton more we don't know about?"

That made my guts twist.

"We should find a way to wipe them all out," I said.

"Like what? Burrow to the center of the Earth and set off a nuke?"

I shrugged. "I didn't say I knew how."

"That's like if I told you a few days ago that we should find a way to prevent all fires."

"Fair enough. Speaking of fire, there's something I want to get your take on."

"Shoot."

I rubbed the back of my neck. "White fire."

"You mean wraiths?"

"That's the thing," I said. "My firefighter said he saw white flames coming out of the TV inside that house yesterday. Before the dragon showed up. It didn't make any damn sense to me. I don't know much about wraiths, but I don't think they hide in household electronics for the hell of it. Do you have any light to shed?"

Donahue rubbed his chin for a minute. "He has to be confused. You know as well as me that you can hardly see anything in a fire. And even with good ventilation, your nerves and your mind can mess with you."

"I thought you might have been a fireman before," I said. "You've got that vibe."

"I was a hoseman for almost twenty years, before the dragons. Anyway, maybe your guy saw one of his crew becoming a wraith and mixed up the order of events. Traumatic shock."

"Yeah, maybe. He was really freaked out when I saw him today."

I still wasn't so sure. DeShawn was great about keeping his head during a fire, despite what happened with the scaly. And I also knew wraiths drew dragons like blood in the water. Something was up.

"So we're still learning about dragons," I said. "What

about wraiths?"

Donahue shivered. "You'll learn more in class, but there's not much we can do about them. A while back, some of our propellerheads tried to capture one. The few who came back had slashes on their bodies and shit in their pants." He widened his eyes. "Damn. And now we have to quarantine Buzzard's Roost because of one dumb civilian. I had a great fishing spot out there."

"Don't you think the 'leave 'em alone' tactic is a little lazy? The wraiths are just as dangerous as the scalies."

Donahue chuckled. "Maybe. But we're already dealing with dragons. I can't even imagine adding ghosts to our workload." He looked at his watch. "Listen, I have to get home. It's taco night. Puck will get you fresh uniforms – you look like a bum, and could use a shower. No offense."

I looked down at my dirty clothes, thought about giving Donahue the finger, but I held back.

"I'm also giving you leave for the firefighter funeral," he said.

Shit. With everything going on, I'd forgotten about the funeral for Theresa and the guys from Truck 1.

Donahue was quick to change the subject. "Any other questions?"

"Yeah," I said. "Where can I use a holoreader to call my wife before she hunts me down with a shotgun?"

"Yolanda should have one," Donahue said. "Tell her I said it was OK."

He pointed down to the lab, where the propellerhead had begun to remove organs from the big, red dragon.

CHAPTER 9

The doors to the lab slid open. A smell of sulfur and burned wood hit me like a truck, and, for some reason, it reminded me of my Grandpa Fred.

Yolanda turned with a start. "Oh! You scared the beep out of me."

Beep? Better watch my language.

"Sorry," I said, showing my palms – a gesture to show I was no threat. "Donahue said I might borrow your holoreader." I held up my old one that was now no better than a piece of charcoal. "Mine got torched and I need to call my wife."

She blinked a few times at my request before digging her holoreader from her pants pocket. "Sure."

"Thanks," I said, eyeing the dead dragon on the slab a few feet away.

I circled around, toward where the scaly's forked tongue hung out of its mouth. I wondered how all those teeth were able to fit. The Fafnir's fire-hydrant-red scales shone under Yolanda's lab lights, and even where the propellerhead had splayed its throat open, the dragon's innards were as crimson as the outside.

I wanted to touch it. But then Yolanda emptied the dragon's stomach into a metal bowl and something that resembled a human arm flopped out. I turned away before losing my... well, I guess I hadn't eaten in a while. Just as well.

I punched my wife's number into the holoreader and waited with my back to Yolanda as the line rang a couple times.

Sherry answered. "Hello?"

"It's Cole."

"You asshole!"

"Don't hang up!" I turned to see if Yolanda was watching, but she'd put on some wireless headphones and bobbed her head to music as she picked through the dragon's stomach.

"You think you're slick, don't you?" Sherry said.

"I've been meaning to call you all day. Things just snowballed, and I kind of got roped into this academy–"

"Academy?" I could almost hear her internal boiler about to blow.

"The smoke eaters. They're needing me to stay here for a bit, while I'm in class. It shouldn't be too long. And I'm sure I can take off–"

"What do they have you doing?"

Her interest took me by surprise. I'd fully expected her to explode and berate me about being away from home.

I was about to tell her about the poppers at Buzzard's Roost, but instead I said, "It's been hell. I've done more pushups and other... strains I never thought I'd have to mess with. I'm feeling my age."

"Are there women there?"

I turned again to Yolanda, who looked up from her work to smile briefly. "There are a few, yes. One of them is my instructor. She's the one who made me do all the pushups."

Sherry made some kind of humming noise, almost a laugh. "Well, you need a woman to put you in your place."

"Don't I know it?" I stood there for a second with my eyes thinned. "Are you OK?"

"Yeah," Sherry said with a sigh. "I'm still mad at you. Fixing the upstairs window and buying me a holostereo helps, but it's not a cure."

"Say what?"

A holostereo was one of the hottest new products in stores. A crazy Finnish invention that played music you selected off the Feed, but it also projected holograms of the artist, putting a concert right in your living room, or a digital dance floor complete with a crowd of partiers for when you wanted to go clubbing in the comfort of your pajamas. Movies would come to life in front of you. The price was also astronomical and not anywhere close to my budget's orbit.

"The delivery men and the repair guy just left," Sherry said. "I'm going to try out the holostereo here in a minute. You think Kenji can dance?"

"I don't... What's going on?"

"I'm trying to enjoy the makeup presents you got me, dum-dum." She said it like I was the one confused.

Maybe I can help you get out of the doghouse somehow, Donahue had said.

I looked up to the empty window, where Donahue and I had been talking and overlooking Yolanda's work.

No reason not to play along. After all, it was my ass Sherry would have otherwise been chewing on. "I hope you like it," I said. "I love you."

"Love you!" She hung up.

I stared at Yolanda's holoreader for a few seconds, confused as hell.

"All done?' Yolanda said, putting the headphones around her neck.

"Yeah, thanks." I returned her holoreader and then pointed to the dead dragon. "Hey, is it OK if... I touch it?"

"Sure."

I ran my hand along the tough scales, keeping away from the gash made by Naveena's sword. The Fafnir's tail hung off the slab and curled into a pile on the floor. When my hand trailed down to the dragon's side plate, I knocked on it for good luck.

"Strange, huh?"

"Yeah," I said. "I still don't get how these help it move underground."

Yolanda frowned. "Some think that."

"I guess I'm not the only one who thinks that theory makes no sense."

Yolanda brought over a handheld circular saw. "Every time we," she began cutting around the side plate, splattering dragon flesh, "try to examine one of these," she directed me to help pull the plate off, "it ends up like this."

I didn't have the benefit of latex gloves, but I helped Yolanda remove the side plate. After we yanked it free, the inside of the Fafnir smoldered; I leaned in and saw only charred bones and ash.

"What's that about?" I asked.

"I'm not entirely sure. It's almost like a self-destruct mechanism. And I can't x-ray it, because the plate is so darn tough. It's impossible. There's no way of knowing what's behind the plates. Besides my own crazy theory."

I strained with the plate in my hands. "Where do you want this?"

"Oh," Yolanda said. "Over there on the counter."

Shuffling the whole way, I dropped the plate onto the counter and leaned against it to catch my breath. Glass cubes lay off to the side, with insects frozen in them.

"What are these?"

Yolanda picked one up and held it out to me. "Cicadas. Periodical cicadas, to be specific."

"You like bugs?"

"No, I hate the darn things. But that doesn't mean I don't find them interesting or less relevant."

I studied the glassed cicada, its large wings and ugly red eyes. "I haven't seen a bug since E-Day."

"They're relevant because I think the dragons follow a similar pattern."

"Yeah, both are considered plagues."

Yolanda shook her head. "You're thinking of locusts. Cicadas are completely different. You see, cicadas spend most of their lives underground until they mature and come out to mate."

That did sound relevant.

"But I heard cicadas come around every seventeen years," I said.

"Or every thirteen years. It all depends on the brood, and there are at least twenty-three broods of cicada so they can pop up at different times in different areas. But with the dragons, I think it's more like every seventeen hundred years."

"What makes you say that?"

"Well," she put a finger to her lips, then said, "Nessie."

"As in the Loch Ness Monster?" I cracked a smile.

"Don't laugh. It was sighted about fifteen hundred years ago. Last known sighting of something scaly-like. All the dragon stories from before, maybe they were all based on true accounts, but time just buried them in fantasy."

I nodded. Yolanda had put a lot of thought into her theories. Having heard the dumbest ideas around the firehouse table and on the Feed, hers were reasonable.

"So they'll just go back underground. We just have to wait them out?"

"I don't think we have that kind of time. The dragon broods are growing bigger and more destructive. Our seismic monitoring system can barely keep up. Best thing you guys in the field can do is stop the scalies when they emerge, and destroy any eggs before the offspring find their way into the earth."

"That sounds exhausting."

"Yeah, sometimes the egg teams don't get to an area in time, especially since wraiths stay around the nests like guard dogs."

"So why don't we find a way to trap wraiths? Get 'em out of the area so dragons don't destroy any more houses. No mating. No more scalies."

Yolanda laughed, sounded like a puppy bark. "Now that's the funniest thing I've heard in a long time."

"What?" I couldn't help my smile.

"That kind of technology doesn't exist. Wish it did, but it doesn't. Except maybe in Professor Poltergeist's made-up world."

"Who?

"Oh, you must have missed that day in class. Here." She walked over to a filing cabinet and pulled out a small disk. "You can watch this on your holoreader. The Canadians made it. For kids, but it does cover wraiths pretty well. They don't get into anything too complex, but it's not like you're ever going to need it."

If it had anything to do with stopping the dragons, I wanted to know about it. When I got hooked on a subject, I absorbed as much information as I could. Ignorant people pissed me off, and I never wanted to be the guy who mindlessly accepted and repeated things he heard off the Feed. Those were Rogola's constituents. But the contents of that disk scared me. Who knew what kind of weird cult shit the Canucks were teaching their kids? I took it anyway.

I set the cicada cube down beside the dissected Fafnir side plate. "You said you had a theory about the side plates."

"Oh." Yolanda laughed, embarrassed. "You wouldn't want to hear about it."

"Sure I would. As far as I can tell, you're the smartest person in the building and maybe the country."

She crossed her arms but smiled even bigger. "The others think I'm grasping at straws."

"I'm not them."

"OK. We were talking about cicadas?"

I nodded.

"Cicadas come out of the ground as nymphs, only able to crawl – dragons are the same way, except they can mate as 'nymphs'. When a cicada finds a spot to molt, they shed their old exoskeletons and flaunt wings."

"Wings?" I asked, hoping she'd said something else.

Yolanda nodded, completely serious. "Wings."

She was right. I didn't want to hear about it.

Smoke Eater Headquarters had a hell of a cafeteria. There were no chefs on staff, of course, but their pantries and fridges were fully stocked, and you could eat whatever you wanted as long as you cooked it yourself and cleaned up afterward.

I made a four-egg omelet with mushrooms, pepperonis, and cheddar cheese. Since they also had a waffle maker and instant batter, I also made a couple – OK, three – waffles with blueberries and whipped cream.

At my age, I'd eat whatever I damn well pleased.

I hunted down Sergeant Puck and got a full issue of uniforms: three green duty shirts, two button-up Class A shirts, a few pairs of pants, some damn comfortable boots, and even a couple pairs of green workout shorts.

Puck then showed me to the commissary to grab some toothpaste and other toiletries on credit. I even found an old paperback book collecting dust in the back of the store. They didn't know it had been there and gave it to me for free.

After a long, hot shower by myself, my body was comfortably numb as I plodded down the hall to the dorm room Puck had assigned me. She'd said I would have a roommate. I had guessed as much. In the fire service, bunking together built camaraderie, and was also cheap on the department's budget.

I passed Afu in the hall, who fist bumped me before entering his own, separate room. So if Afu wasn't my roommate...

Sweet Jesus, don't let it be Thomlin, I thought.

I found my room and fumbled with the door's hand scanner as I balanced my stack of clothes and boots. When I walked in, Naveena stood by a bed in nothing but a sleeveless duty shirt and a pair of red panties.

"Well, if it isn't Old Man River." She gave me her classic smirk, but this time it was different. This time: panties.

Whatever I said sounded like, "Abudee-abudee-abudee."

"You got a problem?" She crossed her arms, and I could tell she wasn't wearing a bra.

I shook my head, swallowing, trying to keep my eyes above her neck.

"Then close the door. Your bed is over there." She motioned her head toward the already made bed across from hers.

I threw my clothes on top of the crisp, green blanket before inspecting the room I'd be living in for the foreseeable future, and not looking at my foreseeable roommate. The bare white walls were made from some kind of plastic, not the dirty, pale bricks I remembered from fire academy. A desk stood between beds placed too close together, but there was no other furniture. With all the advances in technology I'd seen over the years, you'd think they could have given us better living quarters.

Naveena pulled out a holoreader and scooted onto her bed. On her right shoulder, a "Sink or Swim" Maltese cross with crossed lances had been tattooed with indiglow ink, making her arm look like a neon sign.

"This dorm room is kind of plain, isn't it?" I said.

"Donahue believes these rooms should be for studying or sleep. Nothing else." Naveena didn't look up from her holoreader.

I opened the plastic commissary sack and tossed the paperback book onto my pillow.

Naveena looked up. "What's that?"

She rubbed her bare feet together, and I looked away quickly, grabbing the book and holding it up for her to see.

I'm not a dirty old man, I told myself. I'm not a dirty old man.

"Old Man's War," she read the book's title, and snorted before returning to her holoreader. The blue, floating letters made her lips sparkle. "How appropriate. A paper book, huh? That thing must be three hundred years old."

I flipped to the copyright page. "It was first published in 2005. This edition is from 2085. Found it lying in the back of the commissary."

"So you were, what, forty when it first came out?" She smirked.

"What about you?" I asked. "What are you reading?"

"The report on a dragon dissection."

"The Fafnir?"

She cocked an eyebrow and tilted her head. "Well, you're sharp as a tack."

"You don't get this old being a fool."

She laughed a little and it made her chest jiggle slightly.

Why are you looking at her chest? The thought was in Sherry's voice.

What the hell was I doing?

"So…" I cleared my throat, "…do they usually put…" I waved a hand between the two of us "…together?"

She sighed and dropped her holoreader. "Donahue lets me live here rent free. It works out great, since I don't have to commute and miss out on any good dragon calls. The only catch is that they sometimes put new recruits in here. I guess they think it helps some rookies get adjusted, and I can impart my wisdom or some shit."

I pursed my lips and nodded. "Yeah, that's good to know and all, but I mean… why put a man and woman in the same room?"

She swung her legs over the side of the bed. "Did you have female firefighters on your crew, in your fire station?"

"Sure. But I didn't see them walking around in their underwear. They had their own rooms. Department policy."

"Smoke eaters are–"

"Different," I finished for her. "Yeah, I know."

She tensed the muscles around her eyes. It was scary. "Are you not going to be able to control yourself around me? Are you some kind of rabid dog in heat?"

"Of course not. I just–"

"You wouldn't try to fuck Afu if he was your roommate, would you?"

I grinned. "The way that dude's built, I'd be the one trying to fight him off."

Naveena didn't laugh.

"No," I said, dropping my smile.

"So don't come into my house and judge me for getting comfortable. You're a guest in here, and I don't need any lip. Especially from some geriatric rookie who'll probably get killed soon anyway. Lie down and read your old-ass book or go to sleep. Either way, I don't want to hear shit out of you for the rest of the night."

She picked up her holoreader and covered herself with a blanket.

I'd been married long enough to know when it was better not to say anything else. So, I lay down and opened my old-ass book.

The long day and the hell I'd put my body through in Buzzard's Roost draped over me like a ton of bricks. I read maybe a paragraph in the paperback, about a seventy-five year-old man who joined the space military, before exhaustion dragged me into a deep sleep.

I dreamed of dragons.

And panties.

CHAPTER 10

I'd arrived at Smoke Eater Headquarters on Tuesday, and the rest of the week dragged on forever. The next morning in class, Puck handed me a holoreader, like Naveena's, and told me I had to use my own time to get up to speed with the rest of the class.

"Will I get kicked out if I fail the test?" I asked her.

"No one gets kicked out, Brannigan," she'd said. "Read your contract. And the only test is the dragons you'll be facing. Pass or fail. I bet you can guess what failing looks like."

An image of my burned body impaled on a big scaly's tooth came to mind.

Yeah. I'd study my ass off.

Wednesday was all class time. If a dragon call came in, we were unaware of it. We were just the backup anyway. I'm sure Donahue gave us a day to… well, "relax" wasn't the right word – my brain was fried from all the scaly knowledge – but a day where we could wear a clean uniform and feel like we were at least a tiny bit closer to knowing what the hell we were doing.

If I was honest with myself, that popper business was sheer, dumb luck.

"Who can tell me what the lightning theory is?" Puck asked.

Williams' hand shot up. "That dragons have been surviving underground by absorbing energy from lightning strikes."

"Very good," Puck said.

I raised my hand. "Hold on. What? That makes no sense."

"Looks like I have to educate Brannigan on basic science," Puck said, turning to expand a screen. "When lightning strikes, it loosens nitrogen from the air and plants take it in as nutrition."

A helpful animation showed lightning jiggling nitrogen atoms to the earth and smileyfaced trees gobbling them up as they fell.

"The lightning theory suggests that dragons absorb electrical energy the same way," Puck said.

Thomlin raised his hand. "It coincides with dragons shooting EMPs and wraiths being made of electricity."

"Also might be why they're attracted to houses," Puck said. "All that juice running through our homes."

I thought of cicadas sucking up xylem from the dirt.

Puck taught us about Leviathans and how the propellerheads didn't think they were confined to the ocean. She said there was always potential for one to pop up in Lake Erie.

"Is that like the Loch Ness monster?" Thomlin asked, with a shit-eating grin. I wondered if he'd heard Yolanda's theory, was making fun of her. I wanted to sock him in the eye.

Puck grabbed a holographic image and expanded it. "Does that look like some stupid legend to you?"

Hell no, it didn't.

The picture was taken from the deck of a battleship. In the water swam the biggest scaly I had ever seen, and most of it, from what I gathered, was hidden below the surface. It had a wide head like a really ugly tortoise, and an open mouth full of beak-like teeth as it roared at the ships surrounding it. Several rockets were either exploding against its cloud-gray hide or in mid-flight when the photographer chanced a photo-op.

"The Japanese lit this thing up with everything they had the day this photo was taken. Thanks to the camera's instant loading to the Feed, we have the benefit of knowing what these things look like. Unfortunately for the men and women onboard these ships, they were never heard from again. The Leviathan, however, has been spotted a few times since."

"I still can't believe those rockets didn't make a scratch." Williams said.

"Twenty pushups for not raising your hand, Williams. And no, nothing they threw at it penetrated its scales. This wasn't too long after E-Day, and they didn't have the benefit of lasers like we do."

I raised my hand, and waited for Puck to point to me. "How in hell are we supposed to kill something like that?"

"Smokies on the coasts are developing reinforced ships armed with laserfire. And we'll be practicing with our water suits next week," Puck said.

What?

Puck filled the rest of the day with more of the same lectures: different types of known dragons and how to kill them, or, how to prevent them from killing you. Some dragons, like the Leviathan, shot boiling steam from their nostrils. Others produced toxic slime from holes in their back or shot spikes from their tail.

I asked how our ability to breathe smoke and resist heat would help fight those kinds of weird bastards. Puck said that they were unique dragons, and that we'd spend most of our time fighting the true-blue fire-breathing variety, but that it was helpful to know about the others just in case.

She also gave me fifty pushups for my trouble.

After that, we practiced shooting lasers and foam, and cutting cardboard dragons with laser swords. Instead of wearing a full power suit, we were provided with the weaponed arms for practice. I sucked at shooting lasers but wasn't too shabby with the sword. But since none of us were deemed to be proficient, we all had to run a mile and a half around the track.

We were so tired, none of us cared about privacy as we shared the shower room and let the hot water comfort us for a solid half hour.

I avoided my dorm room as long as I could, or, more specifically, I was trying to avoid Naveena. I felt like an ass for what I'd said, and didn't want to admit it or have more opportunity to act like an ass.

That night, I sat in the common room studying scalies on my holoreader, while Afu and Williams watched the Feed stream on the wall – some reality show about robot cops cleaning up the mean streets of Scottsdale, Arizona. I wasn't sure "reality show" was the appropriate genre. Robots: reality?

Afu laughed hard, spitting out his popcorn, when a robocop gave a noncompliant perpetrator a wedgie.

Thomlin walked by, laughing at something on his holoreader. When I looked up, he held it so I could see myself telling the fire droid from Buzzard's Roost to get out of the way before slashing at the screen. I'd seen the clip at least a dozen times.

"Way to make us look good, Brannigan," Thomlin said, walking away and laughing as he reloaded the video clip.

A bunch of the smoke eaters had gotten a kick out of it, and I thought I looked pretty badass in my power suit. Plus, it had pissed Rogola off, which made it ten times better. So I sliced some droids. I didn't see what the big deal was.

The news came on after Afu's robocop show.

"Protesters gathering outside Parthenon City Central Fire Station," the newswoman said.

I sat up and stared at the wall, where the video showed at least a hundred people carrying holographic signs and shouting. My old chief was outside the fire station with a few police officers, trying to get the crowd calmed down, failing miserably.

The newswoman continued. "After Mayor Rogola shared video of smoke eaters destroying city property at a wildfire in Buzzard's Roost, many Parthenon City residents have taken issue with the smoke eaters and their methods."

"Why the hell are they protesting the fire department, then?" Afu said.

"Because we're technically a part of the fire department," I said. "And they're too scared to drive all the way out here to yell at us."

Afu shook his head. "This pisses me off, man. That news lady didn't even say we were there because of dragons. We're not the bad guys. We didn't do anything wrong."

The news cut to a shot of Mayor Rogola in his office. "Haven't I been telling you about these loose cannons? I tell you this now, I'm making it my personal mission to…"

"Can you turn it off?" I asked Afu. "I can't look at that idiot without my blood pressure shooting through the roof."

Afu changed it to a home renovation show that featured homes destroyed by dragons.

On my holoreader, I pulled up the smoke eater contract I'd signed, since everyone kept telling me to read it.

The first section outlined how I couldn't be terminated, but also how I couldn't quit. I had to read that part again to make sure I wasn't seeing things in the floating text.

Apparently, if I left Smoke Eater Division, they retained the right to secure every credit they paid me while I was on the payroll. All the work I'd put in would be for nothing if I left. It sounded ludicrous, and I couldn't see any court approving, but, then again, I had signed the damn thing.

The rest of the contract talked about how I couldn't reveal smoke eater methods to the public and that I would leave all communications with the media to the chief. Well, I'd already screwed that pooch.

I was to stay at headquarters for the entirety of my training, with weekends off, that would conclude with a graduation in just under three weeks. They sure weren't giving me much time to learn everything.

After that, they'd assign me to a crew, and I'd work the standard firefighter-type schedule of twenty-four hours on, forty-eight hours off, with the caveat that the chief could institute a mandatory "all hands on deck" schedule in times of crisis.

So, basically, they were fucking me pretty good, but at least they were paying me for it.

I was burned out from reading and didn't want to watch Afu's show or go back to my dorm room just yet. It was nearing ten o'clock, but I messaged Sherry with my holoreader, hoping she was still up.

You awake? I typed.

Yeah, she responded. I can't sleep. Keep feeling small quakes in the area.

They monitor seismic activity here, I typed. If it might be a dragon, they'd put a crew in the area to keep watch.

I'm not worried. Just watching my holostereo, but I think something is wrong with it.

What do you mean? Can't depend on technology for shit.

I'm trying to jam out to a Thunder Rash concert, she replied, but the signal must be off. A horror channel keeps flashing through every few minutes. Scared the shit out of me and Kenji when it first happened. I had to lock him in his room. He kept barking at the stereo like it was going to bite me or something.

I felt helpless, and it was always like that, even when I was a firefighter. When you were on shift, unable to get away until seven the next morning, the whole world went to hell at home. Never failed.

I'm sure it just needs to be tuned up, I typed. What happened? Some guy in a hockey mask show up in the living room?

No. Lol. I could have handled that. It was a wraith if you can believe it.

I typed so fast, I had to go back and fix my words three times. What kind of sicko would make a wraith horror channel? Or would want to watch that?

No clue, she sent. I called the company and they acted like they didn't know what I was talking about.

Typical.

Yeah, so you're coming home for the weekend?

I smiled. Friday afternoon, I'm all yours. They're not complete jerks to keep me away from you forever. But I'm going to Theresa's funeral tomorrow for a few.

Sherry didn't reply for a while. Afu turned off the Feed and waved goodnight. Williams came through and slapped him on the ass. She then took a different hallway. I was pretty sure they were sleeping together. Hell, I didn't care, they didn't have to hide it from me. Afu would circle around to the other side of the building and go to Williams' room, since she didn't have a roommate. Thomlin had been bitching about how Afu came into their shared room at four o'clock every morning.

My holoreader dinged.

I miss you, Sherry sent. Love you.

Love you, too. I signed off and sat there in the common room alone.

After the chaos of the last couple of days, things were starting to even out. I was getting into the swing of being a smoke eater. I was going to see Sherry on Friday, and she was being very understanding about my new career. I had that warm fuzzy feeling that everything was going great and that all the bullshit and trouble was behind me.

Boy, was I wrong.

CHAPTER 11

I didn't want to go to my room just yet, so I dug out the disk Yolanda gave me and put it into my holoreader.

The video began playing in full screen. A Canadian maple leaf flag blew in the background as text appeared at the bottom, signifying that the video had been government-sanctioned.

The next image was in black and white, outside a computer-generated haunted house, complete with wailing spooks and a witch flying across the moon. The picture faded into a mad scientist's laboratory – the viewer was to assume they'd entered the haunted house – and then the picture changed to color.

A man walked into view, wearing a white smock that hung down to his ankles. His white hair stood straight up as if he'd stuck a fork into a socket.

"Hello, brothers and sisters of the Great White North!" the scientist removed dark-lensed goggles from his eyes, resting them on his head. "I'm Professor Poltergeist and this is where I do all my crazy experiments."

I rolled my eyes. Yolanda had said this was directed at kids, but damn.

"And today," Professor Poltergeist said, "we're going to be talking about those wonderful, wicked wraiths! Ah, I have one here."

A woman dressed as a hunchback pushed out a cart. On top, encased in an enormous glass tube, floated a wraith. It had to be CGI.

"I assure you, boys and ghouls, this is an actual wraith. Not like the fakes you saw floating around my house outside. But don't worry, I'm safe with this glass between us." Professor Poltergeist knocked against the tube.

The wraith snarled and scratched at the glass between it and the professor.

Professor Poltergeist flinched, nearly falling onto his ass. It didn't look like acting.

"This one must have been a real hoser in his day," Professor Poltergeist said, trying to get his composure back. "Where do wraiths come from? Why are they here? What's their relationship with the dragons?"

Some Canadians were just like us, their southern neighbors, and wanted to wipe out the scalies as soon as they could. Most Canucks, however, believed in hardcore conservation of all animal life – even those that destroy others. The concept of a smoke eater was reprehensible to them, and the American government issued a trade embargo to our neighbors in the north after they refused to share their research. As far as Uncle Sam was concerned, the Canadians could sing campfire songs and die on the teeth of dragons all they wanted, but that kind of shit wouldn't fly in the good ole US of A.

I'd also heard a rumor that small sects of Canadians worshiped dragons like gods. I wondered what flavor Kool-Aid they enjoyed.

"Click any of these topics to learn more," Professor Poltergeist raised his hand, and bullet points – typed in old-horror-movie green – appeared at his side. "Don't wait around all day!"

It was an interactive video. Professor Poltergeist would

have stood there griping at me until I chose a topic. So I hit the one that said Defenders of the Eggs.

"The Canadian government would like us to inform you that all of these are just theories," Professor Poltergeist said, before the screen darkened.

The next image was deep inside the Earth's core. Thousands of dragons swam through rock and lava. They were small and computer animated, but that didn't make me feel any better. The video focused on a particular dragon, showing it burrowing its way to the surface.

"When a dragon matures," Professor Poltergeist's voice spoke over the image, "it comes to the surface to eat and mate. And that's where we come in."

The animated scaly burst into a house with a family of poorly rendered humans sitting at a dining table. The dragon proceeded to burn everything down and gobble every member of the family.

"Any lucky enough to be chosen, aid the dragon in attracting a mate."

The family reappeared as glowing wraiths while the dragon shifted the ashes into a huge heap.

"Every living thing contains electrical energy. We think that humans have the exact type of energy that aligns with a dragon's. Thus, wraiths can be born! Depending on the sex of the dragon, it creates the appropriate output to attract the opposite sex."

Another dragon crawled from the ground and the two scalies kissed, producing a giant, pink heart above them.

Goddamn, this was pathetic.

Professor Poltergeist continued, "But that's not all the wraiths do."

The second dragon dug back into the earth while the first stayed behind and laid eggs in the ash heap. After it was done, the dragon returned underground as well.

The wraiths then surrounded the eggs like guard dogs.

"Having done their duty, the dragons leave it up to the wraiths to protect the next generation. Woe to anyone who gets close!"

More humans arrived, looking too much like firefighters. When they neared the nest, the wraiths chased them off screen, returning with animated blood on their claws.

"When the babies have hatched, and burrowed below to grow over the next few hundred years, the wraiths disappear, their job done."

The eggs cracked and the dirt under them stirred. Then the animated wraith family faded away.

"Each nest can have between fifty and a hundred eggs. And the same two dragons can repeat the process with other mates as many times as they want before they pass maturity and their time is at an end."

The picture returned to Professor Poltergeist's laboratory, where he waited by the rest of the bullet points.

I didn't choose any of them. The short video had made me sick to my stomach, and I opted for my dorm room and the hope of a dreamless sleep.

Knowledge isn't power. It's a damned burden.

CHAPTER 12

Thursday morning, Puck ordered us to meet out at the drill field, fully geared up. Some kind of obstacle maze had been set up in the middle of the training field, and a fog had rolled in. The humid air stuck to my tongue, almost making me gag. I guess it would have been too much to ask that my power suit came with air conditioning.

I walked over to where Williams was staring at the giant rat maze in front of us. I asked, "What the hell is this?"

Flinching, she came out of her early morning trance and turned to me. She sighed before looking back to the raised, metal walls and the darkened opening that led into the maze. "Some bullshit."

"Might be fun," Afu said, chewing on a granola bar as he lumbered over.

"That looks like fun?" Williams pointed to the twin yellow ladders rising from somewhere deep in the maze. They connected to a building a hundred feet up, where the faintest puffs of black smoke had begun to flow from the windows.

"I hate heights," I said.

"But you were a fireman," Afu said. "You climbed ladders and shit all the time, right?"

"Only when I had to."

Puck came out of a set of double doors at the side of the main building. Behind her, Thomlin dragged a long dolly carrying some gnarly-looking equipment. Both were in their power suits.

"You're early," Puck said with a smug grin. "Good. I guess the pushups are keeping you sharp."

If she said so.

Thomlin stood beside the sergeant, leaving the dolly behind him.

Puck turned to the jolly ginger and waited for him to do something. When it became evident he was going to cling to her ass like a tick, she grabbed his armored shoulder and shoved him toward the rest of us. "Form up, Thomlin."

The sour look on Thomlin's face only made Williams and me snicker harder.

"You catching up on the material, Brannigan?" Puck asked.

"Doing my damnedest, Sergeant."

Puck rubbed her hands and smiled, wide and scary. So much so, that I noticed, for the first time, she had a small gap between her two front teeth. "Good. This'll prove it."

On the dolly stood a row of edged shields made of glass and another row of pitch black lances. Medieval Times 2.0.

"There may come a day when your laser swords or your foam or something else will fail." Puck paced in front of us. "No one wants to see that day, but we need to prepare for it just in case. Every one of our slayers and cannon trucks have shields and lances like the ones you see on the dolly behind me. There are other tools we use, but these two are the bread and butter of slaying scalies when your power suit is toast.

"The labyrinth of hell you see behind me has caused

more than a few smoke eaters to quit. Legally, I also have to inform you that one recruit was killed during this exercise."

I looked at the other rookies to see if they were buying this bull. Williams swallowed. Thomlin raised his chin, as if defying the maze. I'm pretty sure Afu had fallen asleep with his eyes open.

"You have thirty minutes." Puck held out her holoreader and expanded a picture of a little girl mannequin. "This is Little Susie. Your objective is to rescue her and kill any dragons you encounter on the way. Go on and ask me where Little Susie is located."

"Where is she located?" we all said in a mishmash of tired voices.

Puck grunted laughter as she pointed to the sky. "Way up there in the tower."

The black smoke had fully pressurized inside what Puck called the tower – it looked more like a cabin on stilts. My knowledge of fire science said it would be more productive to inform Little Susie's parents that she wasn't going to make it – nothing could survive that environment – not to mention that it looked like a textbook backdraft scenario. If we were able to make it through the maze and open one of the hatches above the ladders, oxygen would be reintroduced, and then – boom!

This was a setup.

But I'd also been in enough training scenarios to know you didn't correct the instructor, especially one like Sergeant Puke. You just did what was assigned and hoped you made it back in time to watch the Feed.

With this scenario, we'd be lucky to make it back at all.

"Who are my first two volunteers?" Puck put her hands on her hips.

I raised my arm – damn instinct. The fire service fills you with this stupid need to always be the first in line. Thomlin was the other lucky contestant. The rest of the rookies took a few steps back.

"Nice," Puck said, walking over to grab something from the dolly. "One more thing."

Spinning back to us, she leveled a gun with a sphere containing what looked like swirling, red electro-liquid. She shot me first. The red goop hit my armored chest in a splat. My muscles tensed as an involuntary moan left my lips. A subtle vibration ran through my body as if I'd stuck my tongue to a frayed electric wire – it tasted like it, too. Inside my helmet, static sparked from the speakers.

Thomlin raised his hands in defense, but Puck had already shot. When the slime ball hit him, electricity danced over his power suit. The orange glow at the tips of his boots and elbows faded to black.

I gulped air as my muscles eased. I'd been holding my breath. "What the hell was that?"

"Remember," Puck said, "I told you this exercise was about relying on other things besides your power suits. Both of you grab a shield and a lance."

Me and Thomlin both walked to the dolly as if we'd been run over by Slayer 3, wincing and sucking air with each step.

"The soreness will go away in a second," Puck said.

When I put my left arm through the handles of a shield, it widened with a loud click. A hundred tiny hexagons rippled across its glass in a yellow, electric honeycomb design, the light pulsing.

"As an added handicap," Puck said, "your shield is programmed to only take so much damage. When it reaches its limit, it'll flash bright red. If I were you, at that point I'd ditch it before it blows up in your face."

"Is that standard?" Thomlin asked.

Puck spit. "No, but we can't have you huddled in a corner the whole time. This will make sure you focus on the objective and not hide behind a shield."

"I don't get it," I said. "If an EMP knocks out electricity, how are these shields going to work?"

"They run on old-style batteries," Puck said. "They only have a forty percent chance of failure if they get hit with a pulse."

"Well, that's comforting," I said under my breath.

Thomlin tested the weight of one of the lances. "Does the tip shoot out like a rocket?"

"No, Zippy," Puck said with an annoyed sigh. "It's just a big piece of sharp metal."

I grabbed my own lance, which was about as heavy as a set of irons – what firefighters call a halligan and axe combo – and walked toward the opening of the labyrinth. Even the maze's floor was metal, and that worried me. Metal conducts heat. And if we were expected to fight dragons inside this funhouse, there was sure to be fire, even if the dragons turned out to be cardboard cutouts. The maze would become a giant oven.

"Just to be clear," Puck said, following behind Thomlin and me, "your power suits are kaput. You can't jump, you can't shoot, you can't use your laser sword or talk to each other through your helmets. No thermal vision. The only things your suits are good for now is making it harder for the scalies inside to kill you, and for collecting your piss when you get too scared to move. The winner gets the rest of the day off. The loser has to clean every bathroom and shower inside headquarters by themselves. Any questions?"

"Wait," I set my lance against the ground and leaned on it. "There aren't any real dragons in there, right?"

Puck ignored me and poked at her holoreader. Giant,

red numbers appeared on the large wall outside the maze, showing thirty minutes.

Afu whooped. "All right, fellas! Kick some ass."

"No cheering," Puck said. "Ready? Go!"

Thomlin broke into a run like it was a foot race and all he had to do was outrun the old man to the finish line. I jogged lightly behind him. I couldn't give a shit less about beating Thomlin; my goal was not dying, and, as a secondary option, rescuing a fucking mannequin.

A few yards into the labyrinth, a metal door rose behind me, sealing the entrance we'd come through, darkening the maze. The fog drifting above thickened.

"Don't stop, Brannigan!" Puck's voice came through a speaker somewhere in the maze. "Time's a'wasting."

I looked around for the cameras she was watching us with. When I didn't see them, I pushed on, catching up to Thomlin, who stood where the path forked. He had his legs spread as if his body couldn't agree on which way to take.

"Hey," I whispered, but I didn't know why. Sound didn't matter. A scaly could sniff us out if it wanted to. "We need to work together."

"Shut up!" Thomlin looked down one path, then the other. "I'm listening."

I shook my head. "For what? You know how we're supposed to rely on other things? I'm one of the other things."

"I can do this by myself. Don't tell me what to do."

"Having a lovers' spat?" Puck's voice rang off the walls.

"There." Thomlin shifted his body to face the left path. "I can hear it."

Sure enough, after he'd said it, I heard a tink, tink, tink. My brain translated it to be the clawing steps of a big-ass dragon. Thomlin shifted his shield and lance, and then took off in the direction of the sound.

"Wait," I called after him in a stern whisper, "you're looking for the dragon?"

He didn't answer me, but the approaching sound of claw against metal confirmed that I was going to take the other way. If Thomlin wanted to run off and be Captain Big Balls, I wasn't going to stop him, but I sure as hell wasn't going to tag along.

I used to be the king of corn mazes when I was growing up. This wasn't much different. As I followed the path, I only turned when my intuition told me to or I had no other choice. It helped to look up at the ladders and the smoking building every so often to gauge if my inner navigator led me true.

"You're in trouble now, Thomlin," I heard Puck say.

At the next turn, I saw the bottom of a rusty yellow ladder.

Pausing to make sure I wasn't hallucinating, I rubbed my eyes. My suit's metal fingers only smudged the sweat around. I poked my head around the corner, checking for any surprise, pop-out dragons. All clear.

Puck's voice came through the speakers. "Looks like Brannigan has found one of the ladders."

I hadn't been keeping track of how many seconds I had left, but I took my time getting to the ladder. With my eyes, I followed the metal rungs up to the building, trying to decide if I should leave my lance or my shield.

Thomlin's screams echoed through the maze. "Help!"

"Uh oh." Puck's smug, disembodied voice was starting to piss me off. "Your fellow smoke eater is in trouble. What are you going to do now, Brannigan?"

I turned to go after Thomlin, but stopped and took another look at the ladder. The frustrated groan I released could have belonged to a scaly.

Scraping my lance against the floor, I drew a quick

arrow around the corner, and did so at every turn – seeing that I was all out of breadcrumbs to lead me back to the ladder.

The clanking of metal grew louder as I found myself in the center of the maze, where the walls curved, forming a wagon wheel shape. I wondered if I was too late, and the metal clanging I heard was the dragon clawing into Thomlin's power suit like a grandma at an all-you-can-eat crab night.

But Puck hadn't made any commentary, and as I turned into a gap in the wall, Thomlin lay a couple dozen feet ahead of me, on his back and shoving his lance into the mouth of a robotic dragon. His shield was holding off one of the shiny, metal claws and furiously blinking red.

"Thomlin, get out of there!" I yelled.

"Meet Mecha-Scaly!" Puck's voice echoed.

"Shut up, Puck!" I didn't care how many pushups she'd give me.

The dragon raised its head with a rusty whine. Its orange, glowing eyes contracted as if it was zooming in on my face. It was hungry for its new target – me.

Whoever had built it had done a bang-up job. Its horns were long and menacing, its teeth plentiful and razor sharp. The thing had to be as big as a Mack truck, and it was all metal, polished chrome. They'd left out a tail, though. No actual dragon had ever scared me as much as this human-built motherfucker.

Lifting its claw off Thomlin's shield, it scraped him behind like a pile of droppings and lumbered toward me – tink, tink, tink.

Thomlin tossed his shield away as the hexagons hummed louder and vibrated out of control. When it hit the ground, the shield exploded in fire and glass.

He couldn't have thrown it at the dragon?

Thomlin ran off as Mecha-Scaly opened its mouth. It

didn't roar, but a flamethrower had been welded into the back of its throat.

I knelt and raised my shield as flames blasted from the dragon's mouth. With the transparency of the glass, I got a great view of the fire steadily burning away my defense. My shield's hexagons flashed orange.

The only place I could do any damage was one of the dragon's orange eyes. I thrust my lance, aiming for the left orb, but the metal bastard swiped my lance away like it was a twig, twisting my wrist in the process. It snapped so badly, I wondered if my wrist was sprained, if not broken.

Flexing my fingers – no, not broken. It sure hurt, though.

I would have tried retrieving my lance, but, with the same claw, the dragon swung back toward my head. I balled up behind my shield in time for the hit to send me onto my back.

Mecha-Scaly ran on an effective program, because I was in pretty much the same position I'd found Thomlin.

Sweat stung my eyes, blurring my vision, but even a blind man could have felt my shield wigging out, flashing red and vibrating as if the hive pattern contained an angry swarm of bees. Above, the dragon reared back, ready to bite. I rolled backwards, throwing my shield under the scaly's belly. It chased after me with its teeth...

...and then the shield exploded.

I sprawled onto my stomach, ready to say goodbye to the majority of my butt cheeks. More than a few hunks of metal racked my helmet and power suit.

Tink, tink, tink.

Behind me, the dragon clawed in chase, gnashing its creaky teeth. They were the only sounds echoing through the maze, besides my labored breath. A roar might have made me feel a little better about having to crawl for my life, away from a metal monster.

The back half of the dragon was gone. It dragged shredded wire and tumbling metal behind as it clambered after me, a cog or two falling out of the gash. Funky, clear fluid pooled under it and trickled away, outrunning the dragon on its way toward me.

Fuel.

It was in that same moment the dragon's oh-so-intelligent computer decided the best course of action was to breathe fire.

I leapt to my feet when it opened its mouth, running with everything I had. Oh, to shed my armor for a little more speed. What the metal scaly had lacked in a roar was quickly made up for by the inferno that ripped to life behind me. The flames scorched my ass first, and then they quickly radiated everywhere else, even in front of me, thanks to the metal box.

I ran until I felt it safe enough to stop, drop, and roll to make sure I wasn't on fire. After I was done with my tumbleweed impression, I lay there, staring at where Little Susie waited for me to save her, in the building still churning out smoke, high above the maze. I heard the crackling of flames and not the tink, tink, tink of Mecha-Scaly, so I assumed it was safe to take a breather.

Forget the clock. And Puck, and everybody else. I didn't sign up for this. My whole body was like a roasted duck, and I was sure my wrist would swell to the size of a grapefruit before the sun set. Fuck Little Susie. I was going to lay there until someone dragged me out.

A blocky green shape moved along one of the ladders. I sat up.

Thomlin.

He'd found his way through the maze and thought he'd steal all the glory. Not on my watch. Huffing and cussing, I stumbled onto my feet and shuffled in search of one of my scratches on the maze floor.

Thomlin was halfway up his ladder when I reached the other and began climbing.

"Give it up, old man," he shouted, when he noticed me clanging up the rungs.

I said, "That's not what your mom told me last night."

"Looks like we have a close race." Puck would have made a terrible sports announcer. "With only four and a half minutes to go."

Every rung climbed was hell on my body. Every time I grabbed another piece of metal, a flash of white crossed my vision, and I considered dropping to my death as a better alternative. But I fought through it.

Thirty seconds later, Thomlin stood under the hatch leading into the bottom of the building. He raised his hand to the handle as smoke puffed in and out of the cracks.

I could have let him burn to death and fall like a meteor, but instead, I shouted, "Wait!"

I don't know why, given our brief, tumultuous history, but he actually stopped and looked at me, annoyed, but curious.

"That room is prepped to blow," I said. "See how that smoke is breathing?"

He did. "What's that mean? Another dragon?"

Amateurs.

"No." I shook my head. "Backdraft. That room is oxygen deficient. The fire has everything it needs but air. If you open that hatch, an explosion is going to send you to the ground."

He inspected the building above us. "What do we do?"

It was a miracle that he believed me. I looked around, even to the maze far below, and at Puck and the other rookies watching us from the grass. I was searching for... hell, I didn't even know.

Pegs had been nailed into the wood about a foot away from my hatch's handle, painted the same color as the building. You really had to be looking to catch them. I followed the line of pegs up to the top of the building.

Well, this was going to be fun.

"I'm going to climb to the roof," I told Thomlin.

"Why?"

"Making a hole up there is the only way to release the pressure without either of us dying. I'll shout when I've done it. But you'll probably be able to tell."

"How are you going to make a hole?"

I swung for the first peg and said, "I'll figure it out when I get there."

I almost missed the third peg, and swung wildly at the end of a five-inch piece of metal, a hundred feet above certain death. My wrist would have cursed me in shrill syllables if it had a mouth. I'd never experienced pain like that before, and I'd broken more than a few bones in my lifetime.

Looking down wasn't an option as I waited for my body to still before reaching for the next peg.

I passed a window that had been blackened so badly it might as well have been spray painted. Up top, the roof was flat and made of thin plywood. I would have used a pike pole or trash hook – or my lost lance – to check the roof's stability, but I had nothing but my power suit. If I fell through, me and Little Susie would both be fricassee.

With an exhausted sigh, I swung a leg over and tapped the roof with my boot. It didn't feel squishy, but I wasn't confident enough to put my entire weight on it. I looked at my uninjured hand and made a fist. It was awkward using my left hand, but pain had already enflamed the other.

My fist cut through the air and I leaned into it with all my weight. The first hit made a crater and a thunderous snap. Smoke sprang out like black ghosts among flames that clawed against my leg.

Good, a dead power suit was good for breaking shit, at least.

For good measure, I punched the same spot and cleared out a two-foot-wide hole. What little fire that showed itself had extinguished with the release of pressure. I hadn't been expecting that, but seeing how this backdraft was intentional, I wasn't going to question serendipity.

"It's done!" I shouted.

I looked back over the way I'd come and groaned softly to myself. Getting back to the ladder was going to suck even worse.

By the time I got to the first rung, Thomlin was climbing down with Little Susie over his shoulder.

"Hey!" I called to him. "Wait for me."

He looked up nervously, and, laying the mannequin over his arms, slid down the ladder like crap through a goose.

"You asshole!"

Hadn't Thomlin ever seen movies where two adversaries in flight school or on a football team bond during a tough training exercise and share the glory of winning together? Didn't he want to put aside our differences and show that, in the end, friendship conquers all?

Yeah, I guess I didn't want that either.

When Thomlin reached the ground, he took off toward the maze's entrance. I put each of my boots to the side of the ladder, and even though my wrist hurt like hell, I grabbed the sides and let gravity do the work.

I'm not sure how far I'd gotten before I hit a snag somewhere and fell from the ladder. Everything was going fine, but then I was airborne, and the ground met me quick.

And it met me hard.

CHAPTER 13

All I wanted to do was take a five-year nap.

No. Make that six years.

With my wrist on ice, I sat on the edge of an examination table in an air-conditioned lab room as Yolanda, the propellerhead, stirred an aqua-blue mixture in a bowl behind me. The injection she'd put in my arm had numbed my body but had also invigorated me like a quadruple espresso shot with a cocaine chaser. Weird combo. But it allowed me to move without crying out in pain.

Puck had been there earlier while I was tenderly peeling my clothes off. She said she wouldn't make me clean the bathrooms until I'd properly healed. Very kind of her.

After I'd fallen from the ladder, the maze walls lowered into the ground, and the other smokies ran in after me. I told them I could walk just fine, but they made me stay flat on my back. Afu grabbed both my legs while Puck and Williams took an arm. I looked at Thomlin as we passed. He had no one but Little Susie to keep him company.

"He'd be dead if it weren't for you," Afu told me as he shifted to get a better hold of my legs.

"Twice," Williams added. "We watched it all on the

wall outside."

Puck remained silent.

I had to hand it to the power suits. They were tough as hell. Unfortunately, I'd irreparably damaged the one I'd been wearing. Hopefully, the smoke eaters weren't going to take it out of my paycheck.

Before she left the lab, I asked Puck if it was fair to punish me, given that I'd killed the dragon and eliminated the backdraft.

"Little Susie was the objective," she said.

I couldn't hide the pissed-offness from my face. "Little Susie would be six feet in the ground if that was a real incident."

"Maybe," she said. "Oh, I had a smoky retrieve your truck. It's parked out front. I assumed you'd want it for the funeral today."

"My truck? So, you guys have added carjacking to your list of talents?"

"Well, maybe you can give me fifty pushups to help you work out your issue with it." With that, Puck left the lab.

I turned to Yolanda as she came over with the bowl of blue goop. "Joke's on her. It'll be at least a month until I heal up."

"I hate to pop your balloon." Yolanda smiled and held up the bowl. "But you'll be good to go sometime this evening. Like nothing happened."

"What the hell are you talking about?"

She lifted my arm. My wrist looked like an eggplant, but the injection had taken the pain away. A spoonful at a time, she slabbed the blue stuff onto my wrist, and tiny, icy tingles rippled through my bones.

"This solution," Yolanda said, as she began to wrap my arm with gauze, "It's like a super antihistamine and cell booster. It's called Ieiunium curate."

I raised an eyebrow. "So... like... super healing?"

"Close enough."

"Think you can rub some of that on my knee?"

She shrugged and put some on the knee I'd pointed out. "Rub it in."

Yolanda was still wrapping my wrist when I heard a commotion outside the lab. Through the long window, I saw Naveena stomp past, at the edge of tears. Renfro chased behind her, holding out his hands like he was trying to console her, but his voice boomed like he was shouting.

Naveena turned on Renfro and shoved him several feet away. The red-eyed man had to steady himself so as not to fall. Naveena had to be strong as hell to nearly topple a guy as big as Renfro.

"Oh, my." Yolanda said beside me, looking through the window.

Naveena turned and stared into the lab, at me. But the fierce death glare I would have expected was missing. Instead, she looked... sad. And hurt. Not the pain I'd suffered with my wrist; this was deeper, something a spoonful of blue wonder gel wouldn't be able to fix.

I don't know how I knew. Maybe it was that body language book I'd read.

Naveena ran, but Renfro stayed, shaking his head.

"You done with me?" I asked Yolanda.

"Hm?" She turned. "Oh, yeah. You're good to go."

"Thanks."

I stepped out into the hall. Renfro's eyes glowed like coals in the fire. He tried to change his demeanor when he saw me, but it was too late.

He pointed to my wrist. "What happened to you?"

"I'll be fine. What's with Naveena?"

He paused, mouth open, like he was about to lie or make an excuse, but then he sighed and crossed his arms. "You saw that, huh?"

"Are you two...?"

"No!" He shivered as if a draft blew in. Naveena was attractive enough that I wouldn't have expected such a look of disgust. "A dragon call got to her. That's all."

"Happens to the best of us." I nodded.

"It doesn't happen to Naveena. I've never seen her like this."

"It hits hardest with the ones who put on a tough act. What happened?"

He stared at me for a second – he could have been a hypnotist with those damn glowing eyes. "It was a kid," he finally said.

"Shit."

I'd had a few calls where a kid died. They haunt you like a wraith.

"Little boy." Renfro shook his head, almost crying. "We didn't get to him in time and–"

"You don't have to talk about it." I patted him on the shoulder.

"Naveena went nuts on that dragon. Chopped it to hell. There was nothing left but a pile of meat and blood. She's lost it. You think I have crazy-looking eyes? Look at hers. Off-the-rails-bat-shit lunatic."

"OK," I said. "I get it."

"I told her that she needs to talk to someone. But she won't listen to me. What worries me is that now she's done killing that dragon, she'll look for someone else to blame."

"And she'll blame herself, right?"

"Exactly."

I took a deep breath, wondering if I should step into the middle of this cesspit. I mean, it wasn't like Naveena and I were best friends. We shared a room where I was afraid to say anything or even have my bed squeak.

"Just give her a few days," I said. "If she's still like this, you can report it."

He clenched his teeth before saying, "I should report it now."

"No, man." I waved that nonsense away. "You don't want to dump betrayal on top of all the shit she's dealing with right now. Just wait. I sleep in the same room. If I see an opportunity, I'll..." I couldn't believe what I was about to say. "... I'll talk to her."

Renfro widened his glowing eyes. "For real?"

"Yeah."

That seemed to put him at ease. He smiled a little and nodded once, like something had been fixed. "I appreciate you, Brannigan."

"Brotherhood," I said, and made the long trip to my truck out front.

Even though I'd griped at Puck about taking my truck without permission, I was glad to have a taste of my old life, on my way to say goodbye to my brother and sister firefighters. My bandaged wrist only hampered my steering a little, and as empty as the road was, it didn't matter how recklessly I swerved. The drive gave me time to clear my head, although I kept imagining Theresa's wraith every few minutes. But it wasn't the schizoid image of her that DeShawn had set up his light show to avoid. I hadn't lost my marbles yet. I knew the difference between ghosts of the mind and ones that could actually decapitate you, scanning each side of the road for any as I drove toward the city.

Every so often a flash of orange deep in the distance would cause me to jerk my head in that direction, but the flames wouldn't be there, and neither were any scaled monsters scurrying across the ash. I hoped it was just my imagination. It was pretty stupid to be driving out there by myself. If the dragons didn't get me, the under-serviced roads would.

I hammered the accelerator.

A sizeable crowd had gathered outside the funeral home, and a whole row of fire apparatus took up most of the parking spaces, except for three that had been positioned directly outside the funeral home's back door.

Theresa's last ride on the fire engine.

Inside, a cluster of firefighters ribbed me about my smoke eater uniform and how it made me look like a walking pickle. I gigged them back with all the dirt I had on them. Then they asked how many dragons I'd killed. I just said I'd lost count.

We did all this in hushed voices. It was par for a firefighter funeral, but we still wanted to be respectful.

I shook the firefighter hands I needed to shake and asked the same old, "How have you been?" and "How long do you have until retirement?" That last question gave more than a few old firefighters pause; it soured their grapes. They smiled, of course, but didn't answer, choosing instead to walk away to shake more hands and ask more bullshit, ceremonial questions they really didn't care about knowing the answers to. I thought I'd been playing along like a good boy. But something was wrong.

"Glad you made it out, Cap."

I turned to see DeShawn dressed to the nines in a black, pin-striped suit, bald, brown head shining in the funeral home's too-bright chandelier. He reminded me of one of those televangelists that used to be on the Feed, before Congress passed laws to ban them from media.

"You know I'd be here." I shook his hand.

He smiled. "Theresa's segment is first. Her husband asked me to give her eulogy. Said it would be fitting, since we were on the same crew and I'm going into the ministry anyway."

I cocked my head to the side and stared at his proud face for a second. "Are you sure that's a good idea. I mean, with you and Theresa having been–"

"I've repented of my sins. Well, I still have some things to check off, but overall, dub, I feel free."

"Yeah," I dragged the word out as I tried to wrap my mind around his decision. "But I think preaching at a funeral for the woman you were," I looked around for anyone close enough to hear, "banging adulterously is something the Lord wouldn't like."

He put his hand on my shoulder. "I'm a different person now. I'm clean. This is my fresh start. And it's a fresh start for you, too, yeah? As a smoke eater. Good thing. Mayor Rogola just signed every firefighter out the door this morning. This is their last week before the fire droids step in."

"You've got to be kidding me."

"Nope. You and I got out just in time."

I wanted to scream, to break something, but I could only shake my head; my mouth drooped open. That's why everyone was so miffed when I brought up retirement. They'd be getting pink slips instead.

"Come on," DeShawn said. "Find a seat. We're going to start."

I found a seat by a female engineer that Sherry had once been murderously jealous of. It made no sense because the engineer, while being a hell of a driver and operator, was fifty pounds over my personal taste in women and played exclusively for the other team. A snowball would have a better chance inside a scaly's throat than any man would have in getting into this engineer's pants. But wives have their own logic.

Holding gold-plated pickhead axes, our department's honor guard stood at each side of Theresa's closed casket.

The casket floated above a platform that would allow easy transport out of the building and then onto the hose bed of the awaiting fire engine. My morbid mind wondered how much of Theresa's burned corpse they'd been able to find before quarantining the neighborhood.

When DeShawn walked behind the pulpit, the honor guard marched out with quiet steps.

"Theresa Renee Parker," DeShawn began, "was a firefighter."

"Yes!" came a cry from a woman behind me.

DeShawn nodded, clearly enjoying himself.

Some people turn to all sorts of drugs after a tragedy: cocaine, digital heroin, religion. But I think the last one is the most dangerous, because it doesn't affect the physical body. It doesn't affect the spirit either. But it does surge the ego to astronomical heights, to where you can't help but see that every living thing is beneath you.

DeShawn was a junkie, same as any other.

"She cared for her city," DeShawn said.

More hoots of praise and agreement.

DeShawn stepped away from the pulpit and raised a hand over Theresa's casket. "She died so others might live!"

This was getting ridiculous.

I shifted in my seat, and looked behind me to the door. Several of Theresa's family members were on their feet and raising their hands in the air. All we needed was a couple tambourines and we could start a band.

"But I fear that to properly put her soul to rest," DeShawn said, "I must confess something before all of you and God Almighty."

I shook my head furiously, trying to get DeShawn to look at me and catch the hint, but I think he was actively avoiding my line of sight.

"Orlando," DeShawn held hands out to Theresa's

husband, who had been crying softly to himself, but now showed the curiosity of an angry badger. "Theresa and I were sexually involved for the last couple years."

A scream sprang from behind me amid the shuffle of people stumbling over chairs, followed by a plop against the funeral home carpet. Someone had fainted.

I stood to leave.

"Please forgive us," DeShawn said with a smile on his face, like he'd baked the poor widower a cake. "Theresa's soul will be–"

Orlando's huge fist stopped DeShawn's mouth from blathering on. Theresa's husband had rushed DeShawn so quickly none of us could stop him. I can't say DeShawn didn't deserve the attack, and part of me thought he'd wanted this to happen, but when my former firefighter hit the ground and Orlando began kicking DeShawn's side, I had to put a stop to it before I'd have to attend another damn funeral.

More people shouted and scattered like ants while several firefighters stood against a wall and shared a flask as they watched the show.

The kilt-wearing pipe and drum band marched in, adding the spine-shattering whine of bagpipes to the commotion. I didn't know if the band had mistakenly received their cue to enter or if they knew this would be the last time they'd play a funeral and figured their musical styling went well with a kerfuffle. Orlando even began kicking DeShawn to the beat of the big drum.

I grabbed both of Orlando's shoulders, firmly but calmly. I only wanted to calm him down. But he was in full-on rage mode and immediately spun around, clocking me across the chin. The chaos inside the funeral home dropped to dead silence, and all eyes fell on me. I stood straight and flexed my fists, ignoring the ache vibrating through my head.

The look I gave Orlando must have scared him pretty good, because he opened both hands to me in supplication. "Captain Brannigan, I didn't mean it. I was just so mad. Please. I'm done now."

"You're damn right you're done!" I stomped over to DeShawn, trying to keep my balance. Orlando had a hell of a right hook.

DeShawn looked up to me with blood staining his teeth. "My burden has been taken from me. I am a new man."

"Your ass got kicked," I said. "And you're a goddamned idiot."

"I'll pray for you," DeShawn said, the smile gone.

"Yeah." I helped him up and embraced him, the kind of squeeze you give someone you know you're never going to see again.

I turned and pushed my way through the crowd, back to my truck, and then Smoke Eater Headquarters where things made relatively more sense.

DeShawn was right, though. The man I'd known, fought hell with, was gone, even though his body had made it out of that fire. Some people are so afraid of the darkness they'll run headlong into the light and never realize it's burnt them to a crisp.

CHAPTER 14

It was still early when I got back to headquarters, but my room was dark, and the hallway light showed Naveena under her covers, flat on her stomach. I watched to make sure she was still breathing, and then got into bed myself. Like Naveena, I wanted the day behind me as quickly as possible. I fell asleep.

The thing about falling asleep early in the evening, at least for me, is that you end up wide awake at two o'clock in the morning, and after a dreamless sleep I sat up in my bed. Even in the darkness, without the aid of a clock, I was sure 2 AM was a good guess at the time.

My holoreader said it was 1:48. Damn, I'm good.

I turned and faced Naveena's bed. Her breath rose and fell, slow and rhythmic, even though I couldn't see her at all.

All four of the room's walls burst into a throbbing red glow while a shrill alarm bounced off them. Naveena didn't stir, but the pulsing light showed she was facing me and her eyes were wide open. I might have spent more time wondering if she'd been staring at me the whole time, but instead I hurried over and knelt in front of her.

Words scrolled around the room, across the walls – Naveena's name and the address of some orphanage.

Parentless kids were on the rise; so much so, the

government decided to do away with foster homes and make like it was the first depression by throwing masses of them into multi-storied buildings under the watchful robotic eyes of nanny droids.

And now the dragons were visiting.

"Naveena," I shouted over the alarm. "You have a call."

She stared at me for another minute before sitting up violently and slapping her hand against the wall by her bed. After holding it there for a few seconds, the red light and alarm disappeared. Her bed squeaked as she lay back down and turned over.

I raised my hands, even though she couldn't see it. "What the fuck?"

She didn't respond.

I tried again. "Those kids need you. You have to go."

Still nothing.

I looked around in the dark, as if there was someone else around to convince her. Then I got a crazy idea and found my way to the door. If Naveena wasn't going to make this call, I'd do it for her.

Still in my socks, I made it to the slayer bay as Renfro paced in his power suit outside the cannon truck.

"Where's Naveena?" he shouted at me, as if it was my fault.

"She's not coming," I said. "But you have me."

"Oh, hell no!" He began pacing again, shaking his head this time. "You aren't fully trained. We'd both get reamed and suspended."

I opened the bin where a power suit waited. "Sounds better than what might happen to those orphans if we don't hurry up."

Renfro stopped pacing and opted for groaning instead.

I secured my suit and helmet, and walked around to the passenger side. Renfro didn't stop me, but spewed a string of swear words as he hopped behind the wheel.

CHAPTER 15

A crowd of people had gathered outside a ten-story building when we pulled up. Most of them wore robes or pajamas. One guy was walking around with nothing but loose boxers and a bubble vape in his lips. It always amazed me how people would stick their noses into emergencies but would never do anything to help, besides point their fingers as if we couldn't see what was going on.

Renfro and I were the only smoke eaters.

"Just us then?" I asked.

Renfro grumbled and nodded. "Our other smokies are fighting dragons in different parts of the state. We're on our own."

"They're everywhere!" a woman in a pink robe screamed at us as we got out of the truck. "Kids are still in there."

Flames danced behind a few of the upper story windows. No smoke. The fire had no pattern, though. Different floors burned while others had been untouched. I'd never seen such disconnected fire, besides a few arson cases during the corporate wars. Behind the building, the full moon watched.

I hoped it wasn't a wyrm inside that building.

Renfro put a hand on each of the frantic woman's

shoulders. "How many kids are in there?"

"Seven... I think."

"You think?" I said.

"It's the middle of the night," she snapped. "I had to get out too."

"Anybody else?" Renfro asked.

The woman shook her head. "Just the droids."

"Did you see the dragons?" Renfro asked. "What did they look like?"

Glass shattered from above, and what looked like a pterodactyl screeched into the night, flapping its tiny wings and holding onto a screaming little girl's leg as she dangled over the gasping crowd. The shards of glass hit the street, but the dragon kept flying.

My jaw dropped. Yolanda had been right all along.

The little girl swatted at the scaly, but couldn't reach far enough to land a hit. It didn't matter, though. The dragon dropped her.

The crowd screamed.

I said, "I got her!" and power jumped toward the falling orphan.

The girl didn't make a sound, and she dropped so fast, I almost missed her. With one hand, I snagged the girl around the waist and tucked her in to my chest before scraping down the side of the orphanage.

Wobbly, but able to stand on her own, the girl looked at me with saucer-sized eyes. Smoke stained her face, and she coughed several times before asking, "Am I OK?"

"Yeah," I patted her back. "You're just fine. Go find the lady who runs this place."

She scampered into the crowd, and I turned to find Renfro.

The scaly hovered fifty feet above me, breathing a stream of fire that caused me to crouch. Renfro jumped at the dragon, firing his laser gun and foam at the same time. When the dragon moved its flames toward him, it caught a wad of foam in the throat that killed the fire. One of the lasers ripped through the dragon's wing, and the scaly screeched as it spiraled to the street. I ran to where it had landed, still alive and snapping its teeth at my boots. When the dragon began crawling toward me, sputtering flames from its mouth, I stomped on the bastard's head until it quit squawking.

The dragon was small, about the size of a Labrador – a Labrador with bat wings and an alligator's mouth.

"Come on," Renfro said, running up to me. "There are more inside."

I couldn't take my eyes off the dead scaly's crumpled wings. "They're not supposed to fly."

"We'll figure that out later."

I shook myself back into the moment and pointed to the broken window in the upper floor. "Think we should start there?"

"As long as you can make the jump." Renfro checked his power level before launching toward the window.

It was one of those times I should have made the sign of the cross or kissed a pendant or something. Instead, I said, "Ah, fuck," and sailed into the air, following Renfro's arc.

I landed at the edge of the broken window, and Renfro had to grab my arm to keep me from falling backward.

"Thanks," I said.

In the dark, Renfro's eyes glowed red.

I engaged my laser sword and followed him through the dark hallway. The building's power had been killed, and the smoke was cotton-thick. We breathed it with ease. Our thermal goggles showed nothing besides a few places where fires grew, but we ignored them, still checking each room we came to for signs of life. I could hear the distant screaming of something, but I couldn't tell if it was a bunch of orphans or scalies.

When we rounded a corner, I stepped on something hard and bulky.

"Settle down, children." It was a nanny droid on its side, burned and cracked open like the egg it was shaped like. It waved a humanoid finger at us as if we were in trouble and due for a time out.

"These stupid things," I said.

Renfro raised his head to the ceiling. "Next floor up. The other six kids are trapped in a room. A shitload of scalies in the hall outside."

I looked up as well. A cluster of blue blobs was gathered in a room, trying to keep the door closed as a cluster of flapping red blobs bombarded it like a military airstrike. The kids wouldn't last long if we didn't hurry.

We entered the next floor up. The scalies at the end of the hall stopped attacking the door. Resting on the floor or hanging from the ceiling, they stared at us. One of them screeched and flew at us like a dart, snapping its jaws. I swung my sword with a quick phhmm and severed its head. The body skidded along the floor behind us, leaving a trail of blood and a sulfuric stench.

That just pissed the rest of them off.

Screaming and flapping like a bunch of hippies who'd taken bad acid, they filled the hall in a dark vortex. Renfro fired his lasers, only grounding a couple. I got ready to slash my sword as many times as I needed to.

They hit us full force, pushing us to the ground. Even though we'd taken out several of the scalies with gun or sword, there were still too many for us to attack at once. I covered my face and blindly swung, but the dragons weren't even trying to bite my head or blow fire at my face. Instead, they concentrated on my sword arm, ripping at it with their teeth, or torching the armor before I was able to fling them off.

When I stabbed one dragon in the throat, another bit deep into my arm, and my sword went dead, evaporating into the dark.

Oh, shit.

"They took out my guns!" Renfro screamed.

As if they knew what they'd done, the dragons screamed in celebration. A flapper landed on my chest, sending me onto the floor, and breathed deep, its chest swelling like flames inside a balloon. I ripped off my helmet and held it in front of my face.

"Cast!" I shouted as flames curled around my fingers, lapping at my cheeks. "Mayday, mayday, mayday. Brannigan and Renfro. We're in trouble at the orphanage. We're on the fourth floor, east side."

I just hoped the helmet radio picked up my traffic, and that someone was listening.

When the dragon on my chest stopped breathing its fire and inhaled for another go, I thrust my helmet into its maw and heard a crack. I'd broken the scaly's neck. "Eat that, you bastard!"

The other flappers gnawed at my head, one nipping the end of my ear, as I rolled over and swatted away the ones swarming Renfro. He had one scaly in his grip and punched it repeatedly.

"Let's go." I secured my helmet.

"Where?"

"With the kids in that room."

He began crawling toward the other end of the hall, fighting against the scalies to get to his feet.

I squished a couple of the flappers into the wall with my shoulder before jumping into a run. Behind us, the dragons clawed against the wall. When we got to the door, it barely budged.

"Back up, kids," Renfro shouted. He pushed his way in.

One of the dragons flew from the wall, aiming for me. I ducked the attack and followed behind Renfro before closing the door. Inside, I couldn't see the kids' faces – two boys and four girls – but the moon shining through the window illuminated the tops of their heads and a few toys scattered on the floor.

I leaned against the weakening wood and said, "Dragons aren't supposed to fly."

"Don't mind him," Renfro told the children huddled together. "He's new."

I ran over to the window and punched it out. The cool air rushed in as I got a good view of the surrounding, ash-covered neighborhood, peaceful and unaware of the horrible shit we were in.

"What are you doing?" Renfro said. "Now these bastards have another way to get to us."

"Watch your language, dub," I said.

Renfro looked to the orphans. "Oh, yeah. Sorry, kids."

"Anyway," I said, "now we have a way out of here."

"We can't power jump with kids in our arms."

"Why not?"

Renfro groaned. "Can you count? Plus, they're too big and it's too dangerous."

"We can't leave them here," I said.

"I know," Renfro whispered. "But we're low on options right now."

"What if we made more than one trip?" I suggested.

"You barely made the jump to the floor below us. Plus, those sonsabit–" Renfro looked at the kids. "Those dragons bit all the right places in my suit. My power is draining."

"Yeah, mine, too," I said. "Would be great if we had a couple lances right now, huh?"

"They're coming from the basement," one of the kids said. "They won't stop."

"Coming?" Renfro asked. "There are more?"

The kid pointed to a laundry chute that had been tied closed with a Slinky.

I had to hand it to these kids, they were handling the situation like professionals, but I should have guessed as much. They hadn't become orphans from Mom and Dad overdosing on sleeping pills or being in a car accident. Dragons had taken their families. They were used to scalies and the death they brought with them.

"We heard them break through the basement," one of the girls said. "We snuck down to see. There's a big, fiery sinkhole they're coming from."

"Sinkhole?" Renfro looked at me. "This building could collapse any minute."

The girl pointed to the laundry chute. "We can hear more of them coming out."

All of us got quiet and I stared at the rednecked, Slinky lock. I took slow steps toward the laundry chute and held out my hand. If more of those flappers were coming out of the ground, I wanted to know about it.

Behind me, someone's breath quickened as I neared the chute, and I was pretty sure it was Renfro.

I grabbed the chute's handle, ready to pull it open.

Bang!

Wings rattled the chute, as if a thousand rabid sparrows flew toward the roof.

I turned to the kids. "OK, I believe you."

Hard hits rattled the door behind us, almost ripping it off its hinges. Renfro and I both ran to hold it shut.

A snout split the wood, stuck in the crack. The dragon screeched and clawed to remove itself from the door, so I decided to help it out with an armored fist. It fell away, but more of them battered the door, and smoke began to curl from the bottom.

I gave Renfro a look that said, We're fucked! He

returned me the same.

We could have opened the door and tried to fight the scalies off, but the orphans didn't have the benefit of power suits. And I sure as hell wasn't like Thomlin. I wasn't going to sacrifice a bunch of kids just to save my own ass.

I stared longingly at the window I'd broken, still considering grabbing three of the kids and leaping to the ground, when the tip of an aerial ladder appeared just outside.

"Hot damn!" I touched my lips and glanced at the kids. "I mean, hot dang!"

I told Renfro to hold the door as I ran to look out the window.

Truck 1 had arrived on scene and the crew was climbing up the ladder, fully geared up. It went against every department protocol. But there wouldn't be a department as of seven o'clock that morning. These guys were saints.

The captain met me at the window, wearing his air mask. I'd lost count of what shift it was, but I realized from his bulging gut, it was the same guy from a few days before. The one whose job I'd saved.

"Need a little help?" The mask muffled his voice, but I'd learned how to decipher SCBA talk.

"Can you get these kids out of here?" I pointed to the orphans.

He waved his hands to receive them.

I handed off the first kid, who was actually smiling. "And a couple axes, if you don't mind."

Truck 1's captain handed me the pickhead axe he'd been carrying and detached the flathead they carried at the ladder tip. I handed the flathead axe to Renfro, and began hoisting the other kids onto the ladder.

The door behind us exploded in flames.

"Lower the ladder!" I screamed at Truck 1's captain.

With all but one of the orphans out of the room, Renfro turned to face the flood of dragons pouring in, while I raised the last kid, a little boy with a mop of blond hair, to the captain.

One of the scalies flew past Renfro and latched onto the blond boy's shoulders. The kid screamed as he slipped through my hands, but I was able to grab his ankles before the dragon took him on a moonlit flight.

Truck 1's captain dodged the dragon's teeth, unable to make a grab at the boy. I dug my boots into the floor, but the dragon flapped harder and pulled me toward the window. I was afraid the little boy would split in half if neither I nor the dragon relented.

Renfro swung his axe wildly, not used to handling anything besides his laser gun and foam shooter. But after the third try, he chopped the flapper's legs. The boy dropped to the floor and rolled away, but the scaly went berserk, crashing repeatedly into the ceiling and splattering blood all over the room.

Another dragon slammed into my back and bit down on my shoulder. I punched it a couple of times, but seeing how it wasn't letting go and that it wasn't hurting me – yet – I focused on taking out the legless dragon cracking its own skull into the ceiling.

I jumped once and missed as it fluttered away. With my next jump I snagged one of the dragon's bleeding stumps and threw it to the ground. I lifted my axe.

The dragon on my shoulder reared back and breathed fire across the side of my face.

I screamed and rolled, slapping at the fire to put it out. The shouldered dragon didn't let go, and went for a ride as I did what we always told kindergarteners to do if a scaly ever caught their clothes on fire: stop, drop, and lose your shit.

The dragon on my shoulder squawked as if it was having the time of its life.

I got to my knees and grabbed the flapper by the snout, throwing it onto the ground in front of me. It squirmed at first, but an axe to the throat stopped that.

The remaining orphan boy screamed from a corner as Truck 1's captain leaned through the window with a useless stretch of his arm. The legless dragon was army-crawling toward the kid, only a couple feet away, snapping and frothing smoke from its nostrils.

I jumped at the scaly as it readied its fire breath, piercing its back with the pick of my axe. Grabbing the boy, I threw him into the truck captain's arms and turned to retrieve my weapon.

As I was pulling my axe free, another dragon flew in, stinging my eyes with the tip of its wings.

I thought for sure I'd been permanently blinded, but I only spent a moment stumbling around the room with my hand out in front of me, hoping Renfro didn't bury his axe into my neck. A dragon's mouth bit down on my arm instead, jerking me all over the room, slamming me into the walls and a dresser that had caught fire.

I was sure this would be the room where I died. I guess it wasn't a bad way to go – we'd saved a bunch of orphans. But I'd always thought I'd die mid-orgasm, and I was kind of sad a bunch of winged assholes were going to be my ruin.

Despite the noise and violence, I heard the pew pew of a laser gun. Renfro's guns were trashed, which meant it could only have been–

"Brannigan, get down!" Donahue shouted at me through the doorway. He stood among the corpses of several dragons, and was taking aim at the one on my arm.

I dropped to the floor.

Donahue's shot hit the dragon between the eyes, just

inches from my arm. The chief helped me up and blasted two dragons off Renfro.

Puck came in and cut down the rest of the scalies with her sword. "Out the window. Now!"

She didn't have to tell me twice. After three bounding steps, I launched toward the ground outside. The other smokies followed just behind me, landing in a clink, clink, clink of metallic rhythm. Puck held a dead scaly by the throat.

Renfro turned to Donahue. "The kids told us more keep emerging from a sinkhole in the basement. That they won't stop."

"We'll make 'em stop." Chief Donahue pointed to Sergeant Puck. "You and Brannigan clear the area. Me and Renfro will get the cannon ready."

"Are you sure that's safe?" I asked. The building was unstable as it was, but adding firepower to it seemed like a bad idea.

"Shut up and do what you're told." Donahue said. "You shouldn't even be out here, but don't worry, we'll take care of that later."

Order up! Shit sandwich to go for a Mr Brannigan.

I followed Puck, who was strangely silent. We told the crowd to get as far away from the building as possible. No sugar-coating was needed. People tend to scatter when you tell them you're about to blow a nearby building to hell. The dead dragon in Puck's fist helped too.

After the area was clear, I drove Slayer 3, which Donahue and Puck had arrived in, to a safer spot. As the cannon truck moved into firing position, I walked over to Truck 1's captain and thanked him for showing up.

"Not a problem," he told me. "We were parked nearby to watch. I scan the smoke eater dispatch when nothing is on the Feed or if I can't sleep. You're lucky this was one of those times."

"That's illegal, isn't it?" I knew the smokies would be pissed if they realized outsiders could listen in on their calls.

The captain smiled. "I won't tell if you won't. I know it was you who saved my job, for a while anyway. Let's consider us square."

We shook hands and let that be the end of it.

An electrical sound rose in pitch behind me. The cannon glowed green at the base of the barrel, where Donahue stood at a trigger that looked like a racecar steering wheel. When the noise could rise no higher, Donahue pulled the trigger, firing a huge streak of green, iridescent light across the parking lot.

The cannon fire hit the bottom of the high-rise, and the building collapsed at once, no hesitation, no delay. In seconds, chunks of concrete fell and clouds of dust rose into the moonlit night. When the air cleared, a few distant car alarms were going off, and the crowd, watching behind the cannon truck, either cheered or shouted for us to be arrested. There were at least a few quips about our mothers. If none of those people had been at the protests, we'd just added more to their ranks.

Some folks you just can't please.

I listened for any dragon shrieks or the flapping of wings, watched the moon for any escaping flapper crossing its face. Nothing.

I limped over to Donahue as he climbed down from the cannon truck. "Those scalies could fly," I said. "Yolanda said this was a possibility. We're in deep shit if there are more like them. Bigger ones than them."

"Puck's going to give that dead one to the propellerheads to study." He sighed, his eyes half open. "And if anyone is in trouble, it's you and Naveena."

"She wasn't feeling well," I said. "I filled in for her."

"It doesn't work like that," he shouted. He relaxed his

face, and the next thing he said was much softer. "Get in the truck. You and Naveena need to be in my office in the morning. We're done here."

We both turned from one another, heading to different vehicles.

A news drone buzzed above us. I wondered how much of the incident it had captured for the Feed, and if the smoke eaters had a tradition about getting on the news. In the fire department, you had to bake a cake if you made the Feed.

As Renfro drove us away, hover trucks arrived and deposited fire droids to clean up the mess we'd made. It would be another mark against the smoke eaters, making us look like assholes and showing the robots to be the efficient heroes, who only did what they were programmed to do. They didn't make bad calls, they didn't blow up orphanages.

It was going to give Donahue more teeth to chew my ass with.

Renfro and I were quiet, listening to the noise of the road under us. It wasn't until we pulled into Smoke Eater Headquarters that Renfro looked over to me with his red eyes and said, "Well, at least there won't be any wraiths."

CHAPTER 16

"Never, in all my years, have I seen some shit like this."

Donahue's office looked more like a fire chief's workspace than I thought it would. With all the crap I'd been hearing about how smoke eaters were so different from firefighters, I'd have expected something more... unusual.

An old fire helmet sat atop a shelf. Pictures of Donahue and other firefighters hung from the wall, along with commendations and souvenirs of a different life. I'd been right. Donahue and I weren't that different.

There was one photo on the wall that stood out from the rest: Donahue and three other firefighters standing in front of a dead dragon, its head as long as the men and women, standing shoulder to shoulder, were wide. They weren't smiling.

"Are you listening, Brannigan?" Donahue said.

I'd zoned out while he focused on Naveena, and she was mentally off the planet as well. I'd seen that look before. Her give-a-damn was broken.

"Yes, Chief," I told him. "But I think this is a special situation."

Donahue dropped into his chair. "Enlighten me."

"For one," I cleared my throat. "Naveena had a bad call yesterday, and needed to go through some kind of post-incident debriefing. To talk it out."

Naveena sprang to life. "I don't need any counseling, rookie!"

"I'm not saying that." I held my hands up in defense.

Naveena pointed a finger at me. "You're due for an ass-kicking."

"All right!" Donahue jumped to his feet and slammed palms onto his desk. "Both of you are suspended for a week."

"Chief!" Naveena huffed through her nose.

I just sat there and shrugged. One week. So what?

"Brannigan's right," Donahue said.

Naveena and I both sat up straighter.

"He is?"

"I am?"

Donahue nodded. "Captain Jendal, you should have come and talked to me about it if you were having problems."

"It's not… it wasn't a problem," Naveena said, looking at me as if she hated and respected me for the same reason. "It was just a fluke. It won't happen again."

"Good," Donahue said. "You can take the week to make extra sure it won't."

Naveena groaned and stomped out of Donahue's office.

The chief leaned back in his chair and turned to me, rubbing his chin. "It was a Tuesday morning."

"Huh?"

"E-Day. I don't know if it was the same with your department or shift, but when I was on the job, firefighting, nothing happened on a Tuesday. Maybe some old people would trip on a rug or we had to check out a couple false fire alarms. But that Tuesday was a biggie.

"My crew and I were the first to go in to this school

fire, some elementary school. The whole place was lit up. Chief told us to go search, so we did. Before we could find any kids or teachers, the dragon found us."

"Shit."

Donahue blinked a few times, but he stared at the spot just above me. "The dragon snagged one of us. Rookie. Poor kid hadn't been on a month. My captain and I tried to escape, but the way back was burning, so we holed up in one of the classrooms. Radio traffic was horrible. Everyone talking at the same time.

"My captain finally decided we had to take out the scaly. Said he'd use his axe. I thought he was crazy. And all I had was a pike pole. I told him we should just run, find a way outside and call in the Army Reserve or something. But he couldn't do that. As scared as I was, I couldn't abandon him either.

"We found the dragon outside on the playground. It'd smashed through the doors and was trying to snatch a young woman from under one of those round jungle gyms. My captain and I took off our masks, thinking it would be OK since we were outside the building, had no air left anyway. But smoke was everywhere, like a fog. The woman's screams and the dragon's growling were the only things that let us know we'd found it.

"My captain was coughing bad; snot and spit coming out of him. I told him again we should go. But he didn't listen. He charged the dragon with his axe."

I waited for Donahue to continue. He just kept staring off into space, reliving the past. After a minute I asked, "What happened?"

"He dropped to the ground before he ever reached the dragon. Dead. Smoke got him. I tried to get to him, but the scaly turned and scorched his body." Donahue cleared his throat. "When it started eating, I snuck around and pulled the woman from under the jungle gym. She seemed to be OK, besides being scared half to death, but I was too. I helped her over the fence, and that's when the dragon got my leg."

He knocked knuckles against his metal thigh for emphasis.

"Damn, Chief," I said. "Did you at least get a lick in?"

"I shoved my pike pole into its eye. It dug back underground after that. Thankfully, I always carried some webbing in my turnouts, so I tied off my leg and waited for help."

I whistled. "You're a tough old bastard, Chief."

"I'm telling you all of this because I want you to know that I get it. When things go bad, some people run and some people rush in. After that day, I promised myself I would never even consider running away. You're the same, Brannigan. But what you have to understand is that we have rules for a reason. I thought a fire captain would know that."

I sat there twiddling my thumbs. I'd run out of smartass retorts.

"We're done here, Brannigan. See you a week from Monday. I'm sure your wife will be glad to have you home. Be sure to take your holoreader so you can still study."

"Yeah, sure," I said. "Aren't we going to talk about how dragons can fly?"

Instead of answering me, he twirled his chair around to face the wall.

When I got back to our dorm room, Naveena was punching clothes into a bag.

"What are you doing?" I asked.

"Why do you care?" Punch. Punch.

"Look, I never wanted to get you in trouble," I said. "If it was up to me, that dragon call at the orphanage would have gone over without a hitch, and no one would know besides us and Renfro. Shit just didn't go our way."

She stopped filling her bag and glared at me. It looked like she'd put on eye shadow after she'd left Donahue's office. "And telling Donahue I needed counseling?"

"So he'd go easier on you?" I shrugged. "It always worked for my firefighters."

She sighed. "This isn't–"

"Yeah, I got it."

If I had to hear how smoke eaters were different one more time… well, I was glad to have a free week away.

There was a knock on the open door. Afu stood outside, with Williams crouched under him.

"Hey," Afu said. "Puck's letting us go early for the weekend. You guys want to come party with us?"

"Hell yeah," Naveena said.

I snapped my head toward her. This woman, who'd been basically comatose the previous night while being called to kill dragons, someone who was just packing like a thirteen year-old runaway, wanted to go party with a couple rookies?

"Cool," said Williams. She threw her chin to me. "What about you, old man?"

Sherry had been expecting to see me all week, at least I hoped as much. I was horny, tired, and needed a break. But I hadn't had an outing with friends since I was forty. And that had ended with rug burns and a hangover.

I also didn't want Naveena to do anything crazy. That kid dying clung to her like fungus. She wasn't acting like herself, and for some reason I was compelled to watch over her. She was a sister smoke eater. Most people in our line of work just pay lip service when calling it the Brotherhood. But it actually meant something to me.

"Where are we going?" I asked. I held my head outside the car window, enjoying the breeze, and then a chunk of ash flew into my mouth. I coughed and hacked, nearly choking.

Naveena laughed from the front passenger seat and handed back a bottle of bourbon we'd picked up on the way. "Here, grandpa. Wash it down with this."

I took the bottle and drank.

Beside me, Afu took up most of Williams's two-door coupe, singing along with the weird sounds blaring from the car's speakers. I'd refrained from keeping up with modern music. Shit sounded like a cat dying to a hundred and fifty beats per minute. Williams drove, and had made it clear before heading out that, in her car, boys sat in the back.

I felt like I was in high school again.

"So, this amusement park got shut down a few years ago when a wraith wandered into the funhouse," Williams said. "People freaked and they boarded it up. Thing is, dragons never attacked it. I guess it was a false alarm."

Afu said, "Supposedly, it's still operational."

"And we're going to break in," I said, confirming my theory of how the rest of the day was going to go.

"Yep," Afu said. He dug into the backpack he'd brought along, and removed a baggie with glowing pills that looked like bottled television static. "Who wants to spark?"

Naveena turned in her seat, and as soon as her eyes hit the bag, they widened. She stretched out a hand. "Me!"

"I'm driving," Williams said. "I'll pop one when we get to the park."

"What the hell are those?" I tried to get a better look at the pills in the baggie. They could have been radioactive mints for all I knew.

Afu handed me one. "Sparks. They take hologram tech and shove it into this tiny pill. Recodes your brain.

Anything that bums you out gets wiped, and it ups all your senses. You might cum in your pants if the right breeze blows by."

Sounded like a dangerous combo of a lot of the drugs popular back in my day. And Naveena was about to throw one back.

"Naveena," I said, maybe a little too loudly.

She stopped and looked at me.

"I don't know if that's a good idea."

She sputtered her lips. "It's the best idea all week. And you're not my daddy." She took the bottle of bourbon from my hands and washed down the pill.

The drug hit her instantly. She howled and spread her arms, cranking up the music and bobbing to the racket. The other two laughed and joined in. I pocketed the spark Afu had given me and took back the bourbon. I'd need a lot more of it in my system if I was going to deal with these people for the next few hours.

"This is to celebrate Naveena and Brannigan's suspension." Afu popped another of the sparks and dry-swallowed it.

I took another swig of the bourbon in sympathy.

"There it is." Williams pointed through the windshield.

Amid the ashes, a Ferris wheel towered over a fenced-in lot that guarded roller coasters and the other amusement park basics. I remembered the park – Cedar Point. I hadn't been there since I was ten years old, when I threw up on the tilt-a-whirl. Besides a generous touch of mildew on the wood, the place hadn't changed much.

Lake Erie surrounded us.

"I say we hit a roller coaster first," Afu said. His voice was more bubbly than normal, and his eyes looked somewhere I could never see, unless I popped one of those hologram pills.

Naveena moved her arms to the music. "You have to

race me there first."

"Wait," I said. "We're not actually going to ride any of that rundown shit, are we?"

"Wouldn't come out here for nothing," Williams said. She parked the coupe outside the side gate. It had been locked with several chains, and a posted sign declared the area to be condemned. It didn't mention why.

A fucking ghost could have been lurking among rotten corn dogs and funnel cakes for all I knew.

Williams got out and folded her seat to let me exit. Naveena did the same for Afu. I stayed in my seat and watched the women sashay to the gate as Afu opened the trunk. With a sigh and another drink of bourbon, I got out and followed the ladies.

Naveena tugged on the tightly secured chains and laughed so hard she fell on her ass.

"Looks like we're out of luck," I said. "Let's go do something a little less stupid, like human sacrifice."

"This won't take but a second." Afu walked past me, wearing the arm of a power suit. He hit a button and a laser sword extended.

"Hell yeah!" Naveena shouted, and got out of his way.

"Are you stealing equipment now?" I hated feeling like the buzzkill, especially given my age. But damn it, somebody had to have a little sense here.

"No, man," Afu said. "I'm offended you'd think so. This is from your wrecked power suit. I help the propellerheads fix them sometimes. We're just borrowing it."

He slashed the chains, and they dropped instantly, the cut ends glowing like lit fuses. The sword died a second later.

Afu shook the power arm. "Damn. Battery didn't last as long as I thought it would."

Seeing that I was stuck in this adventure, I helped

Williams open one side of the gate. Afu and Naveena slipped through and raced toward the nearest rollercoaster.

Williams tapped me against the chest and ran away, shouting, "I'm going to go find the power."

Cedar Point smelled strange, different from how I remembered. It had the stink of rotten wood mixed with the surrounding lake, but it was all tainted by this... sourness that might have only been in my mind. A scent that said, You're not supposed to be here.

Dusk was a few hours away.

The face of the Cedar Point mascot – a big-eyed, bowler-hat-wearing hound dog – was plastered over a sign beckoning, "Have a howl of a time!"

I'll keep that in mind, dog.

Lights sprang to life all around me, followed by the drawl of ancient, carnival music. I think the singer's name was Marvin Gaye.

The roller coaster, the Iron Dragon, stood a long walk down a cracked-asphalt path. Afu manned the controls as the top-mounted cars waited on a pair of rusty, inverted tracks.

"I want to sit in the very front." Naveena made her way through the labyrinth of metal poles that patrons used to slowly march through. "Sit with me, Brannigan."

I swallowed. "Maybe we should run the coaster by itself. You know, to make sure it's still safe."

"Fuck that," Naveena said, raising the lapbar.

"Wait," Afu said. "That's a good idea."

Naveena huffed and backed away, as Afu pushed a button and sent the coaster on its trial run. We all huddled behind Afu and watched the coaster mount the rise with its slow click, click, click. A minute later it dropped down the other side and swooped through the rest of the track. As it made its way around the last curve, the wheels sparked against the track and the Iron Dragon flew off, crashing through the side rail before plummeting to the dry lagoon below.

There was a lot of noise and dust, but no fire.

Naveena and Afu laughed their asses off and pointed at the crash. I looked at what could have been a really crummy death, especially thinking about what Sherry would have thought – why I hadn't come straight home and why I decided to go on a bender with a bunch of drughead dragon slayers half my age.

Williams jogged up the steps and asked, "What was that?"

"Side effects," I said with a frown.

"Let's go find something else to ride." Naveena pushed past me.

I saw an old favorite, one that wouldn't make me puke or be decapitated. "The carousel," I said.

"You're cool, Brannigan," Williams shook her head, "but sometimes you're just too damn old."

"Look at it this way," I said, "if it doesn't work, we won't be crashing into the funnel cake stand."

"I'm in." Naveena swung under the metal dividers and ran toward the carousel, shouting back, "I want to push the button."

Afu shrugged and wrapped an arm around Williams. When we got to the carousel, Naveena was digging around the control booth.

"Want me to help you?" Afu asked.

Naveena shot him a warhead of a look.

The big guy raised his hands and backed away. He turned to Williams. "Want to come find a horse?"

"Shit," Williams said. "I want one of those big seats and another spark."

They headed off, and I waited for Naveena, leaning my back against the control booth. I don't know why

I stayed. We sure as shit weren't a couple. Hell, I don't even think Afu and Williams were an official item either. But a dynamic had been created by drugs, booze, and an even pairing of male and female.

"There!" Naveena said, lifting her head and flicking her hair back. She smiled at me, and a weird feeling settled in my gut.

The carousel lights sparkled as it began to spin, the horses and dolphins and other animals rising and falling as they raced in an unwinnable contest.

"Come on," Naveena told me, jumping on the carousel as it picked up speed.

Of course, I followed right behind her.

We passed Afu and Williams, who sat in a clam-shaped seat. They'd been kissing, but stopped to giggle and hide their faces when we walked by.

"What do you want to ride?" Naveena asked me, appraising the selection.

I stood beside a winged dragon bobbing up and down, but shook my head. "Let's go classic. How about those horses over there."

"OK."

Naveena took the inside horse, a red-painted mount with its tongue hanging out. I took the gray one beside it. A song played from the speakers, one from long before I was born, but I knew it thanks to my grandpa, who'd played me all kinds of olden tunes.

"Man," I said, holding on to my horse's pole with both hands. "This song is an oldie but a goodie."

"So are you." She smiled, but then looked away and said, "What's the name of the song?"

I thought for a second. "I forget the guy who sings it, but it's called 'Fooled Around and Fell in Love.'"

"Did you dance to it at your prom?"

"Shit." I laughed. "It was recorded like a hundred and

fifty years ago."

We rode together for a few minutes, hearing about a guy who considered himself a player, never settling with one girl, but who fucked up anyway and fell in love. I kept my eyes forward, actually starting to enjoy myself, taking in the centrifugal pull of the carousel and the equally strong tug of the bourbon. The lights above were hypnotic, even though they twitched and threatened to die. The last thing I expected to feel was the cool touch of Naveena's hand.

I scrunched my eyebrows and looked at our linked fingers first, then moved up to Naveena's face as she moved in for a kiss. I tried to retreat, and maybe it was the bourbon, but I slipped the other way and fell right into her lips.

High as she was, she didn't notice it was an accident. She pulled back, leaning in to her fake horse, smiling wide. Her eyes sparkled with carousel lights.

I turned and faced the front of the horse as the ride slowed to a stop.

Oh, shit.

CHAPTER 17

I made up a dumb excuse to go back to the car – claiming to want more bourbon – while Naveena and the others broke into an abandoned concession stand, searching for cotton candy. They said that it was the only type of fair food most likely not to have spoiled. Williams had thrown me her keys so I could unlock the coupe.

The real reason I went to the car was quite the opposite. I wanted to clear my head, regretted drinking in the first place. My best hope was that Naveena would forget anything had happened between us and would return to her regular, grumpy self by the time I saw her the next week.

But what about me?

I wouldn't forget. Bourbon or no. Leaning against the trunk of the coupe, I started wondering if I even wanted to forget. Naveena was swelteringly attractive, and it wasn't like Sherry had been Mrs Wonderful to me lately. What if I went ahead and took Naveena into the tunnel of love and did what came naturally?

No.

What the hell was I thinking? Not only was I married, but Naveena was under the influence of some fucked up, William Gibson shit.

A holoreader rang from the back seat.

Afu had left his backpack in the car, and I knew the sound of the alarm issuing from inside. His holoreader vibrated even as I lifted it from his bag. A flashing red notification said that all available smoke eaters were needed at the address of–

No. No way. This couldn't be happening. Afu had to have slipped me a spark. Hallucinations, yeah, that was it.

I rubbed my eyes and looked again. No mistake this time. A dragon was attacking my house.

Sherry.

I threw the holoreader onto the seat and jumped behind the wheel. Ash flew as I pressed the gas pedal as far as it would go. Williams and the others could be pissed at me all they wanted.

My house.

Multiple smoke eater apparatus filled my street. I had to ditch Williams' car a few blocks down. Smokies I'd never met aimed cannon trucks or huddled together for a plan of attack, while black smoke and flames consumed my house.

They'd set up a laser barrier to block off the scene. It flashed red when I ran through it, and a smoke eater stopped me with an armored hand against my chest.

"Need you to get back, sir," he said to me, annoyed and eager to catch up with his crew that jogged toward the fire.

"That's my house, jackass. And I'm a smoke eater."

He leaned back to study my face. "I don't know you."

"Just ask Donahue," I said, pushing past him. "Where's my wife?"

Smoke eaters stood on my yard and the street out front. A news drone flew in, buzzing, chirping, and pointing its huge lens at my disintegrating abode. One of the smoke eaters power jumped to swat it down. The robot camera maneuvered out of the way and settled on recording the action from a higher vantage.

Gaping holes and jagged glass hung where my windows used to be, including the one that had gotten fixed. The front door stood wide, as the flames grew brighter, more violent. The smoke churned out of every orifice. There was no saving my home, and there was no saving anyone who might have still been inside.

Sherry.

A booming roar came from inside, and then the earth shook as if God was sending my house to hell. I tripped and scraped my knee, tore my pants, cursing, but I could barely hear my own voice over the shaking earth.

When the ground stilled, I got to my feet and grabbed a passing smoke eater by the shoulder. "Where's my wife?"

"Hey, pal," he said, "I just got here."

"She was inside!"

He pointed down the road. "Check the ambulance."

I ran toward the ambulance. A house was just a box to stuff your shit. Let it burn. I only wanted Sherry.

When I made it to the ambulance, the back doors opened and an EMT hopped out, starting when he noticed me.

"My... wife," I got out between huffs of air.

He looked into the back of the box, where Sherry lay on a stretcher, face covered in soot. Kenji sat on her lap, looking around with his rubber tongue dangling excitedly.

I didn't wait for the EMT to speak. I pushed him out of the way and knelt beside Sherry, grabbing her hand.

"Our house," she said, beginning to cry.

I swallowed a lump in my throat. I preferred anger to sobs. "I don't give a shit about the house," I said. "I'm just glad you're OK."

"Language," Sherry said.

Kenji barked and said, "Dangsin-eun eodie iss-eossneunji, deomi?"

Sherry hacked up black phlegm. Wincing, she wiped it off on the blanket the EMTs had covered her with. "The holo stereo–"

"Sir, I know you're upset," the EMT from outside poked his head into the back. "But you need to let us treat her."

I spun on him. "Kiss my ass!"

"Cole," Sherry said.

"I'm calling the police," the EMT said, backing up.

"Tell 'em I'm a smoke eater."

That stopped him in his tracks. He closed his mouth and looked at me for a few seconds before raising an apologetic hand and closing the door.

I turned back to Sherry. "What happened?"

"The holostereo started playing that scary wraith show, and then it exploded in flames. I'd never seen anything like it. White fire. Can you believe that?"

I nodded, rubbing her hand and trying not to bite through my bottom lip.

"The ground started shaking, and I fell. There was so much smoke, so quick. Kenji dragged me from the house."

Hearing his name, my wonderful, robotic dog barked and showed happy eyes with dancing hearts.

I hugged his neck and kissed the cold metal of his head. "Good boy."

"The neighbors called 911 and got me out of there. We started hearing roars coming from the house. But how, Cole? How did a dragon show up so quickly?"

"I don't know. But I'm going to fix it."

"What are you talking about?"

I kissed her and patted Kenji again before jumping out of the ambulance. Leaning my head back inside, I said, "I'll meet you at the hospital. I love you."

I shut the door, and as the ambulance drove away, I heard Sherry yelling from inside – it sounded like my name was used more than once. She wouldn't understand what was going through my mind at that moment, what singular urge drove me back to my burning-down house.

I really wanted to kill something scaly.

The nearest smoke eater truck stood about fifty feet away from my home, and I immediately lifted a bin where I hoped an extra power suit waited.

Lucky me.

I jumped into the power suit and strapped on a helmet. This suit was a foam and laser load out, and it was going to be interesting to see how if I could use it well.

Sink or swim.

Smoke eaters poured out my front door, shouting and waving at those standing by the slayer vehicles. They all pointed to the ground, saying the dragon had gone back under.

From the other end of the street, fire droids moved in to put out the flames. I lifted a hand to extend my therma goggles.

"Get out of here," someone said behind me, grabbing my arm.

I was about to swing a fist into whoever's face, but then I saw it was Thomlin. I should have thrown the punch, but I was surprised to see him outside my house in a power suit. He should have been off for the weekend like the rest of the rookies.

"That's my house," I said. "And what are you doing here?"

"Volunteered for extra duty. And you're suspended."

I could have sworn he was smiling under all those freckles.

"Fuck off, Thomlin." I was ready to fight him, even though I really needed to save my energy for the dragon.

The ground shook again and sent us both to the ground. Huge splits ripped through the asphalt as my house and surrounding homes collapsed from the quake. The other smoke eaters held onto their slayer trucks or dropped flat. A few fell through huge cracks that appeared in the street, unable to power jump to safety, screaming until the bloody end.

This wasn't the type of quake I'd experienced before, where it eventually stopped after a few tremors. This went on...

... until a dragon crawled out from a deep hole in the asphalt just outside my house. The scaly was about my size, but snake-like and feathery. This thing caused all that shaking? It had no desire to attack the nearby smoke eaters; it was looking for a way to escape, darting its head to and fro as it fluttered its long body down the street.

Then another quake shook the ground as a cluster of black horns rose behind the smaller scaly. The horns belonged to an ugly head that held countless jagged teeth and a pair of red-glowing eyes. Then another head appeared, looking the same. A third head followed after that. All three heads and necks met at a single body that rose out of the broken asphalt.

One of the bigger dragon's claws easily squashed a car, and when it had pulled itself from the hole its tail whipped into the air, brandishing huge spikes at the end. One of the heads darted forward and snatched the fleeing dragon in its teeth. The prey screeched once before its predator chewed, snapping bones, and then swallowed.

I wanted to run, to scream and piss myself, but I

couldn't help but watch what was happening in front of me. The neighborhood was supposed to have been evacuated, but that didn't stop curious idiots from sneaking closer for a look. Those curious idiots were now running for their lives, screaming like wraiths.

The three-headed scaly shook pieces of street from its slick hide and roared with all three heads, giving us all a great look at what was about to kill us. It was bigger than any dragon I'd seen in person, taking up the street and towering over what few houses remained standing. The three heads moved independently, taking count of all the smoke eaters surrounding it. Then, with another unified roar, the dragon's side plates fell to the street in strings of green gunk. Then it spread gigantic, black wings.

"OK, Thomlin," I said slowly. "Let's get to a cannon truck." But when I turned, Thomlin was gone, running at full speed toward the dragon, screaming like a madman.

All three of the dragon's heads turned to look at the tiny, shouting man power jumping into the air and firing lasers at it. A few of Thomlin's shots struck the scaly, but they might as well have been raindrops.

The scaly behemoth lifted its tail, flexing the spikes. Thomlin was still in the air when the dragon whipped its tail into his chest, sending him hurtling in the opposite direction. He flew over my head and landed with a metallic crunch.

Several of the walking-stick-sized spikes stuck out from Thomlin's power suit, and he wasn't moving. Me and another smoke eater ran to where he lay. We would have rolled Thomlin onto his back, but the spikes had impaled him all the way through. His open eyes stared at me, dead as a doll's. There wasn't even any blood. His heart had stopped as soon as the spikes pierced his chest.

"He's dead," the other smoke eater said to me.

"No shit, Sherlock."

I hated Thomlin's guts, but I never wanted him to end up like this. He was a brother. Maybe not in the fire service, but something like it. And brothers don't let something like this go unanswered.

I turned toward the dragon and readied my laser gun.

"Cast," I said, prepping my radio. "We have to surround and drown this behemoth."

"What does that mean?" somebody responded. "And who is this?"

"We can't let the dragon fly off and wreak havoc on the city," I said, purposefully leaving my name out of it. Donahue was going to find out anyway. Might as well be later than sooner.

"He's right," someone else chimed in. "This is IC. I want laser fire first. Swords need to stay back until we get it weakened. I never imagined saying this, but we have to take out its wings. Wait for my mark."

"Holy shit, look at that," someone said.

Rubble churned where my house used to be. The fire droids pulled themselves out while we all gawked at the robots stomping toward the dragon. They started shooting their water cannons, and the dragon tolerated them for a while before crushing the closest droid with one of its claws. The other fire droids kept marching on, apparently determined to help kill the dragon.

"Ignore the droids," the IC said. "We can use the distraction."

He called a few names and told them to get on top of any houses still upright and stable.

"What about me?" I asked.

"I don't even know you," he said. "Give me a name."

"Brannigan."

"All right, Brannigan, meet me at the back of Cannon 2. We're going to blow this sumbitch away."

I hurried to the truck and met a baby-faced guy who

could have been half my age.

He almost did a double take. "Shit, you're old."

"Thanks. Tell me what I need to do."

He pointed at the ladder leading to the cannon's aiming system. "Hop up there and aim the cannon at the scaly. Don't shoot until I tell you."

"How do I aim this thing?"

He pointed at me, yelling, "Just use the handles and squeeze the trigger!"

I skipped the ladder and power jumped into position.

The last fire droid ran away from the dragon. One of the scaly heads snatched the robot and another bit onto the legs. The dragon heads split the metal man in half, dumping all of its mechanical organs onto the street.

"Get ready, Brannigan." the IC sputtered into my helmet speaker. "Ready lasers on the roof."

I pulled at the cannon's handles. The barrel lifted from the bedded position smooth as butter. It took only a few seconds to set my sights on the center of the dragon's body. The cannon powered up.

"On three," the IC said.

The dragon spread its wings and hunkered down as if it was going to charge me on top of the cannon truck.

"One …"

The center dragon head stayed forward, on me. The other two split the street and growled at either side, where the laser teams waited.

"… two…"

Something wasn't right. My body hair rose from inside my power suit as the dragon sucked in air. Before the IC could say, "three" the dragon released a wave of energy from each head. I pulled the cannon's trigger but it was too late. The energy wave hit the truck hard, flipping me over the side.

I hit my head pretty bad, but I crawled onto my feet

and peeked around the truck. The laser teams had fallen similarly, and it wasn't until that moment I realized my power suit was dead.

I looked up at the cannon truck lights. They no longer spun or glowed. The engine didn't rumble. The Behemoth had roared another of those EMP blasts, only this time it was on a bigger scale. And, based on the complete silence coming from my helmet, every one of us smoke eaters were just as fucked as our suits and trucks.

I tossed my helmet off and lifted the truck bin where they kept the lances and shields. A few smokies ran past me as I hefted my gear down the street. They could run like little punks. I was going to kill this bastard or it was going to kill me. I was tired of playing the middle ground.

The dragon lifted its wings and beat a few flaps before it was flying, the air whipping against my face and scattering loose gravel.

"No!" I shouted.

The three heads breathed fire in every direction, catching more houses aflame, and roasting a few smoke eaters that hadn't cleared out soon enough. I ran with all I had, ready to climb onto the dragon if I could find a way.

Flapping its wings faster, the Behemoth fed the newly lit fires as it soared over me, headed the opposite direction. I spun on my heels and ran after it. I was able to catch up as the dragon hovered over one of our slayer trucks and grabbed it with all four of its claws.

I saw what was going to happen next, so I threw down my shield and grabbed onto the back bumper as it left the ground. Sergeant Puke's pushups came in handy as I pulled myself onto the truck. I didn't know how high the dragon was taking me, but I could make out a line of house roofs in my periphery.

No time for that.

I began climbing onto the top of the truck. All I had to do was get close enough to shove my lance into a vital part of the dragon. Then, I'd figure out what to do about getting back to the ground.

The wind pounded my ears as I stood just under the dragon's belly. It could have roared my name and the winning lottery numbers and I wouldn't have been able to hear it.

I thrust my lance up to pierce its belly, but the Behemoth's underside moved away from the tip of my weapon, and soon I could see its entire body and the three heads flying away.

The sonofabitch dropped me while I stood on a twenty-five-ton hunk of metal.

Everything went black.

CHAPTER 18

I was in the worst pain of my life, and the thing that made it worse was that I was asleep and could do nothing about it. The vaguest flashes of voices and movement came to me, but it was garbled among the void of agony I couldn't seem to find my way out of.

Eventually, I began to crawl back to consciousness a little at a time, the kind of thing they write about in articles about comas and exorcisms. I was awake, but couldn't open my eyes or move any part of my body – not that I had any desire to further my pain.

Beeps and boops of machines surrounded me. Metal clanged. The unmistakable roll of a chair moved past. Light hit my corneas when I was able to split my eyelids open. Everything was blurry, as if I was underwater. I used to wear glasses before I had laser eye surgery to get onto the fire department. This was a million times blurrier than that recovery.

"Are you trying to determine how high of a fall it'll take to kill you?"

I knew that voice. It was Yolanda, the propellerhead with the blue miracle goop. Recent events were still a little fuzzy, but whatever had happened she'd make sure I was in good shape.

"No," Donahue's voice said, "he's just an idiot. They're

immortal and stick around to make everyone else's lives a living hell."

I meant to say, "Fuck you, too." But it came out, "Blugh mugh, roof."

I guess I had a tube down my throat and cotton shit in my mouth. Had I gotten hurt that bad?

"Well," Donahue said. "I guess there is an upside to this. I don't have to hear your wisecracks. Or at least understand them."

My vision had been clearing up steadily, and I could now make out Yolanda sitting in a chair and Donahue leaning against a metal table, arms crossed with bureaucratic angst.

"I can take his tube out if you need him to speak." Yolanda drummed a pencil against her chin.

Donahue smiled, the sick bastard. "No, I like him better this way."

I still couldn't move my body. My head wouldn't lower, so I tried to see as far down as my eyes would go. Instead of lying in a bed, I sat straight, and it looked like I was encased in a large, shiny, gray metal box, almost like a one-person sauna.

"I'll let Yolanda tell you why you can't move," Donahue said, "and what we plan on doing with you."

Yolanda breathed slowly through her nose and sat forward, flipping the pencil between fingers. "You fell from a significant height while on top of a slayer truck. Honestly, when I heard about it, I thought you'd be in a body bag."

"Don't inflate his ego." Donahue groaned.

"Anyway, this isn't like the small injuries you had before. You're going to have to stay immobile, at least bodily, for about two weeks."

Even though I couldn't move, I tensed so bad, my eyes could have popped from the sockets.

"Settle down, Brannigan," Donahue said. "You aren't in any shape to do anything."

Yolanda tapped the metal box surrounding me. "What you're sitting in is in a beta stage, but we haven't had too many accidents with it in our tests."

For fuck's sake.

"We call it the psy-roll," Yolanda said. "We'll show you why in a second. The good news is that I have you hooked up to several IVs pushing Ieiunium curate, and the psy-roll has a cleaning system for…" she bobbed her head from left to right, as if looking for a nice word, "… when you do your business. You'll have to replace the curate tubes every three days or so. And have someone empty the… other stuff."

How hygienic.

I looked between her and Donahue. If I couldn't move, how the hell was I going to replace the very stuff I needed to heal up? Plus, I had no home to go back to, and Sherry was in the hospital herself.

Shit. I had to see her.

Donahue played with the golden lances on his collar. "I have someone assigned to replace your medicine. And don't think you're going to sit on your tail for two weeks. I have a special task for you."

"Mugh flur dungungh!" I mumbled.

"Oh, hell," Donahue leapt off the table. "Pull that thing out of his throat so he can talk."

Yolanda came at me quick. I would have flinched if I could move. The tube came out like a sword through my esophagus and I sat there dry heaving and swallowing away the shitty taste in my mouth.

But after a while, I was able to croak out, "What did you do to me?"

Yolanda rolled back in surprise, afraid I was going to yell at her. Like I could do anything else.

"We didn't do anything," Donahue said. "Not counting the headache I have to deal with in regard to compensating those injured on Friday, the families of those who died. We lost a recruit because he was so damned gung-ho, he thought he could take on a three-headed dragon!"

"The Behemoth," Yolanda said with a grin. "We heard you over the radio. I think the name fits."

Friday. Donahue had said it with a hint of past tense. How many days had come and gone?

I watched the vein in Donahue's neck twitch. When it settled down, I said, "Did they kill it?"

"Kill what?"

"The Behemoth."

Donahue rubbed his temples, a hand at each side. "No."

"You guys lost a dragon that big?"

"No, you lost that dragon. After it burned half of Parthenon City in an air raid, it flew off where we couldn't track it. The citizens are madder than hell, blaming all of this on us. And I've been trying to figure out how in the blue hell the Behemoth just so happened to emerge right under your house."

"Fascinating development," Yolanda said. "Not only is this the most sophisticated dragon we've ever seen, it's also a scaly predator. It's on top of the top of the food chain!"

She grinned wide, while Donahue and I could only stare at her in disbelief.

"Do you think we could have some privacy for a minute?" I asked Yolanda.

She was only too glad to leave, saying, "Get better, Brannigan."

When the glass doors sealed behind her, I said, "You didn't pay to have my window fixed."

"What?"

"You didn't buy my wife a holostereo."

"Hold on." Donahue looked out into the hall. "You're still out of it. I'll get Yolanda to up your meds."

"Listen! My wife had been seeing a wraith appear out of a holostereo, one she mysteriously received earlier in the week. Someone also came out to fix one of our broken windows. I thought it might have been you, greasing my wife up so she wouldn't try to convince me not to become a smoke eater."

"I did pay for the window, but not the holostereo. I'm not made of money." He squinted, trying to solve the puzzle I was throwing at him. "So, if it wasn't me–"

"Who was it?"

"What does this have to do with anything?"

"Sherry told me that right before the dragon showed up at our house, a wraith appeared out of the stereo again, but this time it burst into flames. White flames."

He sat down, rubbing his hands. "She could have been seeing things."

I shook my head. "My firefighter saw the same thing in the fire you recruited me from. Don't brush this away like last time."

Donahue began bobbing his metal knee up and down. I waited for him to respond. To tell me he'd look into it. To say it sounded suspicious. To give a shit.

He sighed. "I'm not sure what to make of this."

"I sure as hell do. Someone's found a way to capture wraiths, and not only that, use them to draw dragons."

"Catching wraiths is impossible. Besides, who would do something like that?"

"The world is filled with bad people. This is like a new kind of arsonist."

He nodded slowly, looking away.

"So, are you going to look into it?" I asked.

"If it'll get you to shut up, I'll see what I can do. Maybe check with the delivery company, if you know who it was." He groaned. "This couldn't have come at a worse time."

"Well, when it shits, it pours. Have you guys contacted my wife? Told her I'm OK?"

"She knows you were hurt and will be out for a few weeks. She's doing all right, but nagged me up and down for not letting her see you."

"Yeah, she sounds like she's her normal healthy self."

"All right," Donahue said. "We've got to get you ready to go on this trip."

"Trip? How the hell am I supposed to do anything when I can't even wiggle my finger? Plus, I'm suspended, remember?"

Donahue shook his head. "It's already been a week."

A week!?

"I want to see my wife. I want to go after the dragon that burned my house down. I want to find whoever summoned it!"

Donahue drummed fingers against his knees. "You ever try to catch a snake?"

"I can tell there's some Aesop fable type shit you're about to tell me, but I'm not in the mood."

"If you sit outside a snake's hole, it'll never come out. The snake would starve to death before it gave you the satisfaction of nabbing it. So, the best way to catch him is to walk away. If it thinks you're gone, it'll slither out. And that's when you cut its head off with the end of your shovel."

"You have some sick hobbies."

"If what you're telling me about the white fire is true, someone targeted you. The news drone got wrecked along with everything else electrical with that Behemoth's EMP blast. All anyone knows is that a bunch of smoke eaters were killed. So if this snake thinks you're no longer in the picture..."

I raised my eyebrows. "You're going to fake my death?"

He moved his hand in a so-so gesture. "Go on this assignment. It's a classified gig, and you'll be learning things most Americans never will, so that should get you excited. While you're there, get better. Come back ready to kick ass. Or quit, go home, and give us back our psy-roll and the chance to ever walk again."

"There are no soft punches with you, are there?"

Donahue shook his head.

"Sherry knows I'm still alive, right?"

"Of course."

I squinted at him, using my limited skill at reading body language to see if he was lying. I couldn't catch anything deceitful.

Donahue had me on the receiving end of an ass-kicking fest.

I gritted my teeth – the only gesture I had to show my frustration at the moment. "How. Do I. Move?"

"Easy," Donahue said. He grabbed a holoreader. "They connected the psy-roll into your spinal cord. Your brain does all the work. Let's see, it's... this one."

After he pressed a button, my psy-roll shot toward him, wheels humming on electric motors. He dove over the metal table and landed on the floor.

I thought, Stop! The psy-roll stopped. That seemed to work, so I told the contraption to turn towards Donahue and it did. I stared down at Donahue on the floor, who stared at me with blue goop all over his face.

I laughed, even though it hurt. "You bastards gave me a psychically powered wheelchair?!"

CHAPTER 19

"Ow! Watch that thing, damn it." Donahue sped faster down the hall to avoid my psy-roll bumping into the backs of his legs.

I snorted. "Sorry. Still getting used to this box you put me in."

The psy-roll was actually pretty easy to drive. It had wheels like a tank and could traverse over most terrain. I just thought about moving or turning and the box did it. But bumping Donahue's calves was cheap entertainment as we headed for whatever secret assignment he'd conned me into.

The green shirts we passed on the way didn't share my easygoing attitude. They hung their heads and avoided eye contact with me and the chief, even though they wished us a good morning. I heard later they'd just left a smoke eater funeral for Thomlin and the others who'd fallen in the line of duty. After I found out, I felt less than two dead flies.

"So, am I still a rookie?" I asked Donahue, just before we entered the slayer bay. "Or is this secret assignment some kind of promotion?"

"Right now you're just a man in a box who does what I tell him."

"Are you sure there isn't something better I could be doing?"

"What the hell else would you be able to do in your condition?"

"Paperweight?"

He tucked in his lips and exhaled through his nostrils, almost like a dragon. "I need a break from you, Brannigan. And you need someone to resupply your meds and accompany you on the errand. She'll take care of all the things you can't do."

"She who?"

Donahue pushed the door open and Naveena stood there, leaning against the wall and looking ready to tear someone's head off. I was pretty sure my head was at the top of the list. That especially unfortunate, because my head was the only part of my body currently working.

"Oh, shit." I remembered leaving her, Afu, and Williams at Cedar Point. They would be pretty pissed at me.

Naveena didn't say anything, but her eyes looked almost like they'd shoot lasers at any moment.

Donahue stopped just outside the door. "Captain Jendal will take it from here. She has all the information and will make sure you don't do anything stupid."

Yeah, if she doesn't push my psy-roll off a cliff.

I spun to give Donahue a piece of my mind, but he was already gone. Slowly, I turned back to Naveena, who hadn't moved or improved in disposition.

"How'd you get roped into this?" I asked.

"Once you're on Donahue's shit list, it takes a while to get off." She thinned her eyes. Wrinkled her lips.

I swallowed. "Listen, about leaving you guys–"

She came off the wall so fast, it stopped me midsentence. She stood there with clenched fists, but it was enough to intimidate me.

I changed the subject. "So, what does Donahue want us to do?"

"We're going to be presented with some new technology. Something that's supposed to changed our entire approach in dealing with the dragons. Sounds like they're feeding us bullshit, if you ask me."

I didn't ask who "they" were. Really, I was trying to avoid asking Naveena anything, hoping somehow we could get to a place where she neither wanted to hate me or kiss me again. Both of those were too complicated for a man in a box to deal with. A man outside a box, for that matter. I wondered if she remembered our incident on the carousel.

"OK," I said. "Which slayer are we taking? And how am I going to get in it?"

She put her back to me and sauntered into the expanse of the bay. "We're not taking a slayer."

The few smoke eaters who were washing trucks or mopping the floor stared at me, but I didn't know if it was because I was the guy who'd chased after a three-headed dragon and survived a hundred-foot fall, or if they'd never seen a wheeled box operated by a disembodied head.

We passed all of the slayers and cannon trucks that weren't out on a run. That's when I noticed Afu talking to Sergeant Puck outside the old jumbo jet.

"Are you serious?" I stopped rolling.

Naveena kept moving. "Do I have to forklift you onto the airplane?"

I accelerated the psy-roll to catch up.

What I thought was a thick coat of rust on the airplane turned out to be a red-orange, dragon scale design painted on every inch of metal. The jet engines were plasma-powered – I could tell by the lack of turbines – and there were three under each wing.

The coolest toys.

Afu looked at me with the same disdain Naveena had

given me, but Naveena had the benefit of experience.

Sergeant Puck was her same authoritative self, looking me up and down. "You look as useless as a square bowling ball."

Afu laughed as Williams came out of the open airplane hatch and saw me.

"You motherfucker–"

Afu grabbed her shoulders before she could attack. "Chill out, lady. You knew he was coming."

"You guys," I positioned my psy-roll in front of them, "I'm sorry for ditching you. My wife, my house... I lost my mind."

"You lost our respect," Williams said.

A chill swirled in my stomach.

I cleared my throat, "If you can't tell by this box I'm in, I lost a whole lot more than that."

I don't know if that eased their attitude toward me, but Williams didn't give me her death glare anymore.

"Just look at it this way, Brannigan," Afu said. "If you die, you've already got a casket."

He laughed, but Sergeant Puck crossed her arms and nearly yelled, "That's not funny."

We all turned to her.

"We already lost one of you rookies. Or did you forget?"

Afu looked down. "Sorry, Sergeant."

"Now let's get on the plane and get this trip over with." With that, Puck stomped up the open hatch.

"Who's flying this thing?" I wheeled up the ramp.

"Couple of the propellerheads," Naveena said. "They stay out of combat, but fly for us whenever we need them to."

Naveena fastened a seatbelt around my psy-roll, cinching it as hard as she could. I decided not to remind her that I couldn't feel anything with a metal box around me. She might have wrapped another seatbelt around my throat. Sloppily, she placed a pair of headphones on my head before strapping herself in next to me.

Puck told the pilots to shut the hatch, and we were all snug as carpet mice in our harnesses.

"So, are any of you going to tell me where we're going?" I asked. "I don't see why we need a plane for a field trip."

"Where Hell freezes over," Naveena said.

"What?" I looked at the others to see if she was messing with me.

"Canada," Afu said.

I said, "Are you guys serious?"

"Donahue's been trying to get in touch with them for a while," Afu said. "Last week, they finally responded. Invited us to come up and see what they're about."

"Just like that?" It sounded fishy to me.

"Brannigan," Naveena said, "shut up or I'll throw you out of the plane."

I frowned.

Canada. Geographically it wasn't that far, but ideologically they were living on another planet. I already felt unwelcome among my fellow smoke eaters. Now I was headed to a country that stood against everything we were about.

Fun.

The enormous doors opened in front of the jumbo jet and the engines powered up. The air grew tighter as they pressurized the cabin. My nerves made me sweat. I was in a wheeled box with no control over my extremities, and I hadn't been in a plane since the early 2090s.

"This plane got a nickname or some cool designation?" I asked, trying to get my mind off rolling out of the hatch at twenty thousand feet.

Everyone looked to Sergeant Puck, who sighed into

her headset's microphone. "Jet 1," she said.

"What?" I said. "Not Death From Above or Scorcher 5 or something?"

"No," Puck said.

Disappointed, I looked at Naveena, who'd closed her eyes and leaned her head against the side of the cabin. Sleep would have been a help, but I'd already been out cold for a week. I had to ride this entire trip fully awake and nervous as hell.

The jet rolled onto the long stretch of road just outside the smoke eater training field. Within a few minutes, we were in the air and flying at what I could only guess to be Mach 50.

"How long until we get there?" I asked through clenched teeth.

"An hour," Afu answered.

An hour didn't seem long enough to enter a completely different world.

CHAPTER 20

I didn't have the benefit of being able to see out the window like everybody else, who oohed and ahhed like a bunch of school kids when we were in Neo Toronto air space.

Afu's thick arm bumped my head as he pushed for a view out the window. "It looks like those old sci-fi movies from the 1980s. I'm surprised they still have so many buildings intact."

I wondered how my psy-roll would traverse over the ruins.

"Must be like an urban safari down there," Afu said.

"They don't just let the dragons roam free," Naveena said. "I'm sure they have ways to keep them out of the city."

"I wonder how they do that." I said.

Naveena eyed me as if she'd forgotten I was still there. "I guess that's what we're here to find out."

Jet 1 descended and the pilot told everyone to buckle in. A significant amount of turbulence hit us. At least, it was significant to a guy stuck in a box. Everyone stared at one another, like we were seeing who might throw up.

Williams hadn't said anything to me the entire flight, sleeping most of the time. I think she shared my fear of flying. Afu had given her a few green pills to ease her stomach, but I didn't see him holding any spark drugs.

The jet's thruster brakes beat against the ground, and we slowed to a stop.

"All right," Sergeant Puck said. "Everybody out."

The hatch lowered, and Naveena unbuckled me before hurrying out to the open air. Everyone with working legs left me to slowly roll down the ramp by myself. Assholes.

A group of well-dressed people welcomed Sergeant Puck and the others with handshakes, but I was more interested in the city around us. For one, we'd landed in the middle of what used to be downtown Toronto. There were plenty of vacant lots where you could almost see the ghosts of former buildings.

At the corner of the nearest block, a man in a blue bandana smoked a bubble vape outside his shop. Above him, a holographic, smiling moose, electrically bright against the dimming sky, hefted a steak on the end of an oversized knife. As soon as I laid eyes on the cannibalistic hologram, it grew larger and floated toward me, offering me the meat. I zoomed my psy-roll backwards, away from the advancing advertisement.

"Brannigan," Puck said. Her neck tensed as she restrained a yell, morphing her lips into what I guessed she would have called a smile, but it looked more like a bulldog having a seizure. She lifted a hand to a Canadian man in a business suit. "This is Alan Hamdel, Vice President of Yūrei Corporation."

The man nodded to me. I tried to nod back, but hit my chin against the metal top of the psy-roll.

"Sorry," I said. "I had an accident. Now I'm stuck in this box."

"We're happy to accommodate you any way we can," Alan said.

He looked about my age – it was nice not to be the only codger in the group. Gray dusted the sides of his otherwise brown hair, and wrinkles sat at the corners of his eyes.

The others in his party were much younger. Teenagers, from what I could tell.

"Yūrei Corporation?" I asked, turning to Puck. "I thought we'd be meeting with the government."

Puck's eyes shook. She tried another one of those monstrous smiles with Alan. "Don't mind him, he's–"

"Our government is made of corporations," Alan said, keeping his gaze on me. "They were the only ones left standing after the earthquakes. It's just like your city states, but on a smaller scale."

I would have shrugged if I could. "Hey, buddy, you guys can elect Ronald McDonald emperor for all I care."

"Aha." Alan thinned his eyes, then turned sharply, almost militarily, to the side. "Allow me to introduce the rest of my board."

The teenagers hustled over to me, hefting their holoreaders. Three of them were women, two men. All of them wore loose suits with carelessly tied ties. The men had spiked their hair; one had dyed his in golden metallic.

Alan introduced each one to me, but for some reason I only remembered Cheryl.

Before Sherry and I found out that we couldn't have kids – my fault – we tossed around a few names. We could only agree on a girl's name – Cheryl. It was a mishmash of Cole and Sherry.

The young woman in front of me even had red hair like my wife. It was hard not to instantly consider what could have been, if our daughter had looked the same, or if we'd adopted a little girl like the one I'd seen in Sherry's orphanage pamphlet.

Hell. If life doesn't constantly slug you in the gut when you least expect it.

I smiled at Cheryl, and she grinned wider than the others. Sincere. Honestly, if I hadn't been shooting blanks, I would have thought Cheryl was my own flesh and blood smuggled across the northern line.

Naveena stepped closer and leaned a hand on the edge of my psy-roll. "Should we move along, then?"

It was difficult, but I raised my head to get a good look at Naveena. She scanned the area with her eyes, as if something was going to pop out of the ground – or sky. Smart. I should have been doing the same thing. But Naveena herself had said the Canadians must have had some means to keep dragons away. Maybe she didn't believe it.

Why the hell did I?

"Of course," Alan said. "You and Mr Brannigan will come with me and Cheryl. The rest of you will be taken to your lodgings until tomorrow."

VIP, huh? I could roll with that.

"Behave, Brannigan," Puck said as she walked away with the others.

Jet 1 rolled toward a glossy building, where a glass door raised to allow the plane in. Alan led us to a van hovering on the street and told the driver to let me in. Then the side door popped out and lowered a lift to the ground.

"Chief Donahue called ahead and told us you'd be coming, Mr Brannigan." Alan grinned slightly at me, but I didn't sense any smugness. "Miss Jendal, you may sit in the back with me."

"Captain Jendal," said Naveena.

"Yes, of course."

Cheryl got in on the other side, wearing a grin that dimpled her cheeks, and sat next to where I'd be. The lift cradled me into the van, and we floated off toward the center of the city.

"Have you ever been to Canada?" Cheryl asked me. She had a slight French accent, and it suited her.

"First time," I said. "Would have probably visited after I retired, but you guys pulled up the beaver skin curtain. So, that plan got nixed."

"You mean Iron Curtain," Naveena said.

"No, I know what I meant."

"I've always wanted to visit America," Cheryl said. "My duties with the company take up much of my time, though."

"What?" I said. "At your age you should be hanging out with your friends and doing geometry homework. Fawning over boys. Why the hell are in you in a soul-sucking corporation?"

"Many of our country's most productive employees are under seventeen," said Alan. His face sat plain, so I didn't know if I'd offended him.

I turned my head to Cheryl. "Well, if you ever decide to defect, I mean visit, you can always stay with my wife and me. We don't currently have a house, thanks to a three-headed asshole of a dragon, but we'll figure something out."

"Really?" Cheryl said. "Thank you!"

I smiled at Cheryl. Naveena gave me a "what the fuck are you doing?" look. I tried to shrug, but forgot I couldn't move my shoulders. So, I just raised my eyebrows.

I stared out the window at the bright neon advertisements and the crowds of people streaming down the sidewalks. Every other block or so, there'd be an old-style house or shop in the midst of the high-rises and more modern sights. In Neo Toronto, they blended the old with the new. It was completely un-American, and I loved it. One thing these dragon huggers got right was a respect for the past with a simultaneous look to the future.

Cheryl put a hand on my psy-roll to get my attention. "Why do you kill dragons?"

"Cheryl!" Alan said. He hadn't shown much emotion until then.

"Sorry." It sounded like soar-e.

"It's OK," I said. "Let's cut any bullshit and speak plainly."

Cheryl laughed.

I cleared my throat. "Let's say your dad is having a beer in his living room, watching the game – it'd be hockey, here, I guess – and suddenly, the power goes out, the earth shakes, and something right out of the pits of Hell bursts through his floor, burns everything he owns to the ground and eats him for added insult. Wouldn't you want to kill the scaly who did it? Wouldn't you want to make sure that didn't happen to anyone else?"

"I lost both of my parents in an earthquake."

Well, that shut me up. Made me want to reiterate my invitation to the States.

"Revenge is a useless idea," Cheryl said, pulling strands of hair behind her ear. "Especially against something that is only following its nature. It would be the same as shooting the cloud that rained on your picnic."

"If a raincloud can wipe out an entire neighborhood, an entire city, you're damn right I'll find a way to wreck that motherfucker."

Cheryl full-on belly laughed.

Alan, however, wasn't as amused by my American antics. "Perhaps we should refrain from political or religious discussion. This is a business endeavor, after all."

"About that," I said, but didn't get to finish.

The driver hit the brake thrusters on the hover van as a gang of teenagers leapt out in front of us, carrying metal swords, sticks, and rocks. A few of them sat on air scooters. One girl in the front held a leash, and at the other end was either the ugliest and biggest dog I'd ever seen, or a she'd found a way to domesticate a dragon.

The thing looked like a Komodo, except that it had a frill below its neck that flashed with sparks of purple electricity.

Our driver hit ultra-bright high beams in an attempt to blind the gang, but that just got them to throw their rocks and run toward us. A few jumped onto the hood and beat the van with their weapons. We surged into reverse, scattering the punks onto the street.

"Please remain calm," Alan said, climbing past Cheryl and me toward the front seat.

"Remain calm?" I said. "What the hell is going on?"

I couldn't do jack shit if one of the thugs got into the van and swung their sword or dragon at me. A turtle-like head retraction would have been a nice addition to my psy-roll at that point.

"Just relax, Brannigan," Naveena told me. But she didn't have a weapon either, just two good legs to leave me behind.

Alan reached into the glove compartment and removed a pulse gun the size of his arm.

"Don't worry," Cheryl told me. "These street gangs are only minor nuisances."

The way our driver was swerving around street vendors like an experienced Hollywood stuntman, I couldn't see how the situation was either minor or rare.

The van stopped as Alan opened the large sunroof and stood on the center console. Through the windshield, I saw his pulse shots rip down the street, hitting a few of the gang members, including the one holding onto the dragon.

The scaly roared and released a circular blast of electricity. The remaining thugs dropped to the street, convulsing out of their smoking sneakers. For a second, I thought the dragon might take the opportunity to munch on the dead teens, but I was wrong.

Apparently drawn to our high beams, the dragon shook its electric frill at full extension and galloped toward us.

"Drive!" Alan shouted, holding his position in the sunroof.

I thought I heard him begin to chant or pray.

The van lurched into reverse again, but it didn't matter, the dragon was faster than the van.

Naveena cursed. "Dead end behind us!"

Sweat stung my eyes, nearly blinding me. "Just shoot it."

Alan wailed in frustration before firing the pulse gun once, twice, finally a third time. Each hit struck the dragon in its center, blowing dark chunks of meat into the air.

Our driver stopped the van, breathing heavily, and the headlights covered the dragon's lifeless body splayed out in the street. Alan slowly lowered to the front seat, holding a handkerchief to his mouth as he bent over, shaking.

Pedestrians and shopkeepers crept out to see what the hell had happened. When they saw the dragon in the street, they whispered to each other, concern plastered over every face.

Alan rose from his handkerchief and made a phone call with his holoreader. The person on the other end didn't sound happy. Alan answered quietly in short, single words – at least from what I could tell. When he hung up, he turned back to us.

"I'm terribly sorry," he said.

But it took a second for me to realize he wasn't saying it to either me or Naveena. He was speaking to Cheryl, who began to cry without the benefit of a handkerchief.

CHAPTER 21

"We don't have to like it, Brannigan." Naveena sat in a chair behind me, tinkling ice in a glass that held whatever booze she'd found in the mini fridge.

We were in one of the corporate apartments – mine. Naveena had been given a different room at the Yūrei building, but on the same floor, so she could come to my aid if needed.

"They have their own customs and beliefs," she said. "None of our business. We're here to look at some tech we might use, do a little diplomacy, and then go home. Stick to the plan."

I'd parked my psy-roll by the big window overlooking Neo Toronto, a place where the people valued dragon life over their own. Where you could slaughter a couple dozen idiot teenagers, but killing a rampaging scaly was the worst thing you could do. Alan had been dead quiet the rest of the ride, his body tight and shaking. He acted as if he was headed for death row.

Maybe he was.

Naveena and I had been holed up in the company building for the last two days while the rest of the smokies got to gallivant around Neo Toronto. Alan's people kept putting us off any time we asked to see the new technology or anything other than the inside of the

Yūrei building and its too-polite employees. Hell, even the Canadian Feed sucked. The religious shows were the worst. It was just like the old American preacher programs, but Jesus was replaced with scalies. The other shows bored me to tears: talk shows discussing regular problems like divorce and mortgages. Where was the action?!

I shifted my focus from the city outside to Naveena's reflection in the window. "Then let's demand they get it over with so we can go home."

"We don't want to be rude."

"Alan is pretty messed up about what happened with that dragon." I turned my psy-roll to face Naveena. "I'm sure he'd be happy to see us go."

"What about your foreign exchange student?"

I raised an eyebrow. "You mean Cheryl? She seems like a good kid. I like her. You think it'd be alright if she came back with us?"

Naveena rolled her eyes. "No, Captain Savior."

"If she wants to come, I don't see any reason to deny her. And what's with all the damn teenagers? Did all the old people in this city die?"

Naveena tilted her head, and her hair fell across her neck. "One of the staff here told me teen gangs have cropped up in the last few years. They think they're rebelling against the evil corporations in charge."

"I haven't seen anyone who could be over thirty. Besides Alan. Even his board members are test tube babies."

Naveena took a drink and winced. "You're just being a paranoid old man."

"No, I–" A flash of pain echoed throughout my muscles.

"Your meds starting to wear off?" Naveena asked.

I closed my eyes and waited for the agony to dissipate.

"I think so."

Standing and stretching her long arms into the air, Naveena turned and placed a thick metal case onto the bed. "These are supposed to last you for the rest of the week. Don't become a druggy."

She was one to talk.

"And I'm not looking forward to emptying your waste at all. I'm writing you a bill. A big bill. So beneath me."

"It's just as embarrassing for me to let you handle my shit."

Naveena lifted a canister that contained the blue gel, studying the glowing slop before shifting her eyes toward me. There was a lot in that look – mostly an evil mischievousness. Tossing the canister between her hands, Naveena walked around to sit on the bed, giving me a good look at her legs.

"How bad are you hurting?" she asked.

I was about to say it wasn't that bad, but then another flash of agony quaked through me, as if my nerves were waking up and realizing a dragon had dropped me from the sky. "It's… starting to hurt a lot now."

She tongued the inside of her cheek. "I'll give this to you," she held up the canister, "if you answer some questions honestly."

For fuck's sake.

"OK," I said, partly out of curiosity, but mostly because I didn't see how else to get my pain-killing juice.

She held the canister like a gun. "What did you think of our kiss?"

Why, God? Why?

I'm not sure if you've seen many lists of firefighter attributes, but honesty and integrity are right up there on all of them.

"It was an accident," I said.

She harrumphed. "You think it's OK to take advantage

of women in an inebriated state?"

"Sweet Jesus, no! You kissed me. I tried to pull away."

Sweat beaded on my forehead, and I was beginning to think dealing with my pain would be a hell of a lot better than this strange interrogation.

I rolled away from her. Just a little. "Look, we haven't exactly been friendly. But I do think you're good at your job and you're smart. I'm a married man and twice your age. I would never, ever put the moves on you. I swear."

She walked to the window and opened it.

"What are you doing?" I asked.

"Shut up." She held the canister outside. One slip of her fingers and my medicine would drop eight stories to splatter against Canadian asphalt. "I'm asking the questions. Did you consider how I'd get you back for leaving me at that amusement park?"

She pulled the canister back in. Her lips moved into something I'd never seen on her face – a very slight grin.

"Oh, you bastard!" I said.

She shrugged.

"Very funny. Now, can you put my medicine in before I run you over with this miniature tank, please?"

"Calm your tits, Brannigan." She walked around to the back of my psy-roll as another burst of pain hit me. The pain waves were lasting longer each time.

I heard a click and then a warm, numb feeling chased away the pain from my head all the way down to where I guessed my feet were.

"Thanks." I rolled toward the door as fast as I could.

"Don't screw anything up, rookie," Naveena called.

The door slid closed behind me, and I began roaming the building like some cyborg security guard. I could roll until dawn if I had to. Yūrei Corp had a lot of space.

The "night-time" lights were on. Anyone still in the building had gone to sleep. The whole place smelled strange, and I was suddenly homesick. A clock ticked somewhere, but I could never find it. Then one of their weird holographic ads popped around a corner and scared me half to death.

This was the worst one yet – a cartoon dragon that looked like someone on LSD had drawn it. The ad was selling a fizzy, yellow energy drink called Sulfurge! Which, coincidentally, is the sound you'd make while throwing it back up.

I cursed the hologram for a sonofabitch and rolled on.

After riding the elevator to the top floor, where the rooms were spaced out much wider, I rolled by a door where it sounded like someone was punching a slab of meat.

The door slid open, and Cheryl stood there, red around her soft eyes. In the room behind her, Alan was on his knees, shirtless, and whipping himself across his bloody back with a cat o' nine tails. After each hit, he'd grunt and mutter something.

"I'm sorry," Cheryl said to me, stepping into the hall and shutting the door behind her. "Please, follow me."

I rolled with her to the elevator. "Everything OK?"

"Mr Hamdel is in pain."

"Yeah, I could see that." I rolled my eyes. "All that over a dragon."

"They're sacred animals. He feels terrible about what he had to do."

In the elevator, I got a better view of the Neo Toronto lights.

"If you guys really had that big of a hard-on for the scalies," I said, "none of this would be here. It would all be ash."

"Like your cities in America?"

She had me there. Despite the enormity of vacant spaces, Neo Toronto was thriving better than the neighborhoods surrounding Parthenon City.

I hummed defeat. "So, how do you keep the dragons from destroying everything?"

Cheryl shook her head, on the verge of tears again. "You smokers know how we do it."

"Smoke eater. And you guys have made it very difficult for anyone to know what you've been up to. All we have is rumors. I mean, I watched a Professor Poltergeist video, but I knew most of that stuff. This tech Naveena and I are here to look at, is that what keeps your dragons away?"

"No, you and Captain Jendal are here to look at something else."

The elevator opened, and she led me onto the roof in slow steps. The wind blew her red hair in a million tendrils across her face as I rolled beside her.

"If you don't mind me asking," I said, "how old are you?"

"Fifteen," she said, turning to me. "Old enough for the drawing."

The red and blue lights lining the roof reflected off her face, making her look half-angel and half-demon. I looked at the sky and was surprised to see a few stars.

"Is that like a military draft, or a lottery?" I asked.

"Both. Now that Mr Hamdel has killed a dragon, we have to appease them by offering a sacrifice."

Without meaning to, I spun my psy-roll violently, around and around. When I got it under control, I shifted to face Cheryl. "You can't be serious."

She stared at me, and I don't know if it was the wind or her eyes, but the back of my neck shivered. If the Canadians wanted to blame somebody, why not blame Alan? I wasn't for killing people over a scaly, but if we were pointing fingers...

The Canucks were taking this dragon thing a little too far.

"That's terrible," I said. "These dragons don't hold grudges. They're just animals, like you said."

"Divine animals. And most in this country would disagree with you."

"People over dragons. That's my motto."

"What would be worse?" She dropped her stare to the rooftop. "One death? Or thousands? Thousands of yūrei to haunt our streets."

"You mean wraiths?"

"Or ghosts," she said. "Whatever you want to call them."

"Wait a minute. Yūrei. That's the name of your corporation."

She smiled, and it made me feel a little less sick that her country sacrificed people to dragons.

"It's Japanese. A playful name, before the dragons came. Our company started in holographic advertising. Neon ghosts."

"Yeah, I met some of those creepy things."

"Very successful. They have retinal detection, so if someone sees the ad, it zeroes in to pitch the product one on one."

"In America we'd shoot at those things if they came at us selling pudding. Most people wouldn't even realize they were ads until their laser cartridge was spent."

Her laughter was electric.

I couldn't believe I was high above Neo Toronto stuck in a wheeled box. If only Sherry could see me now. She'd love Cheryl. Sherry would have said it was a sign that I'd met this girl. That I should bring her home, no matter what Naveena or the others said.

"Anyway," Cheryl said. "Shortly after the emergence, Mr Hamdel developed the yūrei containment beam, and we've recently voted in favor of dropping our embargo to sell the technology overseas to certain groups. It was very successful. So we've decided to move on to other products. To prevent any more dragon deaths."

"Wait. Containment what?"

She sighed. Even Canadian patience had its limits. "You should know all about this. Your city was one of the first customers of the wraith remotes. Surely you've used them."

The metal of my psy-roll clanged from my jaw dropping onto it. Donahue hadn't said shit about knowing of a way to trap wraiths. And there was no way he'd keep something like that from us, or the city. Would he?

I regained my composure and cleared my throat. "Oh, you know, we have a learning curve to work through," I lied. "But I think we're getting the hang of it."

"Ah." She nodded. "I told that Mr Jenkins it would be beneficial for you smoke eaters to come train with us, but he wanted the equipment rushed to Parthenon City. I'd be happy to go over it with you sometime if you're having trouble."

"I'd like that." On the outside I was smiling.

Inside, I was fucking fuming. Jenkins. Mayor Rogola's lackey. I'd smelled a rat for a while, and across the border I'd finally found it.

As far as Cheryl and the rest of Yūrei Corporation went, I'd play along as if Parthenon City had been a regular ghost-busting haven of the Midwest. The only problem would be getting Naveena to go along without her blowing her top.

Easy, right?

"I did have one question," I said.

"Shoot."

"I get catching the wraiths, but is it possible to uncatch them?"

"Well, sure. What good is it to trap the nasty things without depositing them? You just need a containment area with connected electrical current and glass. They can break out of any other material. We explained all of this to Mr Jenkins. He seemed very nervous, maybe he wasn't paying attention."

Rogola. That bastard had burned my house down, nearly killed my wife. He'd... Theresa and the others, too.

I'd let the cops have a head start, but if they didn't get to him first, throw him in the darkest jail they had, I'd be pounding his face in. It was time to fly assholes and elbows back to Home Sweet Ohio. But this time, we'd have an extra passenger.

"You should come back with us," I told Cheryl.

She widened her eyes. "Oh. I... I don't know. That's kind of a big deal."

"Just a visit. I just want you to see what America is like. You can pack for a week and then we'll fly you back."

"Do you have the authority to make that decision?"

"I'll tell you this," I said, "after I take care of some business, they'll owe me a favor."

Cheryl laughed.

"So what do you say?"

She looked away, biting her lip. "I would have to get permission from Mr Hamdel. The company."

"For crying out loud, you're fifteen." I rolled to her other side and took a big breath of night air. "This is going to sound silly, or crazy, but you remind me... you look like the daughter I never had. And normally I don't believe in coincidences or any of that astrological bullshit, but it feels like I was meant to be here, to meet you. It can't be just to see some doohickey you Canucks invented."

She was going to think I was crazy. I stopped before I got ahead of myself. And since all I had was a head, in the functional sense, that would have been bad.

She stared at me while the wind blew her hair around. Then she said, "Did you really just say 'doohickey'?"

We both laughed.

But then she choked up and looked away.

"I'm sorry," I said. "It must be this medicine I'm on. Makes me extremely spontaneous."

"No, it's all right." She sniffed and wiped her eyes with the back of her hand. "It's just that my papa used to call everything a doohickey. You brought back a lot of memories."

"Now that is a coincidence."

"OK," she said. "After we present our new product, I'll go with you back to America. Just to visit. It'll give me a better understanding of how you operate, and I can share it with the board."

She'd also be a great witness to put Rogola away.

"And you have to pay for everything," she said. "Deal?"

"Done."

I looked out over Neo Toronto and smiled.

But everything changed the next day.

CHAPTER 22

Cheryl escorted me back to my room. I felt like an idiot to ask, but Cheryl was kind enough to place my holoreader on my psy-roll and change the settings to allow for voice commands. She left me with a pat on the cheek and enough silence to drown a brontosaurus.

I searched the Feed for anything on wraith containment technology and came up with a generous amount of fan fiction and conspiracy theories – nothing worth a damn. Everything I could find out about Yūrei Corporation had to do with its holographic advertising before they went lone wolf.

After giving up on that thread, and still unable to go to sleep – because of the recent juice-up on my meds – I decided to look up the history of the smoke eaters. For all their secrets, my new job had a lot more information than the wraith-catching stuff.

Chief Donahue had been on the Cincinnati Fire Department – when there was still a Cincinnati. Shortly after E-Day, Donahue led the campaign to set up a national program to combat the dragon threat. It burned a lot of asses in the National Guard and even the main branches of the military, but seeing how rapid intervention was the greatest factor, the government agreed that dragons would be better handled on a state level. And so, the smoke eaters were born.

The Feed mentioned nothing about our ability to breathe smoke, which I guessed was for the best. The public was already calling for our heads. When they found out we could breathe smoke like the scalies, it would only turn things into a bad X-Men situation.

I hadn't realized how long I'd been surfing the Feed until the sun crept from behind a building and nearly blinded me. It was time to talk to Naveena.

I should have known her door wouldn't slide open for me. So I rammed my psy-roll into the metal until she opened up.

Naveena wore her usual bedtime attire. "What the hell are you doing? It's too early for your shit, Brannigan."

"Grab some coffee," I said, rolling past her into the room. "I have some bombs to drop on you."

She rubbed sleep from her eyes and hit the button on the coffeemaker, grabbing two cups before remembering I couldn't drink anything.

"You can't freak out when I tell you this stuff, OK?"

She draped her arms over the kitchenette counter. Her eyes were half-cracked.

"And you have to believe me," I said.

"Just tell me already."

"Yūrei invented wraith-capturing technology."

She groaned and covered her face. "Really?"

I tried to nod, but slammed my chin against the psy-roll. "Fuck! I keep doing that." I wiggled my jaw. "And they're under the impression we already know about it. That we've already been using the tech. Know why? Because Mayor Rogola bought it from them a while ago, and that means he's behind the recent dragon attacks with the white fire coming out of appliances."

I proudly tucked in my lips and breathed a deep victory. That was it. That was my grand conspiracy theory laid out. Perfect? No. But I thought I covered most of the finer points of my hypothesis.

Naveena rested her chin in a palm. "You know how stupid that sounds?"

"It makes perfect sense!"

Naveena poured her coffee and added a few ice cubes from the mini freezer. "I don't like Rogola or anything, but why would he summon dragons? Even if there is such a thing as this wraith trapper whatever, how does that mean he can put it in…?"

"A TV or a holostereo?"

"Yeah. Sure." She raked fingers through her bed-mussed hair.

"I don't know all the specifics. Something to do with electrical current."

"Who told you all of this?"

"It was in passing, but, Cheryl."

Naveena laughed.

"What?"

She wasn't taking this as seriously as I'd hoped.

"When I was her age," Naveena said, "I would lie to everyone, too. Just make shit up to see if they'd go for it. Made me feel like I had this superpower."

"It's not like that at all!"

Naveena hummed her disbelief.

"Look, play along if they mention it. I asked Cheryl to show us how they can catch a wraith. After she shows us, we can figure out what the hell is going on. Fair enough?"

She took a long sip from her coffee, then winked. "All right, Brannigan. I'll play your game. But you owe me."

"Sure," I said, just happy she didn't completely write it off.

"But then we have to see Alan. We're meeting with Yūrei's president today, and he's going to show us this new tech – the one we actually came to look at."

"Oh, that reminds me," I said. "Cheryl's coming back with us on Jet 1."

Naveena's reaction was... expected.

Cheryl had been called away for business, but had an employee deliver a disk on wraith-catching for us to watch. I groaned when I saw it was Professor Poltergeist again. He held some weird remote thing and kept blathering on about safe distances and the remote's capacity. He was just about to get into the good stuff, when one of Yūrei's teen board members showed up to take us to see the president.

"Relax, Brannigan," Naveena told me as we rode the elevator.

"I'm fine," I said.

The Canadian youngster flirted with Naveena, smiling too big and asking if she liked such-and-such rock band I'd never heard of. He smelled like mothballs, but my disgusted face went unnoticed. Or ignored.

When the doors opened to the thirteenth floor, a gust of cool air greeted us from a dim passageway. The escort wouldn't leave the elevator, but told us Alan waited farther ahead. Naveena and I moved slowly at first, but when the elevator doors closed behind us, we hurried. The blue, metal walls cast our reflections like funhouse mirrors, and the floor lit up in bright white as we passed over it.

The end of the hall opened into a large room, where an enormous apparatus, shaped like an upside down triangle, hung from the ceiling. Wires draped from the top of the triangle and connected to huge computer towers. Like a helmet, the bottom of the apparatus covered a man's head, who sat in a cushy white seat.

Alan Hamdel and the other teenagers stood in a

semicircle around him. When I got closer, I saw the seated man also wore metal gloves that were connected to the apparatus by even more bulky, black wires.

None of them spoke or even moved. My psy-roll wheels were the loudest thing on the entire floor. Cheryl was absent.

One of the teenagers saw us and whispered into Alan's ear. Hamdel nodded and spoke to the helmeted man, who didn't move, but the room filled with a booming voice, amplified through speakers.

"Welcome," he said. "I am Shane Hamdel, President of Yūrei Corporation."

"What the hell is that thing on his head?" I blurted.

Naveena snorted, but quickly put a hand to her mouth.

Alan and the others looked at me as if I'd taken a dump on the floor. Shane's gloved hands flexed as if he was strangling a rabbit in each fist.

I had no right to talk trash about someone apparently confined to a machine, but shit, it was weird. I knew the Canadians had developed some strange technology we'd never seen, but this was ridiculous.

"My son," Alan said, "is present both here and in cyberspace. Our best ideas come from the digital frontier, where all mankind's collective consciousness has been gathering since the invention of the internet. The Source."

"Does he ever get out of that thing?" I asked.

"I can speak for myself, thank you," Shane said. "And no, Mr Brannigan, I never leave. I can assure you it's much more civilized in here than it will ever be out there."

"Hell, I'll give you my psy-roll when I'm done with it, to complete your transformation."

The board members shifted on their feet, avoiding

my gaze. I don't think they quite got my humor, but I'd apparently set them on edge. Alan dismissed the others.

"Thank you," Shane said. "Although I have no idea what you mean. My father will now take you to our Research and Development department in order to demonstrate our newest product. I think you'll be very excited to see what we have to offer. In fact, we're offering it to you at cost. We all want to make the world a better place. Right?"

Naveena kicked my psy-roll and cleared her throat. "Thank you, President Hamdel. We appreciate your hospitality."

Shane squirmed in his seat, as if hearing a female voice sent slugs up his ass. "Now, if you'll excuse me. I hate to be away from the Source for too long. Good bye."

And with that, lights flickered throughout the apparatus, as Shane leaned back in his chair and began to move his gloved hands through the air like a drughead. Alan hurried toward us and extended a hand toward the elevator.

On our ride to yet another floor I asked, "How did your son surpass you in the company?"

A blood vessel twitched in his temple. "This is a democracy, much like your country. The board saw him as the best choice to lead our company. I agree."

"Yeah, but with his head essentially stuck up a robot's ass–"

"Shut up, Brannigan." Naveena said, but the hint of a smile was there.

Alan cleared his throat. "The corporate government views youth and bold ideas as the currency of our age. My son is the embodiment of those ideals."

I was about to make a witty retort, but the elevator doors opened, and the bright yellow sparks of lasers shut me up. I'd been wondering why almost all of the people I'd seen in Canada had been in their teens to late twenties. A ton of older folks – people my age, at least – filled this new floor, constructing cages with laser bars, holographic ads that projected from hovering discs that followed the nearest pedestrian around the room.

"This is our R&D department," Alan said, leading us through all the cool tech.

Naveena and I had to hurry to keep up with him. We came to a large, silver door at the back of the room. Alan scanned his hand over a sensor and the door slid to the side in a blur.

"Please, step quickly." He frowned at me. "Or roll."

We did what he said, and as soon as we'd passed through, the door slid behind us like a knife. The space we'd entered was small, and if I hadn't already been in a psy-roll, I'd have been squatting under the ceiling like Naveena and Alan. A window lay in front of us, looking into another room similar to our propellerhead labs.

Alan hit a button and said, "We're ready to begin."

On the other side of the window, two older people, a woman and a man, worked on some kind of cannon. At the other end of the room, what I'd assumed to be a wall slid open, and another man brought in a yellow-scaled dragon on the end of a chain. A muzzle covered the scaly's snout. It was the kind with only hind legs – a wyvern, I remembered from one of Sergeant Puck's lectures. Even bound, it thrashed with malice, as if it was trying to find a way to kill everyone in the room. I'm pretty sure that was exactly what it had in mind.

"So, you're selling us another laser cannon?" I asked. "It'd be nice if this one didn't take so long to charge."

"Just watch," Alan said.

The man leading the wyvern connected the leash to a ring bolted into the floor. The scaly snapped its head forward, trying to bite him. What the dragon lacked in the use of its jaws was made up for in sheer force as the muzzled snout sent the man sailing into several carts of electronic devices.

Still connected to the chain, the wyvern swung its neck to and fro, trying to pull the muzzle off. One of the researchers ran to help the fallen man, while the woman frantically powered on the cannon.

"Is this supposed to happen?" I asked, but Alan said nothing.

"They need to get out of there," Naveena said. "That's a fully mature wyvern. They're smarter and meaner than most dragons."

"Our researchers know what they're doing," Alan said with an expressionless face.

Just then, the wyvern stared down at its muzzle. Within seconds, the muzzle glowed bright, golden orange as the dragon's flaming breath heated the metal.

"Oh, shit," was all I could say.

The wyvern didn't stop shooting its flames, even when the muzzle fell in black clumps onto the lab floor; it merely redirected the fire at the two men standing closest.

"Get them out of there!" I yelled.

Alan just stared in surprised terror, a hand to his mouth. Naveena shook her head in disgust, backing toward the door.

One of the burning researchers fell helpless onto the ground, while the other ran for an emergency shower. He hit a button to release streams of foam to cascade onto his body. When the foam had done its job and extinguished the flames, he collapsed.

The woman researcher screamed as the wyvern reared back to breathe more fire, but she pulled a trigger at the back of the laser cannon before the scaly could attack. A large ring of blue energy shot from the cannon and enveloped the wyvern, instantly dropping it to the floor.

"I apologize for that," Hamdel said. "Both of you know how unpredictable dragons can be."

While other researchers poured into the lab to collect the burned men and the distraught woman, I turned to Alan.

"Two men died so you could show us a different way to kill a scaly," I said. "What a waste of a trip."

"No," Alan said, pointing to the window. "Something better."

I followed his finger to the wyvern as researchers raced around its bulk to haul their dead coworkers out of the room. The dragon was still breathing.

"Now you don't have to kill the dragons," Alan said, with a smile of zealous pride.

"It's like some kind of energy tranquilizer." Naveena thinned her eyes.

"Let me get this straight," I said. "You want us to immobilize the scalies and, what, put them in a zoo? Maybe follow your example and have school buses roll up to sacrifice kindergartners to them like popcorn?"

"Why kill them if you don't have to?" Alan asked. "This way, you can eliminate the problem without destroying an entire species."

Naveena leaned on my psy-roll. "Because they're a threat to every life, human and otherwise. Entire ecosystems have become ash because one dragon created one wraith that drew in dozens more dragons."

Alan looked surprised. "But surely you've been using the wraith containment devices we made for you last year. There should be no threat of attracting more dragons."

Naveena turned to me. I raised my eyebrows to say, I told you so!

"I think we need a better handle on how to use the

wraith-trapping stuff," I said. "Cheryl said she'd show us how it's done. That video she gave us isn't that great."

Alan nodded. "I can have Masaki or one of the others show you."

"No," I said. "Cheryl said she would."

Alan looked down and cleared his throat, fixed his tie. "I'm afraid she is no longer employed with us."

"What?" I said. "Why? Because she's coming back with us stateside? You can't do that."

"Brannigan, even though you think the world revolves around you, I'm afraid there are more important things I have on my mind besides policing my employees' travel plans. And I had no idea." His jaw trembled as he fought to keep it still.

"Where is she, then?" Naveena asked.

"I can't release that information." Alan rubbed his eyes. "Now, if you'll excuse me, I'll let you finish your stay in our country and we'll be glad to load your plane with our non-lethal cannons. As my son said, we're providing them at cost."

"Let's just go," Naveena said.

But I couldn't let it go. I rolled toward Alan, stopping just in front of him. "Tell me where Cheryl is and we'll leave. We'll even buy your stupid cannons."

"You can't make that call, Brannigan," said Naveena. "And you should just accept that Cheryl isn't coming. It was a bad idea to begin with."

"Naveena," I turned to her, "I will never ask you for anything else if you do me this one solid. Smoke eater to smoke eater. Please."

I didn't know if it was what I'd said, or that I'd said it without a shred of my usual smartass flavoring, but Naveena's face softened.

Alan moved to leave, but Naveena stepped in his way. "I don't like violence, Hamdel," Naveena said, "but

I'm very good at it. Normally I wouldn't care about what you guys do, but I smell a rat. So tell us where Cheryl is."

The wrinkles at the sides of Alan's eyes deepened as he looked from Naveena to me, and then back. He sighed. "They held the Drawing."

Anger flared from deep inside my psy-roll. "Where did they take her?"

"It's too late," Alan said. "I never wanted–"

"Wait," Naveena said. "What drawing?"

"They took her because of that dead dragon," I said. "They're going to sacrifice her to the scalies. This bastard probably made sure it was her, so she couldn't leave the country."

"I never wanted it to be Cheryl!" Alan said. "It was just a… coincidence."

Coincidence. I'd just spoken with Cheryl about that very thing. Despite my doubts about a benevolent universe and all evidence showing that Sherry and I would never get what we wanted, I'd caved to the hope that maybe it was time to do good for someone and fill a decadesold hole in our hearts at the same time. Well, fuck coincidences. You have to take life by the balls and do it yourself.

"We've got to stop it," Naveena told me.

"Damn right," I said.

Naveena grabbed Alan by the back of the neck and pushed him to the door. "Open it."

He waved a hand at the door, and it slid open. Naveena and I barreled through research and development like a dragon out of hell. I didn't even know the psy-roll could go that fast, tilting slightly as we took a corner, and almost throwing me onto my side. We were in the elevator and on the street outside before Alan could send security.

The same hover van driver from before leaned against

his ride, blowing vape bubbles when I rolled up.

"Take us to where they're doing the sacrifice," Naveena shouted.

The driver started and dropped the bubble vape from his mouth. He blinked a couple of times before saying, "What?"

I said, "I'd do what she says."

"I can't leave," the driver said. "I'm waiting for Mr Hamdel."

"Lower the lift and take us to where they're sacrificing the girl!" Naveena pulled out a pulse gun and aimed it at the driver's head.

"Where the hell did you get that?" I asked.

The driver thought he'd be fast enough to lean into the van and dig for the gun in the glove compartment.

Naveena fired the gun straight up, static crackling the air afterward. "The gun isn't there, dummy. I took it after our last joyride."

Who the hell was this woman?

The driver squatted to the ground with his hands up.

In the next minute, we were speeding down the street to where they fed the dragons. I only hoped they hadn't yet rung the dinner bell.

CHAPTER 23

Far outside of Neo Toronto, Canada looked more like the outskirts of Parthenon City, but darker, and not just because night was coming. Brown clouds had blocked our singular star from touching any scrap of this shithole, and the twitchy glow of holograms would be the only light to navigate by.

Then I saw it. Many politicians over the years – before the dragons came, anyway – had run on platforms of building a wall. First, they shouted about a wall to keep Mexicans from crossing in the south, then, later, a wall to keep Americans from crossing into Canada.

Well, we certainly weren't changing their opinion of us now.

The wall ahead was unlike any brick-and-mortar barrier I'd ever seen. If Hell had a gate, it would look like that wall. The thing was made entirely of glass and, like a macabre aquarium, wraiths floated inside, trapped, crammed in like sardines, and giving off their eerie white glow. They clawed at the glass, wailing for anyone who'd listen. The wraith wall had to be at least twenty feet high and as wide as a city block. That's a shitload of ghosts.

The driver stopped the hover van. "I can't drive any closer."

"Why?" I asked. "Flat tire?"

He turned to give me a confused look. "This van doesn't have tires. It—"

"He was being facetious," Naveena said, gun ever present.

That just made him scrunch his face more.

"We need you to keep going," I said. "Take us beyond that wraith wall."

He pointed to where a horde of guards in red uniforms, brown Mountie hats, and sunglasses stood outside the wall, carrying what looked like Uzis. "They won't let you inside. Not only are you Americans, but you kill dragons for a living."

A couple of the Mounties rode mechanical horses that blew steam from their nostrils.

The driver had a point. And I certainly couldn't roll up in my tiny tank with Naveena trotting beside, expecting to be let through without a couple bullet holes to our heads.

"I can tell them she's my date," the driver said. "That I want to show her inside the wall. I'm in good with them." This guy was starting to be a team player. With the teen gang attack, it was probably the most excitement he'd had in years. He pointed to me. "But you..."

I looked to the floor. Several empty metal boxes lay beside me.

"Put one of these boxes on my head," I told Naveena.

She glanced at the boxes on the van floor and looked back at me with wide, incredulous eyes. "That's ridiculous."

"You're right," I said. "But it just might work."

She sighed, but put the box on my head. Soon, we were moving again. The driver turned the corner and stopped before rolling down his window. The Mounties whistled at Naveena, who had to have been exercising some serious restraint. Thankfully, most of the catcalls and flirting was Canuck slang I didn't understand. The driver said he and Naveena would only be a few minutes. With whoops of praise, the Mounties let us through, and after another few minutes, we stopped. Naveena took the box off my head.

"Get out," the driver said, hitting the lever to lower me out of the van. "Please don't expect a ride out of here. I'll be leaving."

I grinned. "Stay where you are, Chuck. We'll be fine on our own from here."

But as I looked around the courtyard, surrounded on three sides by thick, glossy black walls, I quickly realized how big of a clusterfuck Naveena and I had jumped into.

"This'll be fun," I said.

"Let's look behind that one." Naveena ran toward the back wall. At the top of numerous stairs waited a huge, double door.

I spun my psy-roll around and headed for a ramp at the far side of the courtyard. Good thing this sacrificial chamber was wheelchair-friendly.

Drums began to beat somewhere on the other side of the wall, so, with every psychic scrap of energy I had, I pushed the psy-roll as fast as it would go. My treads took the ramp with ease, but the incline quickly put hell on my squat little box.

A deep reptilian roar joined the drums.

"Hurry up, Brannigan!" Naveena shouted, already halfway up the steps.

"Come on, you piece of shit," I shouted at the psy-roll.

My mind pushed so hard I got a headache, so hard I almost thought I'd sweat blood and break my teeth with the effort.

Boom, boom, boom.

My psy-roll took another curve in the ramp, and I tried to rid my mind of acknowledging how far I was leaning back and how easily I could have toppled backwards.

I reached the top of the steps and helped Naveena burst through the door. We entered something resembling an arena, looking out onto a long, wobbly bridge that stretched over a chasm so deep and wide, I couldn't see the bottom. Not until flames flew from the pit.

Around the edge of the chasm and behind a thin wooden rail, drummers banged on oversized taiko drums.

Cheryl stood alone in the middle of the bridge, directly over the hole. Chains held her arms in place.

"Cheryl!" I screamed.

The drummers kept up their tempo, but out of the corner of my eye, I saw a couple Mounties running for me. They didn't look armed.

"I'll hold them off," Naveena said. "You go get Cheryl."

I sped forward, toward the wooden bridge. Behind me, Naveena shouted for the Mounties to stay back.

On the bridge, Cheryl looked up and stared at me, and although it was too far away to know for sure, I think she smiled as a dragon rose from the darkness below.

The scaly was green and snake-like, tall as a building as it rested on a tail deep within the chasm. Its eyes shimmered golden from the fire flickering out of its mouth in small bursts. Long tendrils floated in the air from its snout, and at each side of its body, small claws flexed open and shut. It floated without wings.

I guess I could understand why someone would revere something so large and nearly supernatural. But not me. All I wanted to do was wipe this bastard and others like it from the face of the earth.

Just before I'd made it a third of the way across the bridge, gunshots rang out behind me. Several Mounties had entered behind Naveena and were having a hard time wrestling her to the ground. The other Mounties tackled my psy-roll. It took all of their weight to push me onto my side, and the bridge heaved violently to and fro. But I didn't bother with that. I kept my eyes on Cheryl.

She looked sad, like I'd let her down – I had. The dragon descended as I screamed. Cheryl never made a sound.

And then she was gone.

CHAPTER 24

I was getting a firsthand experience behind one of those cages with lasers for bars. I'd initially thought they were meant for trapping dragons or wild dogs, but I guess they were also good for securing the big, bad American in a robotic wheelchair.

The Mounties stood outside my cage, wearing their crisp, red uniforms and cracking jokes under their breath. I was sure their jollity was at my expense. You could call it a gut feeling – and because a few of them took aim at me with their submachine guns.

I didn't care. Nothing really mattered at that particular moment.

Alan walked in, and the Mounties got quiet, straightening to attention at the sight of him. The older man dismissed them with a jerk of his head toward the door before dragging a chair over to my cage.

He didn't say anything for a while, and neither did I. We just sat there listening to each other breathe. His had a whine and crackle to it, a struggle to inhale. Well, it was one advantage I had on him.

"Mounties," I said. "An interesting choice for national defense."

Alan nodded. "There were certainly more of them than any soldiers, after the dragons came. Very loyal."

"So, what's going to happen to me and Naveena? You going to sacrifice us, too?"

"We don't delight in the Drawing, or the sacrifice. We haven't even needed it for the last two years. Then you came."

"You're blaming me? I didn't make those teen gangbangers release a dragon on us. You did the right thing taking that scaly down, and I was content to let you pout and whip yourself like a dusty rug. But when you feed an innocent girl to one of those things because you think it has feelings? I hope they swallow this country whole. You all deserve to feel their so-called wrath."

Alan raised his chin. "Maybe you're right," he said. "But you won't be here to see it."

So, that's how it was going to be, huh? They were going to sacrifice the foreigner. Well, I'd put up one hell of a fight until the end. That's one thing I could promise, for Cheryl's sake at least.

The door slid open, and Naveena walked in. "Is he ready?" she asked Alan.

He nodded.

"You're going along with this?" I couldn't believe Naveena would throw me under the hover bus. Sure, we had our tussles, but we were smoke eaters. She'd just run into a dragon pit with me and taken on a gang of Mounties.

"We don't have another choice," Naveena said.

Alan pushed a button on his holoreader and the cage's laser bars disappeared.

"Come on," Naveena said. "Or would you rather they sacrifice your old ass?"

"So, you called Donahue?" I asked Naveena on our long walk and roll to where Jet 1 waited for us.

"Yeah. He sounded..."

"He'll understand."

The neon lights of Neo Toronto flickered goodbyes as we left the smothering buildings and skittish crowds. We must have made a name for ourselves in our short stay. Shop owners would close their floating carts when they'd see us coming, and blast down a back alley, leaving behind the smell of thruster ozone and the savor of whatever food they'd been peddling. No gangs bothered us on the way either. Good ole Canadian passive-aggressiveness.

It's the little things, I tell you.

I looked up at Naveena, asked, "You tell Donahue about the wraith-trapping thing we supposedly bought?"

"No," she said. "I didn't want to overload him at once. I'll tell him when we get back."

A holographic ad flew over us, promoting a new Godzilla movie featuring an enemy named King Ghidorah – a three-headed dragon.

"Yeah," I said. "There's a lot I need to do when I get out of this box."

"If he lets you out," Naveena said.

When she stopped walking, I stopped rolling, and she stood there, letting the wind push her hair over her face. She squeezed her hands into fists and all of a sudden it felt like Neo Toronto had piped down to hear what she was going to say.

"Brannigan?"

"Yeah?"

"I'm sorry about Cheryl."

I lost any words. What do you say to something like that? Thank you? Didn't seem to fit. Only a big slice of silence and the pain of guilt swirling within my psy-roll felt appropriate.

Naveena shrugged. "It's a good thing we're never coming back here."

"What do you mean?"

"That's one of the things we had to promise for them to let us leave unscathed. We can't come back to Canada. Ever."

"Good riddance," I said.

"And they'll deny that we ever set foot here. They're still giving us that nonlethal cannon, though. Free. At least Donahue can't be mad about us saving the budget."

"It's all about the bottom line." I rolled ahead, and Naveena had to run to catch up.

"I didn't think anyone would do that," she said, "sacrifice someone to a dragon. I'm sure in your heyday you saw the Aztecs do it. Quesadilla or something."

"Quetzalcoatl," I said.

She was trying to cheer me up, but I wanted no part of it. I deserved to feel like shit. I'd lost my house, my body, and a young woman I could have saved from this terrible country. No one was going to take my guilt away from me.

"Yeah, that's the one," said Naveena. "They killed people to please that dragon."

"It was more like a winged serpent, but basically a scaly. And he abolished human sacrifice. To the Aztecs he represented humanity and progress."

"Oh."

"That's why a lot of Mormons think Jesus visited the natives in the Americas, and the Aztecs called him Quetzalcoatl."

Naveena shrugged. "I guess what I'm trying to say is that religion fucks people up."

I thought of DeShawn lying bloody on a funeral home floor.

"Yeah," I said. "It does."

Sergeant Puck and the other recruits were waiting for us outside Jet 1.

"Brannigan, you could ruin a brass monkey," Puck said. "I haven't had a vacation in ten years and now I'm banned from the one country I actually liked besides our own. Get in the plane before I leave your wrinkled ass."

Return trips always took longer. Maybe it's the excitement of a new place that makes going there fun, and coming back a drag. Add the weight of seeing Cheryl eaten alive, missing Sherry and Ohio, and the desire to leave Canada – the flight home was an eternity.

Afu was the only one who showed me any kindness. When he tried to start up a conversation with me, Williams slapped him across the chest and gave him a look I was all too familiar with when Sherry didn't want me doing something.

I let Afu off the hook and shook my head, letting him know it was OK.

Getting us banned from an entire country was entirely my fault – since nobody was lumping Naveena into the blame. The other smokies would get over it, and if they didn't, oh, well.

I asked Naveena to reload my medication, and then I slept the rest of the trip.

I dreamed about Cheryl. We were somewhere up in the mountains, but everything looked bright and cartoonish. There were no trees, only the hard rock of the mountains and maybe a touch of crayon green here and there on a yellow, dirt path. The clouds had funny black squiggles in them as if someone had drawn them with a black sharpie.

I was on some good drugs.

Dream Cheryl beckoned me to follow with a single curling finger, and I began to cry. It was the kind of deep sobbing that, even though I was dreaming, I could have been crying in the back of Jet 1 for my fellow smoke eaters to see.

I followed Cheryl to a dark cave, deep in the animated mountains. Of course, I knew there was a dragon in there, and of course it would be the three-headed one. A long, black dragon arm snaked out of the cave and snatched Cheryl so quickly I didn't have time to stop it.

I ran to the edge of the cave and hesitated before following into the darkness. I don't know why; I would have gone in head first in real life. That's one thing I hate about dreams. You always become the sniveling, little coward you try so hard not to be.

As I forced my dream self forward, the Behemoth rushed out of the cave, knocking me onto the crayon-colored ground. All three heads surrounded me, but the scaly snouts and obsidian horns were gone, and in their place were the heads of Cheryl, Naveena, and Sherry.

They snatched me up in their teeth and tore my body in three separate directions before I sprang violently awake.

Naveena frowned at me.

"Sorry." My mouth had gone dry. I couldn't wait to drink something. Anything. I still had another week in the psy-roll.

Puck said, "What were you dreaming about, Brannigan? All the pushups I'm going to make you do?"

"Sergeant," I said, "if I can get the use of my body back, I'll be happy to do as many damn pushups as you want."

Puck laughed. "I'll remember that."

Through the porthole, Parthenon City stood below us, and it was the most wonderful thing I'd seen all week.

When we'd landed, and as I rolled down the jet's ramp, Yolanda, the propellerhead, called to me from across the apparatus bay. "Come with me."

"I really need to see Donahue first," I said.

"Chief Donahue wanted me to come get you in his place."

"What for?" I asked, rolling beside her into Smoke Eater Headquarters.

"He said if he saw you, he'd probably kill you."

"Fair enough," I said. "I really need to talk to him, though. And then I really need to see my wife. You guys find that Behemoth yet?"

"No, we haven't had any luck." She waved her card to open her lab's door and let me roll in first. "And Chief's been too busy trying to calm the public."

"What do you mean?"

"Well, after that dragon destroyed most of that neighborhood, the citizens have been pretty peeved, saying that those fire droids did a better job than we did."

"That's ridiculous. Those metal bastards got stomped in seconds."

Yolanda shrugged. "People have been protesting all over the state for the last couple days. Demanding we be disbanded. Honestly, I'm surprised they haven't tried yet."

"They'll calm down as soon as we find that Behemoth," I said. "Surely someone has seen it. Scalies aren't very inconspicuous."

"This one is. We've even put out the word to smoke eaters in other states. Nothing has popped up yet, though some have seen strange shapes on radar. Then it disappears. I've even researched ancient three-headed dragons, like Zmey Gorynych–"

"Gesundheit."

Yolanda smiled and shook her head. "I haven't found anything different from your basic knight-saving-the-maiden dragon folk tales. We're still up the creek on this."

"Can't I get any good news?" I groaned and lowered my head.

Naveena walked in. "You about to crack open this oyster?"

"Just about to," Yolanda said.

"What the hell are you ladies talking about?"

Yolanda was about to answer, but Naveena jumped ahead of her.

"You're getting out of your psy-roll."

My eyes nearly bulged out of my head. "You're just messing with me."

"Nope," Yolanda said. "I'm ready if you are."

"But you said I had to stay in this thing for another week at the minimum."

Yolanda wrinkled her lips and looked at Naveena, who laughed.

"Well…" Yolanda said. "Chief Donahue… I mean, it wasn't my idea to keep you in it for two weeks."

"That bastard wanted me incapacitated for as long as he thought he could get away with!"

"Relax, Brannigan," Naveena said. "I'd say you and Chief are even."

I turned to Yolanda. "Well, come on."

"It'll take a little bit for your muscles to get back in the swing of things. Almost like a really bad case of your appendages falling asleep. And you'll probably notice some… changes."

"I better still be able to use my dick," I said.

Naveena shook her head.

Yolanda put fingers to her lips, looking down with a shy smile before clearing her throat and saying, "Everything will work. I promise. Now, with this first part, you might feel some discomfort."

"Wait," I said. "Discomfort?"

She took out her holoreader and linked to the psy-roll. "Here we go."

"Hold on a–" Feeling entered my body as I realized a tube was lodged in each of my lower orifices and along my spine. They were then forcefully yanked out.

"Ow!" I yelled. "Holy shit!"

Naveena laughed.

"Laugh it up, asshole." I was able to move my hand to rub one of the affected areas inside the psy-roll.

A few buttons later, and the front of the box opened like a casket. Instinctively, I covered my nether regions, not that it really mattered. Yolanda had already gotten a good look at me when she first put me inside the damn psy-roll, and Naveena... well, that was another story.

I looked down at my body. Yolanda had been right about something appearing different. For one, she had shaved most of my body to connect all the electrodes and such, but now, my muscles swelled larger and more refined than before they went into the psy-roll. My chest looked like two boulders above a chiseled stomach, and my forearms and thighs were striated like an anatomical chart. It was more like a swimmer's body than a bodybuilder's, but... hot damn!

I still had gray hair poking out from between my fingers where I covered my junk.

I jerked my head up. "You Captain America'd me!"

"Are you mad?" Yolanda frowned, genuinely concerned that I would be upset.

I laughed, and it hurt a little as my body was getting used to functioning again. "Hell no, I'm not upset. Is this from that blue gel?"

Yolanda nodded, handing me a thin, white robe from a cabinet.

Naveena leaned in to get a look.

"Hey, no free gawking," I said. "Turn around."

She did as I asked as I wobbled to my feet and let Yolanda help me into the robe. I tried to step out of the psy-roll, but couldn't lift my foot high enough and fell forward.

Yolanda caught me and started breathing heavier – I

don't think it was from any physical strain. "You need to take it easy while your muscles wake up. They may look pretty, but they're still not all the way useful."

Pretty, huh?

"That Ieiunium curate is some powerful shit," I said. "You guys need to give some to the hospitals, it could save a ton of lives."

Yolanda frowned. "Well, it's still being tested, and by the time it goes through all the red tape, it wouldn't be as effective. I say we just keep it in house."

I was about to argue with her, when a page came over the speakers in the ceiling.

"All available staff report to the foyer," the voice said. "All available staff report to the foyer immediately. If you're hearing this, that means you."

Naveena turned around. "Let's go."

"What about that thing we have to talk to Donahue about?" I asked.

"Well, he'll be in the foyer, won't he?"

CHAPTER 25

Yolanda gave me a walker to use until I was able to properly move. Along with the old man robe I wore, it really crapped on the wonder of my newly formed body.

Naveena followed beside me as we entered the foyer. A few smoke eaters I hadn't met waited around, talking to Donahue.

I hobbled toward the chief, but Naveena cut me off.

"Chief," she said. "We need to tell you something important."

Donahue turned and looked at me like I was a squished bug on the windshield. "It can wait."

"This is related to what you and I were talking about before I left," I said.

Afu and Williams walked in wearing their dress greens, making me feel like the crazy, underdressed uncle at a family reunion.

"After this," Donahue told me.

"But Chief–"

"Damn it, Brannigan, get in line with Williams and Kekoa, and we'll talk for as long as you want afterward."

Smoke eaters and propellerheads filled the foyer. We were gathered here for something, but all I knew was that I was the old bastard with a robe and a walker.

Sighing, I got in line beside Williams, who looked me

over and snorted, trying to hold in laughter.

I leaned toward her to whisper. "Does this mean we're cool? About the Cedar Point thing?"

She play-punched me in the arm. I took that as a maybe.

Sergeant Puck entered last with a box in her hands.

"All right, everybody," Chief Donahue said, raising an arm in the air. "This is a little impromptu, since we weren't expecting our recruits to be back from Canada so early."

More than a few eyes fell on me.

"But I want to officially open the proceedings to accept our new brothers and sister into the fold. If Sergeant Puck approves of them, of course." Donahue turned to Puck.

Sucking on her teeth, Puck nodded.

This was a graduation? I didn't feel like I had learned a thing, besides a few different types of dragons and the different ways they can kill you.

Not only underdressed, but also underwhelmed.

Looking back at my time in the fire academy, even with all the tests and training evolutions, I'd felt the same way at that graduation.

Donahue said, "Tamerica Williams."

I had never known what Williams' first name was until that moment. She stepped forward from our line.

"Sergeant Puck," Donahue said, "what is your recommendation for this recruit."

"Acceptance," Puck said.

What was the point of all this? Donahue had told me not long ago about the lack of smoke eaters and that the only way out was in a box. We were already "accepted". This was a waste of time.

Donahue opened the box in Puck's hands and took out a badge. He pinned it onto Williams' shirt and slapped it with his palm. "You were born a smoke eater. Welcome to your calling."

I'd never seen Williams smile so big. She stepped back in line as those around us applauded.

"Afu Kekoa," Donahue called next.

My big buddy stepped up, puffing out his chest. He'd tied his hair in a bun for the occasion.

Puck said, "Accepted."

Donahue repeated the same badge-adorning and meaningful words as he had with Williams.

Looking at me, Chief D sighed deeply. That just made me smile.

"Cole Brannigan, step forward."

I wobbled against my walker, ignoring the muffled laughter behind me. My legs were getting better, but not fast enough.

Donahue raised an eyebrow at Puck. "Do you accept this recruit?"

I wanted them to just get on with it. Yep, we're all accepted and ready to slice scaly heads and level orphanages to the ground. Sherry was waiting for me, and I was eager to use my new musculature to release some pent-up sexual energy, and then, after fully recovering, go shove a foot up Mayor Rogola's ass and see him locked up for the rest of his life, and then maybe we could go find us a three-headed dragon before anybody else had to die.

But, you know, let's have a low-key graduation first.

"I wish I could accept him," Puck answered. "But I can't."

The hell?

"Is that your answer?" Donahue said.

Puck nodded, raising her eyebrows in a, "Yeah, I meant it, motherfucker!" kind of way.

I spoke so every smoke eater and propellerhead could

hear me. "Mayor Rogola bought a wraith-catcher and is using it to draw dragons to burn down houses. I don't know why. Real estate fraud, maybe. Personal revenge. He's the reason my house is gone and why a bunch of firefighters and smoke eaters are dead. Just thought you should know before I hit the door and kick his ass without your help."

Puck and Donahue both stood with their mouths wide open. I turned to Naveena, who shrugged. A few of the crowd mumbled among themselves.

Donahue spoke first. "I was going to say that we'll accept Brannigan's old ass anyway."

He walked over with a badge lying in his palm and showed it to me. On the badge, a dragon spread its wings over a Maltese cross bearing two crossed lances behind the great seal of the state of Ohio. Attaching it to my robe, Donahue patted it hard, enough to where I winced.

"You and Naveena," Donahue spoke low. "In my office. Now." He turned to the others. "OK, everybody. Back to work."

Donahue told Naveena to follow him, and I hobbled behind with my walker. The chief stood outside his door, smiling courteously at us.

That worried me.

When Naveena and I were seated, Donahue closed the door and sat very slowly into his chair. Then he let loose. "What is wrong with you, Brannigan? You think you're funny, spreading some lies around about the mayor? Just because you've got a vendetta against him doesn't give you the right to drag dead smokies into your game and try to get everybody else to go along with your nonsense!"

"He's telling the truth," Naveena said, stopping Donahue short as he took a breath to go at me again.

"He... what?"

"Brannigan is telling the truth. I heard it with my own ears. Yūrei Corporation sold Rogola some kind of technology to catch wraiths."

"And then they sacrificed a girl to a scaly," I whispered. It was too unbearable to say any louder.

Donahue stopped talking. He rubbed his chin a few times, as if he was petting a cat, then he bent down to a drawer in his desk and pulled out a bottle of vodka. Without offering either Naveena or myself any booze, he cracked the bottle open and swallowed for at least six seconds.

"Damn, Chief," I said.

Donahue leaned forward and stared at his bottle, saying more to himself, "The Canucks sacrificed someone?" He drank another swig. "This would be a lot easier if you were full of it, Brannigan."

"I can't argue with you there," I said. "But what are we going to do about it?"

"Do you have any real evidence, anything on paper, electronic receipts?"

I looked at Naveena. She sighed and shook her head.

"I'll call Hamdel," Chief said. "But I'm thinking that's going to be tough, since we're on their ban list. Might not even get through. We have to get the police involved. We're allowed certain bends in the law, but we can't storm city hall and kidnap the mayor for something we don't have much evidence on."

"Why don't we just go straight to the horse's mouth and ask him ourselves?" Naveena said.

"Go interrogate him?"

She nodded.

"I have to see my wife," I said.

Sherry thought I was still in Canada. But it would be nice to surprise her.

Donahue stood up from his seat. "No, no. Brannigan,

we need to see the mayor first. Then I'd like to take you to your wife myself. She might be... unsettled by your appearance. The, uh, new body. I had her put into temporary housing until you two are able to find something more suitable. How soon can you be ready to go?"

I eyed Donahue for a few seconds, watching his breathing grow shorter and quicker. He was hiding something. That body language book had never let me down.

"Thirty minutes should be fine," I said.

"I'll meet you out front."

I was about halfway to my dorm when I found Williams. "I need you to sneak me out of here."

"What? Why?"

"Something is up with Donahue. I can smell fishy-rat bullshit better than most, and I need to see my wife."

Williams turned to look down the hall. "Well, OK. I don't know what's going on, but hurry up and get dressed."

"No, Donahue will be looking for us. Just get me out of here. You know where my wife might be?"

"The department has a building they use to house families who've lost their homes to dragons. She's probably there."

I threw my walker away and limped toward the apparatus bay. "Then let's get out of here."

The temporary housing building stood on the north end of Parthenon City, not too far from downtown. Vehicles crammed the parking lot, floating in stasis, while a bunch of kids darted around them, playing tag. Williams pulled up to the front.

"You want me to come up with you?" Williams asked.

I grinned at her. "I have your number if I need you. Thanks for the ride."

Before I closed the door, Williams said, "Hey, Brannigan?"

"Yeah?"

"Do you always look for ways to get into trouble?"

"I think it just comes naturally." I closed the door and waved as she drove off.

I had to ask four different people – all of them looked at me like I was a crazy, homeless crack head – but I finally found out that Sherry was staying on the eighth floor. I stopped at the door, having to take a minute until my head stopped spinning.

Damn blue, chemical shit.

After a few of my hurried knocks, Sherry cracked the door. When she saw me, she swung it wide and greeted me with a fist to the arm.

"Ouch!" I screamed.

She followed the punch up by grabbing my robe's collar and slamming her lips into mine. Jumping, she wrapped her legs around my waist, and we stumbled into the apartment.

I had no sense of direction with my wife glued to my face, but somehow we found our way to the bedroom.

One time, back when Sherry and I were still dating, we had sex six times in seven hours. After that, especially after getting married, we'd averaged around one to two times a month. Now, I don't know if it was my new muscles, or the fact that we hadn't been happily alone together in a long time, but we beat our original record.

By a lot.

The apartment was a small studio with walls so thin, the whole building probably heard us going at it. We didn't even speak.

After the last round, lying on our backs and catching

our breath, I asked, "Want to go again?"

"I... can't."

"Slacker."

"I... must be dreaming."

Smiling, I took a breath and hummed my approval.

"I thought you were dead," she said.

I sat up. "What? I was just hurt and had to go on an assignment. Donahue said he told you."

"Assignment?" Sherry looked like she was going to flip out, but shook it away for later. "Your chief told me a dragon killed you." She scrunched her eyebrows together. "I've been crying for days."

I jumped out of bed. "I'm going to kill him."

"He said some people might come by asking questions about you, but your death and dismemberment insurance was paying for this room and a check would come for me to get a new house. Said we couldn't have a funeral until the investigation was through. I was too depressed to question it."

"Well, did anybody come around asking about me?"

Sherry shook her head.

I searched the room for some clothes. Kenji was asleep, charging beside the dresser. I found a few plain shirts and shorts. I'd have to keep using the slippers Yolanda gave me.

"You're leaving?" Sherry asked, gripping the covers around her.

"I've got to kick a few asses, and then I'll be back to repeat what we just did. OK?"

"It's not your job to save the world, you know."

"Yes, it is." I grabbed the holoreader near the kitchen and asked Naveena to come pick me up. Told her it was important. She said it always was with me.

When I hung up, Sherry was crying and squeezing the life out of her pillow. "Don't die on me again."

I sat on the bed and kissed her. "You remember how you always told me I could talk to you, if I ever saw something on the job that I couldn't shake?"

She nodded.

"Well, I never did when I should have. I used to keep a lot inside. Figured telling you about all of it would just make it worse. If I couldn't protect them, I could at least protect you from knowing about it. I know that's stupid."

Sherry held my hand, cool against my heat.

I said, "This assignment I went on, I saw something that's really gnawing at me."

"You can tell me. Whatever it is."

"I can't," I said. "Not yet. Not until I've crossed some things off my list."

"That's not good, Cole. You can't keep burying that stuff."

I touched her cheek. "I'll give the chief an extra punch for you."

We held each other in silence for a while, and then I left without any weakness in my muscles.

CHAPTER 26

"So you think Donahue is in league with Mayor Rogola?" Naveena asked as Renfro drove us toward city hall.

Naveena had filled her partner in on everything that had happened. He was surprisingly cool with it all.

"No, but he told my wife I was dead," I said. "That he's meeting with Rogola right now just gives me two birds for my one stone."

Naveena had called to see if Donahue was still waiting for me at headquarters, but they'd told her he'd gone to city hall.

"You said he was going to make it seem like you were one of the smokies that died," Naveena said. "Maybe he thought it would be better if your wife thought so, too."

The buildings zipped by in a blur.

"Well, either way," I said, "it was a shitty thing to do, and I'm kicking his ass."

"Let me handle it, Brannigan," said Naveena.

Renfro shook his head. "Just because you can't get fired doesn't mean you can't get in trouble for attacking a superior. We do have dungeons below headquarters, you know."

"What would you do, Renfro?" I asked.

He drove for a few more seconds before answering, "Yeah, I guess I would kick his ass, too."

When the cannon truck pulled up to city hall, I jumped out before the wheels had stopped spinning. Naveena chased after me. Even in my shitty foam slippers, I was putting her to shame as my legs found their full strength. I was never that fast before my fall, at least not since I was seventeen.

"Wait, Brannigan!" Naveena shouted behind me.

Wasn't gonna happen.

The security droids moved in when I burst through the front doors, but weren't fast enough. I passed by the elevator and randomly hit a button inside, sending it up so Naveena would have to take the stairs like me.

I hadn't even broken a sweat when I entered the floor to the mayor's office. His receptionist was in the middle of blowing a big red bubble I popped with a finger as I passed.

"Hey!" She jumped back. "You can't go in there!"

"Watch me."

The door hit Jenkins when I barged in. He crawled along the floor grabbing for the holoreader he'd dropped. Chief Donahue sat across from Rogola, both of them staring at me and frowning. I aimed my fist for the nearest man.

"Brannigan," was all Donahue was able to get out before my knuckles met his jaw. He fell sideways into Rogola's desk.

"I heard you were dead," the mayor said.

When he chuckled, I lifted a chair.

"Stop, Brannigan!" Naveena shouted as she entered the office.

I chucked the chair. Mayor Rogola was still smiling as it left my hands and flew right through his head, briefly sending his image into a flurry of static before it reformed into a belly-laughing simulation.

Fucking holograms.

"Where are you?" I said through gritted teeth. My pulse throbbed from the side of my neck.

"You honestly think I would risk coming down there, with thugs like you, and all the other creepy crawlies that plague our land." Rogola laughed again. "Jenkins, get security to see these losers out of here."

The mayor's assistant scrambled to his feet and left the room. From where I stood, I saw that the back of the sh◻ statues' heads held lenses that projected Rogola's image. Naveena ran over and helped Donahue onto his feet.

"What the hell!?" Donahue said, but I didn't know if it was from me punching him or that he hadn't known he'd been conversing with a hologram.

"I'm going to find you," I told Rogola. "This isn't over."

The mayor never budged – wherever he actually sat. "Yes, it is. All of you are over."

Thuds sounded against the floor, along with metallic clanking. Behind us, droids stomped into the office. One grabbed Naveena.

"Don't resist," the droid said.

"Get off of me." She kicked at the metal man's groin, but it had no effect.

The robot lifted her like she was a five year-old throwing a fit. "Don't resist."

Two others entered and came for me next. I decided not to resist. If Naveena couldn't take down one of these bastards, I sure as hell couldn't, even with a fresh body. They hefted all three of us out of the office one by one.

"Why did you punch me?" Donahue asked as we waited, crammed inside the elevator.

I glared at him, which couldn't have looked that threatening in the embrace of a robot. "You told my wife I was dead."

"Oh." He looked down, not attempting to defend his actions. "Well, I guess faking your death is worth a pile of dung now."

"I'm not worried about the mayor."

"Yeah, well maybe you should be," Naveena said.

We listened to a saxophone solo drifting from the elevator speakers.

"So, what now?" I asked.

"He wasn't giving me anything," Donahue said. "Even when I told him the Canadians had shown us some new toys. I don't want to say any more around these metal bastards."

I looked into one of the droids' blue eyes, remembering that they could be recording us at that moment. "What are we supposed to do?"

"For now, your jobs. Your regular jobs. Captain Jendal, meet the newest member of your crew." Donahue motioned his head toward me.

My new career had officially begun. What terrible timing.

CHAPTER 27

"Hurry!" the old woman shouted through a surgical mask she wore across the bottom half of her face. "It's in here."

You could have heard an axe drop through the surrounding neighborhood. In fact, the old woman's house was the only one with a light on. Standing on her lawn, wearing only a bra and pajama pants, she pointed to her open front door. The woman had six-thirty breasts – both sagging straight down like hands on a clock. I mean, that bra was basically pointless besides saving us the displeasure of seeing them bared to the night air.

Her house showed no fire, no smoke, no sign of a dragon at all.

Renfro, Naveena, and I waved from our seats in the cannon truck to let the woman know we saw her and that we'd be taking care of her problem shortly.

"What the hell is going on here?" Renfro said. "False alarm?"

"Propellerheads didn't see anything on the seismic monitor," I said.

Over the radio, Naveena told the second smoke eater crew, still on the way, that nothing was showing and we were going to investigate. Naveena took the lead, and I followed her toward the house.

"It's in the laundry room," the old woman said, before bending over and hacking into her mask.

"What did it look like?" Naveena asked, as she scanned the house with her therma goggles.

"What does that matter?" the woman said. "It was big and ugly!"

I brought my goggles out too, but nothing showed up in my scan besides a small red blob in the living room. A cup of coffee?

"I want to know what we're dealing with." Naveena threw Renfro an air-slashing hand signal that meant we weren't going to need the cannon powered up.

Making an "OK" with his gloved hands, Renfro threw down a couple wheel chocks and jogged over.

"Hurry!" the old woman said. "Why are you just waiting around?"

Naveena rolled her eyes and moved toward the door.

The house's smell hit me halfway up the front steps. I'd encountered the same stench in the fire service, when we'd go on runs to old folks who couldn't take care of themselves or drugheads who only took care of their next fix. The smell was a combo of shit, cat piss, and old books.

Don't be a hoarder, I thought. Don't be a hoarder, don't be a hoarder.

She was a hoarder.

Inside, we had to traverse stacks of papers, unopened shipping boxes, dolls, cups, and just a whole lot of junk I didn't feel like mentally categorizing. I know the old stories said dragons liked to hoard gold. Why couldn't my fellow humans hoard something good like that? I would have much rather walked into a house full of bling or jelly beans, not a collection of litter boxes that hadn't been emptied since 2082.

"I don't think a dragon would be the worst thing we

could find in here." I held my power suit's glove over my nose and mouth.

Renfro dry heaved into his own glove.

The woman stuck her head into the doorway behind us. "It's around the corner on the left."

Something fell in a distant room – a thud, then the scamper of tiny scratches against the hardwood floor. I wouldn't have put it past this death trap to house rats, or maybe a raccoon, but I desperately hoped against it.

Naveena moved toward the room, trying, but failing, not to touch anything. Around the corner she stopped outside a closed door, scanning it with her therma goggles. "I'm not seeing anything." She retracted her goggles and opened the door. "Shit!"

"What is it?" I extended my laser sword.

"Come see for yourself."

I leaned against the wall and poked my head into the room. Old laptops and bed sheets rose in towers to the ceiling. In the middle of all the junk, a turtle sat on the ground, slowly retracting its neck into the shell.

"Is that a turtle?" Renfro said over my shoulder.

I bent down and picked the turtle up by the sides of its shell. It snapped its sharp beak at my face before going back into defensive mode.

"That's why we weren't seeing anything on the goggles," Naveena said. "Cold-blooded."

I stared into the turtle's hidey hole. "Maybe the lady's titties were dragging the floor and this little guy started snapping."

Naveena radioed the second smoke eater crew, telling them to cancel their response.

"My brother and I used to catch snapping turtles out of a creek when we were growing up," I said.

"I didn't know you had a brother," Renfro said.

I shrugged. "He passed away a few years ago. Heart attack."

What a comment on the world we lived in, that when someone died you felt obligated to tell others it wasn't a dragon, that people did die the good old-fashioned way every once in a while.

We turned to leave, and the old woman met us in the hall with a broom in her hand.

"That's the dragon!" She almost looked like a wraith the way she screamed and slobbered all over her bra. "Kill it!"

"It's just a turtle, ma'am." Renfro held up hands as if she was going to attack him with the broom.

It was a good thing Renfro spoke first and was closer to the woman. I would have thrown the snapping turtle at her and called it a night.

"I saw it breathe fire," she said, eyes darting left to right – basic psycho eye movement.

"Well, we'll just remove it from the premises." I carried the turtle away as it decided to come out of its shell. I grabbed one of its front legs and waved "bye-bye" to the homeowner.

The old woman screamed and almost clawed up the wall. "No wonder everybody in this state hates you. You're all just a burden on our taxes. Can't even do your job."

Renfro stayed behind to console her, while Naveena and I walked out before I said anything more. It also didn't hurt to get some fresh air.

"You guys get these kind of bullshit calls often?" I asked Naveena, as I set the turtle down in the neighbor's bushes.

"Not a lot, but it happens."

"Figures," I said.

"What?"

"I thought I'd left the crazies and false alarms with the fire service."

Renfro backed out of the front door. "Yes ma'am, I understand. You have a good night." He shut the door and turned to us with wide eyes. "Why'd you have to leave me in there alone?"

"Old people love you," Naveena said.

I grabbed the wheel chocks and hopped into the truck, ready to get back to headquarters and finish my shift without another peep.

Tomorrow, Sherry and I were going to look for a new house. Hopefully, the bank would cut us some slack since we'd have to start over from square one. Our dragon insurance claim was stalled. They said further investigation was required. After all the money we'd paid, they couldn't fork over what was due? Highway robbery.

I would've much rather spent the day hunting the Behemoth or thinking of some way to take down Rogola. But the only thing I could do at that point was the one thing I hated to do above all else – wait.

"So, let me ask you something, Brannigan," Naveena said as we drove away.

"I'm an open book."

"With your new body–"

"It's the same body," I said. "It's just been rejuvenated."

"OK, whatever." She turned to look at me, and the lights from the truck's dash put a yellow halo around her head. "You able to get it up now?"

"Damn," Renfro shook his head. "That's asking too much information."

"I never had that problem to begin with." I smiled at Naveena, knowing she was just fucking with me.

"I wonder what's on fire," Renfro said, looking to the night sky through the windshield.

I leaned forward. "What do you mean?"

"I can see smoke drifting up over there, a few blocks away."

"I don't see anything," I said.

Naveena said, "That's because you don't have eyes like Renfro."

"You can see in the dark?"

Renfro shrugged. "I thought you knew. It's not great, but I can see things most people can't."

"Well, let's go check out that smoke," I said.

We might as well make the trip mean more than turtle-wrangling.

"Don't you want to get back to headquarters?" Naveena asked. "Maybe we'll sleep the rest of the night."

I made a pfft with my lips. "It won't take long. Maybe somebody's in trouble, and I can show you youngsters how it's done."

"We fight dragons, not fire." Naveena put a hand to her chin, considering it. I just had to push her a little more and she'd agree.

"We can at least drive by," I said. "It's on our way."

"I don't mind if you don't, Captain" Renfro said.

"Fine," Naveena said. "Probably just a backyard campfire."

"I'll buy you a beer if it's bullshit," I said.

"It's a bet."

"You better buy me one, too," Renfro said. He took the tight residential corners with ease.

The area south of the city had been going to hell long before E-Day, and things hadn't improved. I wouldn't have been surprised if we ran into a wraith around the next bend.

Renfro eased the cannon truck to a stop and pointed through the windshield. "It's coming from over there."

It was still too dark for me to see what the hell he

was talking about. All I saw was an old building that had a second story jutting from the center of the structure, almost like a church, almost like a…

"That's the old crematorium," I said.

Naveena made a disgusted shudder. "Kind of weird to be burning corpses this late, isn't it?"

"Yeah," I said. "Especially since that place has been shut down for years."

Naveena pointed. "Then whose car is that?"

A black hover car, the kind with vertical doors, sat tucked away at the side of the building, behind a few low-hanging branches.

"Shut the truck down, Renfro." I patted his shoulder. "And kill the lights."

He did, although his movements suggested he didn't understand why. Right after the engine died, a man ran out from the back of the building. He was in a hurry, like a dragon was after him.

Renfro dug out the mute bag, the same one they'd put over my head. "Should we take him in?"

"No," Naveena said.

I shook my head. "You guys must love that chokey bag."

With a jerk of the car door, the fleeing man was behind the wheel and zooming away with pieces of the tree branches clamped in the door. When he screeched around the corner, we stared after him with more curiosity than concern.

"What did that guy look like?" I asked Renfro.

"I don't know," he said. "Skinny. Glasses and a bow tie."

"Bet it was Jenkins." I nodded at Naveena.

"The mayor's assistant? What the hell is he doing out…" Naveena stopped as something dawned on her.

I was thinking the same.

Jenkins was destroying evidence.

"Renfro, stay here in case there's trouble. Brannigan, come on." Naveena jumped out of the truck and ran toward the crematorium.

Right on her heels, I made for the side of the building where we'd seen Jenkins exit.

"The way he sped out of here," I said, "I'm sure he didn't lock the door behind him."

I was right. The side door gaped wide open and the thinnest wisps of smoke climbed toward the night. Maybe it was the firefighter in me, but I stopped in my tracks to survey exactly what we were running into. Naveena disappeared inside, unconcerned.

I chased after Naveena into the darkened crematorium, calling her name a few times before I extended my therma goggles and saw her standing around the corner in the next room.

"You guys OK in there?" Renfro asked through our helmet speakers.

"Yeah," Naveena answered. "Brannigan, I'm just past—"

"I see you." I rounded the corner, holding onto the wall.

There was nothing I could trip over, but I kept feeling like I was going to fall into a pit or something. Naveena stood at two vertical doors that looked like they could have been the jaws of a macabre robot.

Pulling at a chain on the side, Naveena opened the doors to the cremation chamber, and even though the place hadn't been used in decades I could smell the scent of burning flesh and gasoline.

The light from the fire allowed me to retract my goggles and get a better look at what lay burning inside – lots of electrical equipment.

"The wraith-trapping shit!" I shouted, running toward

the blazing hole.

"Are you sure?"

"What else would they want to destroy?"

"Well, pull it out."

"I can't," I said, desperately looking for a way to remove any of the equipment that hadn't yet been damaged. "There's no slide or anything. Smells like he used gas."

"I'll go get a tool. Maybe we can save one." Naveena stomped away, just as frustrated as I was.

There wouldn't be time.

I stared into the flames, at the only proof we'd ever have to nail Rogola. My house had burned for nothing. Theresa's death and DeShawn's lapse into pious insanity would be a pointless tragedy, and the Behemoth would destroy a peaceful community somewhere, all because Rogola had summoned it from the earth. It wasn't fair.

But there was no better time to put my abilities as a smoke eater to the test, was there? I jumped into the cremation chamber.

"Brannigan!" I heard Naveena scream behind me.

Fuck, it was hot. I don't mean the kind of hot like sitting too close to the fireplace or when you've been mowing the lawn in the middle of an August day. This was like cutting yourself open and pouring rubbing alcohol all over it. My natural heat resistance and power suit protected me a bit from the flames, but at the same time it was like being inside an oven, inside another oven. Jenkins had really wanted this stuff to burn quick.

When I began smelling my hair burning I was sure I'd done something stupid, but one of the pieces of equipment lay only a few inches from my outstretched fingers, and if I just... reached... a little farther...

Naveena grabbed my ankles and yanked me from the chamber. I fell on my chin and bit into my tongue. For some reason, that was more painful than the heat from the cremation flames.

Naveena was nearly in tears. It was nice to see she cared. "What were you thinking, you dumb-ass, mother–"

She stopped when I spit blood, smiled, and raised my throbbing, heat-thrashed arm.

"Holy shit."

The piece of equipment in my hand looked like an awkwardly-shaped TV remote control, back when they still used to make them, except it also had a metal, coiled pole jutting from the end like a toy ray gun. I didn't know if the thing could trap a wraith or if I'd mistakenly grabbed a really ugly voice recorder.

There was only one way to find out.

Naveena shook her head. "You're nucking futs, you know that?"

She helped me to my feet.

I opened my power suit and crawled onto the ground while Naveena told Renfro we'd be back in a minute. After a few seconds of waiting for the sunburn feeling to disappear from my face, I reentered my suit and hobbled for the door. "Let's go test this wraith-catcher out."

CHAPTER 28

"This is a stupid idea," Renfro said.

"Yep," Naveena agreed.

We were just outside the city, headed for one of the newest quarantined zones. The burns I'd received from the crematorium weren't as bad as they felt, just first-degree – I'd have to slab some of that blue curate on my skin when we got back. Even so, it hurt like a sonofabitch, and I was fidgeting in my power suit like a cat stuck in a clothes dryer on permanent press.

"If this doesn't work," I said, waving the wraith-catcher in my hand, "we won't have the embarrassment of going after Rogola with something they'll call a piece of science fiction memorabilia."

"If this doesn't work," Naveena said, "a wraith will claw your eyes out."

"And if it does work?" Renfro asked.

I smiled. "Then we'll have taken a wraith off the street and can go shove it up the mayor's ass."

"Fair enough," Renfro said.

"It's just a few more miles," I said. "And then–"

"I remember," Renfro said. "I was there that day, too."

I hadn't thought of Theresa in a while, what she looked like, how she used to pour a cup of coffee and dump it into the sink, just to say she'd gotten use out of paying her part of our firehouse grocery dues. It was hard coming back here. But it was the only place I could think a wraith might still be – that collapsed house, where I discovered I could breathe smoke.

I leaned forward in my seat as we arrived at the subdivision's entrance. Hologram ribbons, declaring the area to be closed to the public, glimmered across two brick pillars and soundlessly shattered into fragments of light when our cannon truck drove through them.

Parthenon City and its surrounding neighborhoods weren't the brightest of places at night, but compared to this now dead area, they were dazzling beacons in a sea of darkness. Renfro flicked on a spotlight that hung on the side of the truck.

Naveena said, "It doesn't even look like the same place."

Heaping mounds of cinders lined both sides of the street. They didn't even resemble houses or lawns or the backyard playgrounds kids would play on when ash clouds weren't flying in on the wind.

"Didn't you guys come out for more scalies in this area?" I asked.

"No, we wouldn't," Naveena said. "After they evacuated everyone and taped it off, this neighborhood was left to its own destruction."

"Not enough manpower or time to battle all the dragons that would have emerged after that day," Renfro said. "Safer and cheaper. An egg-crushing crew should have hit this place though. Unless they were busy."

"Busy?"

What a shitty way to operate. I understood why. It just sucked that all of those people, who were minding their own business and trying to live a decent life in these terrible times, had to suffer and lose their houses because of one scaly on one bad day.

"You know," I said, "when I was a fireman, we used to lead these fire safety classes and would tell citizens that going back into a house when it was on fire wasn't worth it, that it was just a house, you could replace it. I don't know if I believe that anymore.

"I mean, a house – a home – becomes a part of you. It's almost like looking in a mirror when you pull up to your place after a long day. It's where you eat and sleep and fuck. You fill it with junk, sure, but I think you also nail a piece of yourself to the walls along with all of the family photos and paintings."

"You're getting too deep for me, Brannigan." Renfro laughed. It had the deep thrum of a bass guitar.

Naveena looked back at me. "I stay at headquarters, remember?"

"Stop here," I told Renfro. "This is it."

There was no house for me to recognize – just more and more ashes – but I remembered the house being in the groove where the road curved, and the legion of cracks in the driveway now revealed after the cannon truck's exhaust had blown cinders off the pavement.

Don't be out here, Theresa, I thought.

"Now what, Brannigan." Naveena said.

"We look for a wraith."

"Do you even know how to work that remote?" she asked.

"How hard could it be? It only has two buttons." One was red and the other black. I wished I'd finished watching that Professor Poltergeist video.

The ashes crunched under my boots when I exited the truck. Renfro stayed where he was. I was glad he kept the engine purring, scared of what I wouldn't hear if he'd shut it off. The silence would be deafening.

"So we're going to split up?" Naveena asked as she came around the front of the truck with a flashlight.

"Don't even play with me right now," I said. "You aren't leaving me alone out here, and we've only got the one wraith-catcher."

She smiled and abandoned the safety of the truck's headlights. I took a deep breath and followed her to where the house used to be.

The neighborhood looked like a graveyard, where the ash heaps resembled freshly covered graves. The ash pile straight ahead had a big hole dug into it, as if something had been living inside. Or still was. I tensed my right arm, ready to extend my laser sword. It was hell enough to think of finding a wraith out here. A dragon on top of that? No, thank you.

"I called you the Angel of Death," I told Naveena, just a little louder than a whisper.

"What?"

"Before I knew what your name was. I called you the Angel of Death. Or just Angel for short." I laughed like a nervous little boy.

"Look at this," Naveena said, she and her flashlight disappearing into the ash hole.

"Get away from there," I said, too late.

I poked my head into where Naveena had jumped.

Ten feet below, she shone her light on a bunch of blood-red egg shells about the size of her head. They lay in broken pieces, and several small holes had been burrowed into the ground.

"Don't expect me to come down there." My voice echoed within the ashen chamber.

"Shut up," she said.

"Sorry, I'm just trying to—"

"No, shut up. I hear something."

I shut up and listened. Behind me, a croak killed the silence. It sounded like the slow close of an old, whiny door mixed with a growling rat.

That's when I spotted the glow, an eerie white light that throbbed from around another ash pile behind me. The croak-growl grew louder.

"Fuck me," I mumbled.

The wraith floated into view, staring straight up as if it had been lobotomized. I placed a hand against my mouth so I wouldn't curse or scream. My first instinct was to run away all assholes and elbows, but I couldn't leave Naveena.

I quickly changed my mind about catching a wraith. This thing could just float off into the dark somewhere else, unaware of our presence, and then Naveena and I could hop back into the truck and forget this whole, stupid idea.

Naveena power jumped from the hole and landed beside me.

The wraith snapped its head toward us and raised its claws.

I'd always avoided placing myself in situations to get a really good look, but wraiths, while all having the distinct odor of burnt flesh and the color of bird shit, do look different from one another, slightly resembling their former, living selves.

This was Theresa's wraith, fulfilling what I'd feared. And she was pissed.

Spreading its mouth wider than humanly possible, Theresa-wraith shrieked over sharp crooked teeth that bled white energy from the tips.

It zoomed for us.

"Fuck!" I ran with all I had, ignoring the pain from my burns as I loped across the ashes.

Naveena ran the other way, as the wraith singled me out to chase. Maybe I looked older and slower.

I zigged and zagged to fake out Theresa's ghost. I even hit my power jump to gain some distance, sailing over another of the ash mounds, but the wraith was too damn fast, and the jump was a waste as the wraith quickly closed the distance between us.

"Brannigan," Naveena said over my radio. "You're going the wrong way, you idiot."

"Great," I said to no one but the dark.

Seeing no other option, I released my laser sword and spun on the wraith, slashing with a big, diagonal wave of my arm as Theresa-wraith reached for me with both of its claws. When the laser made contact, the wraith dispersed into a shower of radiated dust.

"Damn right," I said with a victorious laugh. I wanted to puke from the still-present wraith smell, an odor too much like charred and moldy hotdogs.

Then the glowing wraith particles began gathering together again, croaking out an angry growl as one, ghostly choir.

I looked around for the cannon truck's lights, but the glow of the quickly reforming wraith was the only illumination, and everything else was just darkness. So, I ran for the darkness.

"Cast," I said into my helmet. "I'm lost out here!"

"Stay where you are and we'll come get you," Renfro said.

Naveena cut in. "He can't stay still. He's got a wraith after him. Brannigan, keep it away from you, I'm coming."

Sure, that'd be easy. I kept running into the night.

"Why don't you use that wraith-catcher?" Renfro said.

I'd completely forgotten about the remote in my hand. I guess a dead friend returning to eat your face, kind of removes normal thinking.

Slowing my steps, I looked behind me. The wraith's claws slashed and scraped against the chest of my power suit, leaving jagged grooves in the metal. The grooves burned with white fire.

I ignored the flames and pointed the remote. "Eat this you mother–"

The ground disappeared beneath me. I fell into even more darkness, swallowed by ash. When I met solid ground, I rolled a few times until I lay on my back. I sat up and spit out wads of cinders. Once that taste, and actual char, enters your mouth, it never completely leaves.

Sticky gunk covered my power suit, smelling like a raw omelet. My hand moved against what sounded like crunchy shards. I'd landed on a nest of unhatched eggs.

Above, the wraith appeared at the edge of the ash hole. It screamed even louder when it saw what I'd done to the eggs. As the wraith descended toward me, undead shreds of clothing flapped in its wake. The ash even parted a little.

The wraith-catcher. Where was it?

It had flown from my hand at some point during my fall. I dug through the ashes around me, searching and finding nothing. The wraith's stench thickened and its shriek grew louder. I was well and truly fucked.

The wraith's glow cast my shadow across the ashes in front of me, and that's when I noticed the small, dark shape lying a few feet away.

The wraith swiped at me again as I scrambled forward. This time Theresa-wraith took a chunk from the back of my power suit. I heard metal skitter across the ash. When I grabbed the wraith remote and flipped over, the ghost was on top of me, gnashing its teeth toward my face.

I hit the remote's red button, and a black energy beam blasted from the tip of the coil. It's a strange thing to imagine, I didn't even believe it as I saw it happen, but against the white radiance of Theresa's wraith, a black laser wrapped around the ghostly torso and pulled the ghost into the remote with a short pzzt.

It's a surprise I didn't crush the remote, because I kept mashing that red button even after the wraith was gone. I let go and looked at the wraith-catcher. A rounded rectangle on the side showed a single white light throbbing in the dark. Based on the amount of unlit squares, it looked like I had room to catch a shitload more wraiths if I wanted.

"Brannigan!" It was Naveena. She pointed her flashlight into my eyes.

"Watch where you point that thing," I said.

"Where's the wraith?"

I waved the remote. "Moved to a smaller apartment."

It took a couple of failed power jumps and even more spitting of ash dust, but I managed to climb out of the hole. "Remind me to tell the propellerheads to install GPS in our suits."

"Most of us aren't so dumb we can't find the truck."

"I had a wraith on my ass," I said.

Naveena pointed to the wraith-catcher. "So that thing really has a wraith in it?"

"You bet your ass. I think I can still smell it." I didn't mention whose ghost it was.

"Damn, Brannigan," Naveena said. "You really did it."

We walked back to the truck, which wasn't that far away – a knock to my pride and sense of direction. And while I was glad to have something to use against Rogola, all I wanted to do was get back to headquarters and sleep as long as I could.

"We have to go," Renfro said as we climbed into the truck.

I groaned and leaned back into the headrest. "Don't say it, man."

"Suck it up," Naveena said, with exhaustion in her voice. She took the holo-reader from Renfro. "We've got a report of a Poisonous Pete at 3800 Broadway."

"You guys know it was Pete's Dragon, right. The dragon's name was Elliot."

They didn't say anything, and it was just as well. I was going to try to get a few minutes of sleep on the way to fight yet another dragon. As a precaution, I secured the wraith-catcher in a bin before shutting my eyes.

CHAPTER 29

Donahue insisted I wear my dress greens to accompany him to meet with the police chief. I figured it couldn't hurt.

"So there's no way that thing can get out?" Donahue nodded toward the wraith-catcher in my pocket as we walked toward the big, blue building.

"I don't know," I said. "They had to have some way of putting the wraiths into TVs and stuff. The red button caught it. I don't really want to hit the black button and find out. Know what I mean?"

"Yes. Please don't."

"So, you think we have enough evidence to put Rogola away?" I pulled at the tight collar of my uniform.

Donahue nodded. "Police chief has the final say, but... hell yes, we do."

I remember when the police department used to have precincts all around the city. Now, the cops housed themselves in a singular building the same color as their uniforms. After E-Day, the police got to pick their new headquarters, and I guess they went all out in promoting the whole "blue" thing. We firefighters laughed at it, of course. They were trying to cut in on the same kind of romanticism firefighters had with the color red.

Donahue and I crossed the street and came to the

security shack at the front entrance. A droid stood behind the window, wearing an old school police hat on top of its chrome head.

Donahue took a step back, flinching. "Where's Murray, the regular guard?"

"PCPD is here to serve you," the droid said.

"Damn." I shook my head. "These metal bastards are taking everyone's job."

"We're here to see the police chief," Donahue said. "I'm Chief Donahue with Smoke Eater Division."

"All appointments must be made prior to arrival." The droid's voice was emotionless. The eyes brightened and dimmed rhythmically under that stupid police hat.

"No, I don't have an appointment," Donahue said. "I've never needed one before. I happen to be friends with the police chief."

"Chief, this thing is repeating scripted lines. Let's just go in." I didn't understand why Donahue needed to explain himself to a walking rust bucket.

"Please check in at the front office," the droid said, following us with its glowing eyes as we moved away.

"What in the world was that about?" Donahue asked under his breath, as we climbed the steps to the front door.

I didn't say anything, because I had no clue.

Inside, things just got worse. The whole building was filled with droids. They bustled along corridors, around desks, carrying holo-readers and escorting a few people in handcuffs toward the cells in the basement. A particularly snarky-looking droid sat behind the big desk in front of us. A diagonal burn mark covered its face.

"State your business," the droid said.

I noticed this one didn't say "please."

"Where is everybody?" Donahue flexed his fists, sweat forming at his temples. "Where are all the cops?"

"This is the Parthenon City Police Department headquarters, home to the first all-droid law enforcement agency in the country."

Another robocop brought in a distraught man with a black eye.

"Help me," the man said, so soft I almost didn't hear him. "They're taking over."

The droid behind the desk spun its head to the new arrival and said, "Holding." Its head swiveled back to me and kept going around like it was possessed by demons, stopping again at Donahue after a few spins. "If you have nothing further, you may leave."

The man with the black eye began screaming, even though he didn't struggle against the droid. He knew it was futile. Once the man was behind the corner, the screaming abruptly stopped, as if they'd entered a black hole.

"I need to see Chief Feldman," Donahue said. His frustration had dwindled a little, having seen a robot dragging a screaming man through the halls.

All I could do was stand there and take in all the droids and the fact that the only humans in the building were under arrest. Besides Donahue and I.

"There is no one here by that name," the desk droid said.

"Since when?"

The droid's eyes throbbed brighter.

"What the hell are you droids up to?" Donahue raised his voice.

The droid stood. "You may leave or be removed. You have thirty seconds."

I put a hand on Donahue's shoulder. "Let's go, Chief."

"No," he said. "I want to know why a bunch of robots have replaced every cop in this town and I want to know where all the real people are!"

I put my mouth to Donahue's ear, although I wasn't sure if it would prevent the droid from hearing. "We're in the middle of a bunch of droids who have been programmed to act like cops. We don't have power suits or anything else to defend ourselves."

A little color faded from his face, and his muscles relaxed. Nodding slowly, he turned for the door, picking up speed with every step. I wasn't far behind. That whole place gave me the heebie-jeebies.

"Have a nice day," the droid called from behind.

"In all my years–" Chief Donahue had one hand on the wheel and the accelerator to the floor. "–I've never seen anything like that! This city has gone to pot, and we thought the dragons were bad, but Brannigan, I'm telling you, nothing, nothing is worse than lazy people and technology. They've written our death certificates in the name of convenience."

He'd been yelling since we entered his command vehicle and were safely away from police headquarters. He was all over the road, and I was just glad the wasteland was devoid of traffic.

"Technology is a tool, like anything else," I said, when he finally took a breath from his tirade. "And if it's in the wrong hands, it's a pain in the ass for everybody else. Right now, the wrong hands belong to Rogola."

"We'll storm city hall. Tear it down, brick by brick."

I couldn't believe I was the sensible one in this conversation. "We can't stage a coup. I know you don't mean that. You're just pissed, like me. But even if we were to go down there to kick ass and take names, Rogola is hiding somewhere else. We have to find out where."

"I sent Afu, Puck, and Williams to the mayor's mansion," Donahue said. "He wasn't there either."

"So we have a mayor and a three-headed dragon both off our radar. They couldn't make it easy and be hiding together could they?"

Donahue smiled a little. "Wouldn't that be nice?" He dropped the smile just as quickly as he spotted something ahead. "What is that?"

Crowds of people surrounded Smoke Eater Headquarters, holding self-made holo-signs that floated in the air. As we sped closer, I saw a few of the signs said things like: Worse than Dragons! and SHIT Eaters Go Home! One bare-chested man had animated a drawing on his belly of a dragon fucking a smoke eater from behind.

I love people.

Several speakers towered among the crowd, as if it was a music festival. A woman with dirt-stained blonde hair and a bandana shouted into a microphone. When she saw us traversing the angry mob, she pointed and told them all that, "Here come some more of the very people letting you down, letting your homes burn and your children be eaten. They destroy orphanages and entire neighborhoods!"

The crowd threw rocks and tomatoes, and I think I saw a few coconuts hit the windshield. Really, it was one big waste of pricey produce, but Donahue's truck held up under the assault. The chief grumbled curses as he held tight to the steering wheel.

I've never been flipped off so many times at once in my life. The whole scene twisted my guts pretty badly. I mean, people were supposed to protest the police, politicians, oil barons. They never came after firefighters, or smoke eaters. We were the good guys.

"Citizens of Parthenon City."

The crowd turned from us to see who'd spoken. Donahue drove us toward a sealed entrance around the side of the building, but I was able to take a quick look behind us.

Mayor Rogola hovered above the crowd, flickering in hologram blue. "I'm sorry I can't be here with you in person, but I want you to know I stand with you. This is our city, and we can't stand by and let reckless individuals allow monsters from below destroy our homes and terrorize our communities. They have to go!"

The crowd roared in agreement, as the secret door closed behind Donahue's truck.

CHAPTER 30

Donahue marched straight to the cafeteria, clinking his false leg hard against the tile floor. He made a huge pot of coffee and wouldn't allow me to say a word while he brewed it.

"I guess you saw the mess outside." Naveena ran in, out of breath.

Donahue had his back to us, bending over the counter. He raised a finger and proceeded to chug a mug of black coffee. Then he refilled and repeated. Being a smoke eater was also good for not having to wait on coffee to cool.

I straddled a chair backwards and just shook my head. "It's been a day full of disappointing news."

Donahue received a message on his holo-reader and turned away to read it.

"We need to find Rogola," I said. "Lock him up and make him confess. We have to be the better people here."

"Why?"

I shrugged. "Well, I don't want to kill him."

"No," Naveena said. "I mean, why would he do all of this? He's already the mayor. What more does he want?"

I thought about it for a second and said, "The way the world is now, there really are no more rungs on the ladder to climb. So if you can't grab more, you just squeeze the fist tighter."

Donahue turned sharply. "We're needed in New Mexico."

Naveena blinked a few times in silence.

I dropped my jaw. "What the hell are you talking about? We're losing the city here."

"This is important." He waved the holo-reader in his hand. "The smokies out there found something of ours."

I was about to yell at my chief about how it wasn't the time to be performing any mutual aid or interstate relations bullshit, when he expanded the video feed of one of the propellerheads in our dispatch center.

Donahue held out the holoreader. "Go ahead and tell them, Vicky."

Vicky blew a strand of blonde, curly hair from her eyes. "Hey, guys. We've been hearing reports of burned communities with no sign of what did it and no quakes in the area either. I've only recently detected a southwesterly pattern in these burnings, relative to us. Well, New Mexico smoke eaters just outside of Carlsbad called in on that three-headed Behemoth. They'd take care of it themselves, but they're busy with a bad scaly season and knew we were on the lookout for it."

"How did it get all the way out there?" I asked.

Naveena nudged my shoulder. "It can fly, remember?"

Vicky continued. "They've tracked it to a cavern called Lechuguilla Cave."

"Thanks, Vicky," Donahue said.

"Fun fact," Vicky said, "Lechuguilla is the deepest cave in the US and–"

"Thanks, Vicky!" Donahue closed the feed. To us, he said, "So, how about that? This is exactly what we need to boost public support."

"No." I shook my head. "I want to nail that three-headed bastard more than anyone, but we've got a shit storm in full downpour right here in Ohio."

Donahue harrumphed. "Well, it's a good thing you're not in charge. Get Afu, Williams, and Renfro, and suit up."

God damn that smoke eater contract.

"Can you at least go pick my wife up and bring her here. Shit is getting worse and I don't want her by herself."

"Done," Donahue said.

"You sure about this goose hunt, Chief?" Naveena asked.

Donahue sighed and looked a little betrayed. "Those protesters aren't going anywhere. If they're not afraid to cross the ash to get here, they're in it for the long haul. And, Brannigan, you said it yourself, we had the Behemoth and Rogola both off our radar. Now that one has reared its head–"

"Heads," I corrected.

He sighed. "I don't intend on letting it get away again. The people out there will ease up once they've seen we've retrieved the one that got away. Fair enough?"

There went those two terrible words that got me involved in this hullabaloo in the first place. I still wasn't so sure that the angry mob outside would think it was "fair enough."

"Fine," I said, following Naveena out the door. "Wait, what do you mean 'retrieve'?"

CHAPTER 31

Yolanda was ratcheting something onto the nose of Jet 1 when we entered the bay. It was a huge cannon that smelled like a new toy.

"Hell yeah," I said, standing underneath her. "That big sucker is sure to blow the Behemoth into a million evil pieces. But why are you fixing it to the front of the jet?"

She returned my smile, but guiltily, as if she knew something I didn't. Well, my body language book hadn't been wrong yet.

I thinned my eyes. "What's wrong?"

"This is a nonlethal cannon we got from the Yūrei Corpo–"

"No."

Yolanda was just following orders, there was no reason to unload on her, so I stomped away to gripe at someone else.

Naveena had just finished putting on her power suit and was attaching something to the back of Williams'.

"We are killing this thing in New Mexico, right?"

She answered without turning. "If we have to."

Williams looked over her shoulder to give me a wary glance.

"So, this is what 'retrieve' means," I said. "What a crock. We're supposed to fly down there, kill that

bastard, and then get back here to save our jobs before
the city runs us out of town."

Naveena turned and slapped Williams on the back to
send her away. "Get in the plane, smoky," she said to
me. "Now."

"You don't have anything to say?"

"Sink or swim."

"I hate that motto," I said.

"The propellerheads want a live dragon, subdued. This
Behemoth is like nothing we've ever seen, and they're
going bonkers about it being cannibalistic. If there are
more like this three-header, or worse, I want to know
the quickest way to take them down. Don't you?"

Reluctantly, I nodded.

"Plus, you can look at this trip to New Mexico as a
make-up for the shit you pulled in Canada. You can walk
around now, and you don't have to worry about human
sacrifices–" She covered her mouth with both power
gloves. "Oh, fuck, Brannigan, I didn't even think about
what I was saying."

I shook my head and stomped onto the plane.

Before E-Day, I never thought I would've appreciated
staring at the desert. Back then, I would have told you I
didn't see the big deal. It's just a bunch of sand and tan-
colored rocks, maybe a patch of grass here and there.
There was nothing in the desert.

But after the dragons, I relished seeing any landscape
that wasn't covered in ash. I was still correct about there
not being shit in the desert, for sure, but that meant
there wasn't shit for the dragons to burn. They didn't
call New Mexico the Land of Enchantment for nothing.

"All right," Naveena called out as Jet 1 slowed in its
descent. "Everybody stand up."

I looked from Afu to Williams, standing at either side

of me. They stood up without hesitation.

"What do you mean?" I asked. "We haven't landed yet."

Afu widened his eyes. "You guys told him, right?"

"Damn it, Naveena…" I started to say.

"That's Captain Jendal to you, Brannigan." Naveena stepped past me and hit the button to lower the hatch.

"Oh, hell no!" I backed toward the cockpit.

The air rushed in and beat against my face. I stayed glued to my seat, trying to refrain from vomiting or peeing myself. As scared as I was, it might as well have been a dragon that bit off the back half of Jet 1.

"Come on, Dragon Blood," Williams shouted at me. "Sink or swim."

This wasn't the time for nicknames.

Naveena motioned for everyone to get closer to the lowering door. "Thirty seconds and we jump."

"Jump?" I stood, but my legs wobbled under my weight. New muscles were no match for pulse-stopping fear. "Jump with what? Where are the parachutes?"

"You've fallen from up high like three times." Afu grinned, showing all of his teeth. "What's the matter?"

"I only fell twice," I said.

"Go, go, go!" Naveena ushered Afu forward.

"Sink or swim." Afu jumped. The big man was gone in an instant, not slowly gliding like birds or feathers on the wind. He dropped like a stone.

Did he not realize we were thirteen thousand feet in the air? There would be no swimming and a lot of sinking.

Williams took a few deep breaths through puckered lips, as if she was in Lamaze class. "Sink or swim," she shouted, before throwing herself into the sky.

Renfro went next without saying anything. Naveena motioned me toward her, but I shook my head.

"We have to go now," she said.

"You should have told me we were jumping. Did you even fit me with a parachute or whatever the hell you think I'm going to–"

Naveena grabbed me in a bear hug and leapt out of the plane. My mind went completely blank, even though I screamed for a few seconds. I just couldn't believe Naveena had done it.

She tried to tell me something, but the pressure and wind in my ears prevented me from hearing. While I'm great at reading body language, I never learned to read lips. It would've come in handy right then. As we plummeted toward the rocky desert, I started shaking and squirming. Naveena pushed me away.

Wait!

Maybe I could engage my power jump just before I hit the ground, and that would buffer the incredible amount of force I was building up.

No. How stupid was that?

My mind raced for a solution, no longer in holy-fucking-shit-I-am-going-to-be-a-pancake mode. A rapid beeping interrupted my thoughts, and my power suit took on a mind of its own.

I felt it in the shoulders and my suit's upper back. The momentum shifted, and instead of dropping down, I glided in a slight diagonal line. Then, I turned just a bit to the right. It was as if God had snatched me with two fingers and corrected my course.

Breaking through a small cloud, I saw the other smokies flying in front of me. An apparatus on the backs of their power suits extended almost like wings, and a burning flow of orange energy burned out of it like jet exhaust.

"You motherfuckers!" I shouted, even though I knew none of them could hear me. So, I cast a radio signal through my helmet and said it again.

Afu's laughter came through the speakers first. "Man, you should know we wouldn't let you die. Did you not see Captain Jendal putting the gliders on the back of our power suits?"

I hadn't.

"I wish I could've seen the look on your face," Williams said.

Later, I would kick myself for not taking the chance to appreciate the view and the act of flying over southern New Mexico like Iron Man, but all I could do at the moment was pray my suit kept working, at least until I made it safely to the ground.

"All right, Captain Jendal," I said. "You've had your fun. Can you fill me in before I fill this suit with piss?"

"Our suits are following the GPS we set," Naveena said. "Our suits will land us just near the entrance to the cave, and then we'll go hunt down a dragon."

"What about Jet 1?"

"They're circling, so we have to make this quick."

I refrained from lifting my head to search for the jet. "We have to make what fast, finding the Behemoth?"

"Yeah. And luring it out in the open. Into the sky. That's why Jet 1 isn't landing."

"Ah, shit."

"Hey, Brannigan." It was Renfro. "Don't open your mouth too big. You don't want to lose your dentures."

Everyone keyed up to laugh.

Bastards.

In front of me, the other smokies rose and then dropped altitude. It was kind of like riding in the back of a roller coaster and seeing the front cars drop down first. You knew you were next. And I remembered the last time I was around these people and roller coasters.

I held my breath.

My suit rose on the wind and spiraled down to follow the others. The ground looked like a bunch of giant serpents had coiled through the sand – and that wasn't too far of a reach for the world we lived in. All of us began to circle like a flock of buzzards above a corpse, lowering a little at a time with each pass.

I was the last to land, and I would have kissed the ground if I wasn't afraid a scorpion would sting me on the lips. My glider retracted with a click.

"Lechuguilla Cave is just a few yards this way." Naveena jogged ahead of us, holding a holo-reader.

We all followed after our captain. Afu and Williams hurried to catch up to her, but Renfro and I took our time. One of the things you learn as you get older is to conserve your energy.

Naveena led us to a paved path that wound its way deep into the mouth of the cave. Mouth – that was too accurate. It looked like a deep throat ready to swallow us. When we were just outside the cave, rock rose high above and surrounded us like we were in a stone cup.

"Are we sure it's in there?" Williams asked.

A thin trail of smoke flowed from the cave. The scaly was in there alright, we just didn't know how deep we'd have to go.

"That answers that," I said.

"All right, circle up." Naveena twirled a finger in the air for added effect.

"What's the plan?" I asked. "Walk until we find it?"

"This cave is over a hundred miles deep, Brannigan." Never mind.

"We're going in, but no farther than the Chandelier Room." She brought up a picture on her holo-reader. The image showed white crystals hanging from the cave ceiling, looked like enormous snowflakes. "This is where we'll have to draw it out if we don't find it sooner."

"Draw it out how?" I widened my eyes as understanding hit me. "You don't mean...?"

Naveena pulled out the wraith-catcher and handed it to me. "You're in charge of releasing it and re-trapping it. You've done it before, so..."

"We're going into a deep, dark hole and putting ourselves between a ghost and a three-headed dragon?" Williams sat down, looking like she was going to puke.

"That sounds about right to me." I clapped my hands. "Come on, guys. I'm slowly starting to realize there's no point in arguing logic within this organization. Sink or swim, yeah?"

Afu was zoned out, but this time I think it was from being terrified, and not his usual attention deficit disorder.

I slapped his metal chest. "Yeah?"

He nodded slowly and turned to Naveena. "I'm ready, Captain Jendal."

"Use your therma goggles," Naveena said, "but only occasionally. I don't want one of you tumbling off into the dark because you were too focused on heat signatures. We are not here to kill the Behemoth." She stared at me for a few seconds, until I nodded. "Renfro and Williams will stay at the entrance and will fire off some shots to wrangle it toward the sky. Then, Jet 1 will do their thing. Any questions?"

"Yeah," I said.

Naveena tilted her head toward me. She should have known I wouldn't follow orders blindly.

"What happens if this thing doesn't scare from the lasers? Didn't seem like it gave two shits about what we threw at it last time. And even if we manage to pull this off, how the hell are we going to lug it all the way back to Ohio?"

"We have the technology," said Naveena. "Hope

you're fresh on your rope-tying skills."

"I can go in there with you guys," Williams said, although she still looked sick to her stomach. "I'll be fine."

Naveena said, "I need your lasers out here. You and Renfro are the most important part."

I would have utilized Renfro's night vision, but I didn't want to completely crap on Naveena's leadership. Renfro also happened to be an ace with the lasers, so it wasn't like she hadn't put any thought into it.

"Enough yapping." Renfro pushed past us and leaned against the rock, urging us on with a jerk of his head. "Let's get this over with."

The cave was really beautiful when you stopped to look at it. I was glad the propellerheads took my advice and added flashlights to our helmets. After all, therma goggles didn't help you see everything. We passed pools so clear and deep, I almost stopped to drink from them. The rock formations were like works of art – the ones still standing, at least. The Behemoth had made no effort to tread carefully. Stalactites and stalagmites – I can never remember which is which – lay shattered and crumbled to dust. We passed a few piles of burned bones that made an elephant graveyard seem like Legos.

I nearly threw up when I stepped into a heap of Behemoth droppings.

"This is awesome," Afu said. His voice bounced off the rocks and echoed deep into the cave. He kicked at a group of rocks. "These look like stone dildos coming out of the ground."

I loved Afu, but I wished he'd shut up. Sure, we were trying to draw out the Behemoth, but I didn't want to ring the dinner bell for it either. But after a while, I was bored. We didn't see any more smoke, and the therma goggles weren't revealing anything but a few cooling piles of dung.

"How far have we gone?" I asked.

Naveena checked her holo-reader. "Just over two miles."

"Shit!" My voice echoed as if I'd stuck my head inside a church bell.

Naveena spun on me. "Why don't you just start shouting the scaly's name, Brannigan?"

"Afu's been talking the whole time back there about stone dicks and all kinds of other stuff." I pointed for emphasis.

"I wasn't that loud," said Afu.

"Let's do it here," I said. "The closer we are to the entrance, the better."

"We don't have anywhere to hide here." Naveena held a hand to our surroundings. "And it's not flat at all. We're more likely to get ourselves impaled on a broken rock."

"I'm thinking of conserving our energy and being in a spot we can bail out if we have to. I don't like being this deep as it is."

"That's what she said," Afu snorted.

"Fine," Naveena said.

With all our gabbing, I might not have had to release the wraith at all, but since I'd opened my big mouth and Afu was already creeping toward the cave wall to get away, I held out the remote. I shone my light on the buttons to make sure I hit the right one.

After pressing the black button, a white light shot from the tip of the remote's coil, and Theresa's wraith leapt back out into the world, slashing and shrieking as if I'd only pressed pause on it from the night before.

I gritted my teeth to keep from yelping and ran to where Afu crouched. Naveena backed away slowly, keeping her sword arm forward, even though I'd told her it would do no good.

A roar came from deeper in the cave. And we still had a wraith to deal with.

"The wraith did its job. I'm trapping it again," I yelled to Naveena.

The wraith flew toward me.

"No," Naveena said. "Wait for the dragon."

The ghost stopped and turned to speed toward Naveena. It couldn't make up its mind on who to go after.

"I have to trap it now." I ran at the wraith with the remote outstretched in my hand. I was about to press the catch button when my foot hit a rock, and both me and the wraith-catcher tumbled across the cave floor.

Claws scratched across my helmet, as I scrambled away on my hands and knees, and the wraith's glow illuminated the rocks a foot or two in front of me. I didn't see the remote anywhere, but then the wraith's glow winked out and only my flashlight beam was left.

"Damn, Brannigan." Naveena said behind me, holding the wraith remote. "You're clumsier than a three-legged clown in a banana factory."

Normally, I would have had a good retort for that one. Instead, I said, "So, we just wait around for the Behemoth to show?"

That's when I heard the rocks cracking behind me.

"I don't suppose either of you brought any playing cards?" Naveena asked.

Afu laughed like an old car low on gas.

"Hey, Afu," I said. "How long have you and Williams been together?"

"You knew about that?"

Naveena sputtered. "Even the dragons knew about that, man."

I laughed just before the ground shook and orange

fury set the cave alight. Above me, all three heads of the Behemoth shot out of the dark, spewing fire as its claws and wings crushed through priceless rock formations, throwing a fit like a big, douchebag three year-old. The wraith hadn't only attracted the scaly to us, but it sent the dragon on a rage-filled feeding frenzy, and as far as I could tell we were the only things flammable and edible within the immediate vicinity.

"Go!" Naveena left me, running toward the cave entrance.

Afu was already ahead of her.

My helmet's flashlight bobbed all over the place, and I had to navigate by flashes of visible surroundings as they came. Zigzagging, I ran past an ice-like formation, but one of the Behemoth's heads crashed through it, sending rocky shrapnel all over me.

Teeth clamped just behind my ass, then came the fire.

This pattern wouldn't hold for another two miles. I was either going to die down in that cave, or I was going to disappoint the propellerheads and bring them back another dead dragon.

I could live with disappointment.

Skidding to the right, I spun around. The Behemoth's center head charged for me, spreading its jaws and breathing flames. I power jumped, but aimed forward so I didn't break my neck on the cave ceiling.

I landed on its snout and held on to whatever my hands could find. Unfortunately, my right hand had found the inside of its mouth. The scaly bit down, and an ungodly amount of pressure crushed into my arm. The power armor cracked.

Another head snapped at me from the side. This one grabbed my legs in its teeth, and both Behemoth heads pulled me in either direction. My power suit was obviously not designed with this kind of treatment in mind. My arm was in danger of being ripped out of the socket, my legs ground into pepperoni. It was like two dogs fighting over a chew toy. The third head with nothing in its jaws roared out a victory. I roared back.

I flung myself over and hit the button for my laser sword. The beam shot into the middle head's gums, and the jaws let me go. Using the same momentum, I swung to the underside of the head that held my legs and sliced deep, avoiding my own appendages.

For a second, the resulting roars of pain were a three-part harmony, but with my laser sword I cut it down to an angry duet. I fell hard onto the rocks below, having to roll away from stomping dragon feet as the Behemoth lost its shit.

I flinched when I crawled into a cluster of teeth, but realized it was the severed Behemoth head.

There was no way not to kill this scaly and survive – so I went for its legs. Above me, a different kind of growl burst from the headless neck, then fire exploded from the bloody hole in a continuous stream. I guess one benefit of being a dragon is that you can cauterize your own wounds.

The Behemoth galloped away from me.

"No, you don't!" I latched onto its hind ankle.

The scaly clawed through the cave with dizzying speed as I collided with several rock formations and maybe even a wall or two. If I thought I was lightheaded before, the concussion I was likely suffering made me want to puke.

Stop the dragon, Mom, I want to get off. But letting go wasn't an option.

Daylight shone from above. We were at the entrance. The dragon stretched its wings and flapped, even as it continued clawing against the cave walls.

Renfro and the rest of the smokies waited at the

entrance. They were stunned to see me holding on to the Behemoth's ankle at first, gaping their mouths and staying low to avoid the river of flames pouring from the headless neck. Then they began to fire.

"Stop shooting!" I yelled.

The scaly carried me higher.

Voices sounded through my helmet, but I couldn't understand what they were saying.

I really didn't want to fall again, so I stretched my laser sword and thrust toward the dragon's gut, but just like last time, I missed. And just like last time, I fell. Thankfully, it was from a much safer height. I landed at the edge of the cliff overlooking the cave entrance, rolling to a stop just before I would have dropped over the edge.

I pushed myself to stand and watch the erratic Behemoth pick up altitude. It was much slower having to fly with a decapitation, not paying much attention to where it was going.

"Cast," I said, remembering Naveena's plan. "Brannigan to Jet 1, the dragon is in the air, heading," I checked the position of the sun, "east. It's still low in the air, but it's spewing fire and picking up speed."

"We're on it, Brannigan," Jet 1's pilot replied. "Captain Jendal already gave us a heads up."

Jet 1 flew over my head, so close I could have power jumped to catch a ride. The big cannon hung from its nose, looking more dangerous than it really was. Farther toward the horizon, the Behemoth changed direction and soared straight for our jet.

"What the hell did you do, Brannigan?" Naveena came up behind me, out of breath.

"What? It's still alive," I said, watching the two airborne beasts sail toward each other.

Jet 1 fired the cannon. The beam flashed like lightning,

but missed the dragon by at least a hundred feet. The dragon shot its own beam – an EMP. Jet 1 maneuvered out of the way.

"Oh, damn," Naveena said, almost in a whisper.

The remaining Behemoth heads aimed toward the jet and roared with determination, even as the headless section continued blowing fire. The jet doubled back for another round of Chicken.

"Shoot it," I said, urging the jet to strike before the dragon closed in.

Three streams of fire were spewing out now, as the dragon reared its claws to slash at the jet.

"Fire, damn it!"

At the last minute, Jet 1 fired again, nailing the Behemoth dead center. The dragon heads dangled and no longer spewed flames, but its wings were still extended as it pitched forward.

"It's unconscious, right?" I asked Naveena.

The others had gathered behind us.

"I think so," Naveena said.

"Then why is it still flying?"

"Ah shit," Afu said. "It's not flying. It's falling – straight toward us!"

We all ran as far as we could. I turned in time to see the Behemoth land faces first into the ground, tumbling over itself and sending sand all over us. A few granules got in my eye. This stupid dragon was a pain even while unconscious.

After the sand had settled, we watchfully surrounded it.

Afu kicked the Behemoth. "Uh, you guys? You sure that cannon is nonlethal?"

"Yeah," Naveena said. "Why?"

"This thing's not breathing."

We all watched the Behemoth's middle, hearing

nothing but the song of a wind gust in the distance.

"Damn it!" Naveena said, jolting us out of our trance. "Damn thing must have broken its neck when it hit the ground."

"Necks," I corrected.

"What are we going to do now?" Renfro asked. "Donahue and the propellerheads wanted a live dragon."

In the air, Jet 1 circled for a landing. I sat on the sand and watched it descend in the distance. A job not very well done.

CHAPTER 32

On our way home, Naveena was pacing in the back of Jet 1 when I exited the cockpit and took my seat. "What were you doing in there?" she asked.

"Just talking to the pilots."

I guessed the answer was good enough, because she went back to her pacing and under-the-breath swearing. The others in our crew had their eyes closed, worn out from the strain of nabbing the Behemoth. Renfro was still awake, but looked like he would fall face first at any moment. Hell, I did most of the hard work, and I felt great.

The dragon itself hung about fifty feet below us, secured with magnetic rope we'd had to shimmy under the Behemoth's dead body. The work had taken at least a couple hours, and everyone else had to take a break every few minutes. It wasn't fun by any means, but I kept going as they took turns securing the ropes to make a net around the scaly. When we were done and loaded onto Jet 1, the plane extended a high-powered magnetic claw and picked up the Behemoth like it was a ball of paper.

"You can blame it on me," I told Naveena.

She shook her head and kept marching. "No, Brannigan. As much as I want to, you didn't do this."

SEAN GRIGSBY   299

"So, tell the truth. The dragon died because it couldn't go to sleep like a good, little scaly."

"It was my plan," Naveena said. "I should have known shooting it in the sky was a bad idea. This is on me."

"Well, you know how I feel. It's just another dead dragon. Case closed."

"Easy for you to say, Dragon Blood." Renfro stared at me through heavy-lidded eyes.

"Williams called me that before. What's it supposed to mean?"

"Don't tell him," Naveena said. "It'll just be something else for him to bitch about."

"Well, now you know I won't let it go," I said.

"You don't wear out, and you're jumping on dragons like a wild man," Renfro said. "You don't think that's a miracle?"

"A miracle of science, maybe." I shrugged. "That blue shit Yolanda whips up in the lab is awesome. Ieiunium whatever."

"And where do you think the curate comes from?" Naveena said.

"Don't say dragons."

"Dragon blood," Renfro said. "And while any scaly blood is good for making small-scale medicine for bruises and the like, we only had one supply of live dragon blood. And guess who got it pumped into them while rolling around Canada in a box?"

My jaw dropped.

"Face it, Brannigan," Naveena said. "You've got more scaly in you than all of us."

I felt violated.

Staring at the floor for a few minutes, I noticed the slight turbulence in the air, the muffled conversation of the pilots behind the cockpit door. "So... do I have, like, super powers?"

They laughed, so loud it made Afu and Williams jump in their sleep, although they didn't wake up.

"We're smoke eaters," Naveena said. "Is breathing smoke and resisting heat not enough?"

"I guess I was hoping for something more," I said. "Like x-ray vision."

"You old perv."

Renfro leaned forward. "Yolanda has a theory about why we can do what we do. She thinks before the dragons went back underground all those centuries ago some warriors drank dragon blood or injected themselves with it somehow."

"And their bloodlines kept the scaly code as the DNA was passed from generation to generation," said Naveena. "Our people were going to inject a non-smoky and see if it had any effect."

"So," I said. "I got the live blood because…"

"Because you needed it," Naveena said. "Your death drop changed plans."

I crossed my arms. "I see. So, now we're in the business of manufacturing smoke eaters."

"If we can," Naveena said. "There aren't enough of us. If we can turn the tide of this war without having to rely on random genetics–"

War, huh?

"What about people with cancer?" I said. "Quadriplegics? Those people need that curate more than we need soldiers."

"Dragons are more of a threat," Renfro said. "Shit, Brannigan, I thought you would understand more than anyone."

I wasn't the one being hypocritical here. The scalies were a particular thorn in my ass, sure. But for ages, mankind has put more money, more time, and more brain power toward destruction than healing. And now that we know the thing we're fighting against has the potential to change lives for the better, we hide it from the public and use it for our own agenda?

Same shit, different day.

"So, that's why you're pissed," I said to Naveena. "We had one of the biggest living scalies to farm blood from, and now it's dead."

"Would you guys save the political talk?" Williams stared at us with one eye still closed. "I'm trying to sleep."

"Yeah," Naveena said. "We're almost home anyway."

And boy, did I have a surprise for our entrance.

I looked out the window. The crowd of protesters had tripled outside our headquarters. It looked almost like a rock concert, especially with the huge speakers among the crowd, and the flashing of glow sticks. I couldn't hear anything, obviously, but I hummed a tune, imagining they were jamming to it.

Droids had been brought in for crowd control. I wouldn't let that sour my mood.

Naveena squatted beside me and looked out of a porthole. "Why are we flying in this way?"

"I asked the pilots for a favor," I said.

Naveena glared at me. "What did you do?"

I smiled.

Naveena charged toward the cockpit, but by that time Jet 1 was over the front stairs of Smoky HQ and the weight we'd been carrying abruptly left the bottom of the plane.

"Whoa," Afu said.

Naveena froze and turned back.

I readied to defend myself from any flying punches, and said, "I figured the crowd would appreciate a grand entrance."

CHAPTER 33

Naveena didn't punch me, although I saw in her body language that she really wanted to. As Jet 1 backed into the bay, she jumped out before the hatch had fully stopped lowering, and ran for the front of headquarters.

After exiting my power suit, I ran after Naveena, but when I broke through the doors to the hallway Sherry nearly tackled me with a hug.

"You look great!" Sherry said.

I was in a sweat-soaked smoke eater uniform and was still spitting out grains of desert sand. Wives are wonderful creatures.

Kenji stood on his hind legs beside Sherry, barking and begging for a pat. I smiled and gave him a rub.

"Your chief said you went to New Mexico to nab a dragon?" Sherry said. "Was it hot there? Is the thing still alive?"

Sherry was being exceptionally high-spirited, so much so, I thought maybe Donahue had drugged her just to keep her from demolishing the walls. Whatever the case, he'd kept his word, and Sherry was safe.

"I'm glad to see you," I said, "but I've got to get to the front of the building."

"Kenji and I'll come with you."

I didn't have the energy to argue with Sherry, so I

didn't stop them from following.

Naveena was yelling at Donahue at the front entrance. They both turned to me as I jogged up.

"Well, you really did it this time." Naveena balled her fists. I could have sworn steam seeped from between her fingers.

"Sherry." I extended a hand. "This is Captain Naveena Jendal. My, um… boss."

"Hi," Sherry said, smiling big. "Nice to meet you."

"Yeah," Naveena said.

Donahue scrubbed his face with both palms, as if he was rubbing a lamp, wishing I'd go the hell away. "Brannigan, why is there a dead dragon in front of my headquarters?"

When I'd asked the pilots to drop it on our front steps, I was releasing a little anger. I thought it would be a great way to put the fear of God into the protesters, if not just piss them off. But when Chief Donahue asked me, I figured I'd give him another reason.

"Public relations."

Donahue's eyes twitched, and a low gurgling sound came from deep within his throat.

Kenji barked and said, "Neoneun modu manghaessda."

"Maybe we can still use this," Naveena offered, as she placed a hand on the chief's shoulder. "Show them that we can still get the job done. It'll take some finesse, though."

Yolanda appeared around the corner. "Things are about to get suckier."

Donahue turned at that. "What?"

"Um." Yolanda puffed air from under her top lip. "You're going to want to come with me."

Donahue swore, and I told Sherry and Kenji to wait for me.

Yolanda led us to a propellerhead lab where, on the

other side of the glass, a man sat on an examination table, trembling and cupping a mug. He wore an unbuttoned police shirt.

"So there are some cops still around," I said.

Donahue took a sip of coffee as we all stared at the policeman like a rabbit in a cage.

"He showed up around the time the protesters were gathering outside," Yolanda said. "We thought he was one of them until he showed us his badge."

"And you believed him?" Naveena asked.

"Another propellerhead recognized him, said he worked with his dad." Yolanda crossed her arms and looked at the floor. "I'm just hoping what he's saying is bunk. Or at least that he was hallucinating or something. It's just too crazy."

"What did he say?" I asked.

"I'll let him tell you."

We entered the room slowly, as if the poor guy was a scaly strapped to the table.

"You the chief?" the cop asked Donahue.

"I am. Yolanda says you have something to tell me. What's your name?"

"Billy... er... William Martinez. I'm a sergeant with PCPD. Or, at least I was."

"Yeah," I said. "We were just there. What's with all the droids taking over?"

Martinez looked on the edge of tears. "It was just like any other day. You know? Sometimes you just know it's going to be a bad day, and you're always right. But not this time."

We all waited for him to continue.

He took a drink from his mug and cleared his throat. "Droids came in all at once, aiming lasers. A few cops tried to fight them off, but they got thrown into a wall or held down. We smoked a couple of them, though. But it took so many damn shots, the other droids were on us before we could run.

"Then they brought in Chief Feldman. He told us we were all being let go, including him. That there were droids waiting outside our homes at that moment, and if we resisted…"

Donahue shook his head. "Jesus."

"I have a little girl," Martinez said.

"They would have killed her in an instant," I said.

"I know," Martinez said. "But I still feel like shit. They gathered us all up and loaded us in the back of a truck. Except Feldman. I don't know what happened to him. The droids said if any former cop got close to headquarters, we'd be shot on sight. Then they'd kill our families like they'd promised. Before they locked us up, I saw droids marching people out of the court house across the street. Judges, too.

"We were crammed in that box for hours, sweating our asses off. I was trying to figure out a way to stop the droids. Nobody wanted to listen. They didn't want to risk their families any more than I did. But I had to do something. Finally the door opened on its own. I don't know why, but I came straight here. I knew the smoke eaters could help."

Donahue led Naveena and me out of the room after telling Yolanda to get Martinez anything he wanted.

"Rogola strikes again," I said.

"He fires the police force and replaces them with droids," Naveena said. "The whole legal system is probably gone by now. And he's got the city calling for our heads on platters."

"Because we're better defended than police," Donahue said. "And he probably sees it as a way to boost himself while destroying our department at the same time."

Naveena cracked her knuckles. "There's no way the

police can let this stand."

"Sure they can," I said. "Who would they complain to? The droids are running law enforcement now."

"The government," Naveena said. "The big one."

Even Donahue laughed at that. "I learned a long time ago that the America we used to know is gone. Now it's all city states that have a shared fondness of what used to be and are maybe trading tomatoes for air conditioners and things like that. We're on our own, Naveena."

"We can get Martinez to tell them what he told us."

Donahue shook his head. "He doesn't leave this facility. This is the safest place for him, at least until we find a way out of this mess. We don't mention his name to anyone, and we send a couple of our people to bring his family in, too. That's all we can do for now."

"This is such bullshit." Naveena kicked the wall.

Donahue sighed. "Suit up. Full power armor. The works."

CHAPTER 34

After introducing Sherry to the others in my crew, I showed her how I got into my power suit.

"Nice," she said. "Think you could bring it home sometime?"

"Come on," I said. "I've got a mob to calm."

Afu and Williams were staring out the front doors when we came back. Williams leaned against Afu's arm. Both swore in disbelief.

"Things are getting crazy out there," Afu said. "They brought a shitload of those robots."

I turned to Sherry and Kenji. "You guys should stay inside. I don't trust those things."

Sherry shook her head, humming a negative. "You had me dragged all the way out here and are just going to hide me away? I don't think so. Besides, what can a few hunks of metal do?"

I swallowed, still not thinking it was the best idea. When I opened the door, the protesters' collective roar hit my ears. A synthwave song boomed from the speakers and the people chanted something I couldn't decipher. An army of droids stood at the front of the crowd, hands on their metal hips.

Donahue and Naveena stood hidden from the crowd behind the mass of the dead Behemoth. The dragon smelled worse than when it was alive, like body gas and rotten possums.

"Now what?" Williams asked.

Donahue waved a megaphone in his hand. "Now, I try to clean this mess up."

He walked around the dead dragon and waved to the crowd. They booed him on sight, followed by the same chant that I worked out to be, "Fuck you, smokies!"

It did have a nice ring to it.

"People of Parthenon City," Donahue began.

The music lowered, but still trickled from the speakers.

"I know all of you are upset about the destruction of your homes, the ashen wastes that used to be your neighborhoods. You've lost family. Friends. All because of some ancient species returning, with nothing but destruction on its agenda.

"And we," he waved for all of us to step out there with him, "are all that stands in the way, between the dragons and what's left of our civilization."

We moved to stand beside him. I hated this "We Are the World" treatment, but if Donahue thought it would get these people to shut up and let us go back to doing our job, I guess I had to play along. Sherry ate it up, putting her arm around my armored elbow, smiling as if she was the first lady. Kenji stood silent, watching the droids warily.

Naveena seemed pissed as ever, while Afu, Williams, and a bunch of other smokies looked like they were starring in the school play and had walked onstage completely naked.

I didn't see Renfro. Lucky bastard skipped out on this charade.

"Lying here," Donahue held a hand to the dead Behemoth, "is the most recent dragon to terrorize our city. We travelled over a thousand miles to track it down.

"We brought this dragon back for you. Because that's who we serve. You. Now, if you want us gone, fine. But if you think a bunch of droids can replace us, you won't have a city left to call home. And you'll all be dead within the month."

That shut them up. The only remaining sound was the horrendous music softly bumping from the speakers towering over the crowd. And funny thing, something I hadn't noticed before because of all the other flashing lights, was that the speakers glowed white.

How long had they been doing that?

"Oh, shit," I said, too loudly.

But it had already happened. With an electrical pop, the speakers erupted into white flames and dozens of wraiths crawled out of the inferno like a ghostly factory line.

The crowd tried to scatter. People crashed into each other, were thrown to the ground, trampled over, screaming louder than the wraiths closing in. The droids, who'd been standing statuesque among the crowd, turned with glowing red eyes and raised laser pistols.

"Brannigan!" Naveena chunked me the wraith-catcher remote.

I caught it and grabbed Sherry. "Get inside."

"But what about you?"

"This is my job." I turned her toward the building.

A droid launched up the steps, its eyes flashing red. "Eliminate. Eliminate. Eliminate," it kept saying.

I guess it wasn't as cliché as, "Destroy! Destroy! Destroy!" but the robot had obviously gone apeshit. The metal man grabbed Sherry by the throat.

Kenji bit the droid's ankle, but the metal man raised its leg and smashed my dog against the pavement. Gears and pieces of metal canine shattered and skittered down the steps.

"Kenji!" I screamed. But there was nothing I could do. He warbled out something in Korean before his eyes faded to darkness.

Williams moved in to shoot the droid, but it slapped her across the face, and she fired her lasers over the heads of the crowd.

I ducked low to avoid the lasers and moved in. Sherry kicked her feet against the droid's chest and choked out weak whimpers. The droid hadn't crushed her throat, but it kept its eyes on me, waiting for me to attack. She was bait.

Something tried to grab me from behind, but I dodged and fell forward. The overwhelming smell of burnt flesh and the deafening shrieks told me it was a wraith. I flipped over and kicked at its ugly face, but it would only disperse and reform as soon as my armored boot was out of the way.

The wraith sank its claws into my armored legs. Electric ice ripped into my muscles, pinning me to the spot. Above, the droid, still choking Sherry, raised its metal foot and brought it down toward my head.

I ejected my laser sword. With a slash, the dismembered robot leg landed on my face. The pain was like a firework had exploded in my nose, and then blood poured from my nostrils.

I sat up and shot the wraith with the capture remote. The black light swallowed the ghost, and I had time to turn toward the droid to ram my sword into its chest and catch Sherry before she hit the ground.

She wasn't breathing.

"Help!" I screamed. All my confidence, all my resolve, all my courage stolen from me like the droid had stolen Sherry's breath.

Her skin was still warm against my cheek, and she hadn't gone blue. I tilted her head and gave her two breaths, just enough to see her chest rise.

"Help!" I screamed again.

The ground shook as people and wraiths screamed behind me. In the back of my mind, I knew what that meant, but I was too distraught.

Williams crawled over to me and my wife. "You blow," she said, wincing against a pain in her side, "and I'll push."

I nodded and moved to Sherry's head. We needed to get her out of there, but she wasn't breathing, and I'd always been trained that immediate CPR gave the highest chance of survival.

After I gave two breaths, Williams began compressions. Thirty years in the fire service, I'd performed this too many times to count, too many times to remember each dying face. But I'd never had to do it for someone I knew, someone I loved. The whole world was falling to shit just a few feet away as wraiths and murderous robots wreaked havoc amidst the crowd, but I didn't look up. I was focused on Sherry, on Williams' compression count. I refused to look away.

At least, not until I heard the first dragon roar.

They came from everywhere. Mounds of earth exploded under the wraiths and droids, scattering the crowd into a blind frenzy. Several of the protesters didn't move in time, and flew like rag dolls into the air as a large, blue dragon emerged with fire in its teeth.

"Blow, Brannigan!" Williams shouted.

I gave Sherry two more breaths, then swiveled my head back to the shit storm developing. We were stuck. The rest of the smoke eaters fought amidst the crowd, trying to decide which was the worse threat – droids, wraiths, or dragons.

It was a shit sandwich buffet.

A few smokies had been sheltering several protesters

from a wraith, when a couple poppers emerged from a hole and snagged one of the smokies. They gnawed at either end of him, until the other smoke eaters shot or stabbed the poppers until they stopped moving. Then a gang of droids charged in and snapped one of the smokies' necks. The other smoke eater fought like hell, but the droids fired lasers into his face. When other droids began blasting citizens with water cannons and scattering them across the ground like loose pebbles, I knew things had gone completely insane.

"Get my wife inside," I told Williams as I stood. "Get her to Yolanda."

"What are you doing?" Williams yelled.

I stomped into the crowd and ejected my laser sword. "What I was born to do."

A couple droids tossed a shirtless man toward a snapping, bird-like dragon. I cut both of the droids' heads off and ran after the man. The bird scaly had caught him by the ankle and, with one pinch of its beak, severed his foot. Smoke plumed from the dragon's mouth as it guzzled the morsel down.

The man cried and crawled toward me. The dragon saw its prey escaping and flapped two bat-like wings to float into the air. I met it midflight with a power jump, snatching its long neck with both of my hands. We landed just behind the footless man, and I put every ounce of anger into my squeeze. The dragon's eyes bulged as it snapped at my face, but I bent my elbows with a snap and broke the bastard's neck.

"Thank you," the footless man said. He was bleeding badly.

"I have to take your pants off," I said.

"Yeah, yeah. Just help me!"

I ripped his pants off quickly, but he still screamed from the gushing stump at the end of his leg. As tight as I could, I tied a makeshift tourniquet around his calf.

The propellerheads had begun streaming from the building with gurneys and cots. I handed the man over to two of them and turned back to the mayhem.

I zapped two wraiths that had been clawing after a group of women wearing light-up hats. As the women ran away, their hats' lights disappeared into a developing cloud of pitch black smoke surrounding us all. Most of the protesters were bent over, hacking against the dragon smoke, stumbling blind as the toxins stung their eyes. It had become a warzone.

To my right, a snakelike scaly had half-swallowed someone – their legs stuck out of its throat. A nearby smoke eater sliced the snake dragon mid-gulp, cutting the poor protester inside at the same time.

To my left, a couple droids rode the back of a spiky dragon that looked like a porcupine had fucked a dinosaur. Spike headed straight for me, snapping at passersby that managed to dodge its long snout. As it got closer and I readied myself to attack, I noticed the droids weren't riding the scaly, but had become impaled on its spikes.

The dragon spread its jaws, but instead of fire, purplish gas shot from its throat. I rolled away. My smoke-breathing ability didn't cover poisonous gas.

When I turned over to slash at Spike, it was already on me and biting down hard on my sword arm. I swear, these scaly bastards had a group meeting and knew how to go after our weapons.

Spike threw me into the air, and I soared with no control over my arms or legs. As I fell back toward the earth, the dragon opened its mouth to welcome me into its belly. But a barrage of lasers cut into its flesh. Some lasers contacted the purple gas just before the monster shut its jaws and flopped over onto its side. It exploded in a shower of stinking, scaly flesh.

I hit the ground and rolled over to stab Spike's charred head. Not because I wanted to make sure it was dead, but because it had pissed me off.

An armored hand offered to help me up. Williams, the badass.

I took her hand and stood. "My wife?"

"Propellerheads are working on her. She still wasn't breathing when I left. But I'm needed out here. OK?" She ran over to a woman whose back was on fire and covered the protester with cooling foam.

We ran deeper into the crowd.

The citizens had begun to fight back – against the droids and scalies at least. They used severed droid appendages to swing at dragons swooping from the air. Other protesters shoved a dragon shooting flames toward oncoming robots. Unfortunately, several of these people succumbed to the smoke, or died a fiery death, or were mangled by metal hands. I couldn't have saved them if I tried. I was fighting the same bastards, and I had the only weapon against the wraiths.

I began blasting ghosts like nobody's business. Williams took out any droids that ran or shot at us, while I focused on the undead. Everywhere I turned there was another wraith to zap.

I checked the wraith-catcher remote. Only half full.

Ahead, the black smoke parted violently, and a wraith flew toward me, glowing like a radioactive firefly. It slashed my cheek. Icy fire swelled in my face.

"Son of a bitch!" I shouted. "I hate…" Zap! The wraith was gone "… you…" I trapped another one sneaking behind Williams "… dead motherfuckers!" I shot another two at each side of us.

At the corner of my vision, farther into the smoke, more white light throbbed, teasing me. The job wasn't done.

"Come on," I told Williams.

We ran toward the glow, and when we got there we saw Donahue sprawled with his face toward the smoke-stained sky.

Four droids each had a hold of his armored wrist or ankle. Chief was screaming and cursing the robots for the bastards they were. He didn't see the wraith floating toward him from behind. The droids didn't pay the ghost any attention either. They were too busy pulling Donahue in four different directions. The droid at his metal leg fell backwards when it popped from the socket.

"No!" I ran, ready to slash them all to hell. But the wraith was an even greater threat, so I lifted the remote.

"Chief," a voice screamed to my right. Naveena.

She ran toward Donahue as well. One of us was bound to reach him before–

A fat scaly with a face like rocky lava bounded through the smoke behind Naveena. She didn't hear it coming over the surrounding screams and roars. She didn't see it.

I power jumped and tackled her. The scaly soared over us, biting at the empty air. Williams lit it up with laser shots, but they didn't have any effect. Naveena was already back on her feet and burying her laser sword into the scaly's head.

But we were too late for Donahue.

The wraith got to him first. There was no preamble, or any hesitation its former human self would have taken. It just latched onto Donahue's head with both white claws and ripped his face off. Chief was still screaming when the rest of the droids quartered him. His gory torso fell to the ground, and the robots toppled over, each with a different piece of him still in their grasp.

I screamed. I cried. I'd never had so much hate bubble up in my guts toward these inhuman things, metal and scales and ethereal glow alike. But even in my rage, even in the blackest part of the smoke, I knew they were only tools used by one man. One asshole I'd be seeing very, very soon.

But first.

Naveena took the two droids on the right. She chopped them into a million rusty pieces. I zapped the wraith and began my own slice-and-dice routine against the droids. Williams had to grab my shoulder to stop me slashing at metal men that weren't there any more. They were just piles of gears now.

The smoke began to clear as other smokies finished off the last of the dragons. I didn't see any more wraiths or droids.

Donahue's eyes stared into the distance. He'd bled out, even from where they'd removed his metal leg. His mouth was open, like he had one last thing to say, one last criticism to give me, one final piece of wisdom for Naveena. But he was robbed of it.

A thud hit the ground behind me. Naveena had fallen to her knees. She said nothing.

"Is it over?" Williams asked.

"No," I said. "We need to triage."

"Need to what?"

Naveena spoke. "Separate the ones who can be helped from those who are too gone for it to matter."

I nodded. "Tell the other smokies to start gathering the protesters. If they can't breathe on their own, consider them gone. Anyone who can walk, can help."

Williams gave a thumbs up and ran over to the closest smoke eater. I knelt beside Naveena.

"Donahue rescued me," Naveena said. "Back on E-Day. That's how I found out I was a smoke eater. He found me hiding in the middle of a burning playground. I'd gone to pick my little brother up from school. Did I ever tell you that?"

Donahue had. "You were under the jungle gym."

She nodded as tears streamed down her face.

"I have to go check on my wife."

"I'll go with you." She wiped away the tears with the back of her armored wrist.

We hadn't taken two steps when we heard a roar come from the front of the building. Above the steps, the overburdened metal net snapped like spider web as the hulking monster inside stood and stretched its wings. We'd been wrong. The Behemoth was still alive and now it was awake.

Screams surrounded us. Protesters ran in all directions.

The Behemoth's headless neck no longer spurted fire, but the other two heads looked even more pissed than I remembered. The few protesters who'd run for the building and abandoned their friends froze on the steps when the Behemoth awoke. With clumsy turns they ran back toward us. Two of them didn't make it. Each remaining Behemoth head snatched a protester in its teeth and gobbled them down like blood-filled gummy bears.

"Cancel the triage," I radioed to everyone. "Our main priority is that dragon."

"Line up on me and Brannigan," Naveena said.

The Behemoth took two giant steps that shook the ground and sent shivers up my spine. I really thought I'd gotten a grip on my breathing, but I was huffing like I'd climbed a skyscraper. The other smoke eaters ran or power jumped over to us.

"I thought that thing was dead," Williams said.

"How the hell are we going to kill it?" asked another smoke eater.

The Behemoth finished choking down its meals and eyed the line of us standing in its way. I'm sure we looked like army men stacked in front of it. The two horns on one head flickered with an electric glow, causing the other to curl its head and snarl, like they were having a conversation.

"Killing it would be easy," I said into my radio, and the words tasted like bile. "But we need to keep this thing alive."

"What?" Williams's yell sent feedback through all of our helmets.

Naveena turned to me with a glare, but then comprehension filled her eyes. "Brannigan's right," she said. "We need its blood to help everyone here who's hurt."

"And how are we supposed to do that?" Afu ran up with a severed dragon head in his hand.

"We have to get to Jet 1," I said.

The Behemoth jerked both heads in my direction, as if it had understood what I said, and breathed a wall of fire, daring us to cross. Then, with two flaps of its enormous wings, it sent the flames toward us and sprang into the air.

"Shit!" I ran along the wall of fire, looking for an opening. "Everyone with lasers, focus on its wings."

A million lasers filled the sky, most of them hitting the Behemoth's wings and tearing jagged holes through the leathery skin. With a roar, the dragon pelted us with another of its EMP blasts. I twirled into the air and landed on my side. The others had fallen over into similar positions, and all of our power suits were dead.

"This shit has to quit happening," Naveena groaned.

The Behemoth continued to flap its damaged wings, only managing to hover, caught between the ground and the endless sky.

"Our equipment is shot," Afu said.

Williams said, "So is the scaly."

"Yeah, but it still has fire and teeth." I scanned the

ground for a useable weapon. Dead bodies and pieces of droids littered the ashy dirt. Maybe one of the police droids' laser arms still worked?

My ass.

The Behemoth blasted more fire and glided forward. We had no weapons, no power to jump away. A few of the smokies began digging into the ground, as if that would save them. As if they forgot the scalies came from underneath.

I stood there, ready for what came next. Hopefully it would be quick. As a firefighter, I always accepted burning to death as a possibility, I did my job anyway. Having a dragon chew me to pieces had never been on my radar, though. I wanted to avoid that at all costs.

Naveena grabbed my hand, and when I looked over, she was staring straight at the oncoming Behemoth. No fear, no remorse. This was just another day, brought to a fiery close.

I raised my arms in the air and laughed like a witch who'd smoked too much cannabis. Everyone beside me stared like I'd lost my mind. I pointed up, just beyond the Behemoth. That's when the other smokies cheered and jumped. The dragon roared, still breathing fire, unaware of what flew behind it.

Plasma engines cut through the sky. Coming in hot, just behind the Behemoth, flew Jet 1. Its laser cannon glowing hot with contained energy. Jet 1 fired, striking the Behemoth square in the back. The flames died in its mouth and it collapsed midair, coming down with a heavy thud in front of us.

Afu ran up to the scaly and kicked its side. "Yeah, that's right, asshole!"

"You didn't think I'd miss the fun, did you?" It was Renfro coming over the radio. I could imagine him giving us a thumbs up from the cockpit of the jet.

"I didn't know you could fly," I said.

"I can drive anything."

Puck broke in. "He had my help, damn it."

The smokies on the ground cheered, but just like bad house fires I'd beaten before, there was still overhaul to perform, and that was always the toughest part.

"We still need to gather the wounded," I told everyone.

"Brannigan's right," said Naveena. "Listen to him. Follow his lead."

I was taken aback that she would actually let me run the show, not that I craved the position. I just knew no one else had been trained in mass casualty incidents.

"All right." I motioned for everyone to circle around me. "This is what we need."

CHAPTER 35

We cleared out the Slayer bay to make room for beds and cots and anything else we thought could hold a patient. The propellerheads were in rare form, travelling back and forth from the disaster scene and carrying patients to where they needed to go.

IVs of Ieiunium curate were wheeled in from the lab and injected into the most needful first. As the propellerheads drew more blood from the unconscious Behemoth, more curate was made available, and even citizens with a mild case of the vapors got an IV.

There were going to be a shitload more smoke eaters – if Yolanda's theory was correct.

We'd gotten smarter with experience and had Yolanda remove the Behemoth's ignis glands and hamstrings. I wouldn't call it cruel. We could have just killed it. Still, we'd make sure the Canadians didn't find out. The propellerheads could now reverse engineer the nonlethal cannon and reproduce it in smaller form, fitting every power suit. We could draw dragon blood and cure existing diseases while basically immunizing the public from dragon smoke.

The future looked so bright, I'd have to wear therma goggles.

Sherry was the first person I had to see. I didn't even

care if anyone saw me crying as I ran to where one of the propellerheads had told me to look. My wife lay on a bed in one of the labs with an x-ray cervical collar around her neck and an IV of blue shit plugged into her. She smiled when she saw me.

Ejecting from my power suit, I wheeled a chair over to her side. I kissed her, gently, to avoid hurting her neck. "I never thought of you as the damsel in distress."

"I'd like to see you take a robot hand to the throat and live to talk about it," she said, wincing from the pain.

"Fair enough." I looked toward the IV, watching the drip, drip of curate.

"Kenji," she said, suddenly worried.

"He's in a lab right now. I'll get him back to his old self. We have the technology."

I was terrible at mechanical stuff, but I'd find a way. Maybe get a propellerhead to help.

"They told me this blue stuff will completely cure me," Sherry said. "Sounds too good to be true."

"It's not. This shit will make you even better than before."

"I'm still not cleaning the toilets."

We both laughed.

I gripped her hand, never wanting to let go. But there was something important I had to do.

When I got back to the Slayer bay, the smokies had gathered just on the other side of the door. They all looked up at me when I entered.

"What's going on?" I asked.

A few propellerheads broke through the line, pushing a hovercot into the building. The body they carried had been covered with a sheet, but the area around the face was damp with blood.

Donahue.

We all watched him enter headquarters in silence. Only the distant groans of a few citizens echoed inside the bay.

"We need to elect a new chief," Naveena said.

"Can't that wait?" I said. "We need to nail Rogola while he still thinks we're licking our wounds."

"It's like when there was still a US president." Puck stepped closer. "Your old ass should remember that. If something happened to the commander in chief, the vice president was sworn in."

I lifted my hands. "So, swear 'em in and let's go already."

"Donahue had a will," Naveena said. "And maybe it's not all that legally binding. But we have a code to uphold, and we all want to follow his wishes."

I crossed my arms, feeling the cool sweat trapped in my cotton uniform shirt, and waited for her to continue.

"He wanted us to vote on it."

I looked at each face gathered around me like a sweaty lynch mob. No one spoke, they looked tired and miserable. I was tired and miserable.

"OK," I said. "I vote Captain Jendal. She's got the experience and doesn't take shit from anyone."

No one responded.

"Come on guys!" I pushed through them, wondering if I should take the cannon truck or something more inconspicuous to city hall.

"I appreciate that, Brannigan," Naveena called, "but we already have a majority. We want you as chief."

I stopped dead in my tracks. My mouth wrenched into something that was part frown, part surprised gape as I turned back to all of them. I stared at each face. Some, like Afu and Williams, nodded as if to say, "Believe it, asshole. You got the job."

I cleared my throat and leaned in so I'd only have to

say it once. "No thanks, guys. See you later."

I ran for a car outside, because staying there any longer would cause them to try to weasel me into Donahue's position, just like I had been weaseled in to the Smoke Eater Division in the first place.

I picked Donahue's truck, ironically. I was backing out when Naveena threw open the side door and hopped in beside me.

I groaned. "Aren't these vehicles supposed to lock when you put them in reverse?"

"Let's go," she said.

Time being of the essence, I didn't argue. I just drove.

"So, how are we going to find Rogola?" Naveena asked.

"We don't have to find him," I said. "At least, not his physical body."

CHAPTER 36

Rogola's receptionist was about to press a button to alert the mayor, but Naveena beat her to it.

With a finger to her lips, Naveena wheeled the receptionist into another room. I would do this by myself.

Jenkins jumped at my entrance and ran for the door, throwing his holoreader at me, as if it was a useful distraction. I shoved him with a stiff push of my arm, and like a rubber ball Jenkins bounced off the nearest wall and lay still on the floor. Hell, I hadn't pushed him that hard. Jenkins was either playing possum, or had fainted from being touched.

Rogola had watched this silently, his hologram fingers steepled against his lips. "You can't find much loyal help these days. Or at least any with enough balls not to run." He stood and looked down at Jenkins. "If you can hear this, Jenkins, you're fired."

"Interesting choice of words," I said. "Hosed. Sacked. Let go. They all mean the same thing, but I'll just put it bluntly and tell you: you're finished."

"Now, before you go into your righteous spiel about getting even or justice or some other nonsense, maybe you can hear me out for a second." Rogola moved to stand behind the hologram chair and leaned against it. The image flickered, shimmering blue. "We haven't been very cordial to each other, you and I, it's true. But given how things have progressed, how you've shown that you're good at getting things done... I could use someone like you. I think you could be fire chief."

"Of what? A bunch of droids?"

"There will be positions for those who show they're team players. Plus, droids don't have to be paid. The droid factory only gets paid for each unit. That means more money for you."

"And even more for you." I tightened my lips and breathed hard through my nostrils. "That's what it all comes back to, right? More money?"

"Of course not. It's about helping this city." Holographic sweat beaded down the side of his face. He softened his eyes, putting on a look of sincerity, as if he actually believed he was the good guy in all of this.

"You think summoning dragons to poor people's houses is helping?"

Rogola harrumphed. "Those hovels were barely standing. When we move in and rebuild, things are stronger, cleaner, better."

"And having wraiths and dragons attack civilians? Droids killing Chief Donahue or strangling my wife?"

"Well, you were all supposed to die, weren't you?" Rogola snapped out the words, clicking his teeth. "But that didn't happen. Like I said, we haven't been on the best of terms. But I'm a flexible man, Captain Brannigan. I can see the universe is telling me I've approached all of this from the wrong angle. I'm offering you the olive branch."

"In case you haven't noticed, not much grows around here anymore, outside of a building," I said. "Least of all olive branches. And even if they did, I wouldn't side with you, no matter what you promise me. I don't do what I do for money or power. And I won't tolerate assholes who do."

The mayor threw his chair, and it disappeared out of the hologram camera's view. "You bastards can't even find me. The only person who knows where I am was lying on the floor behind you."

Was?

I turned and saw that Jenkins had snuck out while Rogola and I were talking.

"And don't think you'll be able to get anything out of him. I put an explosive bug in his neck. If I hear him even hint at revealing my location... kaboom. And all I have to do is move somewhere new. I have plenty of places to go. Places no one knows about."

"Seems you have it all figured out."

Rogola snickered. "A wise man knows his enemy."

"And that explosive," I pointed at my own neck, "is that something else you got from the Yūrei Corporation?"

"They make a hell of a lot of interesting toys, don't they?" Rogola reached out of the holographic view and righted his chair, sitting like the victor, the king on his throne.

I pulled out the wraith-catching remote and waved it above my head. "Like this toy?"

"What is that?"

"You know what it is. You thought you had it all wrapped up. But it looks like Jenkins missed one." I wiggled the remote again.

Rogola thinned his eyes, but remained seated.

"I'd been thinking long and hard about how you did it," I said. "Put the wraiths into the TV where my firefighter died. The speakers outside our headquarters. The holostereo in my own house."

Rogola swallowed.

"A Professor Poltergeist video said it best. We all have electrical energy inside us. It's basically what a wraith is

– angry energy created by the scalies." I walked over to one of the sh⬚ statues, the things that were supposed to ward off evil spirits.

"What are you doing?"

I found a compartment on the side of the statue, popped it open, and plugged the wraith remote into an empty jack. "Just returning your ghosts."

I hit the release button. Rogola jumped from his chair, stifling a scream, still unsure he was in any danger.

Hell, I didn't know if it would really work. Until it did.

Dozens of fuzzy wraith images floated into the hologram's beam until, on the other side of the desk, fully embodied ghosts materialized and floated around Rogola, flexing their claws and gnashing their teeth.

That's when Rogola really screamed.

The wraiths added their own shrieks before they tore into him. The hologram camera on the mayor's end tipped over. The image warbled into static, even though the sound of screaming and the tearing of flesh continued.

I turned my back to it.

Sometime soon, a rash of dragons would spring up and we'd know exactly where Rogola had been hiding the whole time.

When I left the office, Naveena stood behind the receptionist with a hand on the trembling woman's shoulder. The receptionist sucked on her vape and blew out a bubble that grew in size as it floated above our heads. It was glowing white.

A few days later, DeShawn sent me a message via holoreader. I thought it might have been an electronic, Christian witnessing tract at first. But I'm glad I didn't instantly delete it because it helped me make a decision about my future with the smoke eaters. And I'd be lying if I said it didn't choke me up a little. He wrote:

"Cap, I want to apologize for what happened at the funeral home. I should have listened to you. I want you to know that I've always appreciated everything you've ever done for me. You were like a father, and I don't just mean to me. Everybody on the job felt like that. I know you never had kids of your own, but you should be proud of how much your leadership and experience helped all of us young punks do the right thing, even when it wasn't the easiest thing to do.

"You're everything I hope to be someday. And even though we've taken separate paths, I hear your words in my head every day, telling me how to be better."

"So are you excited?" Sherry asked as she handed me another screw.

I sighed and began drilling it into the wall. "I'm tired and frustrated with these damn electro blinds."

"The store clerk said these are only a pain when you put them in. After this, we're supposed to love them."

Kenji bounded in and said, "Neoneun igeos-e kkeumjjighae!"

Yolanda had been a life saver in helping me put him back together. I really couldn't have done it without her. She even gave him a better paint job. He looked like a real Dalmatian.

Refraining from rolling my eyes at my dog, I began drilling the last screw into the wall. I hated being Mister Fixit because I was better at wrecking stuff. A horn honked from outside and it made me jump and strip the screw.

"Fucking hell!"

"Cole!" Sherry smacked my bottom. "You're going to have to watch your language from now on. That's not something I want our little girl learning."

"I'll do my best."

The next day we were going to welcome a four year-old girl named Bethany into our home. She was brown-haired and had been giving the orphanage people hell, once tripping a nanny droid to fall down a flight of stairs.

I liked her immediately.

I laid down the drill and patted Kenji on the head. The dog grabbed the tool and ran off somewhere in our new house, shouting something smartass. We'd gotten a good deal on the house since it was near an area previously destroyed by dragons. Even with all the work the smoke eaters had been putting in to keep scalies outside the city with wraith gates, people were still skittish of living near a formerly cordoned area. Almost like avoiding moving into a haunted house. We could have paid it off with my smoke eater money, but considering we had to pay for dragon insurance anyway we got another mortgage and would spend the majority of our money on toys and dresses for Bethany.

Sherry wrapped her arms around me and I gave her a big kiss. Her neck injury was completely gone, along with the tiny amount of arthritis that had been bugging her for a few years. I'd been sneakily trying to test if she had any smoke eater abilities – holding a candle a little too close to her hand, smoking a cigar and blowing the smoke near her face. She slapped away my candle attempts and slugged me in the arm with a baseball for the cigar. That crap wasn't allowed in the house.

"See you tomorrow," I told Sherry.

We kissed again, and I walked outside.

Naveena leaned against the chief's vehicle, wearing her green uniform and showing off a smug smile. The cannon truck was parked behind.

She tossed me the keys. "We'll follow you in."

"I know how to get there."

"Yeah, but you might change your mind midway and veer off the road."

"Have I ever changed my mind after making it up?"

She toed my driveway with a boot. "Brannigan, if I knew what went on in your head, I wouldn't have gone through half the shit we've had to deal with."

"That's Chief Brannigan to you."

"Yes, sir." She looked me over. "That uniform looks good on you."

I glanced down at my orange chief's shirt. "I feel like a walking citrus fruit."

"Come on," she said. "They're waiting for you."

I swallowed a lump in my throat and got behind the wheel of what used to be Donahue's truck. The funeral we gave him was grander and yet more secretive than any firefighter funeral I'd had the misfortune to attend. He'd requested to have his body set adrift on water and burned afloat.

Donahue's wife picked a place just west of the city. The procession had to be the longest in funeral history, with apparatus from both the smoke eater division and the fire department trailing up the highway for the ceremony. Hell, even a few police cars came along in support, not even for traffic control. It was good to have actual human cops back in charge of law enforcement. They were at least a tiny bit more competent than the droids. They'd found and arrested Jenkins in a matter of days. We'd yet to find out if that thing about the explosive in his neck was true.

At Donahue's funeral, Sergeant Puck said a few words, as did Naveena and a few other firefighters Donahue had worked with in Cincinnati. The stories were the best part. They knew a side to Donahue I never did.

I declined to speak.

When it was time, we took Donahue's body off the

top of Slayer 3 and set him on a raft at the water's edge. We all sang an ancient tune from a band called The Doors. Something about lighting my fire. Donahue had put some strange requests in his will.

The smokies with lasers shot at the corners of the funeral raft, where the propellerheads had placed a couple canisters of something incendiary they'd whipped up in the lab. It was supposedly taken from one of the Behemoth's ignis glands. The raft blasted into an instant inferno when the lasers struck. That fire had to have burned for a good hour and a half before the ashes sank down to the lake's bottom.

As far as funerals go, it was pretty nice. I'd want a send-off half as good.

I walked into Smoke Eater Headquarters a different man from when I'd first arrived. Sure, part of it was the way my dress shoes squeaked against the tile floor. The other part was that I was now in charge.

Fire isn't all bad; it can heal as much as it can hurt. But it always changes what it comes in contact with. My personal change may not have been visible – besides the godawful orange I now had to wear – but it'd been a lot deeper than a chemical reaction.

A multitude of faces greeted me when I walked around the corner in the east wing. They looked as nervous as I felt, so that was something. Their eyes widened when they saw me, but they stayed silent, waiting for me to start. Each of them was as different from one another as could be. Some were black, others Asian. Some were white or Latino or a mixture of different races. Half of them looked as old as me or even older. Some didn't even look old enough to drink. Women outnumbered men.

I cleared my throat. "I want to thank each of you for waiting patiently and going through this entire process.

You wouldn't be here if you didn't have at least a minuscule desire to help others." I smiled. "And let's be honest, we have some pretty cool toys."

That got a laugh out of them, even though they still shifted in their seats or trembled slightly.

"I'm Chief Cole Brannigan. I'm new to this position, but not new to a dangerous job. And that's what this is. Each of you will see your neighbors having the worst day of their lives. You have to be their strength. You will face literal monsters, and maybe even some ghosts. But we will give you the training you need to be able to encounter all of these things and more, if you're willing to meet us halfway and give the best you have. Dragon blood can improve and save many lives. It saved your own. We used to be slayers. Now we're evolving into something more productive to society."

I crossed my arms and inched closer to the glass room where they sat. "You were told before that you can leave any time during this recruitment process. I'm here to say that again. If any of you want to leave right now, you have our permission and our well wishes. It's true that our curate saved most of your lives, but please don't feel like you owe us something. You don't. This is entirely your choice. The door is always there if you choose to walk out."

That was something else I changed when I became chief.

A few of the recruits looked around to see if someone would leave. None of them did. I waited an extra minute or so just to be on the safe side.

"All right, then," I said. "This last test is for you as much as it is for us. Our highly trained medical staff is waiting just on the other side of this room in case anything goes wrong. I went through this same step. Don't worry. When the smoke comes, breathe deep."

I hit the button and dragon smoke poured into the glass room, blocking the potential recruits from my sight. Hopefully, they were all able to breathe. Hopefully, we'd have a good number of smoke eaters on the payroll soon. But I wondered if there'd ever be an end to this – the scalies, the wraiths, the ash.

Well, I'm saying right now, there won't be an end to it. There will always be dragons. You can either run, and eventually burn, or you can take up your lance and do what you were born for.

I've made my choice.

Sink or swim.

ACKNOWLEDGMENTS

The first person I have to thank is you. Since you're reading this, you are that special reader, dare I say book-buyer, who actually reads the acknowledgments. I hope you enjoyed *Smoke Eaters*. And if you dig my writing, please keep an eye out for my future books.

Paul Stevens is my agent and I can't thank him enough. His experience and insight into publishing is invaluable. I'm glad he's always there, not only to help brush up my manuscripts and get me the best deal, but also to talk me down when I get too amped up.

Michael Underwood thought this book was cool enough to bring to the attention of the other Angry Robots, and I'm so thankful for his support, as well as his marketing and sales acumen. Phil Jourdan helped me make *Smoke Eaters* even better than I could have imagined. His understanding of story and human emotion is almost god-like. Penny Reeve is such a fantastic publicity manager who always has the best ideas and knows how to sell books better than most people know how to breathe air. Publisher Marc Gascoigne is such a pleasure to work with, and his concept for the cover blew me away. I'm glad he's running Angry Robot, both as a writer and a reader. Speaking of the book cover, Lee Gibbons is a badass. I'm definitely getting that dragon and Maltese cross tattooed on me somewhere not embarrassing.

Special thanks also goes to Lauren Adams, who was such an awesome beta reader and is my number one fan. Jason Nelson will always be my mentor and guide, aka person I vent to. The members of the Pitch Wars 2015 group are some of my closest homies, thanks also to them.

I'd be remiss if I didn't thank all my author friends who've rooted for me on this journey to my first published novel. You guys know who you are, and I wish I had room to add each of your names. Even the smallest kindness went a long way for me.

Finally, I want to thank the women and men of the international fire service, who daily ride out to help strangers in their toughest times. I'm proud to call myself your brother.